Derek Hansen is a former advertising man who walked away at the peak of his career to fulfil a lifelong ambition to write novels.

His first novel, *Lunch with the Generals*, became an immediate bestseller, followed by *Lunch with Mussolini* and *Sole Survivor*. *Lunch with the Stationmaster* is his sixth novel and the third in the Lunch series.

Derek Hansen's work has also been published in America, Europe and the United Kingdom. He is married, has two adult children, and lives on Sydney's northern beaches.

'[*Lunch with the Generals*] is a rare book and a rare story that blazes life and death and love from every page ... the style sparse yet detailed, the sign of a brilliant storyteller'
— *Courier-Mail*

'Derek Hansen take a bow. You have written one of the most entertaining, gripping and powerful novels of the year.'
— *Sunday Telegraph* on *Lunch with Mussolini*

'Another fine effort from Hansen, with complex characters from wartime Germans to Italian fascists to Australian widows'
— *Courier-Mail* on *Lunch with Mussolini*

'Derek Hansen has a knack for making the immediate past come alive with contemporary pain'
— *Canberra Times* on *Sole Survivor*

DEREK HANSEN

LUNCH WITH THE STATIONMASTER

HarperCollins*Publishers*

To Carole

HarperCollins_Publishers_

First published in Australia in 2002
by HarperCollins*Publishers* Pty Limited
ABN 36 009 913 517
A member of the HarperCollins*Publishers* (Australia) Pty Limited Group
www.harpercollins.com.au

HarperCollins_Publishers_
25 Ryde Road, Pymble, Sydney NSW 2073, Australia
31 View Road, Glenfield, Auckland 10, New Zealand
77–85 Fulham Palace Road, London W6 8JB, United Kingdom
Hazelton Lanes, 55 Avenue Road, Suite 2900, Toronto, Ontario M5R 3L2
and 1995 Markham Road, Scarborough, Ontario M1B 5M8 Canada
10 East 53rd Street, New York NY 10022, USA

National Library of Australia Cataloguing-in-Publication data:

Hansen, Derek.
   Lunch with the stationmaster.
   ISBN 0 7322 7508 3.
   I. Title.
A823.3

Cover and internal design by Darian Causby, HarperCollins Design Studio
Cover photography: APL/Corbis
Typeset by HarperCollins in 12/16pt Sabon
Printed and bound in Australia by Griffin Press on 80gsm Bulky Book Ivory

5 4 3 2 1   02 03 04 05

FIRST
THURSDAY

CHAPTER ONE

The blind man walked confidently into the restaurant, automatically counting off his steps to the right-angle turn where the carpet runners intersected and led directly to his table. He had little fear of carelessly placed handbags or briefcases tangling with his feet and sending him flying. Over the six years of its existence, Gancio's Giardino had steadily moved up-market, a tribute to his friend Gancio's skills as a restaurateur and his own guiding hand. Gone were the young secretaries and office workers celebrating the birthday or departure of one of their number, forced by the upward creep of Gancio's prices to look elsewhere. Once, the restaurant had been bustling by twelve-thirty as diners arrived early to secure fast-filling tables. Now it was the province of business men and women, upper management and deal-makers, people whose lives tracked appointments and reservations, and to whom one o'clock signalled the major break in their working day. As Gancio's silent partner and backer, the blind man was pleased with the transition.

The sound of a chair being pushed back confirmed that he was almost upon his table. Milos had stood to greet him. Almost immediately he heard someone begin to whistle the opening bars of 'Advance Australia Fair'. Neil's trademark.

One of the two would claim the right to become storyteller for the next few weeks and he wondered who it would be. He also wondered, not for the first time that day, if he would again be targeted, set up for his unforgiven breach of convention by telling a story that trespassed onto his private life and, in doing so, added a dangerous new dimension.

'Welcome, Ramon.'

Lucio, the short, bald, unlikely Latin lover spoke first. So all three of his friends were present.

'What is it about you?' continued Lucio. 'You arrive and Milos stands for you. Neil whistles the national anthem. I arrive and they just check to see that my fly is done up.'

Ramon smiled. He reached out his hand and felt Milos take it and shake it warmly.

'You are five minutes late,' said Milos. 'You are still upset with us over last week, no?'

'No,' said Ramon evenly. He shook hands with Lucio. 'Upset demands at least ten minutes. I harbour no regrets. I thought I made that clear before leaving last week.'

'I thought you left before us so you could go home and sulk.'

Ramon smiled and reached his hand across to where he knew Neil would be sprawled. Neil was the youngest of them at a fit forty-five and, as though to counter Milos's European courtesies, deliberately went out of his way to be rude and provoke.

'How are you, Neil?'

'Same old same old. Though I have bleached my hair and had a buzz cut. Shame you can't see it.'

'Take no notice of him,' cut in Lucio. 'There is nothing different about Neil. He has not yet resigned from the white shoe brigade and is too Pavlovian to ever change. Now, please, won't you sit down so we can get on with things. I for one am anxious to know who our next storyteller will be. I would like to know the nature of the story, have some indication of where the story will lead us, know whether there will be beautiful women in it and whether or not they will be accommodating. I would like something to whet my appetite prior to lunch.'

'First we must attend to business,' said Ramon. He placed his cane against the table and lowered himself onto his chair in a smooth practised motion. 'There is the matter of payment to address.'

'We're up to date, no?' said Milos.

'Next week our monthly fees fall due. I am proposing we increase them.' Ramon settled back in his chair, the centre of attention, precisely where he most liked to be. 'We have all of us come a long way over the past four years since we discovered our mutual love for storytelling, but one aspect has not. Four years ago we each paid thirty dollars for lunch and wine at our Thursday gatherings. Three years ago we increased our contribution to forty dollars. Forty dollars hardly pays for the wine and grappa let alone the food.'

'What are you proposing?' asked Milos.

'Sixty dollars each,' said Ramon. 'I spoke about this to Gancio but he flatly refused. He reluctantly agreed, after much persuasion, to accept fifty.'

'Done,' said Milos. 'My one regret is that we did not think to do this sooner.'

'Lucio?'

'I would pay one hundred. How can I refuse fifty?'

'Neil?'

'Maybe we can pay fifty and kick in an extra ten each as a tip.'

Milos groaned. 'Sometimes I find it hard to separate the act from the ignorance.'

'What Milos means is, one does not tip friends,' said Ramon gently. 'If we were to offer Gancio a tip he would throw it back in our faces. There could be no greater insult and the insult, I fear, would be terminal. He would not have us back in his restaurant. He sees us as friends not customers, guests in his house not just his restaurant. Yes. His house. This restaurant is more his house than the apartment he lives in. It is also his life. If you see only a restaurateur and not a friend, then, Neil, you are blinder than I. Gancio accepts payment only at my insistence. He would gladly host these lunches for nothing.'

'Just a suggestion,' said Neil affably. 'Now, whose pocket do I have to piss in to get a drink around here?'

'Why do we put up with you?' sighed Milos.

'Because it's my turn to tell a story,' said Neil. 'And you all agree my stories are the most entertaining.'

'So you have elected to pick up the baton,' said Ramon. 'Good.'

'No,' said Milos. 'The baton is not his to pick up.'

'What do you mean?' snapped Neil. 'It's my turn. I always follow Lucio.'

'And Lucio always follows me, no? When Lucio insisted on following Ramon, I had no choice but to defer, but I will not defer twice in succession.' Milos looked around the table for support. 'I refuse to be steamrollered twice. I claim the right to tell the next story.'

'I follow Lucio,' said Neil. 'Always have done, always will. That's how it is, Milos, so get over it.'

'No!' Milos slapped his hands on the table, an action so unexpected and out of character that it stunned his friends. 'I claim the right to tell the next story. You have no choice in the matter, Neil. Neither do I! None of us have. This story has already been too long awaiting the telling. It must be told now. Time is running out, it is running out ...' Milos eased back in his chair to regain his composure.

The blind man heard the urgency in Milos's voice, heard it falter, heard the slight quaver as the last few words fell from his lips. He sensed what his colleagues could clearly see. Incredibly, Milos had lost control, however briefly.

Lucio finally broke the silence. 'For God's sake, Neil!'

'What?'

'Apologise!'

'For what?'

'Tell me, Neil, will the world end for you if Milos tells his story instead?' Ramon reached across the table feeling for Neil's hand. Neil withdrew it so Ramon's hand groped futilely. 'Neil, I may not have eyes but I do have feelings. Bait me as much as you like, but remember this. It is no small thing to refuse to take the hand of a friend.'

Neil relented, slapped Ramon's hand as if giving him five. 'You want me to defer to Milos, right?'

'Is it such a big deal?'

'Since you ask so nicely, I defer. But you'll regret it.' Neil shrugged dismissively and turned towards the kitchen. 'Gancio! How about some service? This used to be a good place before you put the prices up.'

Gancio burst from the kitchen with not one but two bottles of pinot grigio. 'Sorry, sorry. One of my juniors decided to fillet his hand instead of the whiting I gave him. Please accept my apologies and this wine. It's on the house.'

'That won't be necessary,' said Ramon. 'What delights do you have for us today?'

'Antipasti with melanzane, beautiful red capsicum, artichoke, semi-dried tomatoes and wild onions. Linguini with blue swimmer crab. Whiting fillets, lightly grilled with a delicate lemon-butter sauce and polenta. Served with Isabel sauvignon blanc. Good, eh?' He looked around the table for approval.

'Excellent,' said Ramon. Neil and Lucio also made appreciative noises but their reaction fell short of what Gancio was accustomed to.

'What's the matter?' His face clouded with concern as he sensed the tension around the table.

Milos attempted a smile. 'A small cognac, if I may.'

'A cognac? Now?' Gancio was not the only one taken by surprise.

7

'Please.'

'Anyone else?' Gancio glanced around the table but there were no other takers.

'It's Milos's turn to tell a story and he needs fortifying,' said Neil by way of explanation. 'You offer us seafood but I suspect we're heading for another serve of European tragedy.'

'One cognac coming up.' Gancio turned away and headed for the bar.

'Neil, perhaps you'd care to fill our glasses.' Ramon gently pushed his glass in Neil's direction. The glasses were filled and Gancio returned with the cognac. Each man waited for the other to speak.

'Well,' said Ramon eventually, 'is Neil right? Are you going to take us back to Europe?'

'Yes,' said Milos simply. 'I am.'

'Jesus Christ!' spat Neil. 'Can't you reffos leave it alone? Why do you guys insist on bringing all your baggage with you? Why can't you just grab what this country has to offer and make a fresh start? Why wallow in the past?'

'Sometimes it's not a matter of choice.' Milos spoke so softly they had to strain to hear him. 'We are all shaped by our past. It is as much a part of us as our physical being. It shapes the way we perceive things, the way we think and the way we act. We cannot just shake it off as you would have us do, Neil, any more than we can shrug off our own skin. As much as we may try to put it behind us, our past imprisons us. It shapes our present and also our futures. The past is not something easily discarded. Whether we have escaped Nazi Germany, Pol Pot or the Taliban, we can never escape what happened to us there. Never.'

'Rubbish,' snorted Neil. 'You guys cling to it. You love it. You carry your martyrdom with pride. You wear it like a badge. You all have your story which you think the rest of the world is hanging out to hear. Well, sorry, mate, I'll give you the scoop. We're not. What irritates me most is that you think that somehow what happened to you makes you special, superior in some way to Australians.'

'Explain that,' cut in Ramon.

'Okay. Our troops went overseas to fight in two world wars and in Vietnam. But we've never had a war on our soil, apart from a few air raids on Darwin. For some reason, because we have never been conquered, occupied or oppressed, you guys feel we're somehow lacking, that we're lesser people. You scorn us for our lack of baggage, for our easy-going lifestyle, for not having suffered.'

'On the contrary,' said Milos. 'That is why we envy you.'

'Then copy us. Forget the past. Give it away!'

'Ahh, if only it were that easy.' Milos smiled but his smile lacked all warmth. 'Do you imagine for an instant that survivors of the Holocaust can come to this country and forget everything that happened to them? Forget what they saw? Forget their fear? Just because the surf is up? Just because the sun is shining?'

'C'mon, Milos,' said Neil impatiently, 'I'm not suggesting that it happens overnight, but the war ended in 1945. Fifty-six years ago. People have had plenty of time to get over it.'

'Get over it,' said Milos quietly.

'Sure. A bit of counselling. A few sessions with a shrink.'

'And that's it?' Milos shook his head sadly. 'Are you aware, Neil, that there is no cure for post-traumatic stress syndrome, no cure for memories of being dragged from your home and put into cattle trucks and herded off to gas chambers like livestock to an abattoir? There is no cure for witnessing loved ones shot dead before your very eyes. There is no cure for having lived every second of every day for weeks, months and years on end inescapably bound to your worst fears. There is only palliative care, counselling and drug therapy that dulls the brain, deadening not only the pain of the past but the pleasure of living as well. There can be no joy where all feeling is suppressed, no life and certainly no peace. Only death can bring peace.'

'Very dramatic. Heart-rending, even. But I'm sorry, I just don't buy your argument. Time heals, at least where there is a will to heal.'

'You know, Neil, there was a time in my life when I could not even begin to conceive of a people as fortunate as Australians, of a country so blessed, so free and so utterly incredible and wonderful. I am Hungarian and will always be Hungarian, but I see myself as a Hungarian Australian with the accent very much on Australia. I love this country and embrace it with all my heart. But I did not come to this country with the unfettered innocence of a newborn child. I have a past and the past makes demands on me. Some wounds heal but others do not. That is the burden of the past, a past which is unalterable.'

'So we wallow once more.' Neil leaned back in his chair in resignation. 'I warned you all that if I deferred to Milos you would regret it. I had planned a story with humour, unexpected twists, subtle clues and, for Lucio, a fair bit of healthy bonking. Instead you have Milos and the burden of history. God help us. It's all your fault, Ramon.'

'Why? Because I supported Milos?'

'No. Because you changed the rules and brought yourself into your story. Because you drew on your past. You opened the door for Lucio to drag out his baggage and now Milos is dragging out his.'

'I don't recall you complaining when I told my story,' cut in Lucio. 'I gave you the chance to stick the boot into Ramon and you leapt at it.'

'That's not the point. Look — for four years we were perfectly happy to entertain and be entertained. No! More than happy. Ever since that first day our Thursday lunches have taken precedence over everything. We rescheduled appointments and meetings and even organised our travel so we missed as few Thursdays as possible. We found something precious, something we all wanted, in the entertainment and intellectual stimulation, the opportunity to use our brains for pleasure and not just for the advancement of some business deal. Sure, we have a few digs at each other, but duelling egos is part of the reason we come here. Jesus Christ! Wasn't what we had good enough? I thought it was.' Neil's voice had become shrill and he paused to regain composure.

'Have you finished?' asked Ramon.

'No,' said Neil, moderating his voice. 'We were friends yet strangers, satisfied to know nothing about each other or, more accurately, know only what each of us chose to reveal, which, from my point of view, was comfortingly little. Certainly nothing of a personal nature. But you, Ramon, you had to overstep the mark and change everything. Stuff you and your bloody ego.'

'No,' cut in Milos, 'you can't blame Ramon for my story. I said before that this story must be told now. That time is running out. Regardless of what Ramon did, I would still tell this story. I have no choice. It is not just an obligation but a repayment of a debt, as you will see.'

'A debt?'

'Yes, Ramon, a debt. You are owed, all of you, more than you can ever imagine.'

'You owe us nothing,' cut in Lucio.

'Why do you assume the debt is mine?'

Milos looked around the table. He had them. He could almost hear their brains springing into action, saw the quickening in their eyes. He smiled.

'Besides, Neil, you make a serious mistake if you think my story is all doom and gloom. You say you are happy to be entertained and I assure you, you will be entertained. Had you proceeded instead of me, you promised us humour, wit, clever twists and subtle clues. I promise no less. Ramon delved into the Argentina of the Generals and we sat enthralled, sometimes appalled, but we lived every moment and hung on every word. Lucio took us back to wartime Italy and

Germany. In putting his war criminal on trial, he also put us on trial. Both had us on the edge of our seats, taking sides against each other. Do you expect any less of me?'

The story had begun, of that none of the listeners had the slightest doubt. Gancio stood by the table, antipasti in hand, not daring to interrupt.

'My story is the true story of Heyman Milos.'

'Milos Heyman, Heyman Milos.' Neil sighed heavily. 'If you're going to tell your life story, but don't wish us to know it, surely you could have chosen a less obvious pseudonym.'

'This is the story of Heyman Milos. My story. In Hungary, the surname precedes the given name. I will endeavour to present my story as authentically as possible, without embellishment or embroidery. If at times I appear brave, then I was brave. If I give you reason to think less of me, then you are justified in doing so. There is an imperative in the telling of my story and to do it full justice I, too, may have to break with convention but not in any way you could anticipate. Bear with me. It is the nature of the debt that the repaying of it may take an unexpected form. Grant me *egy kis turelmet*. Grant me a little patience.

'If I change the story in any way it will be slight and only to aid comprehension. Magyarul, the language of Hungary, is an orphan. If you search back far enough you will discover it is related to the Finno-Ugric group of languages, but very, very distantly. Suffice to say, knowledge of any other languages will not assist you in the understanding of Magyarul. It is ranked with Japanese in terms of difficulty. It is not my intention to give you a lesson in its complexities and idiosyncrasies so, where necessary, I will anglicise the names of people and places. *Erzsebet*, for example, will become Elizabeth and given names will precede surnames. These are the only changes I will make. At the end of it all you may conclude that there was, and is, weakness in character. This may certainly be Neil's conclusion. But I contend there are some things time cannot

12

heal, can never heal, and that there is no escaping the past. Only in having the strength to accept the inevitability of defeat can there be triumph. I believe my story is a triumph of will, a triumph of character, a triumph of love. I believe that, ultimately, it is a triumph over death itself.'

There was defiance in Milos's voice but also uncharacteristic passion, and the reddening of his eyes spoke of a sorrow they could only speculate upon. Lucio dragged his eyes away from Milos to see if Ramon had somehow picked up on it. The blind man had missed nothing. He fidgeted with his table napkin, folding and refolding it. Lucio and Neil glanced uneasily at each other. What Milos promised made a mockery of both Ramon's and Lucio's breach of their convention. He was threatening to do no less than bare his very soul. The prospect was unwelcome and a sense of foreboding settled over the table.

'*Primo piatto*,' said Gancio emphatically and laid the platter of antipasti on the table.

'*Primo piatto*,' said Ramon pensively. '*Primo piatto*.' He turned to Milos and smiled. 'Yes, the first dish. And beautifully served.'

CHAPTER TWO

Spring 1948

Something was wrong and the two hunters sensed it. Gabriella could hear them whispering above the sounds of her own labouring breath, the crunch of their footsteps and the pounding in her ears. They were arguing softly but urgently. They stopped so suddenly that Milos collided with the younger of them, stumbled and would have fallen had Gabriella not been holding on to him. Had he not been holding on to her. The older and stronger of the hunters slapped his hand over Milos's mouth, held it there so he couldn't cry out. Gabriella could barely see them in the darkness though they were less than an arm's length away. But she saw enough to realise what they were doing. The hunters straightened, listened, sniffed the air and scanned the night with their eyes, as cautious and fearful as the pigs and deer they hunted. Their instincts told them something was wrong. But what? And why? How? Their plan was good and she knew Tibor would have shared it with nobody. Nobody who didn't need to know. Nobody they couldn't trust with their lives.

They stood huddling together on the narrow track. Gabriella felt Tibor push past her, heard him curse the two hunters. Tibor wanted to keep moving but Gabriella was grateful for the rest, however brief. Her pack weighed heavily on her back even though she carried the bare minimum and less than half of what Milos and Tibor each carried. She sucked in the bitterly cold air. It had lost none of its sting in its journey south-west across Russia. It burned her lungs but she could sense it reoxygenating her weary blood, slowing the pounding of her heart, bringing back strength and the will to keep going. Milos wrapped his arms around her to keep her warm.

'We have to leave the trail.' Tibor stood over them. As usual he invited neither comment nor argument.

Leave the trail? Gabriella leaned back so she could look around her. She tried desperately to pierce the darkness but the larch, oak and hornbeam canopy which crowded over the little-used trail was thick enough to blinker their vision even in daylight and deny all but the briefest glimpse of sky. But for Milos supporting and guiding her, she'd have been unable to follow the trail as far as they had. How could she possibly cope if they left it altogether? She wanted to object and protest her inability but knew her objection would be ignored and, besides, she lacked the strength to argue.

The hunters pushed on up the trail for another two hundred metres before plunging sharply left into the bushes. The path they now followed, if it was a path, was steeper, narrower and cross-hatched with roots. Foliage from the undergrowth whipped off Milos's body and stung her face. She clung on to him for a tow, using her free hand to pull her hat lower over her face, and burrowed deeper beneath the upturned collar of her greatcoat. She stumbled often, landing heavily on her knees, but the muffled curses told her she wasn't the only one to trip. Minutes passed agonisingly yet the hunters showed no sign of slowing. Somewhere in the darkness, the summit of Mount Nagy-Milic towered above them. Gabriella wondered how many of its nine hundred metres they would have to climb before beginning their descent to the Hernad River and the relative security of Czechoslovakia, wondered how many metres there could possibly be left to climb.

An hour passed but any reassurance the hunters had hoped to gain by their diversion had eluded them. She could again hear them muttering and arguing. The going was steep but became easier as the trees thinned out and the larches gave way to linden and ash. Finally the hunters paused in the lee of what Gabriella could clearly see was a ridge. She felt no elation at the knowledge that their climb may be over and sank helplessly to the ground. She slipped off her pack, rolled over onto her back gasping for air and closed her eyes. She was vaguely aware of Milos lying down beside her. Above she could hear Tibor in earnest conversation with the hunters. Something was wrong. She heard one of the hunters say how they'd been following pig trails and yet they'd encountered no sign of pigs or any other animals. Why were there no startled pigs crashing away from them through the forest? Why had they heard no deer? Why were there no animals at all? The younger of the hunters crawled up to the lip of the ridge and peered over, listening, listening . . .

'Drink.'

Wearily, Gabriella pushed herself up onto her elbows. In the darkness she could just make out the shape of Tibor kneeling in front of her, bottle extended towards her.

'Water?' she asked.

'Better. *Barack*.'

Gabriella took a mouthful of the fiery liquid, swallowed and felt its warmth suffuse her body.

'Thank you.' She passed the bottle of *barack* to Milos who handed her a flask of water in exchange. The *barack* took the chill off the icy water and she swallowed greedily.

'Not too much,' warned Tibor softly. He took the water from her.

'Is there a problem?' she asked.

'There shouldn't be.'

'But is there?'

'We don't know.' Tibor handed the water flask back to Milos in return for his *barack*. 'We have a steep descent before we rejoin the trails. That is the source of dispute. My friends do not believe the trails are safe. They are convinced there are border patrols and that the patrols have scared off the animals. I believe that is unlikely. However, we have no choice. The trails bisect our path to the boat. At the very least we must cross them. But we will reach the boat much sooner if we use the trails. I believe whatever risk there is, is justified. That is what we will do.'

Tibor rose and rejoined the hunters and began to placate them with his *barack*. Gabriella tried to listen in but their whispers were too soft and easily carried away on the wind. She closed her eyes.

'Gabi! Wake up!'

Milos was shaking her. Wake up? She'd fallen asleep?

'Time to go.'

How long had she slept? A few seconds, a minute? She slipped her arms wearily through the straps of her pack and stood. Just as she turned to Milos to take his arm so he could help her on the final leg to safety, she heard the sound that never failed to chill the blood in her veins. No amount of *barack* could have prevented the sudden surge of fear. No amount of warning could have prepared her.

'Dogs!' Tibor charged at the two hunters, one of whom backed away from him, arms raised. 'Scum! Who did you tell?' He no longer bothered to whisper. The dogs had found their trail and the rules had changed.

'No one! We told no one!' The big man, Janos, stood his ground.

'I should shoot you and leave you here.'

Shoot? Tibor carried a gun? The tone of his voice convinced Gabriella as well as the hunters that he would not hesitate to use it.

'Tibor! We have no time for this.' Milos let go of Gabriella and confronted his brother. 'We've got to go. Now! While we still have a chance of outrunning them.'

Tibor ignored Milos. 'How much did the AVO pay you?'

Janos spat in disgust. His cousin, Laszlo, took another frightened step backwards.

'Who are you? Why do the AVO want you?' Laszlo turned on his companion. 'Janos, who are these people?'

Tibor laughed, suddenly and unexpectedly. He put his gun away. Even in the dark he could see the hunters weren't acting.

'Get us to the boat. Try to run away and I will shoot you. Understand?'

He grabbed hold of Gabriella and dragged her to the top of the ridge. A blast of wind rocked her back on her heels. 'Hold on to her, Milos. Don't let her fall. She falls, we all die!'

The descent was steeper than Gabriella could ever have imagined but there was no time for caution. Again and again she stumbled, on the verge of falling, only for Milos to catch and support her. The hunters led the way with Tibor hard on their heels, keeping them honest. But they were experienced woodsmen. What their eyes couldn't see their feet instinctively knew. Despite Tibor's best efforts to keep up they drew away from him. He realised then that his threat to shoot them was worthless and he could do nothing to prevent them running off and saving themselves.

'Slow down!' he called, not expecting them to, was surprised when they did.

'Give me the girl,' said Janos. 'You are too slow.' He grabbed hold of Gabriella, pulled off her pack and handed it to his colleague. 'You lead.' Without another word he lifted Gabriella onto his massive shoulders. He adjusted her position once so that her waist wrapped neatly around the back of his neck and his arms trapped her knees and shoulders. 'Try to keep up,' he said and plunged into the darkness.

Time and again Gabriella thought she must certainly

explode from his grasp as he plunged down the mountainside. She buried her face in her arms to shield it from branches and to cushion the impact if they fell. When they fell. Janos was strong but he laboured under the effort of carrying her. His breath came in pain-filled gasps and many times she felt him stagger. But any thought of rest was abandoned when they again heard the chilling baying of the dogs. That meant their pursuers had crossed the ridge and had descended to where the forest was thicker and the wind no longer carried away their sound. She felt the hunter stumble once more, barely heard him curse before he slammed into a tree trunk almost knocking her senseless. Gabi could taste blood in her mouth but was too stunned to identify the source. Had she lost a tooth? Split a lip?

'Come on!'

Gabriella didn't know who spoke, only that Janos didn't bother answering before resuming the plunge down the hillside. He charged recklessly through foliage with no regard for her safety or even his. It was all she could do to hang on. She was dimly aware of him turning abruptly left and a lessening of the jarring. The hillside no longer seemed so steep. She opened her eyes and realised they were once more on the trail. Milos was just behind her and Tibor brought up the rear. Her befuddled mind recalled what Tibor had said: the trails were faster and worth the risk. She clung to the fact that the trails were faster, that they'd reach the boat sooner, that the pounding that drove the breath out of her lungs would soon cease, that the aching in her head would pass. But if they could run faster on the trails, how much faster could their pursuers run? She shivered involuntarily, more frightened of the dogs than the men who ran with them. Would they give her to the dogs to tear apart? Terrors she'd tried her hardest to suppress resurfaced. The terrible nightmares took on the substance of premonition. She was unable to prevent the sob that burst from her throat.

'Hold on. Not far now.' The hunter pulled her legs and arms tighter to his body. His breath hissed from his lips and Gabriella could tell by the shortening of his stride that he was nearing exhaustion.

'Arrgh!'

The cry and the thud that followed were unmistakeable. Someone had fallen. Someone behind her. Milos or Tibor.

'Milos!' she cried. 'Stop!' But Janos only ran faster.

'Keep going!'

Who called out? Milos, or Tibor? What did it mean? Were they both okay? What was the point of escaping unless Milos escaped with her?

'Milos!' She called again. Desperately.

'I'm okay! Keep going!'

This time there was no mistaking the voice or the pain it carried. It was Milos. Milos had fallen. She knew he was hurt but how badly? Could he still run? Could Tibor carry him? She wanted to go to his help, to be by his side, no matter what.

'Put me down!' She thumped her fists into Janos's hips. He slowed and swung her onto her feet but didn't let go.

'You must run now, run with me! You cannot go back! Hold on to my arm.'

'No!'

'They are coming. Your friends are coming. Listen!'

Gabi swung back the way she'd come, hardly daring to breathe. Sure enough she could hear the crunching of leaves underfoot and curses. Two people cursing. Two people!

'Now run! They will catch us. Run, girl! Run for your life.'

Gabriella turned and ran, half pulled, half dragged. Somewhere behind her Tibor was doing the same for Milos and she owed it to both of them to do her best. Her head swam and the sticky thickness of blood oozing in her mouth obstructed her breathing, making her gag, making her want to vomit. But there was no time. Milos was behind her. Running for his life.

A sudden burst of gunfire made her cry out. The dogs howled as though cheering this development. She cried out again, scared, panicked, desperate. Another burst of gunfire shattered the night.

'Run! Keep running!' Janos grabbed her by the back collar of her coat, lifting her so that her feet skipped over the trail. 'Nearly there!'

The downward grade steepened without warning and there ahead of her Gabriella could make out a clearing and something else. It wasn't until she splashed into the muddy water that she realised the clearing was in fact the Hernad River and the something else was the boat. The younger hunter was holding on to it as though preventing the boatman from rowing away into the darkness. Gabriella felt hands lift her and drop her unceremoniously into the boat. She lay on the bottom, bruised, battered and exhausted, gasping for breath. Another burst of gunfire split the night and, to Gabriella's horror, it was followed by a sharp, agonised cry.

'One of your friends has been shot.'

'No!'

Gabriella pulled herself up so she could see over the gunwale, turned back towards the trail, her eyes desperately trying to penetrate the gloom. Someone was coming. Milos or Tibor? She heard the splash as the fugitive staggered into the water, heard the splash above the shouts of their pursuers, above the baying of the hounds, the crackle of gunfire. Milos or Tibor? She saw the hunters reach out to haul him to the boat so they could all climb aboard and make their escape, heard the rasps as he gasped for breath.

Milos or Tibor? Tibor or Milos?

Dear God, she prayed, please let him be Milos. Please!

CHAPTER THREE

April 1941

It was not easy being a Jew in Hungary but not always hard. Jozsef Heyman nodded courteously towards the faces he recognised and to anyone else prepared to look him in the eye. People watched from doorways and from windows, often half-hidden behind curtains; without exception, the faces were sullen. Jozsef had no expectation of violence or abuse, no fear of anyone blocking their way and preventing him from doing what had to be done. No, for the most part the people of sleepy Sarospatak tolerated their Jews. What persecution there was came not from within but from without, not from the heart but by way of legislation, from the prejudices and political persuasion of those in power, faraway in Budapest. Though they destroyed lives with the pen not the sword, the bitterness and pain was no less. But Jozsef also accepted that, on this day, it was he who had brought about the dismay and disapproval, the collective sense that his action was both offensive and a desecration, at best an exploitation of their tolerance, at worst cynical opportunism. On this day, he had few friends, even among his own kind. On this day, when he sought to free his two sons from the burden of their inheritance.

Jozsef glanced at the boys by his side, wondering how they would remember and judge this day. Would they recall it with bitterness at his betrayal? Or with gratitude for his courage and his foresight? On his left his younger son, Milos, gripped his hand as though to lose grip would be to lose everything. The boy was clearly apprehensive and, perhaps, even ashamed. Nevertheless he held his head up, as he'd been told to, though his eyes studiously avoided contact with others. Jozsef wanted to hug the boy, do something to reassure him, but this was hardly the right time or place and, besides, there'd be plenty of time for that later. On his right, his other son, Tibor, affected an air of total disinterest. Jozsef had to suppress a smile. His elder son had not been born to be oppressed or denied in any way. Almost fourteen, he was only two years older than Milos but, in truth, a gulf separated the pair. Tibor was tall for his age and his body already showed the promise of the man he would become. Where Milos was timid and sensitive, Tibor was bold and forthright. Where Milos was concerned with consequences, Tibor walked his path regardless, confident he had the strength, intelligence, wit and charm to deal with anything or anyone who crossed it.

As they turned the final corner before their destination Jozsef spotted a group of boys lingering sullenly on the opposite side of the street. He felt Milos's grip on his hand suddenly tighten, yet Tibor showed not the least concern. His older son stared at the boys as if committing their names and faces to memory should retribution be required and, unbelievably, waved at them as though inviting comment. Jozsef knew immediately there would be none. No calls of 'Jew boy' or 'filthy yid' nor the accusatory 'Christ killer'. Tibor simply commanded too much respect. Besides, the circumstances compromised their insults. They walked on, the only sound coming from their shoes on the cobblestones shined by overnight rain. Soon it would all be over and they could get on with their lives, his sons with an immeasurably brighter future.

Jozsef paused briefly at the foot of the steps leading to the church entrance. Once inside, he knew they would be welcome. If not himself, then certainly his two sons who would be greeted as two souls saved from corruption, a triumph of the Holy Roman Catholic Church over Judaism. When Jozsef had told trusted friends and colleagues of his intentions, they'd not only expressed bewilderment at the proposed conversion of his sons but at his choice of the Roman Catholic Church. Sarospatak had achieved fame as a bastion of Calvinism and the Calvinist College was still a dominant factor in the life of the town. But Jozsef had his answer ready. He told anyone who asked that the boys' mother had been Roman Catholic and had practised her faith right up until her death from tuberculosis. Those who knew Jozsef found the answer credible and in line with his claim to be an agnostic. As an agnostic, what would it matter which faith his wife chose to follow? Jozsef claimed he allowed his sons to follow their mother's religion on the grounds that he adhered to no religion himself.

But he had another reason. He was determined not to transfer his sons from one minority group to another. There was strength and safety in numbers and four out of every five Hungarians were at least nominally Catholic. Jozsef had also made no secret of his determination to spare his sons the effects of the *numerus clausus* legislation, the discriminatory laws which severely limited the number of Jews able to enter the professions, or take senior positions in public service, education or the arts. His critics protested that this was his sole motive and deemed his actions an affront to both their religion and the law.

While it was easy to question Jozsef's claims, resolving any doubts was anything but. Nobody in Sarospatak had ever met his wife or even known Jozsef at the time of her death. Nobody knew whether she was Roman Catholic or not. That piece of his personal history had occurred in Budapest, before he was banished to Sarospatak. Nobody could check Jozsef's claim that his wife's religion was clearly stated on the boys' birth certificates, because the documents had been lost when he had been forced to surrender his job and his apartment to his successor. Of course, there were copies in the Budapest town hall, but finding and verifying them took both time and effort.

Jozsef was met at the top of the steps by the priest's unsmiling helper. Old Ignac, or Misery Guts as he was universally known, had served the church in a lay capacity for more than sixty-five years and tended to regard it as his domain. He may have been happy to admit the two boys but was far less convinced about allowing a Jew into the church, even one who wasn't practising. He waited impatiently as Jozsef removed his hat and coat to reveal a shining pate completely devoid of hair except around the back and sides, and a portliness which, together with his short legs, made his body appear oval. The acolyte made little effort to hide his disgust.

Once Jozsef had helped Milos out of his coat, Old Ignac led them down the aisle towards the baptismal font. Jozsef took in nothing of his surroundings. Instead he searched ahead, anxious for confirmation that his clerk and his wife had kept their promise to act as godparents to both boys. His clerk was a good man in his late fifties, gifted with intelligence but lacking in ambition. He had an encyclopaedic knowledge of the great composers and nothing thrilled him more than the emergence of contemporary musical talent. From time to time he performed recitals on the magnificent two-hundred-year-old organ in the Castle Church. Music and butterfly-collecting were what he lived for and he was content with a job that provided enough for himself and his wife and didn't intrude on his real interests. Jozsef smiled warmly when he spotted the Zelks standing in the nave with Father Hegedus and his small entourage, awaiting their arrival. He guessed his clerk and his wife had stayed on after mass rather than face the accusing eyes outside.

'Shall we begin?'

Father Hegedus neither offered his hand nor made any attempt to make Jozsef feel welcome. Clearly the priest was anxious to conclude the ceremony as quickly as possible.

Unlike Jozsef, the boys were no strangers to the church, having attended instruction from the priest prior to their baptism to make certain they understood the tenets of their new faith and what was required of them. Jozsef tried his best to follow the proceedings but was distracted as he finally took in his surroundings. The church was far more austere than he had expected, nothing like the great synagogue in Rakocsi Street. And so much more sombre! Yet it did nothing to dim his determination. He assumed the church would be more lively and welcoming with a congregation in attendance, when voices were raised in hymns. Satisfaction welled up inside him as he watched Father Hegedus make the sign of the cross in holy water on the brow of each of his sons in turn. In his heart he was certain he was doing the right thing. Unlike him, his sons would not be persecuted by legislation. His sons would not have their careers curtailed and their options limited. Neither would his sons have anything to fear from the growing menace of Hitler's Germany. His sons would no longer be Jews but Hungarians.

Milos again held his father's hand as they left the church. The priest had spoken of the joy and elation at being admitted into the faith and taking Christ as his saviour, but he felt none of that. Instead he felt confused and ashamed. Although religion had played little part in his upbringing, his brushes with it had been decidedly Jewish. What now of Hanuka and Yom Kippur? What of the Seders when they had celebrated Passover at his grandmother's house in Budapest where he, as youngest, had been accorded the honour of asking questions? It didn't matter that his father now maintained that to be born a Jew his mother needed to be Jewish and insisted she was not. He had been raised believing he was a Jew and been told every day at school that he was a Jew. How could he cease to be one? He felt no different as a Christian than he had as a Jew. When he went to school he would still be branded a Jew. The boys in the schoolyard had made that perfectly clear. Once a Jew always a Jew and undeniable evidence resided within his trousers. Milos could see no benefit in no longer being a Jew, only humiliation.

Another thought struck him and he closed his eyes as though in pain, unwilling even to consider the possibility. What if ceasing to be Jews meant his father would no longer be friends with Gabriella's father? What if they were no longer invited around to Tokaj Street for Sunday lunch? A month never went by without them going to Tokaj Street for Sunday lunch at least once. What would happen if they never went again? Milos glanced over at his brother to see if the thought had occurred to him. If it had, he gave no sign, but that was only to be expected. Tibor's disinterested expression was unchanged. Earlier in the week, as the day of baptism had approached, Milos had tried to discuss things with his older brother but Tibor had contemptuously dismissed his questions. Tibor never let on what he was thinking until he'd made up his mind. He never admitted to doubts and regarded any form of vacillation as weakness. More than anything, Milos had wanted to ask him what effect their conversion would have in Tokaj Street, but lacked the courage. Tibor would have laughed at him and that would have been unbearable. Milos turned his attention back to the street. The cobblestones were finally drying out and reverting to their normal drab grey. The spring air had not entirely shaken off winter but, out of the shade of the sombre two-storey stone houses lining both sides of the street, the direct sunlight was warming. However, it did nothing to drive the dark thoughts from Milos's head. Were they still going to Tokaj Street?

Milos had been aghast when he heard his father invite Father Hegedus and his new godparents home to celebrate the baptism, and mightily relieved when they had declined. There was a celebration to attend but it had nothing to do with their baptism. When they reached the door of the small cottage provided by the railways, he turned accusingly to his father.

'Why did you invite Father Hegedus and Mr and Mrs Zelk to our house?' he asked.

His father laughed. 'Because it was the proper thing to do.'

'But what if they had accepted?'

His father put his arm around him. 'They would never have accepted. It would have been an embarrassment for all of us. Father Hegedus understood and so did the Zelks. The Zelks are good people and good friends. Now, let's go inside.'

But Milos didn't move. He remained in the cottage doorway blocking his father's entry. He had one more question, one that could no longer wait to be answered.

'Are we still going to Tokaj Street? Now that Tibor and I are Christians?'

His father crouched down so that his eyes were level with Milos's, a broad smile spreading over his face, making Milos feel embarrassed for asking.

'Do you think we would have taken so much care buying Gabriella's birthday present if I thought you'd no longer be welcome there? Would I have insisted you become a Christian if I thought it would end your friendship with Gabriella?'

His face grew serious as he began to appreciate the depth of his son's concern.

'Your Uncle Thomas does not agree with what we've done but he understands why. Are we still welcome in his house? Of course we are. Thomas and I disagree over many things. That is why we like each other. That is why we get on so well. I am certain all his family feel the same. Even Gabriella,' he added mischievously.

Milos turned and raced up the stairs to get Gabriella's present before his blushing made him seem even more ridiculous.

*

How old does a boy have to be before he can fall truly in love? At eleven years of age Milos was too young, but he was also too young to appreciate the limitations of his years. He was impatient to get to Tokaj Street where he knew that Gabriella could not help but be overwhelmed by his present. He knew of her love for the poems of Sandor Petofi and had wanted to buy her a collection of his works. But his father had guided him to a far more singular and precious gift: the magical book *Peter Pan and Wendy*. The book was printed in English, a language Gabriella had been taught by her English governess but, best of all, was illustrated by Mabel Lucie Attwell. One of Gabriella's most treasured possessions was a pixie and toadstool tea set designed by Mabel Lucie Attwell, given to her as a farewell present by her governess. His was the most perfect gift and Milos had convinced himself that for once, in Gabriella's eyes at least, his star would shine more brightly than his brother's. More than that, he believed it was a gift to win Gabriella's heart.

Yet his brother worried him. Tibor had been unimpressed when he'd told him about his wonderful present and had simply smiled when Milos had asked what gift he'd bought for Gabriella. That smile worried him. It was a knowing smile, the kind of smile a cat reserves for a cornered mouse the moment both animals realise the inevitability of the situation. What had Tibor got for her? Milos looked at the flat rectangular present Tibor carried under his arm. It was beautifully wrapped in red paper with shiny bright blue ribbons yet Milos could not imagine how it could possibly be better than his book. He hugged his present to his chest.

Tokaj Street was three kilometres from their little cottage and the overhead sun was making a mockery of the coat his father had insisted he wear. He was hot and uncomfortable but still wished his father would walk faster. The unpleasantness of the morning was past and he had an afternoon in his favourite place to look forward to. And, of course, Gabriella's gratitude.

Tibor was not the only obstacle in the way of Milos's bid for Gabriella's affections. Gabriella was two months older than Milos, at least seven centimetres taller, more confident and far more socially adept. Any onlooker would unhesitatingly match her with Tibor; Milos would not warrant any consideration at all. Milos was fully aware of the advantages his brother had over him, yet remained hopeful. He believed it was only a matter of time before Gabriella realised where her true affections lay. One day he would be taller than her and the two-month difference in their ages would no longer matter. With his increase in height would come the confidence and self-assurance now lacking. Then, he believed, he would be more than a match for his brother.

Even if Gabriella had been born plain and foolish, Milos would still have looked forward to the visits to Tokaj Street with the eagerness of a puppy. He loved the big house his Uncle Thomas and Aunt Katica Horvath lived in with Gabriella, her elder sister Elizabeth and brother Balazs, the eldest. The titles 'uncle' and 'aunt' were affectionate courtesies because the families were not related in any way. Entering the house was like slipping into a big, warm bed, like sipping a bowl of hot, thick goulash in front of the kitchen stove on a winter's day, like entering a storybook in which he was hero and a happy ending was guaranteed. His father did his best to make their little railway cottage cosy and comfortable but it could never compete with Tokaj Street. It wasn't just that the rooms in his uncle's house were large and spacious, the ceilings high and the walls bedecked with beautiful paintings. Or that being there awakened vague memories of the elegant apartment in Budapest in which he'd spent the first six years of his life. Whenever he was inside the house he felt happy, safe and significant. The Horvaths were always interested in what he had to say, supportive of what he did and generous in their praise. Their generosity of spirit extended to everyone and everything and their warmth was reciprocated by all who entered. It was impossible to conceive of sickness or sadness ever finding a niche, impossible to believe that harm could ever come to anyone in this wonderful house.

When Jozsef tapped three times with the big brass knocker in the centre of the heavy oak door, Milos felt a sudden flutter of nervousness. His racing mind rehearsed the words he planned to say to Gabriella when he gave her his gift. He couldn't wait to see her face when she'd unwrapped it. It really was the most perfect present. He glanced nervously towards Tibor. His brother caught his eye and shook his head. Milos realised he was shaking with anticipation. His father gazed steadfastly at the closed door though Milos could see he was trying to suppress a smile. Milos felt his face blush bright red. He shut his eyes and tried to tell himself to stay calm and be less eager but already he could hear the sound of approaching footsteps. The door opened.

'About time!' said Uncle Thomas. He was a tall lean man with kind eyes and a face that always wanted to smile. 'We were beginning to think they'd decided to baptise your father as well. Come in, come in.'

He shook hands first with Jozsef, then Tibor and finally Milos. He also tousled Milos's hair. 'How are you, young fellow?'

'I'm well, thank you, Uncle,' said Milos. He stepped quickly around his uncle, expecting to find Gabriella coming to greet them. He saw his Aunt Katy instead. 'Where's Gabi?' The moment the words passed his lips, Milos regretted saying them. Suddenly everyone was laughing, not unkindly, but nonetheless he was the unwilling source of their merriment. Tibor rolled his eyes and shook his head once more as though in despair of his little brother.

'Don't worry, Gabi's not hiding,' said Aunt Katy. 'Now give me a hug.'

Milos responded politely to her greetings. '*Csokolom*,' he said formally. 'I kiss your hand.' He resolved to not say another unnecessary word until it was time to give Gabriella her present. Nobody would laugh then.

As they passed by the dining room, Milos noted with a slight tinge of disappointment the table cloth and place settings. He'd hoped that tables would have been set up outside so that they could lunch in the garden like they did in summer. That would have made the meal really special and Gabriella's birthday celebration deserved nothing less. Uncle Thomas led them into the drawing room where Gabriella was attempting a new piece of music on the piano. Milos couldn't help but notice the shiny new gold bracelet on her wrist. His shoulders sagged. How could his present possibly compete with that?

The moment Gabriella noticed them, she stopped playing and raced to greet them. She looked absolutely gorgeous and wore a dress Milos hadn't seen before. Another present! He noticed Tibor had slipped his present under his coat, out of sight. Perhaps he'd also noticed the bracelet, and was too ashamed of his gift to give it to her. He thought he should follow his brother's example but his coat was still buttoned up and his package too bulky. He felt trapped. He watched helplessly as Gabriella kissed his father, then Tibor, then turned to kiss him. She kissed each of his cheeks then hugged him. He was overwhelmed, as always, by the fresh smell of her hair, by her touch and her astonishing softness.

'Happy birthday,' he mumbled. 'I see you have a new bracelet.'

'Isn't it beautiful?' She held her wrist up to give him a closer look. 'A present from Daddy.'

It was beautiful. It was as though the craftsman who'd made it had anticipated that Gabriella would one day be the wearer and been inspired to greatness. The more Milos looked at it the more insignificant his present seemed. It hung leaden, like his sinking hopes, a dead weight in his hand.

'Hello, little Christian.'

Milos turned abruptly at the sound of the voice and found Gabriella's brother, Balazs, waiting to shake his hand.

'I hope you haven't seen any lions. You're going to have to watch out for them from now on, you know.' Balazs was smiling.

'The Coliseum,' prompted Jozsef, aware of the boy's confusion. 'The Romans used to throw Christians to the lions.'

'You know how that feels, don't you, Milos?' cut in Tibor.

Milos could feel his face flooding hotly.

'Leave him alone,' said Elizabeth. 'Come on, it's my turn for a kiss.'

Gabriella's older sister was always the first to come to Milos's aid whenever he was being teased. Family aside, he loved her second only to Gabriella. He turned and embraced her, grateful for the distraction. He still cherished the hope that Tibor would fall in love with Elizabeth and so clear the way for him with Gabriella. But Elizabeth was almost fifteen and already a young woman. Even Milos had to concede the possibility was remote.

'Well, aren't you going to give Gabi her present?'

Milos found his father looking straight at him and his throat dried up. Why him and not Tibor? It wasn't fair! Tibor should have gone first, being the elder. After they'd seen Tibor's present, everyone would have adjusted their expectations. He tried desperately to recall his little prepared speech. But when he'd lain in his bed planning his words he'd imagined that he would be alone with Gabriella, not centre stage in front of everyone.

'It's nothing,' he mumbled, unable to meet Gabriella's eyes.

'Nonsense,' said his father. 'Milos went to a lot of trouble to choose the perfect present for you, Gabi, and I'm sure you'll be delighted.'

Heartened by his father's support, Milos handed his gift to Gabriella and kissed her cheeks. He summoned up his courage. There were things he was anxious to say even though he expected everyone to start laughing again.

'Happy birthday, Gabi.' He drew a deep breath but his prepared speech abandoned him and he blurted out the first thing that came into his head. 'You're my best friend in the whole world. Honestly.' Unbelievably, his face began to flush even more hotly. He braced himself for the expected laughter but it never came.

'What a sweet thing to say!' said Elizabeth.

'Thank you, Milos. I'm going to love it whatever it is,' said Gabriella. She put his present down on the chair alongside her so she could put both arms around him to hug him. Milos held his breath and closed his eyes. He hoped with all his heart that he'd hear her reciprocate, but she didn't tell him he was also her best friend. But then she hadn't yet opened his present.

'Show us what it is,' said Uncle Thomas. 'Don't keep us all waiting.'

Gabriella loosened the ribbons that Milos had so carefully tied in a bow and unwrapped the book. There was a brief moment while she absorbed the fact that the book was written in English, took in the title and discovered that it was illustrated by the same artist who had designed her tea set. Her eyes lit up with excitement.

'Mamma, look! Look!' She raced over to show her present to her mother. Milos stood by watching, his heart pounding, as proud as any ten-year-old boy could be.

Aunt Katy looked closely at the book then almost quizzically at Milos, as if seeing him in a new light. 'You found this book for Gabi?'

Milos nodded.

'Your father is right. It is hard to imagine any gift more perfect.'

Milos felt himself grow ten centimetres in height.

'I know you're very fond of Gabi but I didn't realise you understood her so well.' She smiled wryly. 'We've underestimated you. It must have taken you a long time to find it.'

Again Milos nodded. As an afterthought, he glanced quickly towards his father, more than a little guilty at not acknowledging his contribution. He needn't have been worried. His father winked ever so slightly but it was enough. Milos had imagined taking Gabriella through the book, colour plate by colour plate, providing a commentary but, for once, curbed his eagerness. He didn't have to go seeking glory when glory had already found him and pinned him neatly in its spotlight. Uncle Thomas was beaming, Elizabeth was making a fuss over the book and even Balazs, who was far too old for stories of pirates and fairies, seemed impressed. Milos realised with sudden insight that he was behaving exactly as Tibor would, with reserve and dignity. It made him feel grown-up.

'Milos, I really don't know how to thank you enough!' Gabriella left her precious book with her brother and sister and hugged Milos once more. She kissed him again on each cheek. Just as he was plucking up the courage to put his arms around her and express in a hug what his words could not, Tibor spoke.

'I too have a present for Gabi.'

Tibor had taken off his coat. When had that happened? It suddenly made Milos acutely aware that he alone was still trussed up in his coat, every button fastened tightly. He felt upstaged. He could feel the spotlight slowly move away from him and onto his brother.

'Our deepest apologies, Tibor,' said Uncle Thomas. 'Please. Gabi?'

Gabriella slipped out of Milos's grasp. He'd been too slow in claiming his reward, or his brother too cunning. Whichever, the moment was gone and so was Gabriella. She was gone,

gone to Tibor, and all eyes and expectations moved with her. Milos frantically unbuttoned his coat. But the red paper that wrapped the present in Tibor's hand spoke to Milos and warned of his defeat. The deep blue ribbon only added confirmation. Milos felt a chill, as though the night rain clouds had returned to claim the day, covered the limitless blue sky and blotted out the sun.

'What is it?' said Gabriella.

'It isn't a book,' said Tibor, as though nothing could be more boring. Milos winced.

'It must be a record.'

Gabriella kissed Tibor but her attention was clearly on the package in her hands. Milos watched spellbound as his sweetheart untied the ribbon, as helpless as a fly in a web as the spider approached. The ribbon came off and Gabriella carefully removed the wrapping paper so as not to tear it.

'It is a record!' she said.

Milos breathed again. It was only a record. How could a record possibly match his book?

'American!'

Milos closed his eyes. There was no mistaking the amazement and delight in Gabriella's voice.

'American!' echoed Balazs. 'What is it?'

'"Sophisticated Lady",' said Gabriella, reading off the record label.

Balazs whistled.

'Duke Ellington,' said Gabriella in awe. She threw her arms around Tibor's neck and kissed him. Not only on the cheeks, but also on the mouth.

'How in the world did you get hold of that?' said Uncle Thomas. There was a tinge of admiration in his voice, even envy.

Tibor just shrugged and smiled secretively.

'Quick! The gramophone!' said Elizabeth. 'Balazs! Find a new needle.'

Milos felt as though he was outside the window peering in, no longer a participant in anything, a helpless onlooker witnessing events speeding ever faster beyond his control. The room suddenly filled with the exotic, swinging sound. Gabriella and Elizabeth began to sway to the rhythm. Balazs tapped his foot and clicked his fingers to the beat.

'What is that instrument?' asked Gabriella.

'Alto saxophone,' said Tibor. 'Johnny Hodges.'

'It's wonderful.'

'Look! Look at my arms,' said Elizabeth. 'The music is giving me goose bumps.'

They replayed the record the instant it finished and this time Gabriella took Tibor's hand and started dancing with him. Everyone applauded, Milos too, powerless to do otherwise. How did his brother do it? How did his brother manage to beat him at everything they did? He watched Tibor in dismay and fascination. He moved so fluently, held Gabriella so confidently, led her so assuredly. Where had he learned to dance like that? How? When? The spotlight had moved off Milos onto Tibor, there to remain, satisfied it had found its rightful home. Milos's spirits plumbed new lows as he was engulfed by disappointment. His gift had failed him. His hopes had been exposed as fantasies, no more rooted in reality than J.M. Barrie's tale. Gabriella had not drawn closer to him but closer to Tibor.

'Milos?'

Elizabeth, arms outstretched, stood before him. She understood. The fact that she understood and sympathised only added impetus to the tears that threatened to flood his eyes. He fought them back, refused to be caught crying, and danced instead.

By the time lunch had concluded, Milos had forgiven Gabriella for finding Tibor's record more exciting than his book. He'd also danced with her and had sat next to her at the table and it hadn't mattered at all that Tibor had sat on her other side. Milos had never been able to stay down for long at Tokaj Street. Now they were playing hide and seek, the one thing he was better at than his brother. Even though they'd long exhausted every possible place to hide, Milos was inventive and the fact that he was small for his age enabled him to squeeze into places neither Tibor nor Gabriella would even consider. He was always hardest to find and, though he suspected his brother was sometimes less than enthusiastic about looking for him, this time it didn't matter. It was Gabriella's turn to find them.

Milos could hear his father, uncle and Balazs talking together in the dining room and decided to sneak in and under the table. It was important that he was not observed because he knew that ultimately one of them would give him away. He slipped silently into the room on hands and knees and eased himself between the end chair and table leg. Once under the table he paused to see if he had been observed. There was no break in the conversation, no hesitation, no indication that his little manoeuvre had been detected.

The next step was no less delicate. He edged slowly up the table, trying to position himself on the other side of the thicket of legs. If Gabriella looked under the table, she'd expect to see him at the unoccupied end. If she searched more thoroughly, he hoped the trouser legs would shield him. That was the point at which his hiding place would normally be given away. But how could anyone give him away if no one knew he was there? Provided none of the men shifted position and inadvertently kicked him, his hiding place was secure. Milos closed his eyes tight and held his breath to suppress a sudden rush of excitement.

It had never been his intention to eavesdrop on the conversation above him, but now he realised he had no choice. His first reaction was of dismay, fearing the consequences of his father discovering his presence. His father would not be pleased. But his dismay gave way to excitement. He'd never been allowed to listen in to the things men discussed in private and he trembled with anticipation. His father was speaking.

'I'm sorry, Balazs, really sorry that you won't be studying law.'

Balazs shrugged. 'Medicine is also out which is a mixed blessing. I'm not sure my mother could deal with two doctors in the family.'

'So what are you going to do?' asked Jozsef.

'Teach,' said Balazs. 'I have applied to several universities. I will take whatever I am offered. Father says these times will pass. They always do eventually. When that happens I will study law and, hopefully and belatedly, begin my career in politics. It is all a question of patience.'

'Patience!' said Jozsef in disgust. He turned to Thomas. 'And what is he going to do until this magic moment when these times pass? Ten years from now? Twenty years? Teach the children of peasants to read and write until his brain atrophies?'

'There's a chance he will be allowed to enrol as a veterinary student,' said Uncle Thomas. His eyes found a spot on the table so he didn't have to look at his son or Jozsef.

'Dammit!'

Milos winced as his father's fist crashed into the table right above his head.

'A vet! A horse doctor! The cleverest boy in his class. No! In the entire school, in the entire north-east.'

Jozsef settled back in his chair, realising his outburst was doing nobody any good and only served to underscore Balazs's humiliation. 'For God's sake, Thomas. It could all have been avoided so easily. Balazs could be studying law today if you weren't so stubborn.'

'If we converted to Christianity, you mean.'

'Is that such a hard thing to do when your son's entire future is at stake?'

'We are Jews, Jozsef.'

39

'In name only.'

'No, by birth.'

'You are no more a Jew than I am. No more religious. I doubt you even believe in the existence of God.'

'There are many things I don't believe in and I don't believe trading phylacteries for crucifixes will make any difference.' Uncle Thomas kept his voice soft and reasonable. 'It would only undermine our identity, our sense of who we are. These days it doesn't matter who or what you claim to be. If they can find a trace of Jewish blood somewhere in your line, then you are Jewish. That's it. Look at Bela Imredy.'

Jozsef sat silent. Bela Imredy had been Hungary's prime minister up until February 1939 when his political enemies unearthed documents which purported to show Jews amongst his forebears. After that, his resignation was a formality. Thomas used Jozsef's silence to complete his argument.

'A crucifix might have got Balazs into law school, but it may not have been enough to keep him there. Look at the Losonczy boy. His lecturers "lost" pages from his assignments so they could mark him down. Sometimes they misplaced his assignments altogether and accused him of not doing them. It is one thing to study law, another thing to be allowed to graduate.'

'But Balazs wouldn't be a Jew. He would be a Christian.'

'The veneer of Catholicism would not be enough. Sooner or later Balazs would be deemed a Jew and be thrown out of university. Like the Losonczy boy.'

'The Losonczy boy is a Jew. Balazs would be a Christian,' said Jozsef, persisting with his argument. 'That changes the rules. At the very least, it would have bought him time.'

'Huh!' said Thomas dismissively.

'Yes, time,' said Jozsef. 'Perhaps even enough time to qualify. Who knows?' He shrugged, a clear signal that he was prepared to let the issue die. 'Perhaps you are right. In the long run, what will it matter? The way things are, time may become a commodity in short supply for all of us.'

'I assume you are alluding to the war,' cut in Balazs, anxious to seize the opportunity to move the discussion on. 'I am confident Horthy and Bardossy will keep us out of the war. They will preserve Hungary's non-belligerent status.'

'The regent is weak,' snapped Jozsef. 'He only ever made one decision and that was to sit on the fence. As for Prime Minister Bardossy, no one can question his integrity or the earnestness of his intentions. But he is doomed to fail exactly as his predecessor did. You cannot lie down with the devil and remain a virgin. We help feed and supply the Reich. We allowed German troops to cross Hungary to invade Romania. We allowed the Germans to use us as a stepping stone into Yugoslavia. They used our rail lines and even our rolling stock, for heaven's sake. No wonder Britain is threatening to declare war on us.'

'I support Balazs,' said Thomas. 'Britain has enough problems dealing with Hitler. Britain doesn't need a war with Hungary as well.'

He paused as Gabriella knocked on the dining room door. 'What is it, Gabi?'

'Have you seen Milos?'

'Not since lunch,' said Thomas.

'He must be here,' said Gabi. 'Tibor and I have looked everywhere else.'

'He is not in here,' confirmed Balazs. 'We would have noticed.'

'May I look under the table?'

Her father sighed gently. 'If you must, but be quick.'

Milos shrank back as far as he could behind his father's legs and held his breath. What would his father say if he was discovered now? What would Uncle Thomas think of him? He closed his eyes.

'Do you see him?' asked Uncle Thomas.

'No,' said Gabriella.

'Now run along. We'll let you know if we find him.'

Milos could hardly believe his luck. Gabriella hadn't seen him! He opened his eyes and eased away from his father's legs. He'd done it! Now he had to remain undetected until it was safe to come out.

'Have you considered what might happen to us if Germany wins?' asked Jozsef, taking advantage of the interruption. 'Do you think Hungary would be a safe place for Jews then?'

'Why not?' said Thomas. 'Hitler will have gained everything he wants. He won't need scapegoats any more. How can he blame Germany's problems on Jews when he no longer has problems? Germany will win the war within twelve months. Then things will start to settle down again. After all, there have been Jews in Germany for a thousand years.'

'I hope you're right,' said Jozsef gloomily.

'You don't think so?' asked Balazs.

'I hear disquieting things. Perhaps now is not the time.'

'What sort of things?' asked Thomas. 'If you know something, share it.'

Jozsef sighed heavily. 'I may no longer be director of railways but I have maintained a network of contacts, people who remain loyal to me or grateful for one or another reason. That is how I learned that the Germans used our railways to move troops and equipment to Yugoslavia.'

'Go on,' said Thomas.

'I don't wish to be alarmist. In fact, I'm not sure what to make of this information that has been filtering through to me. It is tenuous, to say the least.'

'Perhaps discussing it will help bring understanding,' suggested Thomas.

'Perhaps, but there is precious little to discuss. The Germans have been requisitioning box cars and modifying them with solid doors and locks. Why locks? What would you put in box cars that requires locks? Certainly not cattle.'

'Armaments,' said Balazs. 'Food. Maybe even clothing.'

'Perhaps,' said Jozsef. 'But why would the Germans be sending armaments, food or clothing to Poland?'

'Poland?' asked Thomas. 'Why Poland?'

'Why indeed. Sometimes it is dangerous pulling isolated pieces of information together. In all likelihood, they are unrelated. Particularly when the source is third- or fourth-hand and of questionable reliability. I have heard whispers that these trucks have been left under guard in sidings for two and three days at a time and that people are inside them.'

'People!'

'The original sources claim to have heard people crying out for food and water. They say the stench from the wagons is indescribable.'

'Who are these people?' asked Balazs. 'Prisoners of war?'

'Only if you consider women and children prisoners of war.'

'Women and children. Surely you're not suggesting they are Jews?' asked Thomas quietly.

'I don't know,' said Jozsef. 'I don't know what to think. My contacts in Hungary are good but not so beyond the borders. I'm led to believe most of the movement is from the German–Polish border eastwards, but there are suggestions that some of these trains originated in Germany and Austria. What isn't clear is what their final destination is. There's talk of rounding up Jews and concentrating them in ghettos. But so far it is all rumour, stories passed down the line from one railwayman to another. Railwaymen always like to know the point of origin and destination of trains that use their track. It's in their blood. But to answer your question: yes, it is rumoured the people in the box cars are Jews.'

'It doesn't make any sense,' said Thomas. 'Why would the Germans take Jews to Poland? Poland already has plenty of Jews.'

'Of course you are right,' said Jozsef. 'I'm beginning to wish I'd kept this information to myself, that's if it merits being called information. I've probably alarmed you for nothing.

But if there is any truth to these stories, we had all better hope that Germany loses the war and loses it quickly. In the meantime, you could do worse than become Christians.'

Jozsef smiled wryly, uncrossed his legs and stretched them. They met with resistance and Jozsef realised instantly what it was. His smile vanished.

'Come,' he said. 'Enough of this gloom. I think we should join the others.' He paused momentarily. 'It goes without saying that these rumours are best left in this room. No good would be served by discussing them with anyone else.'

Thomas and Balazs looked at each other, surprised and not a little perplexed. When had it ever been otherwise?

Milos remained huddled tightly in a ball after the men left, too stunned to even consider his next move. He didn't know what to think. He'd been paralysed with fear the instant his father's foot had touched him and was in dread of the consequences. But his mind also raced as it tried to deal with what he'd overheard. Living by the railways, he was familiar with the box cars that transported livestock and tried to imagine what it would be like to be crammed in one for days on end without food or water. What if they had been filled with Jews? What if the Germans came to Hungary, to Sarospatak? What if they knocked on the door of Tokaj Street?

The sun was long gone before Jozsef and his sons left to walk back to their little cottage. They'd filled up on sandwiches and cake before leaving but Milos was also burdened by guilt and his terrible knowledge. As usual, he held his father's hand while Tibor walked alongside them. They walked in silence for the first ten minutes before Jozsef spoke. To Milos's relief, he addressed Tibor, not him.

'So tell me, Tibor. How did you get hold of that record?'

Even in the dark Milos knew his brother's face would have eased into a knowing half smile.

'Contacts,' said Tibor.

'Which contacts exactly?'

'Whichever were needed,' said Tibor. 'You have always pressed upon us the value of contacts. I have learned well, no?'

'I saw the sticker on the sleeve. The price was in Austrian schillings.'

'So? According to the Nazis, this American music is degenerate. All good Austrians are getting rid of it.'

'The record was not new. Did you consider that it may have been stolen? That it may have been looted?'

'No,' said Tibor evenly. 'Did Milos ask for the provenance on his book?'

'That's enough,' snapped Jozsef. 'How do you think Gabi would feel if she discovered that the record was stolen from a Jewish family in Vienna? How would any of them feel?'

'Why would she even think such a thing? I made a list of records I thought would make a suitable present, distributed it to contacts and waited for a response. All I know is the record came from Austria, but who knows how many hands it went through to reach me? It was available. I bought it.'

'Before you try anything like this again you should consider all possibilities,' said Jozsef darkly.

They walked the rest of the way home in silence. With every step Milos feared his father would turn on him and raise the serious matter of his eavesdropping. The moment he stepped through the front door of the little cottage, Milos decided to make a dash upstairs for his bedroom. His father, however, held on to his hand, preventing his escape. Milos realised the time had come to face up to the consequences. He hung his head, mortally ashamed.

'Are you all right?' asked his father softly. He let go of Milos's hand and crouched down with a hand on each of the boy's shoulders. 'Are you all right?' he repeated.

Milos nodded. He was prepared for anger, not for compassion. For the second time that day he felt tears welling up behind his eyes. He turned away.

'You've had a busy day,' said his father gently. 'Promise me you'll put it all out of your mind so it doesn't spoil your sleep.'

Again Milos nodded.

His father smiled and hugged him. 'Good boy. Now think about this. Right now Gabi is in bed reading a wonderful book given to her by a very precious friend. Think about that, Milos, think what your best friend is doing. Think of the pleasure you are giving her. Yes? Now kiss me good night.'

As Milos lay in bed and waves of tiredness threatened to engulf him, he did his best to think of his sweetheart reading her book and taking in every detail of Mabel Lucie Attwell's glorious colour plates. But somewhere off in the background he could hear the rattle of cattle trucks and the despairing cries of their human cargo. He let the tears come and softly cried himself to sleep, vowing that if the Germans ever came to put Gabriella in a box car and send her off to Poland, he'd rescue her. No matter what.

CHAPTER FOUR

January 1942

It took another nine months for the war to reach Sarospatak, and it came not with the crash of cannons but with a knock on the door.

As Jozsef had predicted, Hungary lost its doomed attempt to sit on the fence and toppled over into the Nazi camp as a fellow belligerent, its fate sealed by Germany's attack on Russia. Two months after Gabriella's birthday and a week before his own, Milos stood alongside Tibor by the side of the railway track with their fellow students to cheer on the five young soldiers who were Sarospatak's contribution to the token force Prime Minister Bardossy had committed to the Russian campaign. The token force was Bardossy's last attempt to avert the inevitable. Believing a German victory to be imminent, certainly before the onset of winter, Bardossy sent just enough troops to placate Hitler without totally alienating the West, with whom he was attempting to engage in secret negotiations.

The students cheered and waved their little paper Hungarian flags the moment they spotted the train that would carry the soldiers to the rendezvous with the rest of the force.

It was just the regular service from Satoraljaujhely, the border town to the east, but someone had seen fit to bedeck it with ribbons. Milos waved as enthusiastically as any, obeying his father's instructions. Besides, to do otherwise would have been plain foolish. He was now Christian, one of them, and he'd learned the wisdom of letting himself flow along with the tide. Yet he was confused, his head swirling with contradictions. He'd believed his teacher when the class was told that this was a great day for Hungary, that the soldiers were going to Russia to bring an end to the war. The class had cheered and he'd cheered with them, only to learn that his father felt differently. In fact, he'd rarely seen his father so distraught. The following Sunday, when they'd gone to Tokaj Street, he'd heard his father debating the development with Uncle Thomas and Balazs. When they'd finally left the dining room, no one was smiling and the day had ended early. He was glad he had been forbidden to hide beneath the table.

A marching band played on the station platform between the students and the local dignitaries, filling the air with bright brassy sounds rather than the doleful national anthem. Clearly this was an occasion for festivity. Milos looked along the platform to see if he could spot his father standing among the dignitaries. Normally he would have been proud of him but today felt only concern. That morning he'd shined his father's shoes and helped him put on his uniform, not the one he'd been issued with by the railways but the trousers and jacket he'd had specially tailored. His father had paused midway through dressing and stared at him.

'When the train leaves, I want you to cheer with all the other boys,' said his father eventually. 'Do it for the soldiers, do it for them. I'm afraid history will record this not as the train of heroes but as the train of martyrs. No good will come of this, not for Hungary nor for us. And certainly not for them.'

When the train slowed to pick up the five self-conscious soldiers and the good wishes of the citizens of Sarospatak,

Milos waved his flag with genuine vigour. Like his brother, he kept his true feelings hidden. But if his father was right, how could so many other people be wrong? He waved until the train slowly disappeared around the bend and out of sight. All around him were proud smiling faces. How could this be, if what his father said was true?

Jozsef had also predicted that the troop train which would ultimately transport the five soldiers into Russia would only be the first of many, and that their departure would no longer occasion cheers but dread and despair. Milos fruitlessly searched the crowd for any hint that anyone shared his father's opinion. Surely his father had to be wrong.

It was late January, just seven months later, when the postman knocked on the door of Tokaj Street and delivered the papers that changed life in that wonderful house for ever. A knock had been expected, but not the one that came. If Milos had been aware of the postman's knock, he would have run around to Tokaj Street the instant school finished to comfort Gabriella. As it was, he needed comforting himself.

Milos ran all the way home from school even though his father always warned him about running when the roads were covered in snow and ice. He didn't run to keep warm but because Tibor had refused to walk home with him. Milos had pleaded with him but Tibor claimed he had other things to attend to. Milos was used to walking home alone but this time he needed his brother's company. All he could think of was getting home safely and throwing himself on the bed until all the horrible events of the day had worked themselves out. He changed his mind as he reached the door of the little cottage and instead ran on to the station.

His father's office was in the station building and Milos liked going there after school. When he was younger, he'd been allowed to spin on his father's revolving chair and make patterns with ink on his blotter. But lately Jozsef's little provincial outpost

49

had become unexpectedly busy tracking down rolling stock and scheduling the increasing numbers of special trains heading east, not only on his line but over the eastern part of the northern uplands and the north-east. It appeared that someone in authority had realised the discarded Jozsef Heyman still had value and decided to utilise his skills. His instructions came by phone from the regional centre at Miskolc.

Milos peered through the bubbled-glass office window to make sure his father was alone, knocked once on the door and entered. His father smiled tiredly until he noticed his son's hot and red face and how close he was to tears.

'What on earth's the matter?'

Milos rushed over and buried his face in his father's shoulder.

'Is it Tibor?'

Milos shook his head.

'Then what? Come on. I can't help you unless you tell me what's troubling you.'

'School,' said Milos.

'What about school?'

'They got Izsac Janosi in the toilets. They made him take off all his clothes and pissed on them. Then they made him lie down in the urinal and pissed on him too. He was screaming and begging me to help him.'

'And did you?'

'No.' Milos began sobbing.

'What happened?'

'They told me that if I didn't piss on Izsac they'd piss on me too. They told me I had to piss on the filthy Jew to prove I was a Christian.'

Jozsef pulled his son closer to him and held him.

'You did the only thing you could do. How would it have helped Izsac if you'd had to take off your clothes too and the boys had urinated on you? Tell me, how would that have helped him?'

Milos was silent.

'Izsac isn't the first Jewish boy to be treated this way and he won't be the last. This is exactly the sort of ordeal I want to spare you and Tibor. That is why I wanted you to become Christians. Sometimes you have to do things you don't want to do, things that make you feel bad. But so long as you know within yourself what is right and wrong, and do your best to do the right thing at all times, then you can go to bed at night and know you have nothing to be ashamed of. What happened today was not your fault. Understand? It was not your fault. Therefore you have no reason to be ashamed. By all means apologise to Izsac when you get the chance. And from now on, do your best to make sure you're somewhere else when this sort of thing happens. Understand?'

Milos nodded.

'Apart from that, how are you being treated at school? Are you still being treated fairly?'

'Yes,' said Milos. 'My marks are still good.'

Jozsef nodded. Tibor had told him how all the other Jewish boys at school were being victimised by their teachers, that their test papers got lost or were destroyed when coffee or ink was 'accidentally' spilled over them; and how gangs of boys stole homework off the Jews before they could hand it in and burned it in front of their faces. The Jewish children were being humiliated and made the dunces of the school.

'Sometimes . . .'

'Yes?' said Jozsef.

'Sometimes I think the only reason I don't get beaten or marked down is because of Tibor.'

'Tibor?' said Jozsef puzzled. 'Why would your teachers be afraid of Tibor?'

'They're not afraid of him,' said Milos. 'They like him. He does things for them.'

'What sort of things?'

Milos was aware of an edge creeping into his father's voice and wished he hadn't opened his mouth.

'He gets things for them. Like the record for Gabi.'

'Does he?' said Jozsef, and Milos could tell by the tone of his voice that he'd gone too far. 'And what about the school bullies? Does he get things for them too?'

Milos hung his head. He thought of the grubby, fingered postcards Tibor slipped to the older boys, the shameful pictures of brazen women who bared their breasts and worse. There was no way he could tell his father about them. Besides he'd been sworn to secrecy.

'Come on,' said Jozsef angrily. 'What does he get them?'

'I don't know,' said Milos miserably.

'Don't know or won't tell?'

'Don't know!' said Milos and pulled himself free of his father. 'I don't know!'

Jozsef stared at him for what seemed like ages and Milos didn't dare move a muscle.

'When you see Tibor, tell him I want to see him. I'll be home at five-thirty. Now go.'

Milos went, shamed by his secret and feeling guilty for betraying his brother. He was relieved to discover Tibor had not yet come home and sat down to try and work out what to say to him. No matter how he tried to phrase things, there was no escaping the facts. Tibor would be furious. Seeking distraction, he turned to his homework but couldn't concentrate. Instead he built up the fire in the fireplace, which was the cottage's only source of heat, and went down to the cellar for another scoop of coal. The coal was one of the perks of working for the railway. Jozsef was given a sackful every month throughout winter, though lately it had been reduced to half a sack. Milos had just sat down to toast a piece of bread over the flames when he heard the front door open and his brother throw his school bag onto the floor. Tibor pushed open the living room door and came straight to the fireplace.

'Move over.'

Milos moved.

Tibor stood as close to the fire as he could but it didn't stop him shivering.

'Dad wants to see you.'

'How do you know?'

'I went to see him after school,' said Milos.

'Why? Because of Izsac?'

'Yes.'

'I heard you pissed on him.'

'I had no choice.'

'You didn't have to be there, you idiot. Anyway, what's that got to do with me? Why does Dad want to see me?'

Milos looked away, ashamed.

'What did you tell him, you little twerp?' Tibor grabbed hold of Milos's arm and squeezed it as hard as he could.

'I told him you got things for the teachers so we'd get good marks.'

'What else?'

'I said you get things for the older boys.'

'Did you say what?'

'No! You made me swear to keep that a secret.'

'Good.' Tibor nodded approvingly. He let go of Milos's arm. 'Does he want me to go to his office?'

'No. He said he'd be home at five-thirty.'

'Well, that's just too bad,' said Tibor. 'I saw Elizabeth on the way home, she was riding over here on her bike. Something has happened. She wants Dad to go see Uncle Thomas the instant he comes home. She said we can come too, there's enough food.'

Any anger that Jozsef had built up on the way home dissipated the instant he entered the cottage and heard Tibor's news.

'I think I know what's happened,' he said grimly. 'Quick, get your coats and boots. And put on some dry socks.'

They set out for Tokaj Street in silence and it wasn't until they'd been walking for a kilometre that Milos dared ask the question that had been consuming him ever since Tibor had come home.

'What's the matter, Dad? What's happened?'

Jozsef sighed wearily. He was involved in his own thoughts but the boys deserved an answer.

'A train from Sarospatak is scheduled to connect with one heading to the Russian front in six days' time. All I have been told is that it is a transporter of some description. God only knows where they're getting the carriages from because I don't. I suspect Balazs has been ordered to board that train.'

Milos felt a sense of dread envelop him, but he was puzzled. He was aware of his uncle and aunt's fears for Balazs. Throughout Hungary, all eligible men of military age were being hastily mobilised to rush to the aid of the German army bogged down by Russia's winter. Balazs was a prime candidate for conscription, but for the fact that he was Jewish. Jews were no longer permitted to serve in the armed forces.

'Is Balazs joining the army? Is he going to be a soldier?' he asked.

'Soldier!' his father scoffed. 'They don't give Jews guns. They give Jews other things. Shovels, spades, axes.'

'How can Jews fight with shovels?' Milos asked.

'Someone has to build roads and bridges,' said Jozsef bitterly. 'Someone has to make camp. Someone has to dig ditches and clean latrines. Someone has to do the work so others can fight.'

'Will they give Balazs a shovel?' asked Milos.

'Probably,' said Jozsef. 'It's good that we're discussing this now because I don't want it discussed in front of your aunt. Or in front of Elizabeth or Gabi, you hear?'

'Will I have to go to Russia?' asked Tibor.

Jozsef put a reassuring arm around his elder son. 'No, you have the good fortune to be too young. So does Milos. But if the war goes on ...' He stopped mid-sentence, his brow furrowed. 'If the war goes on, we'll just have to make other arrangements.'

'What kind of arrangements?' asked Tibor.

'I don't know. Almost anything would be preferable.'

'Can Balazs make other arrangements?' asked Milos.

'It's too late,' said Jozsef sadly. 'He should have become Christian like you did. Like our fathers should have. No, like our grandfathers should have. It's all too late now!'

Elizabeth answered their knock on the door and Milos could see instantly that she had been crying. She all but ignored him and Tibor and threw her arms around Jozsef. Sobs caught in her throat as she spoke.

'Father and Balazs are waiting for you in the dining room. Mother is with them. Tibor and Milos will eat in the kitchen with Gabi and I.' Elizabeth wiped her sleeve across her eyes. 'We thought if they came it would be for Balazs. For poor Balazs! But this ... nobody expected this!' She collapsed sobbing on Jozsef's shoulder.

'Tibor! Take Elizabeth with you and look after her. Make her a hot drink. Milos, you look after Gabi. Go. Now.'

Jozsef gently eased Elizabeth away and kissed her tenderly on the forehead. 'Go now with Tibor. Let me talk with your father, see if we can sort something out.'

Jozsef smiled, and stayed put until Elizabeth and his sons had disappeared through the doorway at the opposite end of the corridor. His face darkened immediately. Not Balazs? Then who? The only alternative hit him like a blow to the head. It was so obvious! But if it had come as a shock to him, how much of a shock had it been to them? He slowly opened the door to the dining room and entered.

'Thomas, Katica, I'm so sorry.'

'They need doctors at the front,' said Thomas. He rose wearily from his chair to take Jozsef's hand.

Jozsef turned and embraced Katica.

'Why my Thomas?' she said. 'Look at him. He is not a young man!'

'I thought my age would have excluded me,' said Thomas. 'Besides, I am a doctor not a surgeon. It's surgeons they need not old, rural doctors.'

'What about you, Balazs?' Jozsef shook the young man's hand.

'We've rung around. It seems they're calling up Jewish men between eighteen and forty, and some like my father who are older. They've even called up what few Jews there are still in medical school. They haven't yet got to trainee teachers,' he added bitterly.

'Count your blessings,' said Jozsef. 'Have you considered any alternatives?'

'Like what?'

'Yugoslavia. Try and link up with the partisans. Maybe make your way to Palestine.'

'Who will look after my mother and sisters?'

'Who will look after them when you are called up to Russia?'

Katica gasped and put her hand over her mouth.

'Isn't it enough that they've taken me?' asked Thomas.

'What do you want?' said Jozsef harshly. 'Reason? Compassion? In the middle of a war? These are difficult times and I'm afraid they will only become more difficult.'

He paused, regretting his outburst, and turned to Thomas. 'You are leaving for the front on Wednesday, no?'

'How did you know?' said Thomas.

'There is a transporter heading east into Russia on Wednesday. I know it is not a troop train because we're only given short notice for those. It's somebody's idea of security. Your train will go east through Satoraljaujhely then north to Przemysl, where your carriage will be uncoupled and connected to another train heading east. I don't doubt the train will be carrying Jews to join the labour battalions.'

'Labour battalions!' said Katica. The tears had once again begun to flow. 'My Thomas is being sent away with a labour battalion? But he's a doctor!'

'Are you leaving by train?' Jozsef directed his question to Thomas who nodded confirmation. 'There is only one train heading east scheduled for Wednesday.'

'Jozsef ...' said Thomas. 'I ask you as a friend ...'

'No need. I promise I will do everything I can.'

'Your job with the railways ... it gives you some protection. And there is the matter of religion ...'

'A twelve year old could do my job, but, yes, perhaps it will buy me time.'

'You have been right all along,' said Thomas. 'You at least have taken precautions. I wish I'd listened to you.'

'Then listen to me now. Send Balazs to Yugoslavia. Do it now! Do it tonight!'

'No!' shrieked Katica. 'No ... not Balazs too.' She threw her arms protectively around her son.

'Yes,' said Jozsef. 'Don't wait for the knock on the door. Then it will be too late. Perhaps it is already too late. But staying here leaves you no choices.'

'I choose to stay here,' said Balazs coolly. 'I choose to stay here and take care of my mother and sisters for as long as I can. When I am called to the Russian front I will take my chances along with everyone else. The war can't last for ever. They can't kill us all.'

'That is your choice?' said Jozsef.

'It is.'

'Then God help you, Balazs.'

Elizabeth entered the room with a steaming tureen filled with chicken soup and a bowl of boiled potatoes.

'Aha,' said Thomas. A shadow of his familiar smile flickered across his face. 'The hernia and the pneumonia. One of the advantages of extending my practice to certain peasants. They have no money and pay with what they do have. We don't get rich but we eat well.'

57

*

It was snowing when Jozsef gathered his two sons and left Tokaj Street. The farewells had been long and tearful and no one felt like talking. Milos's head was awash with conflicting emotions, some of which made him feel guilty almost to the point of being sick. Of course he was distraught that his uncle was being sent to Russia and his heart had almost broken when he saw how distressed Gabriella was. But he had comforted her. He had held her tightly in his arms and comforted her. *He* had, not Tibor. Gabriella had cried on *his* shoulder. She had let *him* dry her tears. On this most terrible of days he felt like singing. He was mortally ashamed of feeling that way, but he couldn't help it. All the while they'd been at Tokaj Street he'd held Gabriella in his arms, promising to take care of her, to protect her, no matter what. Unbelievably, in the midst of her nightmare, his dream had come true. How was he supposed to feel?

Milos was still alternating between shame and euphoria when they reached the cottage. His father put the key in the door, then paused.

'Tibor,' he said suddenly, 'Milos told me what you do.'

'It's necessary, Father. We go to mass and confession but it's not enough.'

'Go on.'

'People have long memories. I do what I do because it is the only way. It's the only thing that saves us from being lumped together with the rest of the Jews.'

'I understand.' Jozsef rested a hand on Tibor's shoulder. 'Tibor?'

'Yes, Father?'

'Keep doing it. I do what I can to protect you and Milos, the rest you must do yourselves. Do whatever is necessary. Look after yourself. Look after Milos. You have my blessing, you understand? But promise me one thing. Promise me you'll be careful.'

He opened the door and stood back to let his sons through.

On Friday evening after confessing, Milos decided to test the good offices and compassion of his Christian God. He remained kneeling after completing his penance, remained kneeling with eyes tightly shut even after Tibor had tugged at his sleeve and told him it was time to go. He was dimly aware of Tibor losing patience and leaving him. He prayed as hard as he could, concentrating every fibre of his being, projecting his entire soul into his prayers, desperate to make a deal with God to spare his Uncle Thomas and so earn Gabriella's eternal gratitude. He promised to attend mass every Sunday and confession once a week, to keep himself pure in both thought and deed, and only stopped short of promising to join the priesthood because he'd already committed himself to marrying Gabriella. His pleas were so earnest, heartfelt and intense he believed God could not help but hear and act on them. When he joined his father and Tibor on the steps outside the church he felt unburdened and even joyful. He was aware of them looking at him oddly and was desperate to tell them the good news. Uncle Thomas would be saved!

By Wednesday, the day the train was due to depart, Milos's faith had been shaken to the core. Uncle Thomas had not been reprieved. There had been no miracle, no intercession from above. Worse, his father had forbidden him from accompanying Gabriella to the station to farewell her father. He'd begged, pleaded and thrown tantrums but his father had remained unmoved.

'You and Tibor will go to school as usual and remain there until it is time to come home. I will go to my office as usual. I imagine the station will be crowded with Jews saying goodbye to Jews. There will be soldiers and gendarmes everywhere. If you go there you will be identified as Jews when we are doing everything in our power to convince people you are not. I don't want the gendarmes thinking you are anything other than Catholics, understand? I have discussed this with Uncle Thomas and he agrees it is for the best. You will have plenty of opportunities to comfort Gabriella later. You both will.'

Milos went to school but his heart went out to Gabriella. In his mind he pictured her standing alone on the platform as the train pulled away, a forlorn, tragic figure waving despairingly, her useless cries swept away by a cold, relentless easterly wind. In his mind she was left alone on the platform, alone in the world.

Jozsef went to his office but could not settle. He retreated down the track to the signal box. The day was destined to be gut-wrenching enough without having to witness the despair and defeat on the faces of his dear friends, and on the faces of the acquaintances he'd met at the synagogue when he'd first arrived in Sarospatak, people who had accepted his agnostic views and still helped him to settle in. It was bad enough that they were being shipped off to the Russian front to almost certain death; he couldn't bear to witness the death of their hopes as well. It was only human to cling to some hope, however tenuous and fragile. The hope of a miracle. The hope that maybe things would not be as bad as they feared. Maybe the Russians would surrender. Maybe they would be among those who survived. But Jozsef knew that once they saw the train their flickering hopes would be snuffed out like a candle in the rain. There were no carriages for labour battalion conscripts. Word travels faster than trains and he'd had no need to turn his binoculars on the rolling stock in the siding to confirm the worst.

There were only three box cars for one hundred and seventy-eight men. In each car there was one bucket for human waste, one for drinking water. How many days would it take to reach their destination, most men standing until it was their brief turn to lie down? How many would fail to survive even the trip? Jozsef was ashamed by his exemption, but more so by his inability to change a single thing that might in some way alleviate their ordeal. He was ashamed of his railway uniform. That was another reason why he had retreated to the signal box.

From his vantage point, Jozsef watched as the gendarmes began herding conscripted Jews not onto the platform but into Iskola Park alongside the station, where they formed them into sections. The conscripts wore their warmest clothes and boots and held tightly packed carry bags. But Jozsef knew it wouldn't take long for the icy wind driving in from the steppes to chill every cell in their bodies. Had they been allowed to huddle together for warmth, to seek shelter from the wind, they may have found some comfort. But the gendarmes, as though to reinforce the helplessness of the Jews' plight, insisted they stand in lines.

The conscripts' families who had come to farewell their men were allowed to wait in the street to the east of the station. Gendarmes surrounded them to quell any thoughts of a demonstration. But who was there left to demonstrate? Jozsef could see only frightened women and children, a few exempted students and a smattering of helpless old men. He wanted to go to them and tell them to return home, that standing there freezing served no purpose. But though the men assembled in the park were too far away to be identified as individuals, perhaps their families clung to the hope that they might catch a last glimpse of their loved ones in a window as the train crept past. But Jozsef knew there would be no glimpses because there would be no windows. Just sealed box cars with their doors nailed shut to prevent escape. Just more cause for grief.

It was almost three hours from the time the Jews first began to assemble in the park before the train drew away from the siding and up to the platform for loading. His heart sank as Thomas and the rest of the conscripts were marched up from the park. The timber box cars were old and worn, with gaps between the slats, many of which had split and broken edges. They offered little respite from the cruel wind and the occupants' only hope was that snow and ice would freeze over the gaps. Jozsef was well aware how courageous and stoic Thomas could be, that he would rather lose his life than his dignity. But how was he feeling now as he lined up on the platform and realised that the box cars they'd seen away down the track were not for cattle or cargo but for them? How would he feel when he stepped inside? Would he be doctor and offer what comfort he could? Or succumb to the horror of the realisation that his family and Tokaj Street were now memories and his life as he had known it was over? For ever.

Jozsef raised his binoculars to his eyes, something he'd promised himself he would not do, and searched the sea of faces for Thomas. He found him eventually, still standing erect, still refusing to be bowed. He didn't dare speculate on the thoughts going through his friend's head.

'Good luck, Thomas,' he whispered. Then added, uncharacteristically, 'May you find God, my friend. May God find you.'

He didn't have the heart to search the crowd for Thomas's family in the cul-de-sac. Nor did he need to. He knew with aching certainty exactly what he would see.

Balazs's reprieve was short-lived. Five weeks later, he was rounded up with thirty-seven other Jewish men and marched under guard to the station. If the tactic was designed to humiliate them, it achieved its objective. Jozsef didn't know whether the anti-Semitic propaganda had begun to bite or whether the Gentiles of sleepy Sarospatak had finally decided to show their true colours. A change had come over the town, that much was certain. War unites people against a common enemy, and propaganda had branded all Jews as Communists and Russian sympathisers and therefore the enemy. They ceased being friends and neighbours, bakers and butchers, cobblers and teachers, doctors and lawyers, and instead became somehow responsible for all the suffering endured by Hungarian soldiers on the eastern front. People lined the streets to abuse and spit on the sorry, despondent conscripts as they zig-zagged to the station, gathering one unfortunate from this street, another from that. Doubtless there were some decent citizens who felt ashamed by what their fellow townsfolk were doing, but, whoever they were, they were not in evidence.

Jewish families following along behind were not spared either. Yet they persevered, continuing on through the abuse too numbed by their impending loss to fully comprehend what was happening. It was small compensation that this time families were allowed onto the platform and even permitted to hug the conscripts one last time. Perhaps some found hope in the fact that there was no box car for these conscripts but a regular carriage, albeit one guarded by a contingent of gendarmes.

Jozsef had thought about retreating once more to the signal box but had decided against it. He watched the tearful farewells through his window, coffee in hand, until he spotted Balazs. The young man's courage touched him. Balazs was far too intelligent not to understand the dreadful fate which in all likelihood awaited him, yet he smiled encouragingly at his mother and sisters, comforted them and gave them heart. Perhaps Jozsef realised the truth in that instant: that he was deluding himself by thinking he was hiding his Jewish origins, and it was only a matter of time before he boarded one of the trains himself.

He left the security of his office and walked out onto the platform, pushing his way through the crowd to Balazs. The gendarmes had already begun separating family from conscripts when Jozsef reached the young man. He handed him his mug of hot steaming coffee.

'When you get back, leave Hungary. Go to Palestine. Go where you are wanted. Go where Jews have a future.' Jozsef took Balazs's hand and shook it solemnly.

For a brief instant the young man's composure weakened. He realised immediately what Jozsef was doing, that he was giving him another reason to try to stay alive, a dream to help sustain him.

'Any chance you can re-route this train?' Balazs asked wryly.

'I'll see what I can do.'

Jozsef stepped back to allow the gendarmes to load their human cargo. Soon the conscripts would be transferred to box cars; Jozsef knew the location of the siding where the box cars awaited them. Once inside, guards would drive home the final nails in the coffin of their hope. Jozsef remained on the platform while the train pulled away, ears filled with the wails and cries of those left behind. He suspected he was watching his own fate previewed and wondered how much longer his job would protect him. How much more time would it buy him with his sons?

Up until he'd been stripped of his position and influence and banished to the provinces, Jozsef hadn't thought much about meals, other than that he enjoyed some more than others. Food was something that simply appeared on the table, even while his wife was still alive, a product of the kitchen which was the province of their housekeeper and rarely visited. His exile changed everything and Jozsef had been forced to learn to cook. At the beginning, his repertoire had been limited to frying and baking meat when it was available. But with meat scarce, he'd had to learn how to make soups and stews with vegetables and often no meat at all. His cooking never rose to great heights but he managed well enough. If the boys had any complaint it was that he often cooked enough to last three nights. Three nights of beetroot soup or goulash was as much as any boy could stand.

The evening Balazs left for Russia, Jozsef didn't take his

sons to Tokaj Street to extend their sympathies. He'd learned from Thomas's departure that Katica, Elizabeth and Gabriella needed time alone to come to terms with their loss, and that their presence, however well-meaning, only impeded the process. Instead they stayed home and finished off a spicy stew which Tibor had reheated. As Jozsef watched the two boys mop up the gravy with thick, coarse bread, he made a decision. He decided the time had come to prepare Tibor and Milos for life on the run.

'From tomorrow, you boys will be entirely responsible for what we eat in this house,' he said.

His sons looked at him curiously, not grasping the significance.

'You will buy the food we eat and make all the meals.'

'But Dad ... !' said Milos. 'We don't know how to cook. I don't. Tibor doesn't.'

'Shut up,' said Tibor. He turned to his father. 'What exactly do you have in mind?'

'Food is becoming scarce and also expensive. You will have a budget which you will keep to. You will have to sniff out sources for vegetables and for meat. You will have to make contacts with peasants and deal directly with them. You will both do this, understand? There will be no division of tasks. Tibor, you will teach Milos how to deal with people. You will also both learn to cook.'

Jozsef reached across the table so he could put an arm on the shoulders of each of his sons. 'I am sorry that this has become necessary. Today they took Balazs away. I can't pretend that one day they won't also take me.'

Milos leapt from his chair to throw his arms around his father who'd just expressed his worst fear. Jozsef's oval face eased into a tired smile.

'Enough, Milos, I haven't gone yet.' He gently coaxed his son back to his chair. 'Meanwhile we have time for adventures.'

'What sort of adventures?' asked Milos suspiciously.

'After church on Sunday, why don't we go hiking in the country? We'll pack a lunch and take it with us. See how far we can get. Maybe the following Sunday we'll take the train to Satoraljaujhely and hike up into the Zemplen Hills. We've been far too lazy. It's time we got to know the countryside around us. What do you think?'

'Yes!' said Milos.

'Why east?' asked Tibor. 'Surely we'd be better off heading south-west?'

'East away from Germany or west away from Russia? One day the choice will be made for you, no? My thinking is that forests and hills will serve you better than the wide open plains of the Alfold. Perhaps one day we should explore the caves of Aggtelek. Would you like to see the caves, Milos?'

'Yes,' he said, suddenly serious as he realised the intent of the conversation. These were the other arrangements his father had spoken of and, in typical fashion, was preparing them for. Milos dreaded the answer to the next question but felt compelled to ask.

'When will they come for you?'

'Next week, next year, maybe never. Who knows? One day they will realise that the father of these two fine Christian boys is still nominally a Jew. On that day they may also discover that our little backwater railway can get along quite nicely without me. The point is, Milos, if we wait for them to act, we will have no option but to do exactly as they say.'

'Will you come with us?'

'Maybe.' Jozsef glanced at Tibor. 'Even if I do, I would still want Tibor to lead. I would do exactly what he told me to do without hesitation. Milos, will you do what Tibor tells you to do?'

'Yes, I always do.'

Jozsef laughed. 'Then it's settled. You two are now in charge of meals. And every Sunday from now on, we're going exploring.'

66

'One thing,' said Milos.

'What?'

'Can we take Gabriella with us?'

Nobody came for Jozsef that summer, nor was there a knock on the door in the autumn or even as winter once again took hold. Often during their hikes and Sunday adventures it was possible to forget there was a war on, to forget the threat that hung over their heads. They explored the northern uplands and Zemplen Hills, not just familiarising themselves with the trails and terrain but building up their strength and fitness. Milos put on a growth spurt that saw him not only catch up with Gabriella but pass her. Even Jozsef slimmed down with all the unaccustomed exercise, but he pretended to blame his loss of weight on the meals Tibor and Milos prepared. At Tibor's insistence, they also explored the country south-west, into the great plains where they met their first *csikos*, Hungary's legendary cowboys who tended the herds of cattle and horses. Sometimes Gabriella accompanied them but she struggled to keep up.

Once a month, they stayed in Sarospatak for Sunday lunch at Tokaj Street. Although much of the spark that had made their visits so magical had gone east with Uncle Thomas and Balazs, lunch at Tokaj Street still held an irresistible attraction. It wasn't just another opportunity to see Gabriella that drew the boys but something far more meaningful. They didn't have to cook.

Jozsef and his two Catholic sons still managed to exempt themselves from the random persecutions that affected other Jewish families. People didn't abuse them or throw stones through their windows at night. No one blamed them, as other Jews were blamed, for the loss of a husband, son or brother on the eastern front. No one pissed on the boys in the school toilets. No one spilled ink over their homework. Jozsef continued to count his blessings but the war touched them nonetheless. Agnostic railwaymen and Christians were not immune to its heartbreak.

Thomas's carefully worded letters were infrequent at best, but each one was received gratefully and joyfully in Tokaj Street, providing confirmation that he was still alive. Sometimes they came with a note attached, confirming that the letter had been smuggled away from the front by a grateful patient and forwarded on. Then the letters ceased. There were none from Balazs either. Not once had they received any kind of letter or message from him but that was of less concern. Very few messages escaped the camps of the labour battalions. But they expected to hear from Thomas in his privileged position in the field hospitals. Thomas's continued silence hit Tokaj Street hard. Not even the Sunday lunches with Jozsef and the boys could dispel the growing sense of dread.

Six weeks after the disastrous Battle of Voronezh, in which Hungary's army was virtually annihilated and most of its equipment destroyed, a knock on the door confirmed their worst fears. Thomas was dead. The news burst upon the household with all the force of the Russian shell which had killed him. He had been blown to pieces midway through the battle, doing what he'd been trained to do: trying to save another soldier's life.

Jozsef, Tibor and Milos raced around to Tokaj Street the instant they heard, but what could they do? Thomas had not just been the head of the family but its heart and mainstay, the prop to which Katica and her daughters' plans for the future were attached. His death left them bereft of support, purpose and direction. Jozsef and his sons did what they could. They could comfort but they could not cure. Only time could do that. Only time.

As the weeks and months passed, Jozsef's own fears heightened. Jews were still being rounded up for labour battalions to work mines and factories, and each departing train brought both relief and a warning. The gendarmes were casting their net wider. Able-bodied men were taken regardless of age and they'd even taken some boys as young as sixteen. Tibor was now fourteen and a half. Jozsef realised time was rapidly running out.

*   *   *

Milos stopped speaking and reached for his wine glass, despite the fact that he'd drained it half an hour earlier and it had sat empty ever since. Gancio recognised this as the signal to start preparing their coffees and grappa. Intermission had come at last.

'Why the third person?' said Neil.

Milos ignored him and rubbed his eyes wearily.

'Let's at least wait for coffee before beginning the interrogation,' said Ramon. He turned his head in the direction of the hissing espresso machine.

'I agree,' said Lucio. 'It can be exhausting telling a story, as we are all aware. Particularly one as harrowing as this.'

'Let him ask,' said Milos. 'It's a fair question, one I should have answered before I began. I refer to myself in the third person because I have little choice. It is the only way this story can be told.'

'The only way or the best way?' asked Ramon.

Milos hesitated. 'Both,' he said and leaned heavily on his elbows as though the questioning was taking the last of his energy. 'Of course there are other ways, no? But they are inappropriate. I would find it embarrassing to use the first person. Saying "I did this, I did that" all the time. It is also easier to be objective using the third person. You can understand that, no?'

'Sure. Like Ramon did,' said Neil, referring to the last story the blind man had told.

'Ah, Neil, this is your downfall,' said Ramon. 'You can never resist the opportunity to score cheap points. But look what you've done — you've created a diversion and let Milos off the hook. I don't believe for one second that he chose to use the third person to aid objectivity or because he would find it embarrassing to use the first person. No, there is a more calculated reason and clearly he does not want us to know what it is. Is he using the third person because it is necessary to get to the truth? Or to contrive a fiction? What do you think, Neil?'

'I think it's just a conceit, a tiresome attempt to bring his story to life.'

'Ignore him, Milos,' said Lucio. 'That kind of comment doesn't merit an answer. He's still sore because we made him wait to tell his story.'

'Rubbish,' said Neil. 'It's just that I've heard it all before. The war sucked. People suffered. Jews got trampled on. Where are the twists we were promised, the subtle interplay of wit, a little levity? Entertainment, for God's sake.'

'*Egy kis turelmet*,' said Milos.

'Yes,' said Ramon, 'have a little patience. Milos does nothing without good reason. He builds his stories like the Egyptians built pyramids. Stone by stone. Foundations first. His use of the third person is one of those foundations. If you hadn't interrupted, we might have more insight into his motives. Milos also promised us another breach of our conventions, one we could not anticipate. I think his use of the third person provides a clue to what form this breach might take. Your impatience denied me the opportunity to pursue this.'

'You'll survive,' said Neil.

'That's not the point,' said Ramon. 'The clues are there if you care to listen. If you care to use your brain before you open your mouth.'

'Here you are,' cut in Gancio. He glanced anxiously from Ramon to Neil. 'Coffee and grappa. What's the matter with you anyway? You don't normally argue until the fourth day of a new story.'

'It's the pace of the story,' said Neil morosely. 'I already feel like I've been here for days.' He turned to Milos. 'So where are you taking us next? More wallowing in the past? Where are we up to — 1943? God help us, this story is going to take for ever.'

'I think I'm beginning to understand your problem, Neil,' said Milos. 'Earlier you accused me, and people like me who have escaped tyrannies, of feeling superior because we have suffered and you haven't. That's a distortion of the truth, isn't it? The problem is not that we feel superior but that you feel inferior, because we have lived whereas you haven't.'

'Rubbish.'

'Rubbish? I don't think so. What were you doing when you were twelve years old? Were you being beaten up at school and pissed on? Was your father plucked out of your happy little home and sent away to certain death? No. We all know he wasn't. While your father was teaching you to play cricket, mine was teaching me how to survive. How to survive the Arrow Cross thugs who plucked Jews off the street at random and lynched them. How to survive Eichmann and Auschwitz. How to survive the Russians. You resent the fact that I lived more as a teenager than you will in your entire life. You resent the fact that you will never have any experiences to compare with mine. Never! Admit it, Neil.'

'Crap,' said Neil, but he was clearly uneasy.

'I think Milos has hit the nail on the head,' said Lucio.

'I do too,' added Ramon.

The blind man was intrigued. He was surprised at how determined Milos was to make Neil regret his comments and was beginning to wonder whether there was more to it, whether this was the whole point of Milos's story. Was his attack on Neil premeditated or opportunistic? Ramon suspected the latter. Milos had set out to unburden himself of his past and was obviously irritated by Neil. Then again, he must have known how Neil would react to another European war story. Ramon smiled inwardly at the apparent contradiction. Neil wanted entertainment; Ramon was certain that he was going to get far more than he bargained for.

'You see, Neil,' continued Milos, 'I think you resent my living through some of the most terrible events in history. You feel the fact that I survived them — that I had the wit, strength and courage — somehow makes me superior to you. That's quite understandable, no?'

He paused to let this last barb sink in, aware how much Ramon and Lucio were enjoying Neil's discomfort.

'You may resent me for this, but the truth is, I envy you. I envy you because you will never know fear as I have, never suffer my deprivations, never be in a situation where life and death stand as equals, neither more nor less desirable than the other. I envy the fact that you will never know if you too have the wit, strength and courage to survive.'

'Where's all this shit coming from?' said Neil defensively. 'I just asked where you're taking us next.'

'I'm taking you back again, Neil, where else? This story must run its course. But for your sake I'll skip a year. I'll move the story on. Does everyone agree?'

'It's your story,' said Ramon. 'It will be absorbing however you choose to tell it.'

'If I jump a year to nineteen forty-four, I'll need to fill the gap with a little bit of history. I'll keep it as brief as I can so Neil doesn't fall asleep.'

Milos settled back in his chair, as did the others. The second session had begun.

'The regent, Horthy, and the new prime minister, Miklos Kallay, were still loath to commit themselves entirely as Hitler's allies, despite having sent their entire army to the eastern front to fight Russia. They'd crawled into bed with Germany but refused to believe they were bearing its child. They tried to climb back on the fence instead and committed themselves to another bizarre balancing act. They again sent feelers out to the West to establish a dialogue. They feared Russia even more than they feared Hitler and believed they were doing the West a favour by fighting with the Germans on the eastern front. Their ideal scenario went something like this: the Germans defeat Russia after which the West defeats Germany, whereupon Hungary would open its borders to the West unopposed.

'In the meantime they wanted to keep their hands clean. They imprisoned the leaders of Hungary's Nazi Party, the Arrow Cross, and protected Hungarian Jews from the Germans. By this time, Jews from all over Europe were being taken to the death camps but none came from Hungary. In fact Hungary became something of a haven for Jews from other European countries. In retrospect, this is quite extraordinary. Horthy had a history of anti-Semitism and the Hungarian army was openly anti-Semitic. So why? Simple. Because Horthy wanted to limit the damage when the West ultimately won.

'Yet while Horthy protected the Jewish women and children, he permitted the labour battalions, though he must have known how appallingly the Jewish conscripts were being treated. The lucky ones were sent to work as slave labour in mines and factories. They still died in droves but at a much lesser rate than those who were sent to the eastern front and were at the mercy of the anti-Semitic sadists in the Hungarian army. You know, even the German SS were appalled at the treatment the Hungarian army dished out to their Jews. Horthy wanted to help Germany defeat Russia and in the Jewish labour battalions he had a potentially powerful resource. If only the army had looked after them.

'Instead the army treated them worse than slaves. They arrived at the front after anything up to ten days in the box cars, having had little water and even less food to sustain them. They were weak, dispirited, half dead and half frozen before they even arrived. They were dropped into camps that often had no shelter and no sanitation and immediately put to work. Can you imagine how back-breaking digging that frozen Russian soil must have been? They were forced to work till they dropped, and when they didn't work fast enough they were cruelly beaten. Some were even shot. They were thrown into latrines and defecated upon. Every humiliation imaginable was heaped upon them. Those who didn't die from overwork died from disease or exposure. There were innumerable atrocities. In at least one instance, Jews were used for target practice. Target practice. Live rounds, live targets.

'But Horthy's balancing act, like Bardossy's, was doomed to fail. As the Russian army advanced Hitler became concerned about his unreliable ally and, to protect his supply lines and communications, offered Horthy a simple choice: either full cooperation under German supervision or full German occupation and the status and treatment of an enemy country. Once again Horthy toppled off the fence into the German camp, this time with catastrophic consequences for Hungarian Jews.

'Horthy sacked Kallay and formed a collaborationist government. When the Germans moved into Hungary, so did Adolf Eichmann. He'd already demonstrated his ruthlessness in exterminating Jews from the rest of Europe. Now he was given free hand in Hungary to do whatever he liked.'

CHAPTER FIVE

Spring 1944

People say that if you put your ear to a railway line you can hear a train coming long before it comes into view. Jozsef put his ear to the line through his many contacts and began hearing the names of places like Auschwitz, Buchenwald, Mauthausen and Dachau. His first reaction was disbelief. He dismissed the rumours but they refused to go away, each new rumour substantiating the other and contributing to a mass which could no longer be ignored. One Friday, he took his suspicions to the synagogue on Rakocsi Street and discovered he wasn't the first to air them. Jews who had fled to Hungary from other parts of Europe had brought the horrific tales with them, tales spread in dark, disbelieving whispers from one community to another. Still, people doubted the truth. Such cold-blooded inhumanity was too incredible, too extreme, to be anything but outrageous exaggeration. The scale was simply beyond people's capacity to comprehend. But if others could deny the rumours, Jozsef could not. His visit to the synagogue may not have convinced anyone else, but it convinced him.

When the Germans occupied Hungary in March 1944, Jozsef had little doubt what would happen. The only unanswered question was when. He believed the round-up would start in Budapest, where most of Hungary's Jews were concentrated, and gradually spread out to the provinces. Sarospatak was one of the furthest towns from the capital and he drew heart from that. With the Russians making huge progress west and knocking on the door of Eastern Galicia, he thought the odds favoured them reaching the sleepy backwater of Sarospatak well before Adolf Eichmann. In truth, that was what he wanted to believe, because the alternative was too horrific to countenance. So he believed it. He ignored the advice he'd given Balazs and the stand he'd taken with his sons. Uncharacteristically, having consistently preached the gospel of pre-emptive action and each person taking control of their own destiny, Jozsef decided to wait and see what happened.

To some extent, Jozsef was blinkered by poverty. When he had been forced to leave Budapest, he'd lost not only his position but most of his money and possessions. He'd lost his furniture and his art, which he'd been obliged to sell for a laughable sum to his successor, along with his apartment. All he had brought with him to Sarospatak was the proceeds from the sale, his wife's jewellery and some cash which he'd had the foresight to place in his mother's care. Over the years, much of that money had been dissipated supplementing his meagre salary. Although he was required to coordinate and schedule rail activity throughout the region, he was still paid as a lowly rural stationmaster. Jozsef took pride in the fact that he'd managed to keep himself and the boys well fed, their clothes clean and in good repair, and their little cottage comfortable and warm, despite his circumstances. So when the Germans introduced new restrictions on Jews, being a man with little to lose he didn't heed the warnings.

He was unaffected when, over the following weeks, Jews were ordered to hand over their shops, offices and factories to Aryan management, unaffected when Jews were expelled from the professions, and overlooked when they were expelled from the civil service. He was unaffected when Jews were ordered to give up their telephones, cars and radios, having none to give up. Unaffected when bank accounts were frozen and Jews obliged to surrender their bicycles. When tighter rationing was introduced, he had every confidence in the ability of Tibor and Milos to obtain alternative supplies. The boys had taken their responsibilities to heart and bins of potatoes, turnips, parsnips and beets were hidden in their cellar along with sealed jars of sugar, flour and salt. This food, and the remaining cash he kept stashed away, provided a hedge against tough times. Jozsef had been expecting the restrictions and took the view that they were fortunate they hadn't been introduced earlier. He saw them as harsh but temporary, certain to be reversed when the Russians arrived. The only restriction that caused him to lose sleep was the edict that all Jews and those with Jewish blood had to wear a yellow star-shaped patch.

He was a Jew but because of the importance of his work for the railways his Jewishness was tolerated. His sons were Roman Catholic and only half Jewish. They were not persecuted for their Jewish blood and were generally accepted in the community as Catholics. They had not only been baptised but confirmed into the Catholic Church. They confessed every week and took the sacrament every Sunday. They were Catholics and that was a status he wanted to protect at all costs. Yet they also had Jewish blood and the penalty for Jews not wearing the yellow star was death.

Jozsef believed it was more dangerous to admit to being a Jew than to deny it. He reasoned that if he and his sons were not perceived to be Jews, no one would notice the absence of the yellow star. He instructed them not to wear the patch and elected not to wear one himself. After all, how could his sons continue as Catholics if their father proclaimed himself a Jew?

At first Jozsef was vindicated in his defiance. Most Jews were sufficiently frightened by the German occupation to do exactly as they were told. Yellow stars blossomed and this seemed to keep the gendarmerie happy. Nobody considered the *Mischlinge*, the Jews of mixed blood, and sleepy Sarospatak lacked the manpower to track them down and strictly enforce the edict.

There was a hiatus for two weeks, during which nothing happened to cause Jozsef any particular alarm. But towards the end of April things began to change. It is the nature of railwaymen to keep tabs on who comes and goes, and Jozsef couldn't help but notice an irregular pattern among the arrivals. One day seven men arrived among the usual handful of passengers. The obvious thing that aroused Jozsef's interest was that they were of military age, clearly healthy, yet not in military uniform. They also pretended not to know each other when sly glances and smiles indicated otherwise. Over the next few days more men arrived under the same guise. The only mitigating circumstance was that far more young men remained on the train and passed through to Satoraljaujhely. Later, when he recognised one of the new arrivals wearing the cock-plumed uniform of the gendarmes, he decided it was time to warn his sons.

Dinner was a carefully measured serve of vegetable soup made from dried vegetables and paprika and supplemented with chunks of fresh potato and turnip. There was no bread, coarse or otherwise, to wipe their bowls clean and fill the gaps in their stomachs. The soup was plain and sustaining but barely enough. Jozsef decided to let his sons enjoy it as best they could before voicing his concerns.

'Have you noticed any increase in the number of gendarmes?' he asked eventually.

'We were wondering if you'd noticed,' said Tibor.

Jozsef smiled. His sons missed nothing. Tibor was growing into the man Jozsef had always expected him to become. Already one hundred and seventy-five centimetres tall, raw-boned and strong, he exuded a sense of certainty that went beyond mere confidence. Milos had acquired some of his elder brother's self-assurance but his physique and character would never be as imposing. The boy was bright but far too sensitive.

'They've been bringing the gendarmes in by train,' said Jozsef. 'A few at a time and wearing civvies. I think they're doing it deliberately so as not to cause alarm.'

'There are more patrols now,' said Milos. 'They're stopping more people in the street.'

'I'm not sure there's any need to be overly concerned,' said Jozsef. 'They're obviously just here to enforce the new rules. Fortunately, you'll be as much strangers to them as they are to you. Make sure you carry your baptismal papers with you. If you're stopped they'll have no reason to accuse you of being Jews.'

'So long as that's all they're here for,' said Tibor.

'What do you mean?' said Jozsef.

'Haven't you heard what they've been doing?'

'No.'

'Apparently some of them have been stopping Jews in the street and beating them up. I've heard that many of these new gendarmes are Arrow Crossmen.'

'When did you hear this?' said Jozsef, suddenly alarmed.

'This afternoon. I think it's going to make our little forages a bit more exciting.' Tibor smiled and winked at Milos.

'Arrow Crossmen,' repeated Jozsef. 'Why would they send Arrow Crossmen here?'

'They are gendarmes who happen to be Arrow Crossmen. But it might explain why they came in civvies,' said Tibor. 'How many more gendarmes do you think there are?'

'Between twenty and twenty-five. Most of them went on to Satoraljaujhely.'

'If they work shifts, that means there won't be any more than ten or twelve extra men out on patrol at any one time.'

Tibor sat thinking for a moment. 'That's not many if you spread them around a bit.'

'All the same,' said Jozsef, 'you should exercise caution. I think you should both stay home for a while. We've got enough food. We can get by on the rations and what we have in the cellar. There's no need to take risks.'

'I agree we should exercise greater caution,' said Tibor. 'But the more people there are who think like you, the more opportunities there are for us. Besides, we're invited to lunch at Tokaj Street this Sunday. It's time we repaid past hospitality with something more substantial than potatoes and turnips. Milos and I thought we should take them some meat.'

'Meat! Where are you going to get meat from?'

'I have a contact,' said Tibor. 'Four hundred grams of bacon bones. The price is too high so I guess they must include a fair amount of bacon. It's set up for tomorrow night.'

'Tomorrow night.' Jozsef shook his head. 'I don't think that's wise. I think you should wait a while. See how things are.'

'It's tomorrow or never. That's the deal. If we pull out someone else will take our place. Right, Milos?'

'Tibor's right, Father. Besides, they need something to cheer them up around at Tokaj Street.'

'Okay.' Jozsef raised his hands in mock surrender. He could see no point arguing when Tibor had already made up his mind, and could not find it in his heart to deny the women at Tokaj Street anything that would bring some cheer into their lives. Besides, Tibor was better placed to assess the risks. 'I can't tell you not to go but I can tell you to take care.'

'Yes, Father,' said Tibor.

'And take Milos.'

There were times Tibor wanted to challenge his father's edict on task-splitting. He acknowledged the wisdom of it because he still had much to teach his younger brother, and had to accept that one day his luck might desert him. One day the gendarmes might catch him smuggling food. One day Milos might have to manage on his own. As much as Tibor liked to minimise risk and make sure everything was under control, he had to acknowledge that luck was playing an increasing part in his activities.

Tibor could feel Milos shivering alongside him. They lay on their bellies beneath a neglected stand of apricot trees. With no one to prune the trees, the naked branches hung listless and straggly. The snow that had been threatening all day had finally begun to fall and carpet the ground. Tibor hoped the snow might keep the gendarmes inside where it was warm but knew it was only wishful thinking. It might keep some gendarmes inside. On the other hand, the snow diluted their only advantage: darkness. The peasant's house and small cluster of pens and stables stood out in stark relief against the snow. Tibor realised he had no choice but to use the track carved into the soil by the farmer's carts. To do otherwise would leave a telltale trail of footprints. Sooner or later the snow would cover them, but later might be too late.

'Reverse your coat.'

Milos obeyed Tibor's instruction instantly, even though putting the wet exterior against his clothes would make him colder. He had been expecting it. At the onset of winter, Tibor had given their coats to Elizabeth and asked her to sew in a new liner made from old sheets. She'd done so and, once reversed, the coats blended in with the snow.

'Stay here. The last thing we need is two sets of footprints. If gendarmes come keep as still as you can. If they stop me, I'll deal with it.'

Milos nodded. He hadn't yet learned all Tibor could teach him but he could recognise the risks and see the logic in his brother's instructions.

'Good luck,' he whispered.

Tibor rolled gently onto the pathway so he left no footprints back to Milos's hiding place, stood and set off as quickly as he could towards the tiny house. He didn't reverse his coat but pulled his neck into the collar as peasants did. He also pulled his cap lower over his face and contrived to walk with a typical peasant's bent-back shuffle. Milos found himself smiling despite the danger and his discomfort. His brother had a good eye and a talent for mimicry. Nobody could look at him and think he was anything other than a peasant making his way home. Milos watched until Tibor's shape became blurred by the snow then turned his attention back to his surrounds. He listened for soft footfalls, the crunch of a twig hidden beneath a dusting of snow, the sound of a vehicle on the street in front of the houses behind him, the bark of a disturbed dog.

The house was three hundred metres from the vantage point in the orchard, on a flat plain with few trees and no cover. Tibor had baulked at the location of the handover but had been given no choice. He was mobile and the seller wasn't, laid low by an infected ulcer on his leg. If Tibor was unwilling to take the risk, there were others who weren't. He'd intended to circle around the house and approach from the opposite side to the town. But the snow had left him no choice. He could smell wood smoke and see wisps rise from the little house's chimney. Back door or front? Front. If anyone was watching from the town, if there was the slightest chance he was still visible to them, he didn't want to arouse their suspicions by stealing around the back. He approached the front door and pressed hard against it before knocking. A peasant would not knock on his own front door. It opened instantly and he stepped quickly inside.

Tibor removed his cap and smiled at the woman who'd opened the door. She was plainly frightened, too frightened to respond. Without hesitating he stepped up to her and kissed her on both cheeks. The woman's jaw dropped in amazement and she couldn't help but smile back. That was something else Tibor was good at, something Milos had yet to master. Tibor had the ability to infect people with his own confidence and, by so doing, made them want to do business with him again. That was important. Contacts were becoming increasingly scarce as the gendarmes stepped up their patrols. Every contact had to be managed.

The house was basically two rooms and a tiny kitchen. The larger room was for eating and entertaining, the smaller one was the bedroom. Tibor quickly took in the rack of bacon bones sitting on the table between two candles so that he could inspect it. His glance told him all that he needed to know. The peasants were honest and not out to cheat him. He walked straight past the table and stopped at the bedroom door. A single candle burned inside a blackened glass chimney, throwing just enough light for Tibor to see the man on the bed propped up against pillows, his injured leg swaddled in bandages. He tossed a tiny packet of powders onto the bed.

'For your leg. It's not much but it'll help.'

The man stared back at him, his face barely visible.

'You bring the cigarettes?'

'Of course,' said Tibor.

'I'll take those for the pain.'

Tibor smiled. He'd shown his face and sweetened the trade with the remains of a sulphur compound his Uncle Thomas had once given him. It was all a question of trust. He turned back to the table.

'Wrap it,' he said.

'You don't want to examine it?' The peasant woman could not hide her surprise.

Tibor replied by taking the small packet of Munkas cigarettes from his pocket and placing it on the table. He then handed the woman the small packet of salt, the larger packet of sugar and the bag of flour. She weighed each bag in her hands expertly before sampling the contents with the tip of her finger. She couldn't help smiling.

'How do you get these things?' she asked.

'How do I get bacon?' he replied.

Tibor watched her wrap the bacon bones, trying not to appear anxious. He had three hundred metres of open country to cross. Milos was waiting beneath the apricot trees alone and vulnerable. And they still had to duck patrols back across the river and all the way across town to their cottage. The woman finished her wrapping and handed the package to him.

'Be careful,' she said, and crossed herself.

Tibor slipped out of the door and studied his footprints. The snow was filling them in but too slowly. Realising that if he walked back the same way his tracks would be so deep they'd probably stay there till morning, he stepped over the hump in the track to the furthest rut the cartwheels had made. Once again he affected the peasant's hunched shuffle. He appeared to be watching the path ahead of him but in fact his eyes scanned his surroundings as best they could. Snow was still falling but too lightly to hide him from anyone watching. Despite the fact that he saw nothing out of the ordinary, nothing to cause alarm, he began to feel apprehensive. The lie of the land left him too exposed. If there were any patrols about they would stop him on principle. He wanted to run but instead forced himself to slow down. He stopped as though to tighten the binding on his boots, something he thought a peasant might do but a nervous smuggler, never.

'Idiot!' he whispered, berating himself. If a patrol was watching they'd stop him anyway. He realised his play with his boot was only to reassure himself, or an unconscious piece of bravado to impress Milos. The thought made him smile and he glanced up towards the apricot trees where he knew his brother would be watching him. His smile froze. A match flared briefly in the night. A cigarette glowed. Two dark shapes moved out onto the track fifty metres ahead of him, blocking the way. There was nothing aggressive or intimidating about the way they moved. Their mere presence was intimidation enough. Tibor realised his luck had finally run out.

Milos had heard the gendarmes coming down the path behind him, heard them laughing as they discussed a girl. One of them had finally persuaded her to open her legs. His heart had leapt into his mouth and his breath froze on his lips. He took his eyes off Tibor and slowly turned so that he could see the men. He hoped their conversation would keep them sufficiently distracted so that a cursory look around would suffice and they'd turn back the way they'd come. But they didn't turn back, they kept coming towards him. Closer, closer. Milos held his breath as they drew alongside then stopped less than two metres in front of him. He knew the dusting of snow over his inside-out coat would make him well nigh invisible in the dark unless he'd moved and churned up the snow. Had he moved? No. But surely they could hear him breathing! He almost groaned aloud when he heard a match strike and saw the brief flare.

'Hey you!' called one of the guards. Milos lifted his head, thinking he'd been spotted in the glow of the match. But they were looking away from him and down the path. Straight at Tibor. The sudden flood of relief went as quickly as it came. They'd spotted Tibor! Milos fought back panic. What had Tibor told him to do if the gendarmes came? Stay put, keep still, let him deal with it. Milos had no illusions about Tibor's skills as a negotiator but this time nothing could save him. No amount of fast talking could conceal the fact that he was smuggling black-market food. The best Tibor could hope for was a beating and imprisonment, though execution was a more likely outcome. Why didn't Tibor turn and run? The gendarmes' guns weren't at the ready and weren't cocked. Tibor could put some distance between them and him before they could get off a shot, and there was little likelihood of them catching up with him. But then there'd be the trail in the fresh snow. Milos groaned inwardly.

Why hadn't Tibor turned and run? Possible capture had to be better than certain capture. Yet, unbelievably, Tibor gave no sign of even having heard the guards, though he must have. He just shuffled along as any peasant would who had nothing to hide.

The two gendarmes had resumed their conversation. One of them began laughing. But their attention was fastened on Tibor and it slowly dawned on Milos that that was what Tibor wanted. How, when, would he make his move?

'Old man, don't you know it's snowing?' called one of the gendarmes. Tibor didn't respond.

'Too much *palinka*,' said the other. *Palinka* was cheap, often home-brewed brandy made from whatever fruit was available.

Tibor kept plodding towards them, head down as though deaf. Milos slowly drew his legs up beneath him. They felt frozen and leaden and he was scared they'd let him down. Tibor kept on coming. When he was five metres away he stopped, as if seeing the gendarmes for the first time.

'Too much *palinka*,' agreed the other gendarme. They both laughed.

Milos stood silently and crept closer to the gendarmes. His brother had to have seen him. Tibor raised his hands as though in surrender and started shuffling towards the gendarmes. He began whimpering. Milos took this as his instruction to act, leapt forward and banged the two gendarmes' heads together with all the strength his fourteen-year-old body could muster.

Bone crashed against bone with a sound unexpectedly loud and sickening. Neither man did more than gasp as he crumpled. A cigarette spun into the air, its tip glowing. A rifle clattered to the ground. Milos was aware of Tibor charging, heard a thud and a groan of pain. The gendarme on his right doubled over and fell. The other gendarme tried to raise his hands in defence but Tibor hit him as well. He groaned and collapsed onto the ground alongside his comrade. When one of them tried to call out, Milos panicked. He lashed out with his boot to silence him, felt it crunch into cheek. He lashed out again and again, dimly aware of Tibor kicking the other gendarme, but aware, even more aware, of the rasp of their breathing. He grabbed Tibor's arm.

'Enough! Let's go!'

'Wait.'

Tibor picked up one of the rifles, reversed it and set himself to smash it into the head of the nearest gendarme.

'No!' said Milos.

'Get out of my way!'

'No! If you kill them they'll want revenge!' Milos nodded in the direction of the peasant's house.

Tibor paused, and lowered the rifle.

'You're learning,' he said. 'Let's go.'

They doubled back up the track to where it joined the street. Milos wanted to run but Tibor grabbed hold of him.

'What have I told you? Never run. Running attracts attention. Only guilty people run, only people with something to hide. What if there's a patrol?'

'Two patrols in the one area? On a night like this?' Milos pulled his arm free of Tibor's grip.

'Do you know for sure there won't be another patrol, little brother, or are you just guessing?'

Milos hung his head.

'Right,' said Tibor. 'Now put your coat back on the right way around. And we walk from now on, okay.'

Tibor led the way, pausing at each street corner to check the road ahead. The streets were deserted, as Milos knew they would be. They'd barely covered half a kilometre when Tibor stopped suddenly and raised his finger to his lips for silence. While Tibor stood there listening, Milos scanned the road ahead and behind for a sign of anything amiss. He glanced at the windows of the houses opposite to see if anyone was watching. Nothing. No slit of light where somebody might be watching from between drawn curtains. The houses were small working men's cottages which adjoined each other and opened directly onto the footpath. In some the doorways were recessed, making dark, shadowy places where people could hide. Milos studied each one in turn but saw nothing.

'What are we waiting for?' he asked irritably.

Tibor turned suddenly, grabbed him by the arm and dragged him into a doorway. Almost immediately, a truck turned into their street towards them. The motor was barely turning over as it slowly approached. Milos stared wide-eyed at Tibor. A truck moving so stealthily through the quiet streets could only be one thing.

'Keep your head down, away from the headlights,' hissed Tibor.

Milos turned his back to the street and huddled down, grateful that Tibor had insisted he turn his coat again so the dark side was outwards. His heart pounded as the truck crept slowly towards them. Had they discovered the injured gendarmes already? Were they looking for them? Milos began praying to his Christian God, promising Jesus a lifetime of devotion if only he had the opportunity to live beyond the next few moments.

'Shut up!' hissed Tibor.

Milos realised to his shame he'd been whispering his prayers aloud. Footprints! The moment the thought struck him Milos realised his life was over, that all of the prayers in the world could not help. He wanted to warn Tibor but didn't dare speak. The truck was almost upon them. The gendarmes had to see the footprints in the snow, had to know they were hiding in the doorway. Milos had never been more scared in his life. He buried his head even further into his coat, tried to cover his ears to drown out the sound of the truck, the excited shouts and the inevitable clatter of booted feet. He closed his eyes as the doorway filled with foul exhaust fumes, expecting to open them to a hostile semi-circle of pointed rifles. Suddenly the truck was past them. He remained crouched, still not daring to breathe, waiting for the truck to stop, for someone to notice the footprints. The engine note did not change, merely grew fainter.

'Let's go,' he whispered.

'Wait,' said Tibor.

'Our footprints!' hissed Milos.

'Footprints lead to doorways all over town,' whispered Tibor angrily. 'How do you think people got home from work? Now shut up!'

They waited until the dim red glow of the truck's tail-light disappeared around the corner behind them.

'Walk quickly,' said Tibor. 'Stay close to the doorways.'

Walk. Milos nearly screamed in frustration. He'd had enough. He wanted to go home. But Tibor slowed and became more cautious as they approached the bridge over the Bodrog River. The bridge was a natural bottleneck and a favourite of the patrols. Tibor and Milos slipped into their usual hiding place in a gap between two buildings where they could observe both sides of the bridge. They normally hid there for five to ten minutes before attempting to cross, waiting for a car or truck to pass by so they could use the beams of its lights to search for signs of danger. Almost immediately Milos heard Tibor curse. There was no need to wait for any vehicles to pass by because Tibor could already see all he needed to. The gendarmes had set up a roadblock on the opposite side of the bridge.

'They must have found the men we beat up,' said Milos.

'Not yet,' said Tibor. 'But with so many patrols out it's only a matter of time.'

'We can't stay here.'

'So what do you suggest?'

Milos's mind raced as he examined the options. Swimming the river was out of the question. If they didn't succumb to the cold in the water, they would soon after they got out. Maybe they could find a boat, but people didn't leave boats lying around to be found. He glanced across the bridge to the braziers the gendarmes had lit to keep themselves warm. They didn't look like packing up any time soon. He had no choice but to turn the question back on Tibor.

'What do you suggest?'

'Come with me.'

Tibor turned and headed back down the way they'd come. He stopped when he reached a narrow laneway and began scrubbing all the snow off the pavement. When Milos saw what he was doing he joined in to help.

'Do exactly what I do,' said Tibor, 'but don't walk in my tracks.'

He turned around and, to Milos's amazement, walked backwards into the lane. Milos followed, taking care to leave parallel tracks. Tibor paused briefly where another lane intersected, to make sure there were no patrols, and turned into it, still walking backwards. He stopped halfway along, waited for Milos to catch up, then tapped sharply on the door. Light flickered quickly over them from the bedroom window upstairs. Moments later the door opened and Milos followed Tibor into a small cramped hallway. A short, stocky, unshaven man in filthy underwear prevented them going any further. He held his oil lamp high so he could examine their faces.

'Patrols have closed the bridge,' said Tibor.

'Who's he?' The man waved his free hand towards Milos. It was holding a pistol.

'My brother.'

'What have you got?'

Tibor unwrapped the small rack of bacon. For the first time, Milos saw what he'd risked his life to get. There were six rib bones with a small, dry-looking eye of meat along the top of each rib and thin strips attached to the tails. The man regarded the offering dismissively. He grunted and nodded towards the back of the house. Milos found himself standing in the smallest and grubbiest kitchen he'd ever seen. The man handed Tibor a knife which he used without hesitation to cut the rack in half. The man eyed the two pieces silently for almost half a minute before deciding which to take.

'Any coffee?' asked Tibor. The man snorted derisively.

'Come,' he said. He led the two boys into the living room, the only other room on the ground floor. Two armchairs occupied most of the space. He took the bottom cushion off each and tossed them onto the floor in front of a guttering fire. He went away and returned with two thin blankets. In a moment of unexpected compassion, he poked the fire into a desultory show of life and threw on a single lump of coal.

'I'll let you know,' he said, picked up his lamp and went back upstairs to his bed.

Milos slipped out of his coat and crowded the fireplace. He began shivering uncontrollably from the cold and release of tension. His brother picked up one of the blankets and wrapped it around his shoulders.

'Let's get some sleep,' said Tibor. 'We'll lie together on the floor here. Both blankets over us, our coats over the blankets. They're too wet to lie on but at least they'll help us to get warm.'

'I need a piss.'

'Lift the back window and stick it out.' Even in the faint glow of the fire Tibor could see the shock on his brother's face. 'Don't worry. You won't be the first. Wait, I'll come with you.'

Both boys took pride in their ability to write their names in the snow but tonight neither gave it a moment's consideration. Milos's hand shook so badly with his shivering he was lucky he didn't also spray the frame.

'You did well,' said Tibor, 'back there on the track.'

Milos nodded. Compliments from his brother were rare.

'You were going to kill those gendarmes,' he said accusingly.

'Was I?' said Tibor.

'Yes! You were!'

'Maybe I just wanted to be sure they'd stay asleep until we'd got well away.'

Milos shuddered. How could he argue when all he wanted was to stop pissing, to lie down in front of the fire, get warm and go home.

'What about Dad?' he said through chattering teeth. 'He'll think we've been caught.'

'My friend will wake us when the bridge is clear. He can see it from upstairs. Now button up.' Tibor closed the window. 'Let's get some sleep.'

Once under the blankets, he put his arms around his younger brother to stop him shivering. Sooner or later Milos would warm up sufficiently and fall asleep. Meanwhile Tibor considered their next move. Roadblocks across the bridge were nothing new, in fact, were becoming more frequent as food and supplies became scarcer. But he knew from experience that they rarely stayed in place all night. If things went as normal, the gendarmes would pack up and return to their barracks some time after midnight. Provided they didn't overreact to the attack on the two gendarmes. What then? Tibor sighed. They'd just have to wait until morning and take their chances with the people making their way to work and to school. Of course they'd be searched which meant they'd have to leave behind what was left of their bacon bones. He cursed softly. That was not an acceptable option.

In the little cottage across the river their father would be sitting up by the fire fearing the worst. Tibor pictured the pot of thin potato and onion soup on the stove, waiting for them to come home so they could eat together. He smiled ruefully in the darkness. All three of them would go hungry but there was nothing special about that. Hunger was something everyone in Hungary was getting used to. He closed his eyes.

*

Their host woke them around two in the morning.

'Go quickly,' he said, and added unnecessarily, 'Stay off the main roads. Watch for patrols.'

Tibor almost had to drag Milos away from the house and down the narrow laneway towards the bridge. His brother seemed numbed by the cold and lack of sleep, barely capable of walking. Tibor sat him down in a doorway while he went to observe the bridge. It had stopped snowing which improved his chances of spotting trouble, but not enough for him to be sure they could cross safely. As far as he could make out, the bridge and the road on the opposite side were deserted, but there were dark places that could conceal any number of sentries. But would they leave sentries if they'd abandoned the roadblock? He doubted it. But there would be extra patrols. Cold, angry men kept from a warm bed in the scant hope that whoever had beaten up their colleagues was still out and about. Tibor realised they had no choice. They had to chance it. He doubled back to his brother, dragged him to his feet and slapped him hard across the face.

Milos recoiled in shock and stared fearfully at his brother, eyes wide for the first time that morning.

'Little brother,' Tibor hissed, 'we have to run for it. Understand?'

Milos nodded.

'Then run.'

Tibor turned and bolted for the bridge, with a desperate Milos willing his legs into action, trying hard to catch up. Their breath came in searing gasps long before they reached the bridge but neither slowed down. Milos ran as he'd never run before, never more awake, expecting at any moment to hear a challenge followed by an explosion from a gun. Instead he heard the last thing he expected. Tibor was laughing. Laughing!

Once safely across the bridge they slowed to a walk. Tibor signalled Milos into the shadows of the doorways by the corner of Attila Street and Kossuth Lajos. He checked left and right before waving Milos over. Kossuth Lajos Street was deserted but enough people had walked along it earlier to wear a pathway through the thin snow cover. At least they'd leave no tracks. Tibor watched for three minutes. Nothing moved. They walked quickly in one-hundred-metre bursts from one darkened doorway to another, finally slipping down a side street into relative safety.

Tibor checked his watch. If they kept a good pace and stuck to side streets they could be home by three-thirty. If they were lucky. If they didn't run across another patrol. But the occasional shouted commands, the low rumble of idling motors and the whine of distant sirens urged caution. There seemed to be so many patrols, so many gendarmes, that Tibor couldn't feel confident about anything. He decided to play it safe, doorway to doorway, and check out every street from every corner. Maybe they wouldn't get home until four. Maybe they'd be frozen and exhausted. But if they took care they'd get home. And have something else to put in the pot at Tokaj Street besides potatoes.

CHAPTER SIX

'Coal!' cried Tibor. It was Saturday morning and he and Milos had dressed in their most threadbare clothes. There was no doubting their apparent poverty as they pushed an old, battered pram which they'd partly filled with three scoops of railway coal. The grubby hessian bag hanging from the handle of the pram held six potatoes, a turnip, a parsnip and a large onion. Rain slashed diagonally into their faces, driven by a bitter wind.

'Coal!' echoed Milos. He paused in the middle of the road as if waiting for a response. There was none. He caught up to Tibor. They continued on up the slight grade towards the corner where two gendarmes stood in the shelter of the doorway of a shop once run by a Jewish tailor. The shop, like so many others in Sarospatak, was closed.

'Coal!' cried Tibor as they drew level with the gendarmes. They stopped again, scanning windows and doorways for a response. The rain intensified with a gust of wind. 'Coal!' called Tibor again and despondently resumed walking. The gendarmes watched them pass without showing any sign of interest. Harsh rationing was in force and they could see the boys were trying to trade coal for food. Coal was always scarce in spring but the gendarmes doubted anybody would be foolish enough to exchange precious food for warmth.

The boys turned left then right, all the while drawing nearer to Tokaj Street with their precious cargo. Milos was standing in the middle of the intersection, pretending to look at windows for any response to their offer, when he heard Tibor curse. Halfway up the street four gendarmes were putting their boots into two men cowering on the ground. Even through the rain it was obvious who the victims were. There were few orthodox Jews in Sarospatak but the gendarmes had caught two of them walking home from the synagogue. Tibor wanted to turn back but realised it was too late. They'd been seen and to retreat would only arouse suspicion.

'Coal!' cried Tibor, knowing damn well he'd get no response. Nobody wanted to witness what was happening in front of them, on the pavement of their street. The gendarmes were laughing and taunting the Jews; Tibor quickly realised that it was only a matter of time until the Jews lost consciousness and the gendarmes looked elsewhere for another target to amuse them. 'Do what I do,' he hissed to Milos.

Tibor and Milos were now so close that the gendarmes had begun to eye them suspiciously. Two of them made a move towards the centre of the road as if preparing to block the boys' way. Tibor didn't hesitate. He grabbed a lump of coal from the pram and hurled it expertly at the Jews. He heard it thud into an overcoat where the harm it would do was minimal.

'Dirty yid!' he screamed.

Milos followed suit but without the accuracy. His lump of coal hit the road in front of the Jews and shattered, showering them with dust and shards. The gendarmes laughed.

'Coal!' cried Milos. 'Coal for the filthy yids! One pengo!'

'Yes!' shouted Tibor. 'One pengo per yid!' He held a lump of coal in his outstretched hand as if offering it to the gendarmes.

'Keep your coal, you little thieves,' said one of the gendarmes amiably. 'We'll keep our money. Besides, I wouldn't give you a pengo for all the yids in town.'

The gendarmes laughed and waved the boys on. Tibor couldn't help thinking the Russians were an awfully long way away.

When the boys reached Tokaj Street, they slipped through the side gate and around to the back door of their aunt's house. Gabriella opened it before they even had a chance to knock.

'Come in, come in,' she said. 'You must be frozen. Elizabeth, look how wet they are.'

'Put some of that coal on the fire and start taking off your clothes,' said Aunt Katy. 'Elizabeth, Gabi, go get some of Balazs's clothes for them to put on.' She looked at the pram the boys had dragged with them into the kitchen. Dirty coal-stained puddles were forming beneath it on the timber floor. 'You boys must stop taking such risks for us.' She tried to make her voice firm but couldn't keep the smile out of it.

'If Balazs was here he'd do the same,' said Milos, but he felt as proud as any boy could be. He felt like a hero, at last the equal of his brother.

'I'll fetch you some towels.'

Once Tibor and Milos were dried and dressed, they began unloading the coal into the kitchen coal bucket.

'What's that?' said Gabriella. She pointed to a package wrapped in newspaper which had been lying under the coal.

'A surprise,' said Tibor. 'You can thank Milos for this.'

'No!' said Milos, 'that isn't fair!' His face began to blush cherry red.

'Believe me,' said Tibor, 'I know what's fair.'

'What is it?' asked Gabriella again.

'Something to go in the soup with the vegetables. Good Catholic food.' Tibor laughed and removed the first layer of newspaper. He handed the package to Gabriella. 'Here, you unwrap it.'

Gabriella shrieked when she saw the bacon bones.

'Look, Mamma!' she said. 'Look what they brought us.'

Tibor had given Milos the credit but Gabriella knew her boys well and knew what each was capable of. The look she gave Tibor went beyond admiration to adoration. Though she hugged both boys she might just as well have slapped Milos's face.

Milos smiled through his bewilderment. This time he was also a hero. Tibor had said so. All he wanted was half the admiration and half the adoration. It was his due. He'd earned it. And he loved Gabriella without reservation while his brother only loved her as much as he deemed necessary. Dismay and disappointment were bitter pills but Milos had become accustomed to swallowing them.

'We thought it would be better if you made soup with it today,' he said matter-of-factly, 'so the flavour can go through. Three bones aren't much for six.'

'What a treat!' said Aunt Katy. 'Where on earth did you get it?'

'Make us a coffee and I'll tell you,' said Tibor.

'You bring us coal, vegetables and now this,' said Aunt Katy. 'I don't know how we'd manage without you.'

'What about Aunt Jutka and Klari?' asked Milos.

Aunt Jutka and Klari were two peasant women who came once a week to clean the Horvath home and every autumn to make jam and preserves. Thomas had treated them and their families whenever needed and the two women were almost as close as family.

'We've asked them not to bring us food any more. It's too dangerous.' Aunt Katy ran her fingers through her hair tiredly. 'The gendarmes have also taken our bicycles so we can no longer ride over to see them. We have our rations and what we've managed to put aside. We'll get by.'

'Till the Russians come,' said Tibor bitterly.

'Yes,' said his aunt, 'till the Russians come.'

There was a time when Jozsef and his boys had gone to Tokaj Street as an act of kindness on the part of the Horvaths. When they had been the poor guests in a house of plenty. That Sunday they learned how much their roles had reversed. With their bank account frozen, Aunt Katica and her girls no longer had the cash to buy black-market goods, and no jewellery or gold to sell because that had been confiscated on the day the gendarmes had come for their bicycles. Jews were no longer allowed to own gold and Gabi had nearly burst into tears when she described how the gendarmes had taken the gold bracelet her father had given her on her twelfth birthday, bruising her wrist in the process. The gendarmes had also taken their radio and gramophone, their silver coffee set, silver cruets, silver picture frames and any ornament or trinket they thought might have value. They'd also helped themselves to the preserves and jars of jam and pickles stored in their cellar and taken their last bag of flour, claiming Jews weren't allowed to hoard flour.

'Jews aren't allowed anything,' said Aunt Katy bitterly. She'd adopted the habit of wringing her hands ever since her husband had been sent to the front. It was a habit induced by stress and now she wrung them vigorously as though she was washing them under a tap. 'Except what is so worthless the gendarmes don't bother to steal it.'

'We'll help you out,' said Milos.

'No,' said Aunt Katy. 'You have done enough for us. It's too dangerous now. They shoot people for smuggling food. They shoot black marketeers. And they shoot Jews who don't wear the yellow star,' she added pointedly.

'Still no word from Balazs?' asked Jozsef.

'No,' said Elizabeth quickly. 'We've asked around. Other people have received messages from the camps but no one has received any message at all from the men who were taken with Balazs. No one's heard a word from them or from other workers in the labour camps about them.'

'It's like they just disappeared,' said Gabi.

'Don't say that!' said Aunt Katy. She turned back to the bowl in front of her, tilting it so she could scoop out the last drops. When she laid her spoon to rest she noticed that Jozsef and both boys had stopped eating and left half of their soup. 'What's the matter?' she said. 'You don't like my cooking?'

'I'm not hungry,' said Jozsef.

'Big breakfast,' said Milos.

'I'm not used to such rich food,' said Tibor and laughed. Their lies were so transparent he could not resist turning it into a joke.

'But you must eat,' said Elizabeth.

'Keep it for tomorrow,' said Jozsef. 'We have food at home. Much more than you have.'

'Thank you,' said Aunt Katy simply. The leftovers plus the soup still in the pot would probably see them through two more nights if she stretched it with a little water. The sudden, shameful realisation that she was saving soup left in her guests' bowls made her bow her head. 'I never thought it would come to this. Who would have believed it!' She began sobbing quietly.

'The war must end soon,' said Jozsef softly. He reached across the table and gently stroked Katica's arm. 'The Russians will come and we'll be able to live as normal human beings again. That'll be something, no?'

CHAPTER SEVEN

May 1944

'When they start killing people it's time to go,' said Tibor. He'd given up pleading and trying to argue rationally.

'Isolated incidents like that will always occur,' said Jozsef stubbornly.

'These isolated incidents are happening every day.' Tibor pushed his chair back from the table in frustration and turned to Milos who'd started clearing their dishes from the table. 'Sit down! Leave the bowls where they are. What's a few dirty dishes at a time like this? Sit down and tell Father about the Germans.'

'What Germans?' said Jozsef.

'We saw Germans on the bridge,' said Milos unhappily. He hated confrontation, especially when his father's authority was being challenged. Hated it even more when his father was in the wrong. 'A contact across the river has some *kolbasz*. We were on our way to inspect it and negotiate. People can put anything in sausage, as you know. That's when we saw the Germans and heard about the shootings. We could see them from the corner of Attila Street, there were four of them in an open car. People were milling around too scared to cross the bridge to go home.'

'Are you sure they were Germans? I didn't see any Germans arrive,' said Jozsef.

'Maybe they came by car,' said Tibor angrily. 'Who cares? Train, car or push-bikes! The only thing that matters is this: the town is full of Arrow Crossmen, many of whom have suddenly become gendarmes. They're not sneaking into town on the train any more but driving in on the back of army trucks. There are gangs of them and they no longer care who knows they're here. Now the Germans have come to town. Jews are being stopped on the bridge and thrown into the river. The Arrow Crossmen then use them for target practice. Can you believe that? If the bullets don't kill them, they're so badly wounded they drown. The Arrow Crossmen are doing this for their amusement and no one is stopping them. Don't you see what that means? *No one is stopping them.* They stand there laughing like they have every right to shoot and drown people. We're being softened up for whatever they intend doing to us next. Can't you see that?'

'We?' said Jozsef suddenly. 'But you two are Catholics.'

'We're Jews,' said Tibor. 'Being baptised counts for nothing if you've got Jewish blood. That makes us Jews and there's a bounty on Jews, half-Jews, quarter-Jews and, for all I know, one-eighth Jews. People who inform on us get extra food. A piece of bread or sausage. About what you can buy for a few pengo. That's all we're worth now.'

'I got asked at school today why I wasn't wearing a yellow star,' said Milos.

'What did you say?'

'I told them I was a Catholic. What else could I say?'

'Forget the church,' said Tibor disgustedly. 'I'm surprised that Misery Guts Old Ignac hasn't already sold us out. Maybe he still will if one of our rivals doesn't sell us out first. I can think of at least ten people who would be happy to have us out of the way so they can move in on our contacts.'

'But they haven't,' said Jozsef. 'That has to mean something. They could but they haven't.'

'Not yet. But they will. Someone will. Come on, Father!' Tibor leaned forward on his elbows so that he towered over Jozsef. 'None of this is new to you. You have eyes and ears. You know everything that's going on in this town. It's time you stopped kidding yourself. It's time you faced facts. We can't wait any longer. We can't wait for the Russians because they're too long coming and the Germans are already here. You knew one day this might happen. You've been preparing us for it for the last two years!'

Jozsef's shoulders slumped. He'd been deceiving himself but he couldn't deceive his boys.

'They're not asking me to schedule the movements of trains any more.'

'Why? Because you're a Jew or because they've got something to hide?' Tibor showed no sympathy. He realised Jozsef was giving in and pressed his advantage.

'I don't know.' Jozsef hung his head in defeat. This latest development completed his fall from grace. 'Someone high up has been protecting me. There's no other explanation. Probably someone I helped a long time ago. Someone smart enough not to be seen to be helping a Jew. Maybe they can't protect me any more. Maybe you're right, maybe there's something they don't want me to know. I can't even talk to the engine driver or fireman any more. Or the conductor or the guard. That is also forbidden.'

'It's time to go, Father,' said Tibor firmly. 'How much more evidence do you need?'

'I just can't believe they've come here to round up Jews, which is what you're saying. I was certain they'd take the Jews from Budapest first. Why would they bother with sleepy Sarospatak? Why take twelve hundred Jews when they could take four hundred thousand? It doesn't make sense.'

'Maybe they've started taking Jews from Budapest,' said Tibor impatiently. 'Maybe they've started taking Jews from all over Hungary. All I know is the Germans and the Arrow Crossmen haven't come to Sarospatak just to take our names.'

'Do you have a plan?' Jozsef stared at the table in front of him.

'I want to head north tonight with our winter clothes, around Satoraljaujhely and into the hills. If the snow comes before the Russians, at least we'll have warm clothes to wear. I'll bury them in the little cave Milos found so they won't be disturbed by animals. I'll bury some dried vegetables too, and some jars of pickles.'

'How long will you be gone?'

'Two days, three nights,' said Tibor. 'All going well, I'll be back Friday morning. I want you and Milos ready to leave Friday night. If anything happens before I get back, I want you to leave and hide out in the woods above the farm with the Nonius horses. Do you both remember it?' Jozsef and Milos nodded. 'We'll head north first into the hills until things quieten down, then double back around to the north-east and make our way to Romania.'

'Why Romania?' asked Jozsef.

'Because the Russians will take Romania first.'

Jozsef nodded.

'One change of clothes and one blanket each and as many vegetables as we can carry comfortably. Okay?'

'What about Gabi?' said Milos.

'What about her?'

'I've sworn to look after her.'

'Forget it,' said Tibor. 'She is not your responsibility. She can't keep up and she won't survive in the open. You cannot protect her. I can't protect her. It will be hard enough finding food to feed the three of us. She's better off taking her chances here with her mother and sister.'

'She stays, I stay,' said Milos.

Tibor turned angrily to his father. 'Tell him.'

'I'll speak to Gabriella,' said Jozsef. 'But you must understand this, Milos. As much as I would like to believe otherwise, I concede Tibor is correct. Our decision has been made and you will abide by it. It is time to go and we all go. I will explain the circumstances to Gabi and make sure she understands the difficulties and hardships of joining us. If she decides to stay with her mother and sister, that is her decision. Her decision does not affect ours. Do you understand?'

Milos nodded reluctantly.

'The risks in running away are at least as great as the risks of staying. If we are caught we will be shot. Food and shelter will be hard to come by. We could die of hunger as easily as by a bullet. We will have no friends, only enemies who can profit by betraying us.' Jozsef looked solemnly from Tibor to Milos. 'It is no small thing, what we are proposing to do. Let us think on this one more time before we commit ourselves. Let us all be sure we are taking the right option.'

'We have no option,' said Tibor dismissively. 'You know that. You saw this moment coming. Now is not the time to weaken.'

'Tibor's right,' said Milos miserably. 'You must convince Gabi, Dad. You must convince her.'

'Then we're decided,' said Jozsef abruptly. He turned to Tibor. 'You will go tonight as agreed.'

Tibor grabbed his father's hand. 'You won't regret this.'

'And you will take Milos with you.'

'No!'

'Yes. You will take your brother and come back for me on Friday. Come back for me and Gabi. Now go.'

After the boys had left, Jozsef made himself a weak coffee and sat staring into the dying embers of the fire. He'd accused others of not facing reality, of burying their heads in the sand and not taking precautions to protect themselves. Yet he'd been procrastinating with his own and his boys' safety. They should have been prepared weeks ago, should have fled days ago, should have somehow made provision for Katica and her girls. Jozsef resolved to leave with the boys as soon as they returned, with Gabriella if she was willing and had her mother's permission. On Friday, no matter what, he would turn his back on Sarospatak for as long as the war lasted, and possibly for ever.

'Do you honestly think they'll come and take us away?' Aunt Katica wrung her hands anxiously.

'I'm sorry,' said Jozsef. Elizabeth and Gabriella sat with them around the scrubbed wooden table in the kitchen, the only warm room in the big house.

'Where will they take us?'

'You've heard the rumours, Katy.'

'Surely you don't believe them,' said Elizabeth. 'They are outrageous. The Germans are civilised people.'

Jozsef sighed heavily. 'I believe it is my duty and in your best interests to tell you everything I know. Do I believe the Germans are transporting people to labour camps? Yes. We know they are. Do I believe they're taking people to death camps? May the day never come when we're in a position to find out for ourselves. But, yes, I do believe they're taking people to death camps. The stories of the refugees are just too compelling.'

'What can we do?' said Aunt Katica. 'We can't run away like you.'

'Is there anyone who could hide you?'

'You know there isn't.'

'Then perhaps Gabi could come with us.'

'No!' said Gabriella. 'I'm staying with Mamma. The streets are too dangerous.'

'When are you leaving?' asked Katica.

'Tomorrow.'

'Tomorrow ...' She said the word as though it was a death sentence. She turned away momentarily to regain her composure and fight back the tears that threatened. 'What about Elizabeth? Can you take her too?'

'No, Mamma!'

Jozsef shook his head reluctantly. 'We would love to take you all but ...' He shrugged apologetically.

'Then take Gabi.'

'No, Mamma!' shrieked Gabi. 'I won't leave you. I won't go!'

'I'm only sorry Elizabeth cannot go with you,' said Katica to her youngest daughter. 'After what happened to you yesterday, you know you have no choice.'

'What happened?' said Jozsef quickly.

'Gabriella and Elizabeth were lucky to escape the gendarmes last night,' said Katica. 'I won't let them put themselves in that position again.'

'What position?'

'We didn't want to tell you because we thought you would get angry. We thought your boys might start taking even more risks for us.'

'Tell me.'

'We went to visit Aunt Klari,' said Elizabeth reluctantly. 'She told us she had some eggs and cheese for us. Imagine that, eggs and cheese! She was too scared to bring them herself and thought maybe Gabi and I would have a better chance because she said we wouldn't be searched. She said we're too pretty and well-bred. According to Aunt Klari the gendarmes are reluctant to search young women like us. We thought it was safer for us to go than to ask Tibor to go for us.

'When they didn't search us the first time we crossed the bridge we thought Aunt Klari was right and that they wouldn't search us on the way back. But there were no gendarmes on the way back, just Arrow Crossmen, and they were doing terrible things.'

Elizabeth turned away from Jozsef and started sobbing. Gabi took her hand, tears beginning to spill from her own eyes.

'You don't have to say it,' said Jozsef. 'You don't have to say another word. I know what they were doing.'

'They grabbed Gabi and me. They made us open our coats. We had eggs and cheese in the pockets but they weren't interested in searching us. Aunt Klari was right. They don't search pretty girls unless they think we hide food in our underwear!' Elizabeth's anger and disgust momentarily overrode her tears. 'It was horrible. They had no shame and they said the most vile things to us. We just stood there, too frightened to do anything, too aware of the eggs and cheese in our pockets. Some others grabbed the shoemaker's wife while we were there. She hadn't done a thing, hadn't done anything wrong. She was screaming and pleading with us for help but what could we do? They called her "fat Jew bitch" and then they threw her in the river. We heard a splash and her screams. They started shooting at her. They were laughing and shooting at her. They cheered when one of them shot her and the screaming stopped. We couldn't believe it. One second she's alive, the next she's dead for no reason. Before we could even draw another breath, they threw another two men into the Bodrog. That's when we realised they meant to kill us too. They were moving us to the edge of the bridge when the German officers arrived. The German officers saved us.'

'They saved you?' said Jozsef. 'The German officers *saved* you?'

'They ordered the Arrow Crossmen to release us and apologised to us. At least that's how it appeared. They were speaking German so we couldn't understand. They clicked their heels and bowed slightly and waved us on our way. We could hardly believe it. We were still shaking so much when we got home that Mamma had to take the eggs and cheese out of our pockets for us and help us off with our coats.'

'But the Germans saved you,' said Jozsef.

Elizabeth nodded tearfully.

Jozsef leaned back in his chair. 'I wonder what that means.'

'We didn't hear any more shots,' said Gabi. 'We think the Germans stopped them from killing any more Jews.'

'Maybe the Germans have come to restore order,' said Jozsef. 'Maybe they've come to keep the Arrow Crossmen in check.'

'Do you think so?' said Aunt Katica hopefully.

'It's a possibility,' said Jozsef. 'They saved Elizabeth and Gabi. And they stopped the Arrow Crossmen killing more Jews. You said they were courteous? That they apologised?'

'Yes,' said Elizabeth.

'Then perhaps there's hope,' said Jozsef. 'Perhaps there is hope after all.'

Neither Tibor nor Milos fully appreciated what they were witnessing from their hideout.

'Here come some more,' said Tibor softly.

Milos lifted on his elbows so that he could peer through the tall grass, down the hill and across the fields to the narrow lane. All they knew was that the roads and lanes around Satoraljaujhely were crawling with gendarmes and that the gendarmes were rounding up all the Jews from the surrounding villages and farms. Two days had passed yet they still hadn't reached their destination. They had no way of knowing that the extermination of Hungary's Jews had begun. Or that Adolf Eichmann, contrary to their father's expectations, had elected to exterminate Hungary's rural Jews first. In his obsession to rid Europe of every single Jew, Eichmann had begun his deportations in Hungary's eastern provinces so that he would not lose any Jews to the Russian advance.

'Where are they putting them all?' asked Milos. 'There are so many.'

Below them, another fifty to sixty Jews, mostly women and those too old or too young for labour camps, walked quickly in a tight group along the narrow road towards Satoraljaujhely, driven along like cattle by six armed gendarmes. Except for the smallest children and babies each person carried one small bag. The spring sun had at last decided to put in an appearance and the morning air sizzled with unexpected heat. The boys were too far away to see the sweat on the faces of the elderly and the mothers carrying babies, but they could imagine it. Most of all, they could imagine their fear.

Even from their distant vantage point the boys could hear the guards cursing and yelling at their prisoners, telling them to keep up. It was a scene repeated for the third time that day, the fifth they'd witnessed overall as they'd tried to work their way unseen around Satoraljaujhely. As they watched there was a sudden disturbance. One of the small black-clad figures stumbled and fell, an old woman who had succumbed to exhaustion, frailty or fear. People broke ranks to help her; to the boys, it all seemed to be happening in slow motion. Arms reached to lift the old woman back onto her feet but she struggled in vain. Still she might have succeeded if the gendarmes hadn't intervened. They pushed the would-be helpers aside and dragged the old woman out of the line to the side of the road, while others used their rifles as prods to keep everyone walking. People were wailing and trying to restrain an old man from rushing back to help the fallen woman. Two gendarmes stood over her. There was a puff of smoke, a single gunshot and the two gendarmes rejoined the marchers. Two more sounds reached the boys, almost simultaneously: a chilling cry of despair and the sound of someone laughing.

'They shot her,' said Milos in horror. 'They shot that old woman in cold blood.'

'Keep your voice down!' said Tibor. 'Just watch and remember.'

Incredibly, the gendarmes started singing a coarse barrack-room song, interspersing it with abuse and shouts telling the stunned, terrified Jews to keep up. The boys watched until they marched out of sight.

'Remember everything you see, little brother,' said Tibor grimly. 'These are Hungarians not Germans, gendarmes not Gestapo. Hate them as much as you like but keep your hate safely locked away. There will be times when we have no choice but to move among these men and deal with them. There will be times when we'll have to convince them we're one of them. That's our only hope of staying alive.'

He rose to his knees and slung his pack over his shoulders. 'Come on. It's time to find somewhere safer to hole up.'

They turned and headed uphill deeper into the woods, looking for a place to hide and sleep until evening when they could continue the broad sweep that would take them around the town and railhead. Tibor led Milos higher, across pastures into another thicket of bush where he stopped and assessed the terrain before dropping his pack. They lay down close to the edge of the thicket where hornbeams formed a natural hideout, screened on all sides by overlapping leaves. Tibor had chosen their rest place well. If anyone approached from above, they'd hear them coming through the trees which would give them plenty of warning. If anyone came from the woods below they'd have to cross the pastures where they'd be spotted instantly.

'You sleep first,' said Tibor.

Milos nodded gratefully. He swept leaves into a pile to cushion his body and used his pack as a pillow. He closed his eyes but sleep would not come.

'What are they going to do with all those Jews?' he said.

'What do you think?'

'It's hard to believe.'

'Start believing. You saw what happened to that woman. You heard what happened on the bridge.'

'Yes, but where are they going to put them? Thousands of Jews live around here,' said Milos.

'They probably want to transport all the Jews at once,' said Tibor. 'That's what I'd do. Round them all up, stick them somewhere close to the railway and load as many as possible onto the trains in one go. Can you imagine trains just sitting at the station waiting for this or that piddly group of Jews to arrive? That wouldn't be very efficient, would it?'

'Suppose not,' said Milos.

'If they did that, don't you think the Jews would try to resist? Those who hadn't been taken would run away and hide at the very least. Hardly what the gendarmes would want. My guess is that they'll take the Jews somewhere where the conditions are so bad and so overcrowded that the trains seem like a better alternative.'

'Jesus, Tibor.' Milos took a moment to digest everything his brother had said. It all made such horrible sense. He recalled the way the Jews heading for the labour battalions had been crowded together in Iskola Park and inevitably his brain made the obvious leap. 'Tibor! What if they've also started rounding up Jews in Sarospatak?'

'Then we'll just have to hope Dad was smart enough to make a run for it.'

'What about Gabi?'

'Same rules apply.' Tibor rolled over onto his back.

'We've got to do something! I think we should go back to Sarospatak and tell them what's happening here. Warn them.'

'And I think we stick to our plan. On the way back I'm going to sneak into Satoraljaujhely to see if I can learn anything.'

'Why, for God's sake?' Milos gave up all pretext of trying to sleep and sat up.

'Our survival depends on knowing what the Germans and gendarmes are doing and how they do it. I might learn something that can help Dad and maybe help Gabi. I might even learn something that could save our lives.'

'I'll come with you.'

'No, you'll do exactly what I tell you. If something goes wrong, you'll have to go back alone and get Dad. Got that?'

'I think we should go home now.'

'I think you should go to sleep, little brother. It might clear your head, help you to think straight.'

'I can't sleep.'

'Okay,' said Tibor, 'you keep watch. Wake me in three hours.' He rolled over and rested his head on his pack.

Milos dragged himself into a position where he could keep watch on the fields below them. When his brother's breathing had settled into a regular shallow rhythm he turned to look at him, wondering what made the two of them so different. When had Tibor become so cold and calculating? When had he become so wise?

The boys resumed their journey at nightfall, skirting wide around Satoraljaujhely and heading north-east past eerily quiet villages and farmhouses. They walked with a sense of urgency brought on by what they'd witnessed and the knowledge that their journey would take them at least twice as long as they'd anticipated. The detours were not a huge problem even though they added twenty to thirty kilometres onto the trip. Their legs were strong and their bodies well-conditioned, but even fit bodies need fuel to sustain them. The food they'd taken for the trip was long gone and they had no option but to tap into the supplies they'd intended to bury. Opening one of the jars of pickled cucumbers seemed the obvious step but Tibor was reluctant to do that. Once opened, the jar would have to be finished as the pickles would no longer be suitable for burying. Furthermore, Tibor was uncertain that a diet comprised entirely of pickles was suitable fare for hard hiking. His fear was that the vinegar would sour their stomachs and the salt plague them with thirst. He decided they had no choice but to open the bag of dried vegetables. The problem was, they needed a pot to rehydrate and heat them. Around midnight, Tibor left Milos on lookout while he slipped quietly downhill and into what appeared to be a newly abandoned farmhouse.

Tibor eased through the open doorway, his senses as alert as those of any wild animal on the prowl. Although certain the house was empty, he stood stock still just inside the doorway listening for the sound of breathing or anything that might betray the presence of others. He waited two minutes before striking a match. Perhaps once the room he was standing in had been kept immaculate, but whoever had taken its occupants had made sure they had little incentive to return. Chairs and tables had been overturned, curtains torn from windows and crockery smashed. But for the vandalism, the room was little different to dozens of others Tibor had seen and stood in while negotiating. He quickly scanned the debris until he found the broken menorah he was looking for and, nearby, a stubby candle which had tumbled from it. He lit the wick with a second match and stepped over toppled chairs to the stove which had once provided the little cottage with its only source of heating. He removed a saucepan from the hook above it and then searched the cupboards for a preserving jar with a lid. He found one intact and unbroken, extinguished the candle and headed back to the doorway. He felt no guilt at plundering the home of a Jewish family he'd probably seen being marched along the road to the railhead. The loss did not matter to them any more. They were beyond help, but in this small way they could help him. That was all that mattered.

He searched the yard until he found the hand pump that drew all the water the cottage used and filled the preserving jar. He was about to slip silently away when a sudden flutter made him drop to the ground. He lay there barely breathing, pulse racing, listening for anything that would help him identify the sound he'd heard, where it had come from and what had caused it. Had somebody seen the light from his candle? He thought about the torn and detached curtains and cursed softly. He'd chosen this farmhouse because no others were within its line of sight, at least as far as he could tell. Had he overlooked anything? He racked his brains trying to picture the landscape, trying to recall if there were any trees or hollows that might have concealed another dwelling. But there weren't, he was sure of it. He'd been patient and thorough. Another sound in the darkness! He stiffened and peered across the yard trying to gauge direction, heard the sound again. Tibor exhaled quietly and stood. How many times had he heard it before? How many times had he lain in yards just like this and heard the scuffle of paws on hard-packed soil? A low, dark shape suddenly bolted away into the night. Tibor didn't have to see the fox to know what it was. The smell was unmistakeable. He suspected they were both after the same thing.

Tibor crept over to the coop, a rectangular box raised off the ground by four corner posts, and slipped the latch on the door. He lit his candle once more and saw two hens and a rooster staring fearfully back at him. Tomorrow Gentile villagers would come and take the fowls and anything else they fancied, not realising that another had beaten them to the spoils. Tibor extinguished the candle, closed the door to the coop and set off back up the hill to where Milos was waiting.

'What took you so long?' said Milos.

'I took as long as necessary,' said Tibor. 'Now drink.'

Both boys took a quick swallow of water then Tibor filled the half-empty jar with dried vegetables. They still had a lot of ground to cover that night and this way the vegetables could rehydrate and soften while they walked. With luck they could reach the cave before dawn and boil up their little pot. Salt was sprinkled in among the vegetable pieces and dried chillies; together they promised a breakfast both substantial and delicious.

And in Tibor's pocket there was a precious bonus. Two eggs to boil and carry with them.

'I've come for Gabriella,' said Jozsef. It was Friday morning and he was expecting the boys home that afternoon. He wanted to be ready and packed, Gabi or no Gabi.

115

'You'd better come in,' said Katica.

'Is there a problem?'

'Elizabeth is talking to her now. She refuses to go, refuses to leave me. Every time I pack her bag she unpacks it. Perhaps you could speak with her?'

Jozsef shook his head sorrowfully.

'You must understand, Katy, that Gabi has not trained for this. She hasn't been hiking with us to build up her strength and stamina. Even willing, she will be a burden. Unwilling she would jeopardise all our lives. I'm sorry.'

'Please speak to her!' Tears flooded Katy's eyes.

'No,' said Jozsef. 'I'm sorry.'

'Then will you at least give her until tomorrow morning? Please! I will convince her to change her mind. I'll make sure she is willing. I promise you.'

Jozsef wanted to say no, that he had to go to meet the boys, but how could he? Katy was pleading with him, begging him, and he felt both ashamed and embarrassed. But common sense decreed that he should leave without Gabi. The Germans had called for meetings with the leaders of the Jewish community and he had no doubt little good news would emerge from them.

'Okay,' he said, 'tomorrow morning.'

Katy threw her arms around Jozsef and kissed him. Her relief and gratitude overwhelmed him. Yet it failed utterly to convince him that his decision was anything but foolish.

CHAPTER EIGHT

Satoraljaujhely was not much larger than Sarospatak but it was big enough. Around seventeen thousand people lived there, which made it possible for Tibor to move around and not be instantly identified as a stranger. In truth he was safer in the town than wandering about in the country. Entering and leaving were the moments of greatest danger, when he risked being stopped and his motives and identity questioned. He'd slipped into town in the darkness before dawn and hidden in a disused factory until enough people were about to make it safe to come out. Tibor had contacts in the railway, introduced to him by his father, but the railyards were teeming with gendarmes and hardly a safe place for any Jew or Jewish-born Christian. Nevertheless, these contacts were the only ones Tibor had.

He knew exactly where the station was and where the railwaymen were housed. The stationmaster had a small cottage near the railway, similar to their own home in Sarospatak but half the distance from the station. He'd always been friendly enough but he knew of Jozsef's circumstances and Tibor wasn't certain he could be trusted. Of all the railwaymen his father had introduced him to, the old signalman was the best option. He shared accommodation with colleagues close to the railway line but almost a kilometre east of the station. Tibor's intention was to position himself between the signalman's house and the station in the hope of intercepting him on the way to work. He was certain the old man could be trusted. How many times had he seen his father slip a few pengo to him? Yes, he could be trusted.

Unfortunately Tibor had entered the town by the most direct route, from the north, and the station lay two kilometres south of the town centre. Tibor tagged onto the tail end of groups of people heading into the town to work, switching from group to group depending on where they were headed and which streets they took. Sometimes he'd join up with a single man or woman and engage them in harmless conversation about the weather. Sometimes the responses were surly and suspicious, other times people opened up, glad of the opportunity to talk about something other than the tumultuous events taking place. Tibor got the clear impression that while some of the townsfolk he spoke to were openly supportive of the gendarmes' efforts to round up the Jews, others were apprehensive and possibly even ashamed.

Tibor did what any skilled negotiator would do and mirrored the prejudices and point of view of whomever he was talking to. Bit by bit he elicited information, slowly building up a horrific picture of what had happened to all the Jews he'd seen herded together in the roads and laneways. He was tempted to dismiss much of what he was told as exaggeration, but the stories were consistent and truth beckoned in the sheer barbarism of the detail. Even so, his mind grappled with the numbers, the sheer magnitude of what was occurring and the inhumanity of it all. Tibor was no stranger to fear; he regarded it as a valuable tool of his trade, an emotion that honed his caution to a fine edge, that promoted patience and nourished his instincts. But he was accustomed to it as a reaction to an immediate danger: the untimely arrival of patrols, the placement of sentries, the risk of betrayal. The fear he felt now was part of the air he breathed, all encompassing, more chilling, more deadening. How could anyone deal with such ruthlessness, such lack of conscience and compassion? Tibor began to regret his bravado in sneaking into Satoraljaujhely. He wished he'd listened to his brother and headed straight back to Sarospatak instead.

His temporary companion, a young woman, bade him good day and disappeared through an office doorway, leaving him isolated on the street. His first instinct was a quick and furtive look around to check out the placement of the gendarmes, but he resisted it. There was no place for anything quick or furtive, only for the bold and obvious. But bold was not how Tibor felt. He felt crushed and overwhelmed by his knowledge, and struggled with the unfamiliarity of the sensations. Nevertheless he held his head high and looked around as confidently as he could. There were four gendarmes on the street corner on the opposite side of the road. He immediately crossed the street, walked up to them and paused. His heart began beating faster and he could feel his sluggish blood stirring into action.

'Thank you,' said Tibor, 'thank you for getting rid of all the stinking yids.'

The gendarmes looked at him curiously.

'But I've got a problem.'

'What might that be?' said the oldest of them.

'Now when I go for a leak at school I've got no one to piss on.'

The gendarmes burst into laughter.

'You want to piss on Jews,' said one of them, 'go down to the timberyards by the station. There are thousands there just waiting for you. Tell the guards what you want to do. Believe me, you can't miss.'

This also got the gendarmes laughing. Tibor hitched his trousers around his groin meaningfully, gave them a wave and wandered off towards the station. The interaction restored some of his confidence but he began to wonder if he'd ever be the same again. It was one thing to sit around the table with his father and Milos and discuss the death camps and the trainloads of Jews trundling off to oblivion, and another thing entirely to observe the process first-hand and feel the cold-bloodedness of it. He shivered involuntarily, shook his head as though to rid it of all thoughts so he could start over. After all, he had his survival to consider. And Milos's. And his father's. He needed every scrap of his wits about him.

His route around the town centre led him past the Jewish cemetery and he couldn't help thinking bitterly how little used it would be in the future once all the Jews were gone. Fewer people used the streets he now walked and those who did were travelling in the opposite direction and seemed somehow furtive. Why? The answer struck him like a blow to the head. He wasn't thinking, he wasn't using his brain! He knew exactly where the timberyards were — between him and the station. And he was walking unerringly towards them. He immediately turned eastwards towards the Ronyva River and the signalman's house. What had he been thinking of? Tibor began to shake. The lapse was so uncharacteristic and so unexpected it shook him to his core. He wanted to stop, find a place to hole up and gather his wits, but retained just enough sense to appreciate the dangers involved in doing that. Never run, never act furtive and never put yourself in a position that cannot easily be explained. His rules were fundamental and he silently repeated them.

Tibor skipped across Kossuth Lajos Street. Every town in Hungary had a street named after the great nineteenth-century freedom fighter; Tibor wondered how he would feel if he saw how the street bearing his name was being used. In the distance he could see the barbed wire strung around the timberyard and the factories opposite, see the hastily erected guard towers and wire roadblocks manned by gendarmes. The street was strangely quiet, much quieter than normal for a main thoroughfare. Yet if what he'd been told was true, the timberyard and the factories housed some ten thousand Jews rounded up from every village around Satoraljaujhely and even from towns in Slovakia. There should be some noise and its absence worried Tibor. The timberyard didn't cover much ground and the factories even less, yet ten thousand people were crammed into them. He couldn't even begin to imagine the conditions within, the overcrowding, the deprivation, the hardship. There should be some noise. Of protest! Anger! He slipped down the first side street he came to, pondering the phenomenon.

Soon he would reach the house where the signalman lived. Should he knock, go in and take his chances? What if the old signalman wasn't there? What if the signalman's colleagues were no longer reliable? Tibor realised he could not take the risk and had to hope that he would have the good fortune to intercept the signalman on his way to work. He checked his watch. Shift change was at eight o'clock, in twenty minutes' time. He slowed down. How many times could he walk along the street the signalman lived in without attracting attention? Were there any gendarmes on patrol?

Tibor turned left into the street where the railwaymen lived, strode boldly into the middle of the road and kicked at stones as if he hadn't a care in the world. He had to jump back immediately to allow a truck stacked high with sacks of vegetables to pass by. Another truck trailed some distance behind. Tibor could only speculate on where this bounty was headed. Certainly not to the Jews in their ghetto camps and probably not to the general populace. That left the gendarmes and the probability of extra rations as a reward for a job well done.

Once across the road, Tibor walked unhurriedly towards the signalman's house. The street was busier than he'd expected, with pedestrians in singles and groups heading towards him. Doubtless some were going to the station but the numbers suggested a change of shift in some other form of employment. Tibor thought immediately of the timberyard and factories. Did they need civilians to clean the premises or help process the Jews? He doubted it. But some activity in the area was generating work and it didn't really matter what it was. The extra flow of pedestrians gave him the cover he needed.

A woman smiled hesitantly at him as she passed by. Tibor responded graciously but his mind raced to recall who she was. He finally pinned her down. She was the woman from the bookstore that also sold maps. They'd gone in for guides to the hiking trails and Milos had discovered a wealth of books unavailable in Sarospatak. That had made the bookstore a regular stop whenever their rambles took them through Satoraljaujhely. Who else might recognise him, Tibor wondered. And who might know his background?

'Tibor!'

A gendarme's hand on his shoulder could not have stopped Tibor more abruptly. Panic flared briefly and unexpectedly even though he'd recognised the voice. Again he'd let himself down. It was the old signalman and Tibor, in his preoccupation, had almost let him pass by unnoticed.

'Erno!' said Tibor and even managed to project delight into his voice. But it wasn't altogether convincing and he could see concern flicker in the old man's eyes. He threw his arms around Erno's thin shoulders and was relieved to feel him reciprocate.

'Tibor! Tibor!' he cried, and burst out laughing. Then softly into his ear, 'In the name of God, what are you doing here, boy?'

He took both of Tibor's hands and dragged him to the side of the road into the driveway of a warehouse where grain had once been bagged for transportation. He kept his face smiling but there was no smile in his words.

'For God's sake, boy, can't you see it's not safe for you here? Can't you see what's happening?'

'Tell me what you know,' said Tibor.

The old man rolled his eyes. 'Where do I begin? What do you know?'

'They've rounded up ten thousand Jews for transportation. They're keeping them in the timberyard and nearby factories.'

'Ten thousand!' snorted the old man. 'There are fifteen thousand poor souls crammed in there. Fifteen thousand, for God's sake! I've seen the transportation orders. Get back to Sarospatak and warn your father, that's if it's not already too late.'

'What do you mean?'

The old man looked around to see if anyone was watching them. He slapped Tibor's arm jovially. He smiled but his eyes were hard and angry. 'Trains have been running day and night up from the north-east province, all of them packed full of Jews being deported to Poland. There are ten trains originating from here scheduled over the next three days, an average of twenty-six box cars per train. Each box car will be filled with Jews with no room to move or even sit down. Figure it out. All fifteen thousand Jews will be gone by Tuesday. Who do you think will be next?'

'Where are they taking them?'

The old man spat into the dust. 'If you believe the Germans, they're all being taken east to help with the harvest. If you believe the schedules I saw back in the station, they're heading north then west into Poland.'

'What will I tell Dad?'

'Tell him to run.' The old man slapped Tibor's arm again but this time there was moisture reddening his eyes. 'He's a good man, your father. Tell him not to believe anything the Germans say. They came here, arrested the Jewish leaders and held them to ransom. They promised to release them once they got the money and they did. Then, when they wanted to concentrate the Jews in the timberyard, they told them they would be well treated. The Jews believed them. Well treated, my arse! You don't treat animals like that. Now they're telling them to board the train to the Ukraine to help with the harvest.'

The old man paused.

'Just tell him to run! And you, boy, you get away from here as fast as you can. You go warn him, you hear?'

'Count on me,' said Tibor. He took the old man's hand and shook it. 'Thank you, Erno. I'll tell my father what a good friend you are.'

'If you ever need me, I'm here,' said the old man. 'Others too. Your father has a lot of respect. Now go before we arouse suspicion. Go!'

Erno kissed Tibor on both cheeks, faked a laugh and spun away.

'Wait!' said Tibor. 'It's better for me if you walk with me to the corner.'

The old man stopped and turned, checked Tibor as he walked past.

'Listen.'

Erno brought his finger up to his lips to silence him. Tibor was dimly aware of a train pulling slowly into the station, the rattle of the trucks and the release of steam, sounds which were background music to his life and barely noticed.

'It has begun,' said the old man.

Personal discipline was Tibor's strength yet he wanted to deny all he had learned and run. Instead, he fought his instincts and strolled as casually as he could back towards the town centre. Once again he found himself walking against the flow of pedestrian traffic and this baffled him. Why? Why weren't the people at work? Where were they heading? As soon as he posed the question he knew the answer. He took a closer look at the people flowing past him, noted the almost celebratory attitude among many and the hard, cruel look of others. He realised what was happening was probably the biggest thing that had occurred in the town since 1919, when Communist partisans and Slovaks had used Satoraljaujhely and its surrounds as their battleground. All the same, Tibor found their attitude hard to reconcile. It was true many people disliked Jews, and certainly some might have thought they had solid grounds for the hatred, but he couldn't help wondering what exactly the Jews had done to deserve the fate awaiting them. What had they done that their appalling suffering should command an audience of heartless, cheering onlookers?

Milos would have snapped, Tibor knew. Would have thrown everything away in a futile act of outrage and fury or dissolved in hopeless anguish. Either way, his actions would have sealed their fate. He was glad he'd left Milos in the forest so that he didn't have to bear witness, glad he'd protected his little brother from that.

A burst of gunfire interrupted his thoughts, followed by an outburst of cheering. There was more gunfire, more sustained, more deadly. Some people started running to see what was happening, others stopped in their tracks, apprehensive, concerned. Tibor kept on walking. Somewhere behind him in the railyards Jews were dying, shot down for the crime of wanting to stay alive. It cheered Tibor to know that not everyone was going meekly like lambs to the slaughter, but resisting and refusing to board the trains. Ultimately it would make no difference. Other than that dying here in defiance had a dignity which dying in Poland did not.

Once Tibor had passed through the centre of the town, the number of gendarmes on patrol diminished until there were none. He guessed they'd all been assigned to the railyards to prevent escapes or attracted there by the shooting. He faced his biggest risk leaving the town precinct but decided not to wait until nightfall. Circumstances had changed. He didn't expect to encounter gendarmes but if he did he believed he was skilled enough to avoid them. His confidence and strength returned with every step away from the station, the timberyards and the now hateful town. It was almost as familiar to him as Sarospatak, but something had changed at its heart, something had been lost, and its place in Hungary's history tarnished for ever.

Tibor and Milos took extraordinary risks in their haste to reach Sarospatak and warn their father, Aunt Katy, Elizabeth and Gabriella. They travelled non-stop through the night but also well into the dangerous daylight hours of morning. For the sake of speed they surrendered the concealment of the fields and woods and travelled openly down laneways, their only concession being to choose those which were lined by cherry trees and poplars and afforded some cover. They could not abandon caution altogether and took to the fields the instant they heard voices or the sound of approaching vehicles. Yet they made good progress until they neared their home town when, once again, they encountered patrols and bands of hapless Jews being marched along by gendarmes. Neither boy needed telling what that meant, and their fears for the safety of their father first, Gabriella and her family second, drove them on.

But their movements were so restricted! Even travelling by night they had to exercise extreme caution and on two occasions nearly stumbled into gendarme camps. Mostly the gendarmes took over Jewish property in the villages, using them for sleeping quarters. But there weren't always villages where the gendarmes chose to rest and in these instances they took over farmhouses that had belonged to Jews. With limited accommodation, some gendarmes were forced to put up tents and sleep outside, certainly no hardship in the balmy late spring weather, but a trap for the weary boys. If the sentries had been alert, or in some cases even awake, Tibor and Milos would certainly have been captured.

Although Sarospatak was barely twelve kilometres by rail from Satoraljaujhely, the circuitous route the boys were forced to take trebled if not quadrupled the distance. Yet they arrived at the outskirts of Sarospatak barely thirty hours after leaving Satoraljaujhely, exhausted and with stomachs crying out for food.

'Let's go in now!' said Milos desperately. The hands on his watch ticked past eleven. 'It's dark enough. It's quiet enough. We can be in and out in no time.'

'No,' said Tibor quietly. The horrors of Satoraljaujhely were behind him and once again he employed the caution that had kept them alive. He had no doubt that they could reach their little cottage undetected but wasn't sure what they'd find when they got there. Their father? A new stationmaster? Or gendarmes using the cottage as a billet? It was precisely this lack of certainty that urged caution.

'Then what?' said Milos. 'Lying here is doing nobody any good.'

'I'm thinking,' said Tibor.

'Jesus, Mary, Mother of God!' said Milos impatiently.

Tibor laughed bitterly. 'I don't think your God's listening. I don't think anyone's God is listening.' He paused momentarily. 'But you've given me an idea. Come.'

'Where?'

'I've seen the light. I know where we can find sanctuary.'

'Where?' demanded Milos again.

'Have faith, little brother,' said Tibor, 'have faith.'

He led Milos around the back of the rail line away from the river, hugging the privet hedges that bordered the outlying houses, all the while checking the cloud cover to make sure the moon would not break through and reveal their presence.

'Where are you taking us?' hissed Milos.

There were several ways across the railway lines that would ultimately take them to their cottage but Tibor steadfastly ignored all of them.

'Can't you guess?' said Tibor.

'Do we cross the railway?'

'No. Now if you can't guess, shut up.'

Milos ducked lower and followed his brother in their practised stooped run.

'This way,' said Tibor and ducked between two lines of privet hedge. He stopped and waved Milos to do likewise. He put his finger to his brother's lips for silence. Mosquitoes hummed and somewhere in a nearby ditch a frog croaked. But from the little cottage on the other side of the hedge came another sound. Mozart. Even in the dark Tibor could see the recognition dawn on Milos's face.

'My God! What are you doing here?' The man had responded quickly to Tibor's knock on his door. 'Quickly, come inside, come inside. Lonci! Lonci! Come see who is here!'

Milos couldn't help smiling. Have faith, Tibor had said, but he'd failed to make the connection. But how had Tibor made the connection between his blasphemy and their godparents? He allowed his father's clerk to usher him inside, worrying at them both like a small dog with a recalcitrant sheep.

'Have you eaten? Have you eaten? No, of course not! Lonci!'

He led the boys into a tiny kitchen, cramped even further by the small wooden table and two chairs.

'Only if you can spare the food, Mr Zelk,' said Tibor.

'Ha! You are our guests. We are your godparents. You can take the food from our mouths and we would give it gladly. But yes, we have food. Of course we have food. Don't you know your father gave us a bag of vegetables, when?... Thursday afternoon, not three days ago!'

Tibor's eyebrows rose. Sometimes his father amazed him. Was he prescient, he wondered, or just covering all his options?

'We've been away,' said Milos.

'Of course, of course,' said Mr Zelk. He clasped his hands together unhappily. 'Otherwise you wouldn't be here.'

128

'What do you mean?' said Tibor sharply, far more sharply than he'd intended.

The old man turned to him in horror. He caught sight of his wife on the stairs in her nightgown, her hands suddenly shooting upwards to cover her mouth. 'You mean you don't know?' he asked incredulously.

Tibor closed his eyes and slumped down into the wooden chair. Suddenly weariness overwhelmed him. They were too late, too late.

'What's happened?' said Milos. 'Tell us what's happened.'

'When?' asked Tibor.

'Two days ago. Your father knew what was going to happen which is why he gave away his vegetables. He knew.'

'For God's sake,' said Milos, unwilling to believe the obvious until it was spelled out to him in all its horror, 'what happened?'

'They've taken him,' said Mr Zelk simply. 'They rounded up all the Jews on Saturday morning. They've crammed them into the old warehouse just off Kazinczy Ferenc Street. All of them in that little old warehouse.'

'You poor boys.' Mrs Zelk finally plucked up the courage to join them. Tears flowed down her plump cheeks and she put her arms around Milos. 'You poor things,' she said again.

'Is there any way in or out?' asked Milos.

'No,' said Mr Zelk. 'The warehouse is heavily guarded day and night. The only Jews that come out are taken away to be tortured. The gendarmes seem to think Jews have gold and jewellery hidden under every bush. I have talked to people who have heard the screams. The gendarmes also boast about their finds.' He shook his head sadly.

'Any news of our father?' asked Tibor.

'None,' said Mr Zelk. 'That would be asking too much.'

'We have friends in Tokaj Street,' said Milos. 'Have the gendarmes cleared out Tokaj Street, do you know?'

'I'm sorry,' said Mr Zelk. 'I'm sorry for you and for your friends. Yes, they have cleared all of Sarospatak and all the surrounding farms and villages. Now, let Lonci prepare you some food. You look starved.'

Milos's head fell onto Mrs Zelk's shoulder. Never in his life had he needed comforting more than he did then. His father taken! And Gabriella. Two of the three people most precious to him. But what comfort could a friendly shoulder and a stroking hand possibly offer? A despairing wail broke free from his throat and he began to sob uncontrollably.

'Their army is pulling back into the Ukraine and desperately needs transportation but what do the Germans do? Instead they use their trains and carriages for this,' said Mr Zelk disgustedly. 'But why should I look for sense where there is none? Why should I expect sanity when it's clear the world has gone mad?'

Tibor didn't respond. What was left to say?

The railwaymen's uniforms Mr Zelk had found for him and Milos were a thin disguise at best; their faces were too well known, especially around the railyards. They stood on the tracks looking back down the line at the locomotive and enclosed cattle trucks which were already in position at the station. A light mist and the grey dawn light hid much of the detail but Tibor already carried most of that in his head.

'The engine driver and fireman are German,' said Mr Zelk. 'The guards are Hungarian but doubtless they will be changed somewhere before the border. Geza Apro is acting stationmaster. He is the only one of us allowed on the platform during loading.'

Tibor nodded. Geza Apro had been his father's signalman. He was a man of little ambition and equivalent intelligence. Yet he was good company, enjoyed a laugh and was, above all, loyal. Geza would not betray them.

'Who is in the signal box?' asked Tibor.

'I am,' said Mr Zelk. 'I change the semaphore from red to green when the train is ready to depart. I also have three more non-stops heading up the line to Satoraljaujhely.'

'Who switches the tracks?'

'Geza.'

'Would he allow us to do that?'

'Maybe. But you would be exposed. Someone would be bound to recognise you. The gendarmes are looking for you. Your names have not been crossed off the registry of Jews.'

'Then how?'

'Don't even think about it,' said Mr Zelk. 'Why risk everything now? I will get word to your father somehow. Geza will help.'

Tibor met this suggestion with stony silence. His eyes flicked to Milos. He was like a zombie, not speaking, not smiling, not crying, just mutely obeying instructions. His brother was a risk he couldn't afford to take. But somehow, somewhere there had to be a solution.

The world ended for Jozsef when the boys failed to return. He had little doubt what had happened. Two boys on the run in the open with so many patrols about, there could only be one outcome. The numbness that enveloped him made it easy to accept the inevitability of his own fate.

He'd sat up through Friday night waiting for the telltale sound of the key in the back door that would signal the boys' return. He'd delayed his visit to Tokaj Street to collect Gabriella because he couldn't bear to leave in case Tibor and Milos returned. He'd stalled until just before noon when he realised he had no choice but to make for the rendezvous or, at least, find somewhere to hide until nightfall. His one hope was that the boys had realised the danger in coming home and holed up at the meeting place instead. He'd gathered up his bag and taken a last look around the little cottage. Even then he'd paused, listening for a tap on the window or a scratching at the rear door, anything that would indicate that his sons had returned. His spirits had lifted momentarily when he heard footsteps on the street outside. But the knock on the door that followed was one of authority, not of two fugitive boys, and in that instant Jozsef knew that all his plans and decisions were meaningless. They were no longer his to make. He'd offered no resistance.

Jozsef had expected to be taken to a temporary ghetto but he'd imagined it would occupy several streets and buildings, not just an abandoned warehouse. The warehouse, Jozsef soon discovered, didn't just concentrate the Jewish populace but despair of the deepest, darkest kind. No one had anticipated the nightmarish conditions, the overcrowding, the lack of amenities and the absolute inadequacy of the sanitation. No one had foreseen the abandonment of all hope. Some wept, some withdrew, some lost their minds.

Through the horrors of Saturday afternoon and the resignation of Sunday, Jozsef trawled the sea of bewildered, disbelieving, fearful faces for information on Tibor and Milos. But nobody had seen or heard from them. He clung to the slim hope that his boys had made it back to the rendezvous and were hiding there, waiting for him. But as more and more Jews were rounded up and packed into the warehouse, Jozsef's despair grew. What chance did his boys have against such thoroughness? Tibor was resourceful but the enemy were everywhere.

As the days passed and there was no word, he began to accept that his sons were lost, that all his plans for them and all his preparations had, in the final analysis, amounted to nothing. They were gone, captured, tortured, or shot dead in the fields. All because he had procrastinated and failed to act when they still had time to act. But *had* he failed them or was the enemy just too strong and all his precautions never anything other than futile? He tried his hardest to believe the latter.

His one act of courage was to put on a brave face for Katica and her daughters, to comfort them and encourage them to believe the lie that they were being taken out to the plains of the Alfold to help harvest grain, to pick fruit and tobacco. Even in this, he was aware that he was aiding the enemy in their cause by placating fears and stifling resistance. But the lie helped the women and gave them hope when the dreaded alternative offered none. It was the positive side of that great flaw in the character of human beings that makes them believe what they want to believe when all evidence indicates the contrary.

Now, as the gendarmes began lining them up for the march to the station, Jozsef guessed that around eight hundred Jews from Sarospatak had been crammed into the warehouse and half as many again from surrounding villages. One trainload, somewhere between twenty-four and twenty-six box cars. Jozsef could envisage the loading and the renewed disbelief on the faces of the unwilling deportees as they were jammed into every centimetre of the box cars, when they realised the purpose of the two buckets, when they realised what little human dignity remained was a luxury no longer available to them. How many times had he witnessed it before? How many times had he previewed his own deportation? He recalled the bravery of Thomas and Balazs and determined to hold his head up like them and not be bowed. But sometimes he believed that the weight of his loss, the burden of his two lost boys, was heavy enough to bring Samson to his knees, and he hoped desperately that somehow he would bear up until it no longer mattered. These were the thoughts he carried as he stood in line, his small suitcase in one hand and his free arm around Gabriella.

It was a day devoid of mercy. The sun beat down upon the assembled Jews from a clear blue sky without hope of relief. There were no clouds and no breeze to summon them. Ordinarily, Jozsef would have greeted such a day with a smile, but now it seemed as if nature also conspired against them. They didn't march to the station but shuffled, a miserable line of humanity, mothers soothing frightened children, elderly husbands supporting elderly wives, boys and girls wide-eyed with fear holding the hand of any adult who'd take theirs. Around him Jozsef heard muttered prayers in Hebrew and wondered what these people now expected from their God. A change of heart from the Gestapo overseers? A change of policy from Berlin? The vanguard of the Russian advance? Prayers and hopes were the foolish machinations of minds that refused to accept reality. Reality was the leering, brutal faces of the gendarmes and Arrow Crossmen, the quiet approval and satisfaction of the German overseers, the crowd of hostile citizens of Sarospatak who'd come to see the back of their Jews. Reality was the box cars.

Jozsef clasped Gabriella's hand firmly and stuck closely to Katica and Elizabeth. It would be intolerable and the last straw for any of them to be separated now. He didn't blame Gabriella for his capture; it had been his decision to wait and his fault that they'd waited so long to act. His only regret, one he felt deeply in his soul, was that he hadn't been with his sons when the axe fell upon them.

Gendarmes counted the front of the line up into sections like so many sausages. Seventy-five in this group, seventy-seven in that, each led to a box car and forced in under a barrage of threats. Signs on the sides of the box cars proclaimed the occupants to be 'German Workers-Resettlers' but few were prepared to believe them. As their turn approached, Jozsef took a last look at the town that had sheltered him and finally rejected him. He saw his replacement, his one-time underling Geza Apro, standing in front of his old office, staring at him as though deliberately trying to catch his eye. Geza turned and nodded almost imperceptibly towards the signal box seventy metres down the track. Jozsef followed his look, puzzled. To his amazement, the semaphore arm dipped twice, slowly but quite deliberately. He stared hard at the window of the signal box, excitement and relief beginning to flood through every vein and artery in his body. Yes! Yes! There at the window, three signalmen where there should only be one! A godfather and his two godchildren!

'Move! Move!'

Jozsef heard the gendarmes but stood momentarily transfixed, filled with joy and pride. The angel of death hovered over him yet his back straightened and his chin rose in defiance. Eichmann was good but not good enough. His boys were better.

* * *

Eventually the blind man broke the spell that had descended over the table. He reached over to where he knew Milos would be and patted him on the arm.

'Let me get you a coffee, my friend. You have certainly earned one.'

'Thank you, Ramon, but not yet.' Milos ran his hand through his thinning hair wearily. 'I haven't quite finished.'

'Not finished? I thought ...'

'I'm sorry if I gave that impression. It is my fault, no? I paused too long while I gathered my thoughts. I've talked too much. I've journeyed to places I left behind a long time ago and the effort has worn me out.'

'Then leave it until next week,' said Lucio. 'The first part of any story is always the hardest, and this time clearly harder than most.'

'No,' said Milos, 'I will finish now so I can have a clean start to next week's episode. All I want to cover is how Tibor and Milos felt at seeing their father herded onto the train to Auschwitz.'

'Poor buggers,' said Neil. 'I can imagine.'

'Can you?' said Milos, suddenly bitter. He turned on Neil. 'You can imagine how Tibor felt, can you? I don't think so!'

Neil recoiled in his seat as though stung.

Milos bored into him. 'Tibor could see his father's relief that his sons were still alive and his pride that they had the audacity to send him a message. But that only made him feel more guilty. For ignoring Milos's plea to return home when they'd first seen the Jews being rounded up. For continuing on to the cave to stash their winter clothes. For taking more time to see what was happening in Satoraljaujhely. For not considering the Germans and their gendarme lackeys could ever be as efficient and as ruthless as they were. If he'd listened to Milos there was every chance he could have got back to Sarospatak in time to pluck his father out of their little home and escape into the Zemplen Hills. Instead, Tibor was forced to watch his father being herded into a cattle truck, having witnessed the horrors of Satoraljaujhely and knowing that his father was going away to his death. To a terrible death. Tibor, the family provider, the fixer, had got it wrong the one time it really mattered. Blame is the sharpest of blades and it cut through to his soul.

'Can you imagine how Milos felt? He was still only fourteen years old. Can you imagine the devastation he felt, shredded by an overpowering sense of loss and also by more than a fair share of guilt? He felt jointly responsible with Tibor for having failed to rescue their father in time. But Milos, more so than Tibor, had suffered a double blow. What now of his solemn promise to protect Gabriella from the cattle trucks, what now of his vow to rescue her, to marry her, to spend his life with her, to love her as much as any human being can be loved? His streaming eyes flashed back and forth from his father to Gabriella until they and his life as he'd imagined it were swallowed up by the ugly black hole in the side of the cattle truck. No more father. No more Gabriella.'

Milos slumped back in his chair exhausted.

'Thank you, Ramon, I will have that coffee now.'

'I think we all need coffee now.'

Ramon waved his hand to attract Gancio's attention, heard him respond almost immediately.

'I'm sorry, Milos, and I apologise,' said Neil. 'I concede there is no way I could possibly know how the two boys felt. But, for what it's worth, having listened to you I'm beginning to get some idea.'

'No, Neil,' said Milos coldly, 'you have no idea. You can have no idea. No idea at all.'

SECOND
THURSDAY

CHAPTER NINE

There was only one topic of conversation as the four friends sat down to lunch and that was the storm that had broken over Sydney as they'd made their way to the restaurant. It had begun with high winds and rain before the rain had turned into hailstones the size of golf balls, which had smashed office windows, dented cars and blocked drains causing roads to flood.

'As soon as I heard on the radio the hail was coming I drove up onto the footpath beneath a shop awning,' said Neil. 'Beauty of a four-wheel drive. The car alongside me at the kerb, a WRX, looked like some madman had gone over it with a ball hammer. Its alarm was screaming like a stuck pig. Did you get caught?'

'I pulled off the Western Distributor and parked under the freeway,' said Milos.

'Good thinking,' said Neil.

'I agree, but it wasn't my idea. There was a guy in a new Porsche in front of me. Judging by his reaction he heard about the hail the same time I did. When he speared off under the off ramp I just followed. What about you, Lucio?'

'I got here early. I was already in the car park.'

Ramon couldn't help smiling. As far as he was concerned, the storm was as welcome as the first fine day of spring. It had provided the distraction Neil and Milos needed to allow the hostility that had built up between them to dissipate. He was delighted to hear them discussing the storm as if the tensions of the previous Thursday had never happened. But would they resurface and, if they did, who would be the instigator? He no longer believed Milos had deliberately set out to target Neil with his story; Milos's bitterness had been genuine, and the intensity of his attack on Neil more a product of emotion than planning. Yet the anger and outbursts were so atypical of Milos. Were they induced by the story or was Milos simply laying foundations for his tricks? Milos rarely did anything without thinking carefully about it first. But was this the exception?

'What about you, Ramon?' asked Neil.

'Me? I came by taxi. As always.'

'Did you get caught?'

'Yes. It sounded more like shrapnel falling on the car than hailstones. The driver was afraid the windows would break. He wanted to stop.'

'And did you?'

'No. I told him to keep driving. What do I care if the windows break? I can't see out of them anyway.'

Ramon smiled again as his friends burst out laughing. This was the mood to begin the second day's storytelling. If Lucio chose to tell one of his ribald stories now it would be perfect. So long as they could stay laughing through lunch. 'I wonder what delight Gancio has for us this afternoon,' he said. 'Anyone know?'

'I know the first course,' said Lucio. 'Spaghetti, served with the juices of roast lamb cooked with rosemary and garlic.'

'Spaghetti with dripping?' said Neil. 'Is that a cholesterol hit or what? If Hitler had've had Gancio's recipe he wouldn't have needed Zyklon B. He could have got the same result just buying the Jews lunch.'

'Jesus Christ,' groaned Ramon. Lucio rolled his eyes.

'Just testing,' said Neil. He started to laugh. Ramon was relieved to hear Milos join him.

'Do I dare ask where you are taking us today, Milos?' Neil asked. 'Back to Hungary?'

'Of course.'

'Any chance you could move the story on twenty or thirty years?'

'No chance, Neil. I'm taking you right back to that signal box at the instant we left it last week, to two brave but shattered boys waving goodbye. You see, Neil, Jozsef wasn't the only one to spot the boys in the signal box. So did a boy from their school, a boy who'd been taken to the station by his anti-Semitic parents who wanted one last chance to tell the departing Jews exactly what they thought of them, a boy who'd already grown to dislike and distrust Tibor Heyman. His name was Istvan Kiraly, a little rat-faced weasel of a kid who some boys thought was a bit of a freak. But he was much more than that. Oh, yes. The interesting thing is, he and Tibor were alike in more ways than either would admit. Both were intelligent, more mature than their years would suggest, and both were confident in their abilities. They could have become friends, but instead they were destined to become implacable enemies. I'll tell you more about Istvan Kiraly after lunch, provided your arteries survive the pasta.'

* * *

Istvan Kiraly heard the cows stirring beneath him and guessed it was time for milking. The cows served as alarm clock in a household too poor for such luxuries. He poked his elbow into the back of his brother who was fast asleep in the bed alongside him. His brother's response was a sleepy snarl and a retaliatory arm thrown in his general direction. Istvan ignored it and swung his feet to the floor. When was it ever different?

143

The beasts below heard him stir and shuffled expectantly. He sat on the bed and waited until his eyes had fully opened and adjusted to the dark. Hay was also stored in the loft which doubled as bedroom for himself and his brother so candles and lamps were forbidden. Istvan shivered in the cold, rose and pulled his nightshirt over his head. A cow farted voluminously but Istvan barely noticed the smell as the foul gases rose and permeated the loft. It was what he lived with every day of his life.

Besides the bed, the loft was furnished with a wooden chair and a dressing table with four drawers that skidded on worn runners and no longer closed properly. He pulled the chair towards him. His clothes were stacked upon it in the order in which he put them on, the reverse of the way he had taken them off the evening before, so he could dress easily and quickly in the dark. He pulled on his shirt, his trousers, his coarse knitted jumper, his patched socks, his boots and finally his jacket. He raised the trapdoor and was engulfed by the smells of warm animals, manure and urine. The cows shuffled and ruminated as they waited for him to climb down the ladder and ease the discomfort in their distended udders. But Istvan had things to do first, which the beasts well knew. Their lives, like the boy's, were governed by routine.

Istvan grabbed his cap off the nail by the stable door and walked quickly towards the small mud-brick cottage. The back door swung outwards on hinges that he kept well-greased so his duties didn't wake his father. He slipped out of his boots and tiptoed between the bed where his grandparents lay snoring and his little sister's bed, and past the bed where his parents slept, the bed in which he, his brother and his sister had been born. It was also where his father, his grandfather and his great-grandfather had drawn their first breaths. Doubtless over the years the bedboards had been replaced, along with the mattress and bedding, but the family still regarded the bed as though every part was original. In all probability, Istvan's great-great-grandfather and his father before that had also been born in that cramped and uncomfortable bed, but nobody bothered thinking back that far and there was nothing to be gained by doing so.

The Kiraly cottage had also undergone changes over the centuries — new roofs, rebuilt walls, cramped extensions — but the pounded earth floor had simply shed layers so that it lay a good twenty centimetres below the doorstep, almost to the level of the footings. Throughout the centuries there had been one constant: the Kiraly cottage had always sheltered more mouths than the Kiraly land could reasonably support. And this had always been a source of discord and unhappiness.

A fire flickered weakly in the hearth in the cottage's one other room, and that was where Istvan headed. His first duty of every day was to build up the fire so that his parents would have the benefit of its warmth when they finally rose. He added a few sticks, no more than kindling, and once they were alight added two small logs. Not so much that his father would belt him for wasting wood, nor so little that his father would accuse him of forgetting to build the fire up and belt him for that. Life didn't have to be hard, Istvan had learned, so long as you understood how people thought and how things worked. After placing a kettle of water over the flame, he briefly warmed his hands before retracing his steps to the stable. That was something else he'd learned. Cows were less likely to kick him if his hands were warm.

'Sandor!'

'I'm coming!'

'Dad's already stirring.'

Istvan smiled when he heard the sound of his brother's boots being dragged across the floor of the loft. His father was in fact dead to the world but it didn't hurt to hurry Sandor along. His brother was lazy and rebellious and it frustrated Istvan when Sandor made no effort to understand how the

145

world worked, to comply and use his knowledge to his advantage. Instead his brother practised a pointless brinkmanship, leaving his duties to the last minute, not completing them satisfactorily or not completing them at all. His rebelliousness brought their father's wrath down on both of them. Certain things had to be done and they were best done and dispensed with as quickly and with as little fuss as possible. The fire had to be built up, the cows had to be milked, the chickens fed and the eggs collected. They had to muck out the barn and the pig sty, taking care to stack the manure so it could be used to fertilise the crops. They also had to gather parsley roots to crush into a tea for his grandparents' rheumatism. These things had to be done and done before their father rose from his bed. They had to be done.

Istvan lit the oil lamp which was strung on rope over a beam so it couldn't be knocked over accidentally and burn the barn down. He walked the first cow into the milking stall, perched on his little stubby-legged stool, placed the milk pail beneath the cow's udders and squeezed. The milk steamed as it squirted into the pail. Behind him he heard his brother's boots scraping on the ladder, heard him fart. What was one more fart in a barn shared with four cows, a bull and a calf?

'Here.'

Istvan took the enamel mug from his brother, scooped up some warm milk from the pail and handed it back. Sandor drank it greedily. Istvan scooped out another half mugful, drank it himself and lay the mug down by his stool. That was breakfast over and done with. Both boys wanted more but that was not an option. Their father knew almost to the squirt how much milk his cows produced and monitored the output carefully. Spare milk became cheese and cheese became pengo and pengo made life bearable.

Istvan filled two pails and covered the milk with wooden lids that jammed down tightly. He carried the pails outside

146

and set about mucking out the barn. Both boys had their duties but Istvan also had the responsibility of making sure Sandor completed his. Istvan worked quickly and automatically, all the while planning his day and working out the best way to approach the people he needed to deal with. The sooner he finished his work and the sooner he left the cottage for school, the more time he'd have to think about life's other possibilities and how to make his escape. Istvan was determined to break with the family tradition of subsistence and disappointment. His secret agenda was to be the first first-born Kiraly in generations to leave the farm.

With his duties finished, and having satisfied himself that Sandor's were also nearing completion, he carried the two milk pails into the cottage. Once again he kicked his boots off at the door, leaving them in the middle of the step to remind his brother to do likewise. Once inside he woke his sister and gave her some milk. Though only nine years old, she already had the heavy limbs and big hands that marked her as a peasant and equipped her for a life of drudgery. She had the unenviable task of waking their father.

There had been a time when Istvan's father, Gyorgy, had made a determined bid to improve the lot of the Kiraly family. Their land was leased, part of a vast estate owned by one of Hungary's noble families. The bulk of their main crop, wheat, went in rent and taxes, leaving them barely enough grain to grind into flour for their own use. So Gyorgy created a market garden where he could grow potatoes, sweet corn, beets, onions, leeks, cucumbers, herbs and chillies to grind up into paprika. He increased the number of hens and added geese, doubled the number of cows to make cheese and kept two breeding pigs. He dug ditches to prevent flooding and irrigation trenches to keep his vegetables watered during dry spells. Somewhere along the way his back cracked under the loads he subjected it to, yet he ignored the pain and soldiered on. The truth was, his family's circumstances were improving.

For the first time in generations, the Kiraly family had a brighter future to look forward to. Suddenly there was money for more livestock, for new bedding, new boots and new clothes. Then the landlord responded to the improvements he'd made to their property by increasing his rent.

On that day, Istvan's father accepted defeat. He had no rights of appeal, in fact, no rights at all. His one hope of avenging the injustice lay in joining the Smallholders Party and campaigning for land rights. But there was little he could do for the pain in his back. By the end of each day, the pain was so bad he numbed it with alcohol, the only medication available to him, but this took savage toll on the available pengo and on his temper. The *palinka* made life tolerable for him but frequently intolerable for his family.

Istvan's younger sister woke their father every morning by massaging his back, without which therapy he couldn't even rise from his bed. Every morning he began by cursing her but gradually her strong hands loosened the frozen and spasming muscles and with the lessening of the tension came a lightening of his mood. But no amount of back massaging could ease the morning *palinka*-induced headache or the fact that he faced another day of hard work and bleak prospects. The potential for explosion was always there, which was why Istvan worked so diligently to ensure neither he nor his brother gave him any cause for complaint.

'Let me see your boots before you put them on.' Istvan stood by the back step waiting, as he always did, for Sandor to finish getting ready for school.

'They've split more,' said Sandor.

The soles were worn through but the real problem was with the stitching and the uppers themselves. The stitching and the leather surrounding the stitching had rotted, and the uppers had worn so thin the cracks in them had started to split. As hard as he looked there was little to suggest they were capable of repair.

'They're far too small anyway,' said Sandor. 'My feet are bursting out of them. Just sitting in class I could feel the leather split.'

Sandor's boots had been handed down for the last time and the problem had been occupying Istvan for days. There were no old boots for Sandor to step up to and no money to buy any. With the war on and leather — any leather — at a premium, replacing boots was hard when you didn't have money to pay black-market prices.

'You shouldn't have worn these kicking footballs around,' said Istvan irritably. 'And kicking Jews hasn't helped either.'

'They were falling apart anyway,' said Sandor. He glared at his older brother.

'Don't say anything to Dad. Keep wearing them until I find you some others, okay?'

Istvan handed the boots back to his brother. It didn't bother him that Sandor, although a year younger, was ten centimetres taller than him, raw-boned and strongly built and more than fifteen kilograms heavier. What bothered him was that he was expected to wear clothes handed down from Sandor and his brother didn't respect or look after them. Sandor's boots had been ear-marked for him.

'Where are you going to get boots from?' asked Sandor. There was no real curiosity or wonder in the question, more an undertone of scorn.

'Leave it to me,' said Istvan. 'Now let's go.'

He treated his brother's question dismissively but it was reasonable enough. Where could he get boots from even if he had money to pay for them? Where could he get boots when he had nothing to trade except the clothes he stood in, his school bag and books, and an ancient wooden chess set his grandfather had given him? The chess pieces had been carved during long-forgotten, cold winter nights, not by his grandfather but by one of his ancestors, and much of the intricate detail had been worn smooth by generations of

149

fingering. Nothing in the Kiraly household was ever thrown away. Nothing was ever wasted. But that still left him with nothing to trade.

They had to walk six kilometres to school and Istvan used the time to try and come up with a way to approach the one person who could help him find new boots. He prided himself on his ability to get inside other people's heads, to see the world as they saw it, to sniff out their prejudices and perceptions and even to predict their actions and reactions. He knew exactly what people thought of him and used it to his advantage.

Whenever he beat his schoolfriends or his teachers at chess they always demanded a replay, unable to accept that this undersized runt had outsmarted them. Inevitably, when he won the replay they'd dismiss their loss as bad luck. Istvan just didn't look like the sort of kid who could beat anybody at anything. He didn't mind that he was rarely given credit for his victories because he understood the power inherent in being underestimated and, in fact, delighted in the misconceptions surrounding him. He was smarter than anyone credited him with being, did better in class than anyone expected and spoke confidently when required to give talks. If his teachers had a criticism it was that he never volunteered answers to questions even though they were sure he knew the answers. He only responded if questioned directly. Istvan was a listener and an observer. Through listening and observing he learned how to manipulate people and exploit their weaknesses.

This was one of the things that made him so good at chess. He appeared to play to his opposition's strength, all the while luring them into his trap. People were rarely gracious when he closed the trap on them but Istvan didn't mind in the least. He knew that one day his life would revolve around the skills he was honing, though just how he had no idea. Nature had given his intellect the perfect camouflage and that had to be worth something, to someone, somewhere.

The problem Istvan was mulling over as he approached the school was the fact the one person he was certain could get him boots was also the one person whose head he couldn't get into, whose thoughts eluded him, whose actions he couldn't predict and whose power intimidated him. They were classmates but beyond that their orbits rarely intersected. Could they do business and, if so, what would be the cost?

Two games of soccer were already in progress in the concrete quadrangle in the middle of the school buildings. Four groups of boys shouted, scuffled, kicked and tackled, wearing away the leather on their boots and shoes with a disregard that never ceased to amaze Istvan. There in a nutshell was the difference between the Kiraly family and others, as clear a definition of his family's circumstance as anyone could want. He sensed Sandor becoming agitated alongside him.

'Go on,' said Istvan. 'Just make sure your boots last another couple of days.'

He watched his brother race off, whooping and shouting to his friends, grimaced as Sandor threw his school bag carelessly against a classroom wall where other bags lay strewn. For some time Istvan had entertained the notion of taking his brother with him when he escaped, but Sandor unwittingly seemed hellbent on ridiculing the idea. Sandor wasn't cut out for anything other than manual work; was no more or less than his father in the making, one day destined to take over the cottage, the land, and a life that promised nothing. Istvan was happy to see his brother enjoy himself now, knowing full well there would be precious little of that later in his life.

He walked around the quadrangle and down a pathway that ran between two of the school buildings and the main gate. On the left was an alcove formed by the enclosed stairwell and the end wall which was sheltered from the wind and caught the morning sun. Some students ran around to keep warm but Istvan was one of those who headed straight for the alcove. He was always among the first there and set himself up in his usual place where he didn't intrude on others and was largely ignored. It was important to appear to be doing nothing different. He had to make his approach seem casual, almost a whim. He set up his chessboard to reflect a move he'd seen in a book borrowed from the school library and pretended to be studying it.

His target was anything but a creature of habit but most days he walked to school with his brother, even though they usually split up the moment they arrived. He was also a Jew and, according to Istvan's father, the very worst kind of Jew: one that pretended he wasn't. Gyorgy believed the family that owned the estate they lived on was Jewish, though they professed not to be. The estate manager certainly was, and it was the estate manager who had increased their rent. His father blamed most of his and Hungary's problems on Jews, believing that before the war they ran the country's industries and businesses for their own benefit and were the instigators of every conspiracy aimed at suppressing peasants and workers. Istvan went along with his father's views, for to do otherwise courted trouble, but he didn't embrace them like his brother did. He had no place for prejudice or racial stereotyping, because it created unreliable expectations. Individuals, he'd discovered, rarely reacted in a generalised, stereotypical way. Nevertheless, he couldn't help thinking his father's antipathy might be well-founded where his target was concerned.

He packed up his chess pieces and board and joined the steady flow of students into the quadrangle to wait for assembly. It was apparently accidental that he happened to find himself walking alongside Tibor.

'Boots,' he said softly.

Tibor appeared not to have heard though Istvan was certain he'd picked up on it. He also realised that Tibor would judge his desperation by how quickly he repeated himself, so determined to say nothing.

'For you?' said Tibor eventually.

'Sandor. I wondered if you'd come by any.'

Istvan allowed Tibor to steer him out of the traffic to a quiet spot against the wall of the library. Assembly was still minutes away so they had time to talk.

'What have you got?' asked Tibor.

'Vegetables, eggs, cheese,' said Istvan, knowing it wouldn't be enough and, even if it was, he still had the problem of prising the produce away from his father.

'What else?'

'Nothing.'

'Then how do you expect to trade?'

This was the crunch. Either Tibor bit or he didn't and Istvan had no reason to believe that he would. But Tibor did strange things, often the least expected things, which was what made him so unpredictable and hard to fathom. But his unpredictability opened an avenue for exploitation and this avenue was Istvan's only hope.

'I'll play you chess for the boots.'

Tibor's eyes narrowed slightly.

'Why would I do that?'

'Why not?'

'Two reasons. One, I can get good money for boots without risk. And two, you never lose when you want to win.'

Istvan could feel Tibor's eyes boring into him and began to wilt. *You never lose when you want to win.* How did Tibor know he deliberately threw games? He wasn't aware that Tibor had ever watched him play. Istvan was suddenly assailed by doubt, an uncomfortable, unfamiliar sensation of being out of his depth. Unexpectedly, Tibor began to smile and Istvan couldn't help responding.

'What if I won?' said Tibor. 'What would I win?'

'My chess set.'

Tibor rocked back on his heels. His eyes narrowed once more as though he was considering the proposition.

'The chess set is worthless except to you,' said Tibor. 'If I won I would take something that is precious to you, worthless to me, and you still wouldn't have any boots for Sandor.'

'That's a risk I'm prepared to take.'

The bell rang for assembly.

'What's Sandor's boot size?' said Tibor abruptly.

Istvan told him.

'I can get a pair. They're old but well-cared-for.' Tibor's voice had become that of the deal-maker, impersonal, factual. 'They've been coming to this school longer than any of us. But the stitching is sound and there's at least a year's wear, probably two, in the soles. Interested?'

'We play for them?'

'No,' said Tibor. He smiled faintly, turned and walked away.

Istvan watched him go, trying to come to grips with the sudden turn in their conversation. Against all odds, Tibor was going to bring him boots. So he'd been right in identifying Tibor's avenue of exploitation. But any jubilation was tempered by a growing wariness. He had no idea what price he'd have to pay, only that Tibor had found something in him that he wanted. Istvan was at a loss even to speculate what it might be. All the same, boots were boots and he felt an irresistible urge to smile.

The following morning Istvan waited for Tibor in the shelter of the alcove. He'd told Sandor what was happening and his brother had scarcely been able to believe his good fortune. He would have a pair of boots that would keep his feet dry and warm and the bonus of being able to keep his old boots to play football in and muck out the pig sty. Istvan had impressed upon him the need to look after his new boots, making him understand that there could be no more until the war was over.

Istvan laid out the chess set in front of him. With no price agreed he still entertained the hope that Tibor would play him for the boots. He watched the gate carefully, saw Milos arrive by himself and waited until the school bell rang. But there was no sign of Tibor.

Istvan wasn't unduly concerned. He didn't know Tibor well but he had every expectation that he would keep to his word. That was the way the Jew operated. He spotted him in the classroom and tried many times to catch his eye without success. Significantly, Tibor did not so much as glance in his direction, as though he'd thought about the deal and decided against it. Istvan had the feeling that as far as Tibor was concerned he was no longer of consequence. His sense of elation evaporated and instead he felt bitter and betrayed. A deal was still a deal even if half the detail had yet to be agreed.

He decided to confront Tibor at the first recess, but found him surrounded by other boys and deep in negotiations. He turned away. To interrupt meant he would have to impose himself upon the group and reveal a side of his character he'd worked hard to conceal. Sometime, somewhere, he'd get the opportunity to confront Tibor, one on one, and then he'd make his move. He was just conceding the accuracy of his father's prejudices when Sandor came running up, eyes glowing, his old boots tied around his neck by the laces.

'Istvan! Look! They're fantastic.' Sandor stopped in front of him. 'They've even been shined.'

Istvan stared at the boots on his brother's feet. Everything Tibor had said about them appeared to be true.

'Take them off,' he commanded. 'Let me look at them.'

Sandor obliged. Istvan examined the soles, the stitching, the tongue and lining but, beyond the inevitable scuffs and wear in the soles, couldn't fault them. Yes, they were old, but they were also top-quality boots and they had been looked after. He couldn't help thinking they were far better than Sandor deserved.

'They're what I expected,' he said. 'Put them back on and remember — no football in them.'

'Don't worry, I'm going to look after them,' said Sandor. He said it with so much conviction Istvan was almost tempted to believe him.

Istvan watched his brother run off and turned his mind to the price. Clearly it would be high, though what exactly he was expected to pay was beyond him. He couldn't even begin to guess. It troubled him that the Jew had outmanoeuvred him. Once he'd handed the boots to Sandor, Tibor had left him no room to bargain, denying him any basis for further negotiations. It was a deliberate and calculated move to put him at a disadvantage. Istvan cursed silently but at the same time had to concede the cleverness of it. The Jew could now demand almost anything.

Istvan wandered back to where he'd last seen Tibor and this time succeeded in catching his eye. In fact, he got the distinct impression the Jew was keeping an eye out for him. He stopped and leaned up against a classroom wall and waited for Tibor to finish with the boys he was talking to. Having lost more ground in the negotiations than he could ever recover, Istvan nevertheless decided to make Tibor come to him. A small victory on a battleground littered with unaccustomed defeats.

'Sandor happy?' asked Tibor.

'Yes, as you knew he would be.'

Tibor smiled. 'It was worth it just to see his face.'

'Really?' said Istvan. 'I thought the price would be higher than that.'

'Oh, it is,' said Tibor.

Istvan's eyes narrowed. 'What do you want?'

'You have nothing to give me now,' said Tibor amiably. 'But there might be something you can do for me in the future.'

'Like what?'

'I don't know,' said Tibor. He held out his hand to shake Istvan's. 'But you'll know when the time comes.'

*

Ten months later, Istvan stood with his father, brother and other like-minded citizens of Sarospatak alongside the railway line to hurl abuse at the Jews who had employed them, worked for them, made their bread, mended their shoes, set broken bones, repaired painful teeth and spent money in their shops and on their products and produce. While they were not allowed into the station, Gyorgy had insisted on coming early and had grabbed a position as close to the platform as the gendarmes permitted.

Istvan could clearly see the faces of the Jews as they were herded into the cattle trucks, saw the looks of fear, the tears, and heard the sobbing. He was surprised to discover how many people he recognised, many of whom he'd never suspected were Jews. They were people who were as much a part of ordinary, everyday life in Sarospatak as he was. As hard as he tried, he couldn't see any of them being part of an international Jewish conspiracy. If they were, they'd done an amazing job of hiding it.

His father and the people around him were making so much noise, nobody took any notice of the fact that he wasn't. Instead Istvan retreated into his role as observer, watching, listening, learning. When he spotted the stationmaster, he thought it was ironic that he should be taken away by one of his own trains. He was studying the man's face when he saw him suddenly look up and peer intently. At what? The signal box? There was little that Istvan missed and, although he was hardly at the best of angles, he saw the unexpected dipping of the semaphore. A signal? He checked back to the stationmaster, saw the smile spread over his face, noticed the straightening of his back and the lifting of his head. He turned again to the signal box. From his low angle he saw mostly reflections of clouds in the windows, but then he glimpsed movement inside. There were people inside; somebody who could put a smile on the face of a man being taken away almost certainly to his death. Istvan looked back at the stationmaster as he was herded into a box car and suddenly understood.

There was a bounty on Jews, hardly a fortune, but the Kiraly family were in as much need of a little as they were of a lot. A few pengo could buy some *palinka* for his father to numb his pain, a purchase from which the whole family would benefit. His sister needed clothes. Maybe he could buy some cloth with the bounty. He grabbed his brother's arm.

'Tell Dad I've got some things to do,' said Istvan. 'Tell him I'll see you both back at the cottage.'

His withdrawal caused little consternation. People were grateful for the chance to edge a little closer to the action.

CHAPTER TEN

'What will happen to them?' Milos's voice was barely a whisper yet the fact that he had a voice at all surprised him. His heart was broken and his entire body was numb, not paralysed so much as lacking the volition to move. At that moment, a bullet from an alert gendarme would have been a blessing.

Tibor pulled Milos back from the window gently but firmly. 'I don't know what will happen. Nobody does. All I know is what will happen to us if we don't move quickly and keep our wits about us.'

'I promised Gabi I'd rescue her.' Milos still stared hopelessly out of the window.

'I know. So Gabi and I could get married,' said Tibor bluntly.

Milos swung around, his red eyes wide in disbelief.

'You've always had trouble facing reality, little brother, but times have changed. This is reality. Grow up or we won't leave this signal box alive.'

It was all too much for Milos. His loss, the humiliation, the truth. His shoulders slumped, his chin fell onto his chest and he began sobbing as only the heartbroken can. Tibor grabbed hold of his brother and held him as tightly as he could. He let half a minute pass, a minute, all the while holding Milos's head tightly against his shoulder to muffle his sobs. But sympathy was limited by their circumstance. He pushed Milos away and shook him.

'Never mind Gabi,' he said. 'Did you see the look on Dad's face?'

Milos nodded and, despite everything, smiled weakly.

'Worth the risk?' asked Tibor.

Milos nodded again and his weak smile broadened. The moment his father had looked up and seen them at the window, he'd wanted to shout for joy.

'Good,' said Tibor. 'Now put Dad and Gabi out of your mind. Gabi is strong and Dad will look after her. She will look after him. As much as anyone can. Now, come on. From now on we must think only of ourselves. You know what we have to do.'

'Go with God, boys,' said Mr Zelk. His eyes were red-rimmed and he shook his head sorrowfully. 'That they should do such a thing to your father.'

'We can never thank you enough, Mr Zelk,' said Tibor. 'You are a true friend. Whatever happens to my father now, you know he will always be in your debt. We will drop off the uniforms at your house sometime this afternoon.'

'Keep them,' said Mr Zelk. 'A uniform gives you identity. At a glance you are not Jews but railwaymen. You may need an identity in the days ahead and, besides, these old uniforms won't be missed.'

'Thank you again.'

'Remember, you can always rely on the church.'

Both boys hugged their godfather, made their farewells and descended the stairs. Tibor strode purposefully out of the signal box and along the track to the first set of points, Milos hard on his heels. Each carrying a spike Mr Zelk had given them, they prodded the points like a couple of fettlers, squatted as though studying them, rose and continued on.

Nobody took any notice of them; the loading of the Jews was so much more interesting. Once they'd put some distance between themselves and the crowd of spectators, Tibor dropped the spike where he knew Mr Zelk would find it and led Milos down from the line and over the wooden railing to the street.

'Mr Zelk was right,' said Tibor. 'We'll keep our uniforms on.'

In fact the uniforms gave them more than an identity, they also gave them anonymity. Two youths wandering the street may have aroused interest but not two railwaymen. Their uniforms announced who they were and what they did, and people's interest extended no further. Even if anyone had noticed them slip down the side of what had been the stationmaster's cottage, they probably wouldn't have given it another thought.

Tibor found the back-door key exactly where he expected it to be, jammed between the downpipe and the brick wall, hanging on a wire hook from the bracket. It had let them in every day when they'd come home from school and on the nights when they'd been late home from their forays for food. Believing that the railway cottage would have been handed on to Geza Apro or used as a temporary billet for other railway staff, Tibor didn't hesitate to open the back door and enter. He grabbed the meat knife from its drawer as he passed through the kitchen but he needn't have bothered. On this busiest of days for the railwaymen of Sarospatak, he expected the house to be deserted.

Ever cautious, Jozsef had kept some emergency money in the house, in a baking-powder tin jammed behind two loose bricks in the cellar wall. It wasn't the cleverest of hiding places but Jozsef had always felt that if they ever had need for it, they'd also need to be able to get to it quickly. Tibor ordered Milos to stuff the money into his pocket while he grabbed whatever was left of the potatoes, onions, beets, dried vegetables and chillies and shoved them into a hessian sack. There was disappointingly little. Either their father had been very good at giving their stocks away or the basement had been plundered. They took off upstairs to their bedroom. The room was a mess with a mattress thrown between their two beds, both of which were strewn with clothing. Their father's room mirrored their own. Clearly the cottage was temporary lodgings for someone. Milos opened the wardrobe door expecting to find railwaymen's clothes jammed in with theirs, but instead stopped dead in his tracks.

'Tibor!' Milos stepped back in shock.

Tibor stopped rifling through the drawers and looked up to see the gendarme jackets and trousers draped over hangers.

'What are we going to do?' asked Milos. Fear has a way of focusing the brain and, for the first time that day, Milos forgot about his father and Gabi.

Tibor laughed. 'Piss on them. Grab what we want. Piss on them again before we leave.'

'What if they come back?'

'And leave the Jews to load themselves onto the trains?'

Tibor continued to open drawers and stuff underwear, socks and gloves into his sack. He grimaced angrily when he looked up and saw Milos still staring at the wardrobe. 'Come on, Milos! Our coats!'

'Ssshh! Listen!'

Tibor froze. Milos wasn't looking at the wardrobe but at his feet. The boys stood stock still, knowing full well that any movement would bring a squeak from one of the floorboards. They had lived with the squeaks, knew there was no way of avoiding them and had even tried to make tunes out of them. They heard the back door close. Tibor shot a quizzical glance at Milos who nodded in response. Yes, he'd closed the back door behind him. So someone had come in. Was he still inside the cottage or had he gone straight back out again? The boys waited, as immobile as statues, hardly breathing. If someone was still in

162

the cottage, the floorboards would tell them. And they did. There was someone downstairs, walking lightly. The boys looked at one another. There was another sound, quite unmistakeable, of a chair being pulled out from the dining table and someone sitting on it. They were trapped. There was no escape from their window and, given the state of the floorboards, no way of sneaking up on the intruder. They had only one choice.

Tibor picked up the meat knife he had lain on top of the tallboy. He nodded to Milos. The boys could be quick down the stairs and they knew exactly what they had to do. But would they be quick enough? Could they get down there faster than a gendarme could pick up his rifle or pull out a pistol? Tibor motioned to Milos to take the sack of food and clothing, took a deep breath and charged.

Tibor didn't run down the stairs so much as leap down them, one hand on the banister to steady himself. He'd done it a hundred times before and hit the hall floor on the balls of his feet. He launched himself into the main room ready to kill. And found Istvan, rocked back on a chair, his feet on the table and a knowing smile on his face.

'Checkmate,' said Istvan calmly.

Tibor stopped so abruptly Milos collided into the back of him. He glared at his one-time classmate.

'I could have killed you!' he hissed. He turned to Milos. 'Relax. It's just Istvan, playing his games.'

'What are you doing here?' gasped Milos. His heart was still pounding so hard it threatened to break his ribs.

'I saw you in the signal box,' said Istvan. 'Nice touch. Your father certainly appreciated it.'

'Did you follow us?' asked Tibor.

Istvan shrugged dismissively. 'I left before you did and hid in the back garden. I knew you'd come here.'

'Why didn't you report us?' Tibor still had hold of his knife.

'We made a deal,' said Istvan. 'You said I'd know when it was time to pay.'

A slight smile crossed Tibor's face.

'How did you know?' asked Istvan. 'Back then, how could you know?'

'I didn't,' said Tibor. 'I took out a lot of insurance. But I always felt you were my best investment.'

'Why?'

'You were never going to stay on the farm. You're far too clever. I watched the way you played with the other kids, how you trapped and manipulated them. I figured one day your skills would make you a powerful man, probably in politics. I thought it might be handy to have someone in a position of power owe me a favour.'

'Were they Milos's boots?'

Istvan was clearly flattered by Tibor's comments and sought to change the subject.

'He'd outgrown them.'

'Sandor's looking after them as best he can. Unfortunately, his best is not very good.'

'What now?' said Tibor. The time for pleasantries was over. His voice turned cold. 'Our house is being used to billet gendarmes.'

'I'm sorry,' said Istvan, obviously alarmed, 'I had no idea.'

He pushed his chair back and stood.

'What do you want from us?' Tibor towered over Istvan.

Istvan looked at the knife in Tibor's hand as if noticing it for the first time. 'Acknowledgement. That's all. That all debts are paid.'

'They're only paid if you keep your silence,' said Tibor. He pointed the knife at Istvan's throat.

'That's understood,' said Istvan. 'If I wanted to report you, I would have.'

He held out his hand. Tibor hesitated momentarily then threw the meat knife so that it thudded point-first into the top of the table. He took Istvan's hand and shook it solemnly.

'We're all square,' said Tibor.

'Hopefully next time we meet we'll be on the same side,' said Istvan.

'Aren't we now?' said Milos.

'No,' said Istvan evenly. 'Now go.'

Back on the street, Tibor and Milos were acutely aware of the difference in their appearance. Two railwaymen did not attract attention but two railwaymen carrying a sack would. They realised it was only a matter of time before people's curiosity led to recognition.

'We need to find somewhere to hide till dark,' said Tibor, 'and we need to find it quick.'

'What about your contacts?'

'You tell me who I can trust,' said Tibor. He looked around him but the street was deserted. 'First we've got to get out of these uniforms in case Istvan blabs.'

'He wouldn't,' said Milos. 'You made a deal.'

'Grow up,' snapped Tibor. 'He didn't sell us out at the station because we had unfinished business. It's the way his mind works. He followed us all the way to the cottage just to tell us he'd seen us. Just to even the score card, to let us know that he finished on top with us in his debt. We're not dealing with honour here but ego. Now that everything is settled, now that he's had his little victory, I wouldn't bet against the little shit reporting us for the bounty. Now think, Milos! Where can we go that's safe?'

'Mr Zelk's?'

'He's risked enough for us.'

'Geza Apro's?'

'I trust him. Do you trust his wife?'

'Then we only have one choice,' said Milos.

'Where?'

'The church. Like Mr Zelk said.'

His brother nodded reluctantly.

They walked quickly, sticking to side streets as best they could, grateful for the fact that most of the people who

165

wished them harm were still down at the station while the rest kept to themselves indoors and uninvolved. When they reached their destination, the boys quickly climbed the stone steps and ducked in through the open doorway as quietly as they could. There were women at prayer up near the front so they slipped into one of the rear pews before anyone had a chance to turn around. They knelt and Milos closed his eyes, welcoming the chance to pray for the safety of his father and Gabriella.

'There's no time for that!' hissed Tibor. He too knelt as though in prayer, but kept his head partly raised and his eyes wide open watching the confessional. If he was right in assuming the women were saying their penance, Father Hegedus would soon emerge to see if anyone else was waiting. All they had to do then was catch his eye.

Both boys bowed their heads lower and covered them with their hands as though deep in prayer as a woman rose and walked up the aisle towards them. The vulnerability of their position became immediately apparent. Two railwaymen in church, midweek, at this hour? Of course she'd want to look to see who they were. The boys held their breath, listening for a change in the sound of her footsteps as she passed by.

'God be with you,' they heard her murmur as she passed their pew. They tensed. What did that mean? That she recognised them? Or that she simply sympathised with two young railwaymen who, God knows, had much to unburden themselves of on this terrible day.

Moments later an old woman left the confessional and knelt down a few rows back from the altar. There were seven women in all, scattered among the first few pews. Milos turned his head so he could observe the confessional. He expected Father Hegedus to appear at any moment.

'Come on, come on!'

Tibor's strained whisper startled Milos and he glanced

quickly at his brother. Tibor was growing increasingly anxious and this was not something Milos had witnessed often. To his dismay, a woman rose from among the front pews and shuffled over towards the box to make her confession.

'For God's sake, Milos, get over there and make sure you're next to confess. If we stay here much longer someone will recognise us. I'm going to sneak over to the side away from the doorway.'

Tibor quickly checked each of the women. None looked like leaving. 'Go now,' he hissed.

He watched his brother slide away along the pew to the side aisle, rise and walk quickly to a pew near the confessional. He took a quick look around to make sure nobody was watching and shook his head. He had to keep Milos busy and on edge to prevent him sinking into despair. He needed his brother to keep his wits about him.

Milos knelt and fixed his eyes on the confessional. For once he had the leading role not Tibor, and this gave him the courage to hold his nerve. He had to get the timing right and keep his head down when the woman in the confessional left, yet be quick enough to take her place before any of the other women could. Then he'd have Father Hegedus to deal with. Milos prayed silently but didn't dare close his eyes for fear of the unwelcome images he would see. He had to put the memories of the day aside, close the door on them, until better, safer times when they could be released and dealt with. Behind him he could hear Tibor shuffling to a new position, dragging the sack along with him. To his surprise, he could also hear soft murmurings from the confessional although the words were indistinct. But at least he knew Father Hegedus was taking confessions. There was no mistaking the sound of his voice. Milos had heard it often enough. He tried to imagine how his confession would go.

'Forgive me, Father, for I have sinned. I neglected to board the train with all the other Jews.'

The curtains parted, interrupting his thoughts. Milos covered his face with his hands and peered through his fingers. To his horror, the woman took only a couple of steps from the confessional before pausing and gazing intently at him. Unbelievably she took a tentative step towards him. And another. He expected her to point a finger at him and denounce him as a Jew. Instead, to his utter amazement, she knelt alongside him.

'Milos?' she whispered.

Milos's throat was as dry as parchment. He turned to look at her, eyes wide with apprehension.

'Milos?' Realising how much the scarf she wore over her head masked her face, the woman eased it back so Milos could recognise her.

'Aunt Klari!'

He had a sudden urge to throw his arms around the big woman but fought it back. Such affection in church was bound to attract attention.

The woman smiled and then bit her bottom lip as though to stop herself from crying. How many times had Milos gone to Tokaj Street when the two peasant women were making jam? How many times had he helped them stir the pots? How many times had Aunt Klari or Aunt Jutka given him the ladle so he could lick it clean?

'What are you doing here?' she whispered urgently.

'What are you?' said Milos. 'I haven't seen you here before.'

'They took Mrs Horvath and Elizabeth and Gabi, my two beautiful girls. They were always good to us. I came to ask God to protect them.'

At the mention of Gabriella, Milos couldn't help but bow his head.

'Though why I should think God will protect them when He allowed them to be taken is beyond me.' The big woman sighed and wiped her eyes with the back of her hand. 'God disappoints me.'

Milos didn't know what to say.

'But why are you here? Why aren't you hiding somewhere safe?'

'We thought we could hide here,' said Milos.

'Shhh,' said Aunt Klari. She waited while another woman shuffled past into the confessional, fortunately too preoccupied with her sins to glance in their direction. Aunt Klari waited until the curtain was drawn before turning back to Milos and snorting derisively. 'Father Hegedus would hide you until nightfall but Old Ignac would make sure the gendarmes were waiting when you left. Come, you and Tibor are safer with me.'

Milos rose obediently, caught Tibor's eye and nodded towards the door. Milos left with Aunt Klari and Tibor followed soon after. Suddenly the streets seemed safer for the addition of Aunt Klari. Two young railwaymen carrying a sack for a large, middle-aged woman was the very picture of ordinariness. They strolled along as though they didn't have a care in the world, chatting and even laughing occasionally, as would be expected. But their manner belied the nature of their conversation.

'The bridge is safe,' Aunt Klari assured them. 'There are no patrols. All the gendarmes and Arrow Crossmen are at the station. For them, today is a festival,' she added bitterly.

'Did anyone recognise you at the church?' asked Tibor, ever cautious.

'I rarely go,' said Aunt Klari. 'Sometimes Easter, sometimes Christmas Eve. I confess even less frequently. I doubt Father Hegedus even knows my name. As for the other women, I am just a peasant woman they sometimes see in the street or at the market. They would have to search a lot of houses to find where I live.'

'Even so, we will leave tonight,' said Tibor.

'No. Stay, rest up, get back some strength,' insisted Aunt Klari.

'We have another problem,' said Tibor, and told her about Istvan. 'If he's talked, the gendarmes will be looking for two Jews dressed as railwaymen. Someone will remember seeing you walking with us.'

'Then stay tonight at Jutka's,' said Aunt Klari. 'If he has talked, the gendarmes will come for you tonight. I will tell them two nice railwaymen helped carry my bags and point to the horizon when they ask where you went. If they don't come, tomorrow you can come back and stay with me.'

'You're very kind,' said Milos. 'Tell me, did you offer to hide Aunt Katy and the girls?'

'Of course! So did Jutka. Mrs Horvath wouldn't hear of it. She said it was too dangerous for us. I offered to take Elizabeth and Gabi, both or either, but they wouldn't leave their mother. Your father tried to persuade Gabi to go with him to join you two, but again she refused. She was determined to stay with her mother. Now they are all gone, all gone.' Aunt Klari sniffed and began weeping softly.

All gone. Once again Milos was enveloped by sorrow and a sense of loss that left him feeling empty and hollow inside. It was a day filled with shattered hopes and dreams. He'd lost his father to the Germans and Gabi to both the Germans and Tibor. Tibor had never mentioned marrying Gabi before and Milos had never even considered it. He'd never imagined Tibor marrying anyone. His brother was just too independent, too aloof. In his dreams, his brother had moved on and he had stepped into the void and Gabriella's love for Tibor had become love for him. That was how he'd always believed events would transpire. The Germans had broken his heart but his brother had ground the remnants to pulp.

Milos stared silently at the path ahead of them which led out across the flat, sunlit farmlands eastwards towards the Ukraine. The Germans were losing but the Russians were still hundreds of kilometres away in East Galicia. Months away. Tonight he and Tibor were safe because of the kindness of this peasant woman and perhaps they'd be safe for two or even three nights. But what then? Their country had disowned them. The majority of smallholders and peasants supported the Arrow Cross. Gendarmes were everywhere. Their lives were worth less than the sheep that grazed on the stubble of the crops, and they were fair game for anyone with a rifle. He and Tibor were fortunate to have survived until nightfall. How could they possibly survive until the Russians came?

CHAPTER ELEVEN

The box cars had only ever been intended as transport but they served Eichmann in ways he had not foreseen. By the time they arrived at Auschwitz, those within had suffered so much and were so exhausted and dispirited they had no will to resist their captors.

Jozsef had observed the loading of labour battalions and had seen for himself how little room there was in box cars filled with sixty or more people. Yet now that he was in one himself, he found them more cramped than he'd ever imagined. He was jammed into a standing position away from the walls, unable to sit or lie down. Katy, Elizabeth and Gabriella were no better off, jammed together still holding their meagre possessions in the one small bag they'd each been allowed. Already the heat was unbearable and the stifling air was foul with the smell of sweat and fear. Children were complaining and women feeling faint. Yet the door had not yet been sealed and their journey hadn't even begun.

'Eighty-two. I count eighty-two people!'

Eighty-two people. Jozsef groaned. No wonder the box car was crowded. He strained to see who the strident voice belonged to but his view was blocked. He guessed it came from a man somewhere near the doorway.

'We are overloaded!' the voice protested. 'It's not right! There are too many people in this carriage. You must take people out!' The voice switched to broken German and repeated the message. He heard laughter from someone on the platform. The voice repeated its protest in Magyarul.

Jozsef shook his head at the unreality of it all. Was anyone protesting the deportations? Was anyone protesting the fact that they were being transported in box cars? No. The lone voice was protesting the injustice that too many of them were being deported in one box car.

The sound of doors being nailed shut came closer and as it did the voice by the doorway became more hysterical. It irritated Jozsef. What did it matter, seventy-five or eighty-two? There was not enough room for fifty, not enough water for fifty, and people were going to die from the heat, from suffocation and from dehydration whether seven people were unloaded from their box car or not.

'You can't do this!' shouted the voice. 'You can't do this! It's not right! There are eighty-two people in —'

A single shot cut off the voice. Women cried out in fright and children screamed.

'Now there's only eighty-one,' said a gendarme. 'That should make everyone happy!' He laughed again as the door was pulled closed and nails hammered in.

The box car was plunged into a darkness broken only by thin strips of light from the gaps between the slats. Somehow the gloom seemed to make the air hotter. Silence fell, as though everyone was waiting for the next development, apprehensive, too frightened to speak in case they too were singled out for summary execution. If any of them had needed confirmation of the worthlessness of their lives, the sudden explosion from the gendarme's gun had provided it.

Jozsef felt someone take hold of his arm.

'Jozsef Heyman? The stationmaster?'

'Yes,' said Jozsef.

'Izsaac Ornstein, the tailor. Someone must take charge here. We must have order. Would you take charge?'

'Why me?' said Jozsef.

'You were the stationmaster. You know about trains.' Izsaac Ornstein raised his voice. 'Listen, everyone. Someone must take charge. I propose Jozsef Heyman, the stationmaster. He knows about these things. Everyone agree?'

There were a few murmurs but no dissent.

'There you go,' said Izsaac. 'Now tell us what we should do.'

'All I can tell you,' began Jozsef hesitantly, 'is what I saw the men of the labour battalions do. Those on the outside must stand against the walls of the box car. Those in the middle must sit in rows, knees up and taking as little room as possible, with their bags in their lap. You must sit in rows so that people can get through to the lavatory bucket. Do this please.'

Jozsef remained standing while around him his fellow deportees began sitting down. There were protests immediately as the limitations of space became apparent.

'Squeeze up close together,' said Jozsef. 'No one will be comfortable but we will all be less uncomfortable. That is the best we can hope for.'

A whistle blew from the eastern end of the station and was answered by another at the western end. Geza Apro saying his farewells. Jozsef wondered whether his boys were still in the signal box or had already left, having succeeded in their objective.

'The train is about to start moving. Everyone who can should sit now.' Jozsef squeezed himself into what little space there was around him, felt Gabi take his hand. 'In one hour, the people standing will change places with the people in the row in front of them, then one hour later with the people in the second row, and so on. Everyone will have a turn standing and sitting.'

The train jolted as the couplings reacted first to the pull of the box car in front, then to the weight of those behind. With a clanging of steel, a squeaking of wheels and the fear-filled sigh of fifteen hundred deportees, the train slowly began its journey north-west to Poland.

'There is only one bucket of fresh water,' said Jozsef. 'We do not know how many days our journey will take or whether our bucket will be refilled along the way. Therefore there will be no water for anyone until tomorrow, then only one mouthful per person.'

Jozsef expected protests at this restriction but it seemed everyone was now too numb.

'If you brought water or liquids with you, I advise you to drink them sparingly.'

'What about the children?'

Somewhere in the gloom a young mother still sought to protect her children, wanted more for them, wanted better, wanted assurances.

'Children will be treated the same as everyone else,' said Jozsef. 'The same for the sick. Now, please. I am no different from you. I need time to sit with my thoughts.'

'Thank you, Jozsef Heyman,' said Izsaac.

Jozsef bowed his head and felt sweat roll down his face and drip from the end of his nose. He wanted to tell everyone not to give up hope and provide a reason to endure. But what grounds did he have to make such a statement? None. The box car was already insufferably hot and a weariness cut through to his bones. The euphoria that had enveloped him on seeing his sons alive and as daring as ever dissipated in the utter dreadfulness of the box car. He wondered how his sons felt now that they were finally alone with the whole world seemingly lined up against them. How would they fare? How long before they sat in a box car just like this?

Alongside him Gabriella whispered encouragingly to her mother. He gently touched her on the shoulder.

'I saw them,' he said.

'Who?'

'Tibor and Milos.'

'Tibor and Milos?' said Gabriella.

Jozsef smiled at the surprise and delight in her voice. 'They were in the signal box. They came back just in time to let us know they are still alive.'

'I think Milos also came back to rescue me,' said Gabriella, suddenly solemn. 'He always said he would.'

Jozsef leaned away from Gabriella so that he could free his left arm. He put it around her and pulled her close.

'Milos would do anything for you. This time there was nothing he could do. But, yes, that would have been his intention. When all this is over, Milos will find you, Gabi. You can count on it.'

'If Tibor had promised to save me, he would have,' said Gabriella. 'He didn't because he knew it would be impossible.'

'Tibor will be waiting for you too, when we come home.'

'Yes, he will,' said Gabriella. 'Both your boys love me and I love them too. I carry Milos's book in my bag but Tibor in my heart.'

Jozsef pulled his arm free so Gabriella could tell her mother and sister about the boys' daring return from the dead. Already his back ached for lack of support and his throat craved the touch of liquid, any liquid. A slight breeze filtered through the cracks in the slats but did little to dispel the heat or the stink. A baby began crying plaintively and another joined in. How far had they come? One kilometre? Two? How far was their destination in Poland? Two hundred kilometres? Three hundred? More? He closed his eyes and tried to imagine their route. East to Satoraljaujhely, then north to Kassa, Presov in Slovakia, Tarnow in Poland, then where? West to Krakow? His railwayman's mind juggled options until he realised the futility of what he was doing. What did it matter where they were going or what route they took? Death awaited them wherever they went.

Jozsef realised he must have dozed off in the stifling heat when a woman trod on his hand. How long had he been dozing? Seconds? Minutes? The woman continued on her way to a chorus of protests, all the time apologising profusely. Clearly from the general perturbation, the woman was about to make first use of the lavatory bucket. People were squeezing together to make room for her but were also anxious to get as far away from the bucket as they could. But where could they go? Jozsef sat horrified as the consequences slowly dawned on him. Eighty-one people. One bucket.

The gloom of the box car obscured some of the poor woman's indignity as she squatted but nothing could mask the explosive noises of her diarrhoea or the smell.

'I'm sorry! I'm sorry!' the poor woman kept repeating but her apologies served no purpose. Some people began retching with nowhere to expel their vomit except between their knees. In moments the entire box car filled with sickening odours and the protests of people whose clothing was fouled by the vomit washing across the floor. Jozsef realised then that things would not get any better until they disembarked and would probably become unutterably worse. The same thought must have occurred to Gabriella because she began weeping on his shoulder.

Four hours passed before it was time for Jozsef and the three women in his charge to take their turn standing against the side of the box car. Their legs ached with stiffness from being forced to sit in one position for so long. They did what others before them had done and turned to face the wall, mouths open so that they could gather as much as possible of the sweet outside air filtering through the slats. Jozsef caught glimpses of scenery through a crack and it brought a reminder that beyond their confines the real world still existed. For one hour at least he could shut out the smells, the noises and the constant squabbling over space, the moans of the sick and frightened and the pathetic complaints of babies. The longer

Jozsef peered through the crack, the more he recognised landmarks from his expeditions with the boys. There was Mount Nagy-Milic. The recognition brought no cheer. He saw enough to confirm the route they were taking but also their lack of progress. In four hours they'd barely come forty kilometres. He sighed wearily as the train slowed, knowing that once more they were to be shunted into a siding to wait until the line was clear.

Though Jozsef had no idea which regional centre would be controlling the movements, he could imagine the frenzy in the rail office as clerks struggled to come to terms with the activity on the lines under their jurisdiction. How many trains had Eichmann commandeered? How many trains did it take to drain Hungary of its Jews?

The box car shook as it crossed points diverting it onto a siding. Slowly the train wheezed to a halt. Jozsef rued their change in fortune. What little breeze had managed to filter through the slats now ceased and immediately the box car seemed to heat up. Gazing through the crack, Jozsef couldn't help thinking back to earlier, better times when he was still in control of his destiny, when he had brought the boys past similar sidings on expeditions into the hills. Why had he ignored all the signs? Why hadn't he cleared off with the boys while they still could? He thought of all the places they could be now, if only he'd acted sooner. He wondered if Gabriella was thinking the same thing.

'We came this way hiking,' he said softly. 'You came with us one time, before we went to the caves at Aggtelek. Milos insisted. You drove Tibor crazy by insisting on stopping all the time to pick wildflowers.'

'I wish we'd kept walking,' she replied. 'I wish we'd kept walking and never come back.'

'So do I,' said Jozsef. 'So do I.'

They spent the night in the siding, trying to sleep, leaning against the legs of the person behind them and the shoulders of the people next to them, amid arguments and the hourly shuffling of people taking their turn to stand or sit. In the middle of the night the lavatory bucket overflowed. Filth was already so widespread it almost didn't matter.

'Attention, everyone,' said Jozsef in his role as leader of the box car. 'Everyone look for cracks in the floor. Look at the joins in the corners of the car.'

'Here,' called a voice towards the rear, 'there is a chip out of this plank. There is a small gap through to the track. What do you want to do with it? Work on it so we can escape?'

Jozsef told him his intentions.

'No!' cried the man in alarm. 'But I have to sit here!'

'We'll all move up a bit,' said Jozsef. 'I need volunteers. If we cannot get rid of the solids, at least drain the liquid from the bucket.'

'I will help,' called a man near the bucket.

'And me,' called another.

'How do we get the bucket to the hole?' asked the first volunteer. 'Do we pass it overhead?'

'No!' came a sudden and vehement chorus.

'Only joking,' said the volunteer.

Incredibly, despite everything, people found it in themselves to laugh. But that one brief, nervous moment was the only lightness in a night longer and more terrible than any of them had ever experienced. They had no way of knowing that the delay in their progress was a by-product of Eichmann's ruthless efficiency. He was delivering more Hungarian Jews to the gas chambers and crematoria of Auschwitz than the plant could handle. He was ordered to temper his enthusiasm; in short, to slow down. Many of the deportees were to live one day longer as a result.

Tibor and Milos spent the first night at Aunt Jutka's in case the gendarmes came, and two more at Aunt Klari's, grateful for the opportunity to rest up and plan their next move.

However they felt about Istvan, he kept his word and no gendarmes came looking for them. Nevertheless, after dinner on the third day Tibor decided to move on.

'We can't stay here,' he told Aunt Klari and her husband, Andras. 'Sooner or later we will be recognised which would be dangerous for you as well as us. Besides we can't go on eating all your food.' He pushed his empty plate away from him into the middle of the table.

'Where will you go?' asked Aunt Klari.

'What do you think, Milos?'

Tibor deliberately involved Milos in the discussion. His brother had become worryingly quiet and withdrawn.

'East,' said Milos eventually. 'We can't wait for the Russians to come to us, we have to go to them.'

'Makes sense,' said Tibor. 'Except east takes us into the Ukraine and they have been the Germans' staunchest allies. It's as dangerous for us there as it is here.'

'What about Romania?' said Milos.

'Romania, Bulgaria, both good options,' said Tibor. 'According to Dad, the governments of both have resisted the deportation of their Jews. But for how long? Look what happened here. Besides neither of us speaks Romanian or Bulgarian.'

'So what do you suggest?' snapped Milos. 'Yugoslavia and a boat to Palestine?'

'Probably not an available option,' said Tibor, deliberately provoking him. 'Come on, Milos, use your brain. Work it out!'

Milos closed his eyes and began to review their options. There were times when his brother irritated him to the point of screaming. What option had he overlooked? From Tibor's manner, it had to be something obvious. He thought back over their recent escapades and the answer dawned on him. He'd been right, the answer was obvious.

'Satoraljaujhely or the north-east province,' said Milos. 'It doesn't matter which. We go where the gendarmes are no more. We go where the gendarmes have been. Where there are no more Jews.'

Andras grunted approval and a rare smile appeared on his weathered face.

'Won't that be dangerous?' said Aunt Klari.

'All we can do is lessen the danger,' said Tibor. 'Of course there will still be gendarmes in Satoraljaujhely and the north-east. Some Jews are bound to have slipped through the net and some gendarmes will have remained behind to hunt them down.'

'When will you go?' Aunt Klari rose from her chair, as anxious as any mother.

'Tonight,' said Tibor. 'Around midnight.'

'I will give you some sausage to take,' said Aunt Klari. She turned and shuffled over to the cupboard that held their meagre supplies of food. 'Some bread too, and potatoes and fresh fruit.'

'Potatoes we have,' said Tibor. 'And we can get our own fresh fruit. There are many abandoned farms. But thank you for the bread and sausage. One day I will repay you tenfold.'

He rose and followed Klari to the cupboard, put his strong arms around her and kissed both of her cheeks.

'Be careful,' said Andras. His inflection and concern echoed Jozsef's and Milos felt a knife turn in his heart.

They left just before midnight, not for Satoraljaujhely but for the north-east province which, until the deportations, had been home to the largest concentration of Jews outside of Budapest. Before the building of dams and levees to control the Tisza River, the countryside had been swampy, prone to flooding and difficult to access, making it something of a sanctuary against the Turks and other invaders. Over the centuries its inaccessibility had also attracted gypsies, and while many had also been rounded up by the gendarmes, Tibor guessed many would have escaped. He admired them for their cunning, for their determination not to change their ways and their obstinate refusal to yield to authority. Most of all he admired them for their inbred instinct to survive. There were bound to be gypsy resistance groups and Tibor hoped to link up with one of them.

They decided to cut due south towards Northern Transylvania through the parts of the north-east province where they believed the gypsies would most likely be, travelling only by night and sleeping by day in stands of poplars and birches, or in the outbuildings of deserted farms. Tibor and Milos had become familiar with the towns and the countryside alongside the railway lines of the northern part of the north-east on expeditions with their father. They'd even ventured as far east as the town of Zahony. But, for all their travels, they'd always entered the north-east province by train, never on foot. They had forty kilometres of unfamiliar, rolling countryside, farms and apple orchards to cross before they reached the little rural railway that dead-ended at Dombrad and territory they recognised.

They made slow progress, moving cautiously, aware that they weren't the only people using the night for cover. They hid beneath hedges and in ditches whenever they heard footsteps or muffled voices, circled wide when they smelled smoke from cooking fires. Occasionally at night, and sometimes during the first light of dawn or the last light of evening, they caught glimpses of shadowy, furtive figures, people like themselves who'd also gone 'into the black'. The boys made no effort to contact them and did everything possible to conceal their presence. It worried Tibor that there were so many refugees at large, many of whom would be stealing to survive. Inevitably the gendarmes would conduct more sweeps.

The boys had another reason for not approaching the refugees. It was apparent from the way they moved that many were townspeople with little idea of how to survive in the open. Tibor was concerned that they would try to latch onto them, adopt him as their leader and become a burden to them. He could not allow that to happen. The going was perilous enough as it was.

It took them four nights to cover the forty kilometres to Dombrad. Milos remained in hiding with their sacks of vegetables and clothing while Tibor again donned his railwayman's uniform and walked along the railway into town. Dombrad was a small place and he guessed the residents would be on the lookout for strangers. Doubtless some homes would have been broken into, gardens plundered for vegetables and adjacent farms raided for chickens and eggs. There would be no sympathy for any Jew or gypsy caught in this town, where the people despised them and blamed them for every loss they'd ever suffered. But a railwayman wasn't a stranger, Jew or gypsy. Railwaymen were railwaymen and while the residents of Dombrad were familiar with their own stationmaster, fettlers and signalmen, new faces did come and go, particularly with deportations and conscription.

With no train due the station was deserted, as Tibor had expected it to be. He walked through it and out onto the street. He'd met the stationmaster on three occasions, each time with his father, and on their last visit had given him a recording of Strauss by the Vienna Orchestra. Another investment in the future, one he hoped to draw upon. The stationmaster lived in an unprepossessing, two-storey corner house, smaller even than the cottage in Sarospatak. Tibor knocked boldly on the door. The stationmaster's wife opened it.

'My God!' she said. Her eyes widened with fear and her hand rose to cover her mouth.

'I have been asked to inform the stationmaster of a change in schedule,' said Tibor loudly. He tucked his railwayman's hat under his arm. 'May I please come in?'

The woman stepped aside to let Tibor through. He found the stationmaster dressed and pulling on his boots.

'Good morning,' said Tibor. 'I believe you are an admirer of Strauss.'

'Tibor! Good God! What are you doing here?' The stationmaster rose and took Tibor's hand. His eyes narrowed. 'Did anyone see you come here?'

'Maybe. If they did, all they saw was a railwayman coming to visit his stationmaster.'

'Is your father with you?'

'No. Just Milos.'

Tibor told him what had happened to Jozsef, even about their farewell from the signal box. The stationmaster was visibly upset.

'I'm sorry, Tibor, very sorry. But what can anyone do?'

'I need information,' said Tibor. 'What is the strength of the gendarmerie around here? Do you know if any further sweeps are planned? You know as well as I that the countryside is crawling with homeless gypsies and Jews.'

'There are only two gendarmes left in the area. The rest have been reassigned special duties. I think you know what they are. But I know assistance has been requested to round up the escapees. It could come any day. Maybe on tomorrow's train. In the meantime you need to watch out for Arrow Crossmen and the older boys from the farms. I'm told they go out hunting every night and don't take prisoners.'

'We've heard shots. What about further south?'

'As far as I know it is the same. Look, Tibor, you can't trust your contacts any more. There are new men in the railways, not Arrow Crossmen but they might as well be. Everyone fears the Russians which makes them want to help the Germans. You got lucky with me but you can't count on your friends remaining your friends. Understand?'

'Who can I trust?'

'No one. Me, maybe my crew, I don't know.'

'My father once mentioned a Pole, on the main line somewhere.'

'There is a Pole, Stanislav I think his name is. His foot was crushed somehow. Years ago now, while your father was still director. Your father helped him keep his job, maybe even sent him money while he was recovering. It's the sort of thing Jozsef did. He lives near Demecser with his wife. He's a signalman, I believe. Your father is still remembered down there for what he did.'

'Thank you,' said Tibor.

'Can I give you anything?'

Tibor glanced over to the doorway leading into the bedroom. Two small children, no older than three or four, watched him suspiciously, half-hidden by the door. Their bellies had the swollen look of hungry children everywhere.

'We have food,' said Tibor. He could almost hear the stationmaster's wife sigh with relief. 'All we needed was information, which you have given us.'

'Tibor, before you go — Jews and gypsies are being shot on sight. So are deserters. You're a man now, no longer a boy. People might not think you're a Jew but they may mistake you for a deserter. Have you thought of that?'

'Many times,' said Tibor. 'Now, would you walk to the station with me and out onto the track? It would help if it appeared you were giving me instructions.'

'Of course,' said the stationmaster.

He turned to his wife. 'There is a little coffee left in the pot. Give the boy that while I finish pulling on my boots.'

Once night fell, the boys resumed their journey south, looking for a Pole neither of them had ever met. If the man was now their enemy, their journey was over. If he was their friend, he might put a roof over their heads for a night. If he'd kept his eyes open he could even provide them with information which might help them to survive a little longer.

CHAPTER TWELVE

When Istvan parted company with Tibor and Milos he had every intention of reporting them to the gendarmes. Why not? The boys meant nothing to him and his family needed the money even if it was only a few pengo. Besides, there was something satisfying about scoring twice off the one trade. But there was a disparity which troubled him. Reporting the Jews was only worth a few pengo but not reporting them had been worth a pair of boots. The fact that the trade had taken place over a ten-month period was irrelevant. This discrepancy intrigued him: the fact that one piece of information could have such different values. His fertile mind played with the possibilities and he quickly realised how information, used cleverly, could lift his family's fortunes.

Instead of reporting Tibor and Milos, Istvan went to the town hall and asked to see the register of Jews. What were a few pengo when there was the possibility of riches? At first the clerk was not obliging. He glared down at the diminutive, rat-faced youth and demanded to know why he wanted to see it.

'I've been to the station,' said Istvan. 'It's my belief that not all the Jews have been deported. The Heyman brothers were not there. I want to know who else wasn't.'

'So you can find them and collect the bounty?' said the clerk.

'Yes,' said Istvan.

The clerk smiled indulgently. He didn't think the little creep could find his arse with both hands. Nevertheless, he endorsed the boy's sentiment and brought him the register.

'The Germans are very efficient,' said the clerk. 'You will find a cross alongside the name of every Jew who was deported. Any names you find without crosses are Jews who escaped, are missing or dead. Good luck.'

'May I borrow a pencil and some paper, please?' said Istvan. The clerk sighed wearily but obliged.

Istvan quickly skimmed down the list of Jews. Every name had a cross alongside it. It was the same for the next page and for the one after it. On the fourth page he found two crosses missing. Tibor and Milos. The next page brought him no joy either, and he was beginning to wonder whether he was wasting his time. But he reminded himself that Tibor and Milos had escaped and, if they could, so could others. On the sixth page his patience was rewarded. There were four names: Max, Martha, Rita and Mark Lantos. Istvan smiled triumphantly. He knew Mark Lantos from school.

The boy had been in Sandor's class, one of the Jews most often pissed on and kicked until he'd stopped coming to school. His father had owned a factory making light fittings and lamps, including a range based on American designs which had admirers all over Hungary. When Jews were forbidden to own or run businesses he'd had to surrender his company to his employees. What had happened to them then? Istvan headed up a single page with the name Lantos, entered the parents' names then the offspring and, alongside Mark's name, the boy's age. Beneath that he wrote their home address and the address of the factory. He had no need to write down the factory's address because everyone knew where it was, but not to do so seemed careless and unprofessional. He left the rest of the page blank, knowing he'd fill it in as he learned more about the family, and turned to a clean sheet. He turned over to the next page on the register and scanned the names for missing crosses. Istvan didn't realise it but he'd begun his first dossier.

The dossier grew by four pages, four more families, before Istvan handed the register back and left the town hall. There were other names to pursue but he had enough to work on for the time being. As he walked towards the Lantos factory, Istvan tried to recall an image of Mark's father. In years gone by he had visited the school to watch plays put on by students and listen to the school orchestra. Istvan could recall seeing the entire family sitting together in the audience. Chubby little Mark with his weak jaw and soft body, his effeminate ways. His mother on one side of him and his sister in the middle next to her father. She was younger than Mark, he remembered, and she had played with her long hair, straightening her curls then letting go so that they sprang back. His mother? No, he couldn't recall her in any detail but his father ... there was something about him. Yes! He was older than the other fathers, older than his wife. That was it! Istvan remembered being surprised by how old Mark's father was, which would also explain why he hadn't been sent off to a labour battalion. That was something else to add to his notes. But it wasn't like having a photograph or a clear memory. Istvan realised he could probably pass Mark's father in the street and not recognise him.

The exterior of the factory told Istvan nothing he didn't already know. When he looked down the driveway into the rear yard, he saw boxes being loaded onto the factory truck, an old Ford with no doors on the cabin. So the factory was still operating. On an impulse he decided to go into the office. His initiative brought an immediate reward. The Germans and the gendarmes may have been efficient at getting rid of the town's Jews but they'd been somewhat less thorough in getting rid of their photographs. There on the wall was a picture of the company's founder: Mark's father. Istvan studied it, committing it to memory. The photo had been taken when Max Lantos was younger but Istvan could now put a face to the figure in the audience. He was making progress.

'Can I help you?'

Istvan dragged his eyes away from the photograph to the middle-aged woman smiling at him from behind a desk. Her hands hovered over a typewriter and she peered at him over glasses she'd pushed down her nose. Why was she smiling so benignly? Istvan didn't know her and he was equally certain she didn't know him. Then he realised. She was smiling in response to the smile he couldn't restrain when he'd spotted the photo.

'Do you sell lamps direct?' asked Istvan.

'Not normally, but we do make exceptions when we have stock to clear. But right now we're flat out making factory lights. Most are sent on the train to Germany.'

'Is he the owner?' Istvan nodded towards the photo.

'Was the owner,' corrected the secretary. Her face became pensive as she looked at the photo. 'He's a Jew. He was deported.'

'Deported?' said Istvan.

'Yes. His whole family was. Along with all the other Jews.'

Istvan felt suddenly deflated. They had been deported? But why was there no cross against their names? Was he the victim of bureaucratic bungling? He stared at the secretary. Could the Germans or the gendarmes have made a mistake? Could they have made the same mistake with all four members of one family?

'Is there anything else?' The woman's face had become hard and her voice cold. Her eyes had narrowed and she squinted at him, suddenly cautious.

'Did he have a son called Mark?' said Istvan.

'Why?'

'There was a Mark Lantos in my brother's class. Some of the other boys gave him a bit of a hard time. But I liked him.' He added the last statement out of pure instinct.

'I liked him too. He was a lovely boy,' said the secretary. Her gaze softened and she smiled again. 'The whole family were nice. Everyone liked them.'

'If they're all gone, who runs the factory now? The Germans?'

'No, our manager, Mr Kadar. Mr Kadar was our chief designer and technical director.' She sat up in her chair and pulled her glasses upright. 'I think it's time you ran along. I'm sorry I can't help you.'

Istvan left the factory office far from disappointed. Either the woman genuinely didn't know what had happened to the Lantos family and was assuming they'd been deported, or she was protecting them. *'The whole family were nice. Everyone liked them.'* Then there was the matter of the factory operating at full capacity. Many of the businesses the Jews had abandoned had not reopened. Others were failing for lack of experience and direction. Some limped along. Yet the Lantos factory was operating as though nothing had happened. As though Max Lantos was still at the helm. Yes! A surge of excitement surged through Istvan's thin body. As though Max Lantos was still at the helm!

Istvan returned home and entered the new information into his dossier. On paper the information gained substance, became fact, and offered itself up for analysis and re-interpretation. Istvan was intrigued. If the Lantos family had not been deported, where would they be hiding? Who would be hiding them? *'Everyone liked them.'* He underlined these words. Everyone liked them and the factory was still operating at full capacity. That was the most telling point. If Max Lantos was still influencing the factory's output, then there had to be a close association with someone in the factory. Most likely someone running the factory. Istvan fought back his excitement. He already knew where his information was leading him, indeed the conclusion was obvious. But he relished the process and took too much delight in each step to skip over even the most minor detail. On paper the logic became concrete and inarguable. Who had a house big enough to hide four people, two of whom were adults? Did the manager, Mr Kadar, have a big house? Istvan didn't know but he assumed it would at least be bigger than the homes of the other employees. Had Kadar taken over the Lantos house? Though Istvan couldn't picture exactly which house the Lantos family had lived in, he knew the street and it was lined with big houses. The houses were big enough for two, even three families. Istvan folded the pieces of paper that made up his primitive dossier and slipped them between the pages of a schoolbook, the power of his knowledge bringing him more pleasure than he'd ever imagined.

Immediately after school the following day, Istvan walked around to the Lantos house. As he turned into the street he saw removalists carrying furniture into a house a hundred metres away. He checked off the numbers and realised it was the house in which the Lantos family had lived. Two removalists were standing behind the truck discussing the best way to get the bed upstairs.

'Who's moving into the Jew's house?' said Istvan.

'Who do you think?' said one of the removalists.

'The new boss of the factory?' offered Istvan hopefully.

'No chance.' The removalist spat onto the pavement. 'The Deputy Mayor. Fancy people get the fancy houses. Let's see if the prick keeps it when the Russians come.'

His mate laughed humourlessly.

Istvan walked away towards the Lantos factory. He needed to establish where Mr Kadar lived and the only way he could do that was to follow him home. This presented two problems. One, he didn't know what Kadar looked like. And two, his father was expecting him home to help dig the silt out of their irrigation trenches. If he didn't go home, he could expect painful retribution. But if he did, his plans would be delayed. He decided to risk it. If necessary he could try telling his father he'd worked out a way to guarantee a constant flow of money into the family. His father might be intrigued enough by the prospect of a constant flow of *palinka* to listen. But whatever happened, he could never tell his father that his plans involved Jews.

Across the road from the Lantos factory was a small joinery that had once made furniture to order for Sarospatak's gentry. It was another business that had been run by Jews and folded after a couple of desultory attempts to keep it open. Istvan climbed the wire mesh fence and hid behind the timber still stacked in the silent yard. His hiding place gave him a good view of the factory's front door. Istvan assumed the factory would close like the others at around five and that Mr Kadar would leave shortly thereafter. But how? Would he have a car? Possibly. But if he had a car, would he also have access to petrol? Istvan doubted it. Any petrol would be saved for deliveries in the factory truck.

Istvan had no watch but had no trouble knowing when five o'clock had come. He heard voices up and down the street as workers spilled out of factories and headed for home. Within minutes, workers began leaving the Lantos factory, not by the door to the office but down the driveway from the rear of the building. Istvan smiled. He was certain Mr Kadar would not leave that way. Out of interest he counted the number of employees. Eight men, three women and a boy not long out of school. He'd expected more. Two more men followed, one of whom chained and padlocked the driveway gates. Istvan turned his attention to the factory office at the front of the building. There were two windows either side of the doorway with lace curtains which prevented him from seeing in. But he could tell the lights were still on.

He grew restless. He'd instructed his brother Sandor to go straight home and help their father, asked him to really apply himself to digging out the silt in case he was late. But Sandor was easily distracted and lazy at heart. Istvan had never intended to be so late and he began to worry how his father would react. If Sandor had done a decent job, he'd probably get off lightly. If not — well, that didn't bear thinking about. Istvan didn't blame his father for his fits of violence. Instead he blamed the system that had exploited his father's hard work, robbed him of the benefit and left him with crippling back pain. It wasn't hard to remember his father in earlier days, when he was always joking and playing games with him, when he'd pick him up and throw him over his shoulder like a bag of wheat and race along the banks of the ditches, threatening to throw him in. His father deserved better. They all deserved better. Istvan's eyes suddenly narrowed as the lights went out across the road.

The secretary emerged first carrying a leather satchel, then a gentleman in a pressed suit and tie. Mr Kadar! It had to be. He locked the door behind him. The secretary waited on the pavement and spoke to him. Mr Kadar glanced around furtively before replying. They exchanged more words for half a minute or more, both of them on edge, before the secretary passed him the satchel and they parted company. Istvan gave the factory manager a forty-metre start before scaling the fence and following. Mr Kadar walked quickly and Istvan had to hurry to keep up. A smile briefly lit Istvan's face when he realised where the man was headed. It wasn't long before Mr Kadar turned into a street bordered by houses which, although by no means grand, were certainly substantial. Istvan crossed the road to distance himself but needn't have bothered. Mr Kadar turned into the fourth house without looking around.

Istvan quickly scanned the house, taking in as much detail as he could. It was one in a block of similar three-storey houses that ran unbroken the length of the street. It was still daylight yet the curtains were drawn at every window except for those on the ground floor. He checked the neighbouring houses: without exception the curtains were drawn back. What did that prove? Nothing or everything?

He shivered involuntarily as a tremor of excitement ran like an electrical charge down his spine. He could see the evening's entry into his dossier, see the form it would take and the substance it would assume. Istvan kept walking past the house, fighting back the temptation to take another look at it. His mind raced. What had been in the leather satchel? Papers probably, yet it had bulged as if it contained something far more substantial, something the slim bag had not been designed to carry. Could they be work samples, light switches and sockets? Perhaps. But at a time when people were trading gold bracelets and crucifixes for eggs, it could be that it held something much more valuable and vital than electrical fittings. Especially if the man carrying the bag had four extra mouths to feed.

Over the next few days, Istvan made a point of walking past the Kadar house, sometimes in the morning, sometimes in the afternoon, taking special note of the curtains. On the top floor the curtains were never drawn back during daylight hours, on the middle level only occasionally and on the ground floor most of the time. He concluded that either the top floor was closed off and not being used, or was being used by somebody or some people not entitled to be there.

He raced through his chores every morning so that he was free to continue his evening stake-outs of the factory. His dossier recorded that Kadar always carried his leather satchel and on only one other occasion did he have cause to be curious about its contents.

On the sixth evening, Istvan went to the factory straight after school and settled down in his usual place in the timber yard. He listened for the sound of voices in the street, knowing almost to the second when the first workers would appear in the driveway to leave the Lantos factory. Everything had a comforting familiarity and having his knowledge confirmed boosted both his ego and confidence. But if the movements of the workers were predictable, what of his own? The inexperienced spy was about to learn a painful lesson on surveillance and the perils of conforming to a pattern.

He was crouched in his hiding place behind a stack of weathering timber waiting for the office lights to go out, when he was grabbed from behind and jerked roughly to his feet.

'What?' he cried.

Everything blurred as he was swung around and thrown hard against the old joinery shop wall. Istvan gasped as the impact drove all the air from his lungs. The back of his head whiplashed into the wall and the sudden sharpness of the pain momentarily immobilised his senses. He cried out again as a fist thudded into the side of his face. His assailant turned him, wrapped his enormous arms around him from behind, lifted him and pinned him helplessly against his chest. Istvan felt like a child again, impotent and overwhelmed. His father had often chased him and grabbed him that way in a bear hug. In their games Istvan would keep on running, his legs windmilling wildly in mid-air as he tried to get away. But this was no game and this wasn't his father.

'Is this the little shit?'

The voice came from somewhere above Istvan's head and the anger and malice in those few words scared him more than the beating he'd received. He forced his eyes open, saw the secretary and Mr Kadar staring back at him, saw them nod.

'Right!'

The world revolved in a dizzying blur in front of Istvan's eyes as his assailant spun around, lifted him over his head and hurled him to the ground. There was an explosion of light when his head crashed into the ground. He was dimly aware of a crushing feeling in his chest and of pain shooting up his right arm. A boot thudded so hard into his stomach it lifted him off the ground. Hands grabbed the front of his jacket and once more he felt himself lifted off his feet.

'Talk to me, you little shit.'

Istvan tried to focus on his assailant but failed.

'Who are you?'

'Isssch …' said Istvan. Blood filled his mouth and he gagged.

'Oh shit! You filthy little shit!'

Once again his head exploded with pain as his assailant slapped him hard across the side of his face. Istvan forced his eyes to focus, saw his blood splattered down the man's shirt and across his face.

'I dunno what you think you're doing, you little shit, but hear this. If I catch you spying on the factory or Mr Kadar one more time, I'll finish you. Understand? Finish you. You'll be just another corpse floating down the Bodrog.'

'Yeth,' said Istvan.

'Now, why are you spying on us, what have you found out?'

Istvan said nothing. His brain was struggling hard to organise his thoughts but failing miserably. He would have confessed to anything, agreed to anything to stop the beating, but he could form neither the thoughts nor the words. His assailant slapped him again, exacerbating his plight.

'What do you know?'

'Nothing.' It wasn't evasion, simply the easiest answer.

'Nothing. We'll see, shall we?'

Istvan braced himself for retribution but had no idea what form it would take. Suddenly he was flying through the air, flying backwards, doubled over from the unbelievable impact of a fist into his stomach. He hit the ground and slammed into the wall. He couldn't get air into his lungs, couldn't stop the terrible burning pain in his stomach.

'Just remember this.'

Istvan tried to look up through the veil of pain that masked his senses and his sight. His assailant was standing over him. Istvan braced for another kicking.

'If I see you anywhere near here — no, if I ever see you again — you're going for a swim. Understand me? A swim. With bricks in your pants. I dunno what you think you're doing and I dunno what game you think you're playing, but forget it. Understand? Forget it!'

Istvan's whole body arched in a spasm and he vomited. Blood and sludge. Sludge and blood. He sucked in air almost as a reflex to the vomiting. The shock of the attack was beginning to wear off and every part of his body shrieked with pain. He groaned, trying to take stock of what might be broken and what ruptured. Then the terrifying thought occurred to him that his assailant might have done enough damage to kill him, that he might actually be dying. He began to sob.

'You pathetic little shit,' said his assailant. 'I should finish you off now but you're not worth messing my boots.'

Istvan was dimly aware of the man turning and walking away before he lost consciousness.

It was the cold as much as the pain that finally brought Istvan around. Overhead, the stars shone from a clear black sky but there was no moon to help him get his bearings. The inside of his mouth was caked in blood, so was the back of his head where it had hit the wall. Water. He wanted water. His need for it almost overrode his pain.

He reached over to a stack of wood, used it to help him lift himself up onto his feet. The moment he was vertical a film descended over his eyes and he thought he'd fall. But his hold on the timbers was good and gradually his head cleared and his sight returned. There was an old wooden bucket in the yard. The metal ring holding the top part together had broken which was why nobody had bothered to steal it. Rain had gathered in the bottom, not much, but enough to wash out his mouth, rinse his face and wash away some of the matted blood on the back of his head. There were even a few drops left to swallow.

It hurt to walk but he could do so, not straight-backed by any means but bent over so he could nurse his injured ribs. He edged slowly towards the fence so that he didn't stretch or load up bruised and battered muscles. He took a deep breath, prepared himself for unbearable pain and dragged himself up and over the fence. He rested a moment to catch his breath and let the pain subside, then set off for home. What he couldn't understand was why his assailant had asked him questions and then made it impossible for him to answer them. He'd wanted to answer to stop the beating but he'd needed time. He would have promised anything to stop the beating, even given away his grand scheme, if only the man had stopped hitting and kicking him. Why hadn't he given him the chance?

When Istvan heard the vehicle turn into the street behind him his first thought was that his assailant was coming back, that it was the company truck stalking him, the old doorless Ford. But then he remembered watching the driver lock the gates behind him as he did every night, leaving the old Ford parked in the factory yard. He stopped and turned around. It would be a patrol, had to be a patrol.

The truck stopped just behind him. Two gendarmes with torches got out.

'It's just a kid,' said one.

'Christ Almighty!' said the other. 'What happened to you?'

Istvan spun them a story of how he'd been trying to sell some eggs when two men had jumped him, stolen his eggs and beaten him up.

'Serves you right,' said the first gendarme. 'Trading on the black market is illegal.'

'My father has a bad back,' said Istvan. 'I wanted to buy him some *palinka* for the pain.'

'Where do you live?' said the second gendarme.

Istvan told him.

'We're going near there. Hop on the back.'

It was fully five days before Istvan felt he'd recovered enough to leave the house. His time indoors wasn't wasted: he added to his notes and made his plan. He was determined his work would not be for nothing, and neither would his beating. His assailant had erred badly and now someone had to pay for his mistake. Someone had to pay and he knew exactly who and exactly how.

The following evening after dinner, he slipped out of the house and walked all the way to the Kadar house. His ribs and legs still hurt but not enough to deflect him from his purpose. When he reached his destination he walked smartly up to the door and rang the doorbell. The factory manager answered the door and for a moment stared blankly at Istvan, at a loss to understand what a poorly dressed peasant boy was doing on his doorstep. Then he noticed the bruises and recognition dawned.

'You!'

'You need to talk to me,' said Istvan calmly. 'Or should I talk to the gendarmes instead?'

Even in the dark he could see the blood drain from the manager's face.

'You'd better come in.'

Istvan had never set foot in a house remotely like it in his life, a house with real carpet, polished timberwork and what appeared to be fabric on the walls. His senses were swamped. Everything about it looked, smelled and felt different to anything he'd ever known. People could live in the hallway alone. Mr Kadar led him into what Istvan thought was an office, but far grander than the one at the factory. Dark shelves were crammed with books and untidy stacks of files. The files looked out of place and it occurred to him that they were possibly a recent addition. There was a fireplace, the fire set but unlit, and above it a painting of bare-breasted women in a forest glade surrounded by nymphs and cherubim playing on harps and flutes. Istvan had seen similar paintings in books in the school library but had never imagined he'd ever actually see one framed and hung.

The manager pointed to a chair. The chair was covered in dark green leather, studded so that the padding rose like so many even-shaped humps. But more intimidating was its sheer size and height. It had not been designed for the likes of him. Istvan feared he'd disappear in it.

'I'll stand, thank you,' he said.

The manager looked at him closely for the first time. Istvan turned his head slightly so that the bruises on his cheek would be more obvious under the light. Mr Kadar averted his eyes.

'Sending someone to beat me was foolish,' said Istvan. 'Sending a fool to do it compounded the error.'

'What do you want?' snapped the manager.

Istvan smiled. Mr Kadar was clearly a man who used bluff and brusqueness to cover a shortfall in confidence and his height and naturally stern expression to intimidate. But Istvan was immune to his theatrics. He'd dealt with bullies all of his short life. 'There is a bounty,' he said.

'I'll double it.' Mr Kadar glared at Istvan.

'Four bounties, doubled,' said Istvan.

'Agreed.'

'Each month.'

'What?'

'It's good business,' said Istvan evenly. 'What's to stop me taking one payment then going to the gendarmes? Your best interest is served by making sure I keep my mouth shut this month, and the next, and all the months after. You are aware of the penalty for harbouring Jews?'

Mr Kadar scowled at him. 'How did you know?' he asked suddenly.

'I didn't,' said Istvan, 'not for sure. Not until you tried to scare me off. But you are a careless man, Mr Kadar.'

'What do you mean?'

'It is in my interest for this arrangement to continue and it won't unless you make a few changes.'

'Go on.'

'The Lantos family are listed on the register of Jews as not having been deported. You can't change that but there are other things you can do. The Lantos factory operates as though the owner was still in control. You must have seen from your own observations that this is not normally the case with Jewish businesses.'

'I was his partner. I am perfectly capable —'

Istvan cut him off. 'You bring home food in your satchel which I assume others bring to the office for you. You keep the curtains drawn over your upstairs windows. What have you got upstairs that you don't want people to see? These things were obvious to me and they will be obvious to others. You are also too soft, Mr Kadar. Your man should have killed me.'

'What's to stop him killing you now?' the manager said softly.

Istvan smiled. 'Do you really think I'd come here without taking precautions? The game is over if anyone so much as lifts a finger. Now pay me, Mr Kadar. And pay me again on the first of every month.'

The manager angrily reached into the pocket of his jacket and withdrew his wallet. He peeled off some notes and added a few coins from his pocket.

'I believe that is the agreed amount.'

'You will send the man who beat me with the next payment,' said Istvan. 'Four o'clock outside the station.'

He snatched the money, turned and strode from the room. On his way out he noticed things he'd missed on his entry. The chandelier in the hall, the intricately moulded ceiling and the gilt-framed mirror. He paused at the door to allow the manager to open it.

'I have a dossier on you, Mr Kadar. Move the Jews or miss a payment and your dossier will wind up in the hands of the gendarmes.'

Istvan turned and walked off into the night.

With the money snug in his pocket he forgot about his pain. Yet he'd seen the bundle of notes in the manager's wallet and knew he could have asked for more. That was something to bear in mind when he faced his next target. There were three more names on his list and another dossier to begin. He'd already made up his mind who to pursue next. This time his observations would be more circumspect and his dossier more precise. But the result! Istvan jiggled the coins in his pocket as though they were trophies. The result would be the same.

* * *

Gancio interrupted Milos by bringing coffees and grappa.

'What's this?' said Milos.

'I anticipated the end of this chapter in your story and signalled to Gancio,' said Ramon. 'It is a long time since we finished our lunch, a long time to wait for coffee. I assumed you would pause here for a break.'

'You assumed wrongly,' snapped Milos. 'It is not yet time.'

'I apologise,' said Ramon.

'This session is not complete. There is more to tell. Another five or ten minutes. All you had to do was be patient.'

'I'm most sorry, my friend.'

'I accept your apology but you have upset the balance of my storytelling.' Milos hunched over his coffee and stirred it angrily.

'Normally we put sugar in before we do that,' said Neil.

CHAPTER THIRTEEN

Dawn came but brought no relief from the suffering and no further progress. Jozsef was standing with his forehead resting against the planking as the sky brightened and features of the landscape slowly became discernible. The top of Mount Nagy-Milic was shrouded in cloud but there didn't appear to be any rain. Somewhere on the other side of the mountain there was a shallow cave where his sons had hidden vegetables and winter clothing. It occurred to him that his boys might be there, holed up, warm and dry. Perhaps they even had a view east and could see the train. The thought cheered him, even though in his heart he knew it was the faintest of hopes. The train was slow but it had made much faster progress than the boys could on foot.

The box car was quieter than it had been all night; people had finally succumbed to exhaustion. Their weariness came as a blessing without which sleep was impossible. Sobbing, snoring, squabbling, praying, moaning, talking, cursing, defecating. These things had been constants until people had simply become too worn out or, in their utter hopelessness, had embraced defeat and retreated within themselves. The clouds that hid the summit of Nagy-Milic gave him hope for a cooler day and a lessening of the craving for liquids. During the night an argument had broken out when a woman was caught scooping water from their one bucket into a cup to give her children a drink. Jozsef had been called upon to adjudicate.

'You have forfeited your share tomorrow,' Jozsef had told her. 'However you may have some of mine.'

'Ours too,' Elizabeth had cut in.

The young mother had begun to cry, possibly out of gratitude but more probably from shame.

'Let her have her share,' said a woman somewhere in the half-light. 'A mother will always help her children. Besides, what does it matter now?'

In the end nobody had either the strength or the will to continue the debate and the matter ended. What worried Jozsef most was the increase in the number of people suffering from diarrhoea. They'd had no food and as yet shared no water yet somehow the contagion was spreading. Perhaps it was a legacy from their temporary incarceration in the warehouses prior to boarding. Of more concern was the fact that Katica and Elizabeth had both begun to complain of cramping pains in their bellies. He couldn't imagine how they must feel, to be sick and fevered on top of the deprivations. Shortly he would have to distribute everyone's ration of water. How could he do that except by a common drinking cup? How could he prevent the diarrhoea spreading?

At seven o'clock, once he'd surrendered his place against the wall and resumed his seat, he gave the order to distribute the drinking water. Someone provided a cup and a woman provided a spoon she had brought so she could feed her child. Jozsef guessed the bucket would contain five litres of water when full, but it had never been more than three-quarters filled and some water had splashed out during the stops and starts. The spoon became the subject of a debate between Jozsef and the people around him before they reached agreement that it probably held ten millilitres of water.

'Give everyone one hundred mils,' said Jozsef. 'Measure it once and make a mark on the cup so everyone gets an equal share.'

Jozsef's decision was met with an angry swell of dissent. Others could also do the mathematics and eight hundred and ten mils from a possible four litres seemed unreasonable.

'We have come just forty kilometres in twenty hours,' said Jozsef. 'Who knows when this train will get under way again. Who knows how long it will be before we reach our destination. We must err on the side of caution.'

Once again there was a murmur of discontent.

'However, provided our train gets under way, there will be another distribution at five o'clock this evening.'

Jozsef accepted the silence that followed as agreement. What more could he expect? Another one hundred mils wasn't a lot to look forward to but it was something, and Jozsef realised that he could help people cope if he always told them when the next drink would be.

Five more agonising hours passed before he heard their German guards shouting to one another, heard the forward guard's whistle reprised from the rear and the unmistakeable sound of a train creaking back into life. This development was greeted with sighs of relief and even weak cheering. Jozsef shook his head in wonder. Yes, the train was moving again but each revolution of the wheels took them further from their homes and everything they'd known. From their jobs, their hopes, their aspirations and from the lives they'd built for themselves. Each revolution also took them closer to death.

To Jozsef's surprise, the train passed first through Kassa and then Presov without stopping. It was as though the rails had been cleared of traffic overnight and through the morning to make way for them. By late afternoon they were in the part of Poland the Germans had claimed as the General Territory and by evening had cleared the junction at Tarnow. Whatever their destiny was to be, it was fast approaching. As a railwayman Jozsef had made it his business to find the location of the town of Oswiecim. He realised they were not far from Krakow and that Oswiecim was not far west of Krakow. He also knew the German name for the town and the rumours attached to it.

Jozsef had promised to look after Katica, Elizabeth and Gabriella but, like Milos, was denied the opportunity. He could do little more than pay lip service to his promise. He wiped Katica's brow when her fever began to rage and helped Gabriella carry her to the lavatory bucket whenever the pains in her stomach became intolerable. Gabriella shielded her mother with her skirt in these moments of indignity, but humiliation had become the norm and the least of her problems. Nobody noticed any more. Nobody cared any more. As the evening progressed, Elizabeth's suffering began to parallel her mother's.

For a while people had managed to put aside their fears as they struggled to cope in the overcrowded carriage. But now the steady, relentless progress of the train forced them to confront them. For most, their experiences in the detention centres prior to boarding and in the box car had thoroughly exorcised any faint hopes of compassion or mercy. The nature of their enemy had been made plain to them. Yet some people still clung to the faint hope that there was truth in the words on the side of their box car. Perhaps they *were* being taken to be resettled in work camps. Those with family contracted into family groups, fearful but supportive, believing that as long as they stayed together they could cope. This was their only remaining strength. Children clung to parents, wives to husbands, husbands to wives, brothers to sisters. They pooled their strength to face up to whatever lay ahead of them. And it was now that Jozsef really missed his sons. He stood guard over the three women he'd promised to protect and did so conscientiously. But though he cared for them and helped them he was not one of them. If anything, sickness had drawn the Horvath women closer together and, consequently, further from him. He understood, but it didn't help lessen his feeling of aloneness.

What chance would he have in a work camp? The hiking he'd done with the boys had improved his fitness but he couldn't begin to compare himself with the boys in the box car, the boys and young men the age of his sons. And there were the manual workers, older men with arms like the trunks of fruit trees, powerful shoulders and chests. If anyone was to survive, he believed they would be the ones. What of the women? Maybe there were factories in the work camps for women. Maybe there'd be work for him there too. Or maybe the work camps were a myth and their destination was to be their final destination.

He glanced around him but the darkness yielded little. Yet he knew. Minds were travelling down the same path as his. The box car had never been quieter. Jozsef became aware of the weight on his right-hand shoulder. Someone was always leaning against him and it had ceased to trouble him, but this wasn't just someone, it was the closest thing to family he now possessed. He stroked Gabriella's hair but got no response. The girl who one day would have married one of his sons, probably Tibor, and become his daughter-in-law had finally given in to the effort of nursing her mother and sister. Soon he would have to help Katica or Elizabeth to the lavatory bucket and he wondered how he could slip away without waking her.

He sensed the train slowing and tried to find a gap in the slats opposite, but people were standing in front of them. He tried to check his watch but could not read it no matter how close he held it to his face.

'What do you see?' he called softly to anyone against the box car sides who cared to look and answer.

'Signal lights,' said a voice eventually. 'Outlines of buildings. And more tracks.'

'Krakow or Oswiecim?' said Jozsef.

The train continued to slow until it was clear that it intended to stop.

'What do you see now?' he whispered.

'Platforms. Railway platforms. And German guards. Guards and dogs.'

'What else?'

'Prisoners. Prisoners with buckets.'

'Can you see any signs, any station signs?'

'No. Yes! Krakow.'

The train ground to a halt with a shriek and clanging of metals. Jozsef felt Gabriella stir and gently stroked her hair. He heard banging and wrenching and the sliding of doors. Harsh German commands and dogs barking. The door to the box car slid open and two guards stood silhouetted against the weak station lights, guns at the ready, shouting at them in German.

'Buckets. They want the buckets,' someone translated.

'Pass down the buckets,' said Jozsef. He glanced at his watch. Five minutes to midnight. 'If you can scoop out any of the water on the way, do so.'

Prisoners appeared at the open doorway to exchange the buckets for fresh ones, one refilled with water. Nobody inside the box car expressed relief or joy at the exchange. They were far too preoccupied with the menace of the weapons pointed at them, the snarling dogs and the malice on the face of the soldiers. Already Jozsef could hear doors being nailed shut once again but in among the clamouring he also heard names being called and piercing cries of despair that sent a ripple of fear through the box car.

'Elizabeth Horvath! Gabriella Horvath!' A German officer with a clipboard stood in the doorway.

What? Alongside Jozsef Gabriella started suddenly as if woken from a bad dream.

'Elizabeth Horvath! Gabriella Horvath! *Schnell! Schnell!*'

'Quick! Get to your feet.' Jozsef pushed sideways to make room. 'I'll bring Elizabeth.'

'No!' said Gabriella.

'Yes!' said Jozsef. 'This could be your chance!'

'No!' She tried to get away from him but Jozsef grabbed her, stood and forced her to her feet. He felt around for her bag before realising Gabriella had strung it diagonally across her shoulders.

'Here!' shouted Jozsef. 'Gabriella Horvath!'

People leaned and rolled out of their way.

'Mama!' screamed Gabriella. 'Mama!'

'Here,' said Jozsef. Two grim-faced guards glared up at him. He kissed Gabriella and smiled encouragingly. 'Gabriella Horvath. Here she is.'

One of the guards grabbed Gabriella and pulled her off the train, catching her as she fell. Gabriella began screaming.

'Elizabeth Horvath! *Schnell!*'

'I'll get her.' Jozsef pushed his way back into the box car and grabbed hold of Elizabeth's arm.

'No! No!' said Elizabeth desperately. 'I have to go to the lavatory.'

'There's no time! Don't you see? Now come!'

He pulled her to her feet, roughly, desperately, as though sensing he was in a mad race against time. Up and down the train, doors were being hammered shut. Any second he expected to hear the whistle that would tell him he was too late, that he'd failed, that whatever chance was on offer had been denied her.

Elizabeth was crying but he ignored her and dragged her to the door. Auschwitz was Auschwitz and could anywhere else be worse? This was Elizabeth's chance. He was determined to make sure she took it.

'See! See!' he cried triumphantly. Sweat poured off his face and he gasped for breath. 'Elizabeth Horvath. You want Elizabeth Horvath. Here I have Elizabeth Horvath ...'

Just as the officer reached up to pull her off the train, Elizabeth's legs buckled, her bowels failed her and she defecated wetly.

'Ahhh! Jew bitch!' shouted the officer and recoiled. He withdrew his hand, turned angrily to the soldiers around him and barked orders.

'No!' cried Jozsef. 'Wait! Wait! She must join her sister!'

But the door closed.

Jozsef barely had time to catch a glimpse of Gabriella standing on the platform between two soldiers, eyes and mouth wide open in disbelief and horror. Alone. Abandoned. Cut off from her mother and sister, stranded in a nightmare from which there appeared no prospect of awakening.

CHAPTER FOURTEEN

Tibor and Milos became thieves. For three months they crept around the north-east and Northern Transylvania, referred from one sympathetic railwayman to another, chasing rumoured gypsy partisan groups and, most enticing of all, partisans who were allegedly Jewish. They met others like themselves, also on the run, and exchanged rumours, but contact with partisans proved elusive to the point where Tibor and Milos gave up. They might as well have been chasing ghosts, spectral figures such as they themselves were fast becoming.

Through July and into August there had been easy pickings as orchards of apples and apricots ripened, but harvesting soon accounted for the supply. What windfall fruit remained quickly deteriorated and became inedible. Fruit had filled their bellies but it had fallen far short of fuelling their bodies. Their skin tightened over their eyebrows and cheeks, their eyes receded into hollows. Bones not muscles now defined their shoulders and chests and the hunger in their bellies never left them. They lived like foxes, wary and cunning, holed up by day and on the prowl by night.

They stole from people with little left worth stealing, peasant farmers whose crops were plundered with impunity by soldiers and gendarmes. They stole to live, raiding vegetable gardens often beneath the windowsills of cottages and under the noses of their owners. They were careful never to steal too much from the one yard and mindful of covering their tracks. They stole carrots and turnips by plucking them carefully from the ground, cutting off and replanting the tops so the morning would reveal no evidence of their visit. When they dug up potatoes they set the plant back into the soil it had come from with some potatoes still attached to the roots. They stole cucumbers and, on a few occasions, beat the farmer to his cows and fled into the night with their milk. But every raid risked discovery and the penalty was not capture but the sudden explosion of a rifle and the finality of a bullet.

The boys craved protein and fats but weren't alone in that. Sometimes they found mushrooms in the forest but were denied the mushrooms in the fields: others with more entitlement also wanted them and the boys could not take the risk of venturing out onto open ground in daylight or even in the weak light of dawn. Occasionally they were lucky and raided chicken coops for eggs. But passing soldiers also craved fat and had taken so many chickens to throw in their soup that hens and eggs were scarce. For the soldiers a fowl was one meal, but for the peasants who relied upon the eggs it was the loss of many. The boys, at least, understood that.

Early in September, having failed to link up with partisans, the boys were forced to make a decision. One option was to circle back through the north-east province with the intention of heading north to Satoraljaujhely and Mount Nagy-Milic where their winter clothes and vegetables were stashed. This offered the comfort of re-establishing contact with their friends in the railway, people who would shelter them for a night or two, let them sleep without fear, let them wash themselves and their clothes and share their humble meals. Often they were strangers who had never heard of their father and who owed them nothing other than a vague obligation to assist fellow railwaymen. But, tempting as the prospect was, both boys realised it would be a journey filled with peril.

With the collaborationist government in power, Arrow Crossmen were no longer constrained by gendarmes or the Germans. With the full blessing of the government, they now ran rampant across the countryside baying for the blood of Jews. The alternative was to head east once more and try to make contact with the Russian forces, now less than three weeks away on the other side of the Carpathian Mountains. The Russians were an unknown quantity but they weren't torturing and shooting Jews for pleasure.

The boys were weary of dodging gendarmes, Germans, Arrow Crossmen and angry peasant farmers and decided to head east. If both they and the Russians made good progress, Tibor figured that in two weeks they could put themselves beyond the reach of those who wanted to kill them. This was the determining factor.

That evening the boys baked four potatoes in the embers of their fire, ate one each while they were hot and kept one to eat cold for breakfast. That night, with the breeze blowing from the south-east, they heard for the first time the far off rumble of artillery. That the Russians had begun another offensive to push over the Carpathian Mountains and up into the heartlands of Hungary on the very night they'd made their decision to head east seemed like an omen. The spring had long gone from their legs but the sounds of battle were music to their weary souls. Salvation was no longer a faint hope but had acquired the substance of reality. Salvation, safety, survival was within earshot, within walking distance, within reach. They hiked all through the night, slept through the day, baked four more potatoes and hiked again.

The boys felt relatively safe as they skirted around the town of Arad, convinced that, with the might of the Russians poised to roll over the Carpathians, the Germans had too much on their plate to concern themselves with a few displaced Jews.

They were right about the Germans but failed to consider the Arrow Cross.

The Hungarian fascists struck just after dawn when the boys had settled down after a long night's hike. Cautious as always, they had dossed down on a wooded slope not far from a small village. They intended to spy on the outlying buildings during the course of the afternoon to choose the farm which could best replenish their food stocks with the least risk. When the gunfire erupted, their first thought was that the Russians had broken through. Their excitement overcame their weariness and they raced through the woods to a point which overlooked the village.

They expected to see tanks, Cossacks or a ring of troops surrounding the village, but there was nothing that would explain the volleys of gunfire. Whoever was shooting was inside the village.

'It's not the Russians,' said Tibor.

'Then who?' asked Milos.

Tiny figures suddenly broke free of the village and raced across open fields towards the woods that sheltered the boys. There were families clutching children and running in a group. Others, male and female, simply ran to save themselves. Behind them came men in country hats and short, tight, fur-collared jackets. They stopped to fire their rifles and the tiny figures running ahead of them crumpled and lay still.

'Arrow Cross,' said Tibor.

'But the Russians are so close!'

'Tell them,' said Tibor. 'Come on. If even one of those Jews makes it into the woods, those bastards will follow.'

The boys turned and ran back to the hollow which had been their hiding place. Behind them another sound joined the pandemonium.

'Oh shit,' said Milos. 'Dogs.'

They grabbed their meagre possessions and ran.

'Where are we going?' asked Milos.

'To the stream.'

The stream took them back the way they'd come and towards the road the Arrow Cross had driven in on. There were open fields to cross before they could regain the shelter of more trees. But Milos didn't complain. He was just glad Tibor had a plan. At that point, any plan would do. As they ran downhill Milos felt his legs getting away from him, forced by gravity and his momentum to run faster than they were capable of. His muscles, weakened by lack of food and the exertions of the night, could no longer check his speed and he fought to remain upright. But it was a task beyond him.

Milos pitched forward as he overstrode, slammed into the ground, bounced and cartwheeled down the slope. He grabbed at clumps of grass, dug in his heels and fingers, dug in his knees, and desperately scratched and clawed his way to a halt. His head hurt and his right knee burned as though on fire. He lay still trying to regain his breath before remembering that delay, any delay, was a luxury neither of them could afford. He pulled himself up into a sitting position. Way ahead of him Tibor had reached the base of the hill and was sprinting towards a sparse grove of poplars. The poplars weren't their destination but the thicket beyond where a stream wound back into the foothills.

'Tibor!' he cried, but in his winded state his voice lacked force. 'Tibor! Wait!'

Even in full voice, Milos doubted he could have made himself heard. He dragged himself to his feet and almost collapsed. His right knee refused to support his weight. In despair, he shaded his eyes from the morning sun with his hand, and caught a fleeting glimpse of Tibor disappearing into the poplars. When he brought his hand down he noticed it was smeared with blood.

Gunshots. Dogs.

Milos spun around and scanned the tree line behind him. Nothing. Not yet. He pulled his shirt off as fast as he could and bound it tightly around his right knee so that it couldn't bend. His sack! Where was the sack he'd been carrying with the last of their food? Back up the hill about six metres. He groaned and dragged himself uphill, grabbed the bag and started back down. He hopped and dragged, hopped and dragged, each hop threatening to generate more forward momentum than he could control.

More gunshots. The baying of the dogs rose in pitch. Milos gritted his teeth and ran. The pain in his knee made him want to cry out, shrieked at him to give in. But giving in meant death and Milos had fought too hard and too long to lose everything so close to salvation. He reached the poplars, dragged himself into their cover. At least now there was a screen between him and any pursuers. But the relief he felt was shattered as he reached the other side. There was no Tibor. He looked at the distance he had to cover to the next stand of trees and his heart sank. Suddenly he felt angry towards his brother, angry and bitter. Why hadn't Tibor waited for him? Why had he abandoned him? All the way down the slope he'd imagined Tibor waiting for him on the other side of the poplars, waiting to throw an arm around him and help him down to the thicket.

He spotted the dried remnant of a broken branch and grabbed it. It was thick but was it still strong enough? Milos decided to find out. Using it as a prop he set off for the thicket, distributing the load between his injured knee and the stick. It helped.

More gunfire. And a scream. And dogs going mad.

Milos ran for his life, praying that if he was spotted, a bullet would get to him before the dogs. He could taste salt and realised he was crying. Crying from pain, from frustration, from the fear that it was all going to end so needlessly. Suddenly he was in the thicket. Despite everything, he'd made it into the thicket without being spotted. He cried out as hands reached out and grabbed him.

'What the hell happened to you?' said Tibor angrily. 'Quick, climb onto my back. Hang on to both bags.'

Tibor staggered down to the stream, plunged in up to his knees and with grim determination began wading upstream. Milos lay hard against his brother's back, concentrating with all his will on performing the one task Tibor had left him. Hang on. On to the bags, on to him. Milos tried closing his eyes but dizziness forced them open again. He listened for gunfire, for shouts that said they'd been spotted, for the baying of dogs that had latched on to another quarry, but every sound seemed to merge together with Tibor's laboured breathing and the splash of his pumping legs. His head started spinning and the sounds became peripheral to the thumping in his ears.

'Milos.' Tibor had stopped midstream. 'Whatever happens, just lie still.'

Tibor twisted and swung Milos off his back and into the cold water. The cold snapped Milos to his senses.

'What are you doing?'

'The bank's undercut. We can't outrun them. We have to hide here in the water beneath the bank.'

Tibor pushed Milos under the bank and lay on top of him so that only Milos's head was above water. He stuffed their two sacks under Milos's head for support. Grass and weeds overhung the bank and there was a small bush dipping precariously over the water. It wasn't much of a screen but Tibor hoped it would be enough to shield them from anyone searching from the opposite bank.

Milos lay still, trusting his brother, letting the cold water numb his aching knee and soothe his brow. Soothe his brow! He had visions of the water washing away the blood on his head and flowing downstream in a telltale pink trail.

'Blood. Head,' he murmured.

'Shhh!' said Tibor fiercely.

Then Milos heard them. The quiet, determined voices of hunters, their soft footfalls, the panting of their dogs. They were above them. Standing on the bank above them. Time stopped. Milos closed his eyes. Holy Mary, Mother of God ...

They lay there for seconds which seemed like minutes, minutes which seemed like hours, not daring to blink, not daring to breathe. Milos began shivering and quickly the shakes became uncontrollable. He pictured his shivering radiating ripples out across the stream.

'I think we've had enough swimming for one day,' said Tibor softly.

He eased his head out from beneath the bank and took a quick look around. Encouraged, he quartered each bank and methodically checked foreground, middleground and background. He saw nothing and heard nothing. Their hunters had moved on.

'Let's go.'

Tibor helped Milos out from under the bank, threw his arm around him and half-carried, half-dragged him across the stream. He helped him up the bank and over the brow of the ridge and looked for a hiding place where the sun's rays could penetrate and put some warmth back into their bodies. They heard more gunfire but it was distant now. Tibor couldn't help wondering at the mentality of these Arrow Crossmen and their need to kill the last remaining Jews before the Russians arrived. He found a sunny glade and collapsed into it, both of them lying still, cold and exhausted.

'I thought the blood from my head would give us away,' said Milos eventually. 'It was just like that time we sheltered from the gendarmes in the doorway. Remember? I was worried our footprints would lead the gendarmes to us.'

'I remember,' said Tibor. 'You still haven't learned anything, little brother, have you?'

The Arrow Cross killed hundreds of Jews in and around the towns of Csermo, Arad and Lugos before retreating away from the advancing Soviets.

Tibor and Milos spent the day drying out their clothes and sleeping. As soon as it was dark, Tibor left Milos nursing his injured leg and crept down the slope to an outlying farmhouse. Jews had run from this farmhouse and been gunned down before they'd gone one hundred metres. Dogs barked, but their barking didn't worry Tibor. They were not hunting dogs but farm dogs, still spooked and jumpy from the events of the day. Tibor was cautious but didn't expect any trouble. Sooner or later the Gentiles of the village would help themselves to whatever had belonged to their Jewish neighbours but, for the moment, Tibor thought they'd be as jumpy as their dogs and hesitant to venture anywhere.

He went straight to the vegetable garden and took all he could find: a few small turnips and parsnips. It wasn't nearly enough. He pushed open the back door. Nobody stored potatoes in outdoor bins any more; if the family had stored potatoes they'd have to be somewhere inside. Tibor had no matches so felt around the fireplace and its cast iron stove for a tin or box that might contain some. He found a tin that rattled, opened it and found three matches inside. He struck one and used it to find a candle and light its wick. The candle revealed a room as sad and depressing as any Tibor had ever seen. A cradle, no more than a wooden box on rockers fashioned from the arms of a wooden chair, sat on the floor by the fireplace. Whoever had grabbed the baby had also grabbed its bedding in their haste. There was a table and three chairs, but six bowls upon the table. Tibor closed his eyes and recalled the desperate flight from the farmhouse. Grandparents, parents, child. Three generations wiped out. A pot of weak, thin soup sat on the stove. A few framed family photographs hung on otherwise bare walls, and tattered books shared two shelves with crockery, an iron kettle and an exhausted teddy bear. Grimly, Tibor began opening cupboards and soon found the family's food store. Eight potatoes, three small turnips and an onion. Maybe somewhere else there were vegetables which had been sliced and dried but in his heart Tibor felt he'd uncovered the family's wealth.

Eight potatoes, three turnips, some parsnips and an onion. That plus two small potatoes and a few withered carrots they'd saved had to see them through until they met up with the Russians. Tibor tied the vegetable sack to his waist, lifted the pot off the stove and carried it to the doorway where he snuffed out the candle and slipped it and the two remaining matches into his pocket. The soup was weak and watery but Tibor couldn't let it go to waste.

Their narrow escape from the Arrow Cross made them even more cautious. They rested that night and the following day to give Milos's knee a chance to heal, and to see if the Arrow Cross returned. They didn't. Nevertheless the boys kept away from roads and farmhouses, staying high in the hills where the going was hard but the trees and cover were thickest. The sounds of battle were now constant, like the distant rumblings of a faraway storm. By night they saw flashes and the reflected glow of unseen fires in the clouds.

They climbed for seven nights, picking their way among rocks as the vegetation thinned and the spine of the mountains pushed up through the sparse soil. Their plan was simple. To get as close to the front as was safe, hole up and let the battle pass over them, after which they could declare themselves to their liberators. On the eighth day, low clouds and driving rain forced them to find shelter.

They followed shallow trails made by goats, sheep, shepherds or brigands, perhaps a combination of all four. The mountainside had become so steep and rocky that they had little choice. But Tibor had another reason for deciding to stick to the trails. If there was shelter to be found, he argued, someone or something would have found it and the trails would eventually lead them to it. Tibor was proved right when they found a sheltered cavern by the side of the trail. Animal droppings and ashes from cooking fires testified to prior occupation but Tibor overrode Milos's concerns.

'Of course people sheltered here before us and they'll shelter here after we're gone,' he said. 'Right now it shelters us.'

'What if someone else comes?' said Milos.

'Who?' said Tibor. 'Who else would be mad enough to be so high in the mountains with the Russians on the charge? Us and people with the same reason to be here as us. If there are any Jews hereabouts, they're welcome to join us.'

'What about patrols?'

'How many have you seen? And why would they patrol up in the clouds where they can't see anything anyway?'

Tibor seemed happy enough so Milos let it go. But he wasn't satisfied. For nearly four months they'd avoided people and avoided hiding in obvious places. He watched as Tibor pulled a cooked potato and a small raw turnip from his pocket and ate them, taking a bite from one and then the other. Milos followed suit. The brothers lapsed into a routine established over months. Food first then sleep, each of them taking turns.

When the rain eased they could hear the boom of artillery and the explosion of shells. Sometimes they thought they could hear the grinding of trucks from the pass below, but whether they were climbing or descending in low gear the boys couldn't tell. Soon they'd have to decide whether to press on or stay put and let the battle pass by. If pushed, their food could last them another two days, but what if the Russians got held up? Or worse, driven back? Hunger would probably decide their course for them.

Tibor stretched out on the floor of the cave and pulled his coat tightly around him. It was mid-September and too early for snow, but the rain had brought a chill and a warning that snow was not far off. Milos silently accepted that he would have to take first watch. But what was there to watch when the clouds cut visibility to five metres, less when the rain pelted down? Milos leaned against the cave wall, made sure he was a little

221

uncomfortable so he wouldn't fall asleep. He wished they had a match left and something to build a fire. Memories of earlier days and nights of sleeping out filled his mind. His father always made sure they had matches, and finding kindling and fuel for their fire was always the first priority when they made camp. They had meat and dried vegetables and paprika to make their soup with. Salt and pepper. Sweet coffee to finish and blankets to wrap around their tired bodies. He remembered Gabriella's look of horror the first time she slept out with them when she realised she had to sleep on the ground.

Gabriella.

He hadn't thought of her for so long. Where was she, he wondered? Would he ever find her again? He leaned his head against the wall and let the memories flood back. The three of them, lying on grass, heads together, bodies radiating out like equally spaced spokes of a wheel, gazing up at a clear blue sky, with no reason to believe that they wouldn't live for ever. The little patch of lawn at the rear of Tokaj Street had been soft beneath them and their little bellies had been filled with Aunt Katy's cooking. Sunday lunch at Tokaj Street, a lifetime ago. He knew Gabriella had favoured Tibor then and had tried not to show it, but he wasn't cast from iron and he'd been hurt. When he'd put on his growth spurt and begun to assert himself he'd honestly believed things were beginning to swing in his favour. All of which made Tibor's declaration of his intention to marry Gabriella all the harder to bear. But Tibor was the hero, the strong one, the leader; they were qualities which impressed Gabriella and areas in which Milos could never compete. His way was softer, the way of understanding and compassion, sensitivity and attentiveness. Tibor was the rock, but he was the patient water that wore the rock away. Milos smiled inwardly at the metaphor. Maybe things would be different when Gabriella returned. Maybe she'd come home weary of war and heroics and simply want someone who understood her, protected her and loved her absolutely. The prospect was so enticing, so far removed from his situation that, despite the cold and discomfort, he began to smile. But his smile froze in the making when he heard the click of a rifle bolt being drawn.

There were seven of them, saturated, unshaven and filthy. They seemed as surprised to see the boys as the boys were to see them. But they were armed and the boys were not and their surprise was transitory. They stared at the boys, assessing their strengths, checking for weapons. They relaxed once they realised the boys were in no position to cause them trouble. One of them spoke in Romanian.

'We're Hungarian,' said Tibor.

'Ahhh,' said another, the largest of the men. His hair and beard were wild and long and as black as a crow. His eyes also appeared black, set back in a deeply tanned face. To Milos he looked how he'd imagined the pirate in *Peter Pan and Wendy* would look, a long time ago.

'You!' The big man pointed to Milos then to Tibor. 'There!'

Milos shot to his feet and crossed the cave to Tibor. Tibor pulled himself up into a sitting position.

'Who are you? Deserters or Jews?'

The big man spoke like a Hungarian peasant which Tibor suspected he probably was. Pro-Arrow Cross and anti-Jews.

'Catholics,' said Tibor. 'Who are you?'

The big man grinned. 'So what are Catholics doing hiding in my cave?'

'Catholic mother, Jewish father,' said Milos.

'Got any food?'

Tibor pointed to the sack between him and Milos. One of the men pounced on it and plucked out the remaining vegetables: one small turnip and two small parsnips. He handed them to the big man.

'Pity,' said the man. He managed to sound genuinely disappointed. He handed the vegetables to one of his comrades who transferred them to another sack, then sat down and slumped up against the wall. His men took that as a cue to sit, though one man remained standing with his machine pistol at the ready.

'Are you partisans?' asked Tibor.

'Partisans!' The big man laughed as though he'd just heard the best joke of his life. His comrades joined in.

'Who are you fighting?' Tibor persisted, sensing that he had to engage the big man or risk being taken out and shot. He suspected he already knew the answers to his questions. He glimpsed watches on both the man's wrists.

'This man and this man, they are deserters from the Romanian army.' The man pointed out two grinning comrades. 'This one is a deserter from the German army.' Their guard nodded. 'The rest of us deserted from what was left of the Hungarian army after Voronezh.' His eyes narrowed. 'Do you have any idea how many of us the Russians killed?' He glared at the two boys. 'Five divisions. One hundred thousand men.' He spat into the dust. 'The Germans set us up as targets, the Russians shot us down.'

'What are your plans?' said Tibor.

'Plans?' The big man started laughing again as though the idea of having plans was ludicrous. 'Let me ask you, what are your plans?'

'Hide in a cave till the front passes by, then make contact with the Russians.'

'That is a good plan,' said the big man. 'For Jews.'

'Catholics,' corrected Tibor.

'Your father was a Jew. That makes you a Jew.'

'Hail Mary full of Grace, the Lord is with thee. Blessed art thou amongst women, and blessed is the fruit of thy womb, Jesus. Holy Mary, mother of God, pray for us sinners now and at the hour of our death. Amen.' Milos looked the leader of the deserters squarely in the eye. 'That makes us Catholics.'

'Catholic Jews.' The big man roared with laughter at his joke. 'That makes you Catholic Jews.'

224

'You didn't tell us your plans,' said Tibor.

The smile left the big man's face. 'The Germans shoot deserters on sight. As for the Russians . . .' He spat again. 'We sent three men to negotiate with them, to offer our services. The Russians heard them out then shot them dead. They knew we were watching. They made sure we saw their reply. That, my young friends, is how the Russians negotiate.'

'So?' said Tibor.

'So!' said the big man. Any trace of humour had fled from his face. 'So we shoot Germans and Russians and steal their weapons. We shoot peasants and gypsies and steal their food. We shoot refugees for whatever they've got. We shoot people like you for your food and your clothes. We kill to survive. We've taken your food. After we've shot you we'll take your clothes.'

'Let us join you,' said Tibor.

The big man's eyes narrowed. He stared at Tibor, long and hard, searching for any sign of fear. 'Why?' he asked.

'We've been stealing food for four months and killed nobody. People don't even know we've stolen their food until we're long gone.' Tibor told them how they stole carrots and replanted the tops, how they stole turnips, parsnips, potatoes and eggs. 'We can steal food for you.'

'I'll think about it,' he said.

'Take as long as you like,' said Tibor.

The big man again roared with laughter, and this time translated for his Romanian and German colleagues. He gave them all time to share the joke before his smile turned to a snarl.

'Janos! Light the goddamned fire! You!' He pointed to the German standing guard over the boys. 'Shoot them if they move.' He turned to the boys and smiled. 'We're going to eat but you are not. It's fortunate that you are not hungry.'

Once the deserters had eaten and their hunger was at least mildly satisfied, Tibor began singing melancholy Hungarian folk songs. He prodded Milos to join in. At first their ballads aroused suspicion but it didn't take long for the Hungarian deserters, including the big man, to add their voices. The weak fire in the centre of the cave drew their eyes like a magnet and the doleful singing helped draw out memories. Everyone saw in the flames what might have been and it united them in loss. The Romanians didn't know the words Tibor and Milos were singing but recognised the melodies. They sang in their own language.

At any other time Milos would have been moved by the sad beauty of it all, but he guessed what Tibor was up to. His brother had picked the moment when their captors felt their tiredness most keenly and were most vulnerable. He was trying to befriend them. It was hard to shoot people who were friends and were joined in song. Milos was under no illusion that it would save them in the long term but it just might be enough to help them survive the day.

The rain eased as night fell and by ten had ceased altogether. Stars shone coldly from a clearing sky. Once again they could hear the grinding of trucks in the pass but something was missing. The sounds of battle which had been a constant backdrop to their days and nights had ceased. The silence drew the big man and some of the deserters to the mouth of the cave. Tibor could tell they were apprehensive.

'The calm before the storm,' said Tibor. 'The Russians are setting themselves to advance.'

The big man turned and snarled at him. 'So now the boy is a military genius?'

But the words were hardly out of his mouth before the sky lit up with flashes and the boom of heavy artillery followed, rolling over the hills and down into the valleys. Whatever the weapons were aimed at was beyond the next ridge and out of sight, but they felt the impact when the shells landed and exploded. Puffs of dust showered from the top of the cave and the ground beneath them shook and shivered as though in fear.

For the first time, the boys were close enough to the front to hear the rattle of machine guns and small-arms fire.

The big man pulled back into the cave. 'Fire!' he snarled.

His comrades rushed to kick dirt over the flames. The cave plunged into darkness. Only the stars were visible at the cave entrance and the shadowy silhouettes of the men on guard.

'Tonight, maybe we use your plan,' said the big man. 'We let the war roll over us.' He laughed mirthlessly. 'If not, tomorrow we pull out.'

The boys leaned back against the cave wall, eyes wide open, awestruck by the sounds of a battle more ferocious, more powerful and more destructive than anything they'd ever imagined. Somewhere in the darkness one of the Hungarian deserters began to pray softly.

The war didn't roll over them but sometime during the early hours of the morning the heavy barrage ceased, replaced by sporadic but intense bursts of fire, suggesting the combatants were engaged at close quarters. The Russian advance had begun. At first light, the big man led them from the cave. Tibor was expecting a helter-skelter retreat away from the front but instead saw how the deserters had managed to survive for so long. This was no rabble bunch of brigands but an efficient military unit, each of them knowing exactly what was required. The deserters fanned out, moving in short, quick darts from one rock to another. The boys and the Hungarian deserter appointed to guard them stayed hidden until the big man waved them forward. They crouched low and did their best to copy the deserters. Run and hide, run and hide.

The entire group rendezvoused at an outcrop overlooking the pass. Tibor risked a glance between two boulders and saw the Germans in full retreat. The narrow mountain road was jammed with trucks towing eighty-eight-millimetre anti-tank guns and others carrying the survivors of a beaten army. Retreating soldiers also marched along the side of the road.

'There!'

Tibor turned around to see what the big man had seen; he was pointing across the valley. Tibor studied the hillside opposite, a sector at a time as his father had taught him, trying to see what had caught the brigand's attention. He saw movement. Tiny grey helmeted figures withdrawing.

'Up here.' This time it was one of the Hungarian deserters, uphill from them.

When the big man crept over to see what his lookout had spotted, Tibor followed. He found a crack between two rocks and tried to trace back along the deserter's line of sight. He saw tanks crossing a bridge over a steep rocky gully but that wasn't what caught his eye. There were grey uniformed figures dangling below the bridge on ropes, working their way among the supports. Tibor realised immediately what was happening: the Germans were going to blow up the bridge. He heard the big man curse. More soldiers were withdrawing, this time on their side of the hill.

The big man darted back to his original position, Tibor and the deserters following. Nobody said anything but Tibor and Milos suddenly found themselves the centre of attention. Tibor was first to realise what was wrong and his blood turned cold. The deserters were looking to the big man for what, for them, was an easy decision. Their situation was rapidly deteriorating and there was no room in their well-oiled military unit for two boys.

'I'm sorry,' said the big man and shrugged his shoulders. He nodded to the Hungarian guarding the boys and pointed back uphill.

'What's happening?' said Milos, suddenly fearful.

Tibor didn't respond. Obviously the big man didn't want to alert the Germans to their presence so had ordered that the boys be shot on the other side of the ridge. The deserters had already begun moving off, absorbed once again in the business of survival. To all intents and purposes Tibor and Milos had already been forgotten. Their guard prodded Tibor with his rifle.

'Come,' he said. 'And keep down or I shoot you now.'

Milos felt the blood drain from his face. He wanted to cry. Safety was on the other side of the bridge, so close they could actually see it. Nevertheless, he did as instructed, following hard on Tibor's heels, hoping with all his heart that his resourceful brother would come up with a plan in time. But there was so little time. And what plan could Tibor come up with against a man with a gun? What if his brother couldn't save him this time? What if their road was destined to end here? Tears began flooding Milos's eyes and he wanted to hug Tibor and thank him for all the other times when his wit had saved them both, or at least let him know how much he loved him before the bullet ended his life.

They reached the lip of the ridge and plunged over. Tibor kept going as though heading back to the cave. The guard let them go almost fifty metres before calling a halt.

'Kneel!' he ordered.

Milos knelt. Tibor sank only to one knee.

'Don't shoot us!' begged Tibor. 'I heard you praying last night. You are Catholic, no?'

'Shut up!'

Any hope Milos had entertained that his brother would somehow conjure up a plan vanished. Tibor was begging, begging for his life. The sound of his brother's voice shaking and pleading was the last thing Milos had ever expected to hear and it shocked him deeply, heightening his fear.

'Please. You are Catholic. You know how important it is for us to make our final confession. What difference will another minute or two make? Please, I beg you, do this for us.' Tears overflowed Tibor's eyes and rolled down his cheeks.

'Ah shit!' said the guard nervously. He looked around as though to check that none of his comrades were watching. 'Okay, be quick.'

'Will you hear our confession?' begged Tibor. Milos had doubled over, quaking with fright, lips moving in silent prayer. 'Please hear us!'

'Hear each other's! I've no time for this!' The guard nervously checked back to the ridge line. All the while his comrades were getting further and further away.

'For the love of God, please hear our confession,' insisted Tibor. He turned to Milos. 'Look at him! How could he hear my confession? Look! He has pissed himself. Do this for us and for yourself. You should be thinking of your immortal soul.'

'My immortal soul,' scoffed the guard. 'Not even God can absolve the things I've done.'

'But you prayed to God last night. We heard you. God heard you. Now hear us.' Tibor's voice had become more strident, more desperate. 'One day this war will be over and you can look back on this morning as the beginning. Today could be the first day of your atonement. God notices these things.'

'God damn!' said the guard. 'But I'm warning you, you better be quick.' He relaxed and the barrel of his rifle lifted so that it now pointed slightly upwards, away from the boys.

'Do my brother first,' said Tibor.

Milos had doubled over so far his head almost touched the ground. Tears streamed down his face and dripped from his nose. The guard dropped to one knee alongside him.

'Forgive me, Father, for I have sinned,' began Milos, his voice so faint and broken the guard had no chance of hearing him.

'Speak up, I can't hear you!' The guard leaned closer to Milos and put his hand on his shoulder. 'For Christ's sake, pull yourself together!'

'Forgive me, forgive me ...' said Milos. He leaned forward as far as he could and launched into a barely audible litany of sins.

'Speak up or I give up!' said the guard, clearly exasperated and uncomfortable with his role. 'How in God's name can I absolve what I can't hear?'

In frustration he bent right over, put his ear alongside Milos's lips. It was an act of kindness but also an act of folly. Tibor launched himself at the guard and brought a rock crashing down on his head. Milos screamed as the guard collapsed onto the ground, groaning and barely conscious, a deep groove in his head where his skull had caved in.

'Oh sweet Jesus!' said Milos. He rolled over onto his side and vomited, screamed again when a rifle shot exploded alongside him. He looked up and saw Tibor standing over the dead guard, the rifle smoking in his hands. Blood, bone and brain splattered the ground. He flinched as Tibor fired another bullet into the guard's body.

'Stop it! Stop shooting!' Milos was shaking like a leaf in a storm as he sat up, a victim of a tumult of emotions. Fear, relief, gratitude, horror.

Tibor turned to face him, eyes bright and face flushed, holding the rifle as though it were something precious.

'They were expecting two shots.'

Milos stared up at his brother in horror. He'd seen the same look on his brother's face when he'd raced past him on the bridge over the Bodrog, laughing at the thrill of the danger. At that moment Milos glimpsed a stranger, someone who in a flicker of an eye had become a killer.

'He was going to shoot us, Milos,' said Tibor defensively. 'He was going to shoot us!'

'You killed him! Don't you feel anything?'

'For him? No!' He kicked the deserter's body. 'Saved! That's what I feel. Saved and alive. Now, come on, little brother. Dry your eyes and wipe your nose. We've got to make contact with the Russians.'

Tibor dismantled the rifle so it couldn't fire and threw it away. He bent over and began running back up to the ridge, leaving Milos little choice but to run after him.

Tibor tried to stay high because he knew that the German infantrymen were heading lower as they withdrew from their positions defending the crest of the pass. But he soon realised the impossibility of his plan. The bridge spanned a rocky ravine which was perhaps sixty or seventy metres deep and quickly broadened out to a steep valley. There was no way of reaching the other side without crossing the bridge. He cursed silently. If the Germans blew up the bridge, the Russians would be delayed for days if not weeks. Tibor couldn't wait that long. They had no food and no prospect of stealing any without retracing their steps back down the mountain, a mountainside crawling with Germans and, by nightfall, probably heavily defended. He realised they had only one option but never in his wildest dreams had he envisaged a plan so fraught with risks.

'Milos! Come here!' He waited for Milos to dash from the cover of the rock he was sheltering behind and join him. 'Look. See through here.' He leaned back so that Milos could peer between a cluster of rocks to the pass below. 'See the bridge?'

'Yes,' said Milos.

'We're going to cross it.'

'What?'

Milos stared at his brother as if he had gone mad. He checked back to the bridge to make certain he hadn't been mistaken. He hadn't. German trucks were crossing it in groups of three and four and German soldiers streamed across on both sides. 'It's impossible.'

'Not quite, little brother, but you must do exactly what I tell you. Don't let me down now. Forget what just happened back there. Forget everything. Just concentrate on getting over that bridge. We wait until the last German has crossed and then we make a run for it. We can do it. It's not as long as our bridge over the Bodrog.'

'What if the Germans see us?'

'They'll shoot us.'

'You're crazy, Tibor! Even if we get across the Russians will shoot us. You heard what that deserter said.'

'That's just it,' said Tibor. 'They're deserters. We're not. We're Jews.' He smiled ironically. 'Now come on. We'll circle around into the ravine and come up below the bridge. There'll be German soldiers around so don't get seen. Don't hurry. Do what those deserters did: move, look around, move. If you see any Germans, just take cover and stay there. Okay?'

'I'm scared.'

'Good. You'll run faster.'

Tibor turned and led the way. Ahead of them they could hear an almost constant rattle of machine guns and small arms. Occasionally they heard a solid boom and the thud of exploding shells ripping apart pieces of the mountain. Somewhere ahead of them were Russians in tanks.

It took until the sun had cleared the top of the mountains for the boys to work their way into position. Traffic across the bridge had thinned dramatically; what they saw were the tattered remnants of a rearguard. Trucks filled with wounded and dying. Trucks with heavy machine guns and rocket launchers. Hollow-cheeked men in grey hanging off them. The retreat had been sounded and the remnants abandoned their positions by whatever means they could.

The boys watched the vehicles pass, hoping each would be the last, staring across the bridge for any sign of further traffic, listening for the sound of engines under load. The gunfire ceased. The boys glanced at one another as they realised the significance. Tibor stared across the now empty bridge and back down the road behind them. Somewhere on the hillside not far from the road was a group of German engineers waiting to detonate the charges that would destroy the bridge. He decided to wait five minutes. If they hadn't detonated the charges by then there could be only one reason why: the Germans had not just been ordered to destroy the bridge, but to destroy as much Russian armour as they could at the same time. The five minutes ticked by without any further soldiers or vehicles appearing. It suddenly occurred to Tibor that maybe the Germans were also waiting five minutes to give stragglers a chance. If that was the case, what chance did they have?

'Come on, little brother,' he said grimly. 'It's now or never.'

He broke cover and began sprinting across the bridge, Milos hard on his heels as always. The bridge was steeper than it had appeared and the boys were soon gasping for breath. They heard rifle shots behind them and began zig-zagging. They cleared the bridge with forty, thirty, twenty, ten metres ahead of them before they rounded the bend that took them out of sight of the Germans. They made the corner and slowed, legs rubbery, chests heaving. Tibor half expected to see vehicles, German or Russian, appear around the bend eighty metres ahead of them.

'Keep going,' gasped Tibor.

They made the next bend, slowed and peered cautiously around it. The road was clear but for a damaged and disabled German truck. Tibor jogged up to it and waited for Milos to catch up. Both boys leaned against the truck and sucked in huge breaths.

'We made it,' gasped Milos. 'We made it!'

'Not yet. Take off your coat and shirt,' said Tibor.

'What? Why?'

'Take them off! For Christ's sake, Milos, stop making me repeat myself.'

Tibor stripped down to his trousers and rubbed his hand in the pool of oil beneath the truck's broken motor. 'Here.'

The oil was black, thick and the consistency of treacle. Tibor used it to paint a large Star of David on Milos's chest, almost from neck to navel so nobody could possibly mistake it.

'Now do the same for me,' he said. He glanced quickly uphill. Milos had heard it too. The heavy clank of metal, the scraping of metal tracks on asphalt. 'Hurry!'

Milos hurried. The Star of David he drew was erratic but still recognisable.

'We're going to run to meet the tanks,' said Tibor. 'If they turn out to be German, dive off the low side of the road and roll away as far and as fast as you can. Don't stop to hide behind rocks. Rocks are no cover from a tank. If they're Russian, shout and wave your shirt like you've never been happier to see anyone in your life. Understand? Be happy!'

Tibor stared momentarily at his brother, then threw his arms around him. Milos reciprocated. 'This is it, little brother. Just pray our luck still holds.'

They started shouting before they even reached the next corner, whooping and cheering and waving their coats and shirts. They turned the corner expecting to see tanks. Nothing. There was nothing on the road up to the next bend seventy metres away. Yet the clanking sounded close, so close. How far did sound travel in the mountains, Tibor wondered. Well, if they could hear tanks while they were still far off, maybe the Russians in the tanks could hear them.

They ran on, yelling and screaming, up to the next corner and nearly stopped dead in their tracks. They'd found their tanks, but they were bigger and more menacing than they'd ever imagined, not just one or two but an entire column. Foot soldiers hung off every one of them like pears on a particularly productive tree. Despite their shock the boys kept running, waving their shirts and cheering. The lead tank stopped. The muzzle of its gun lowered and swung towards them.

'Ignore it,' shouted Tibor. 'Keep waving.'

Soldiers spilled off the tank and crouched alongside it, weapons pointed at the boys.

'If they were going to shoot they would have,' said Tibor breathlessly. 'Keep waving.'

The boys slowed as they reached the tank.

'The bridge is mined!' yelled Tibor. 'Explosives. Understand?'

The Russians stared back expressionless.

'Look!' said Tibor. He ran to the side of the road, dropped his shirt and coat and began drawing in the dust with his finger. He drew the bridge, then drew crosses on the supports. Two Russian soldiers eyed his drawing suspiciously. Tibor stood, threw his arms in the air and shouted, 'Boom!'

The Russian soldiers raised their weapons.

'Look!' said Tibor urgently. He pointed to his drawing, looked at the soldiers and saw no sign of comprehension whatsoever. He turned around to the tank. Surely someone smarter was in charge? He glanced up at the officer at the tank's turret hatch just as the officer issued a command. Two soldiers immediately rushed forward and grabbed hold of Milos while the two nearest Tibor grabbed him. They dragged them both to the side of the road. The tank engaged gear and began moving forward.

'No!' screamed Tibor. He jerked free of his guards and ran in front of the tank holding his hands up. 'Stop!' he yelled. 'Boom!'

This time he could see he had the attention of the officer in the turret. The tank stopped and the officer climbed out. He jumped down onto the road and grabbed Tibor's arm, pushed his face right in front of Tibor's as though trying to read his mind.

'Look,' said Tibor. He pointed to the side of the road. The officer nodded and followed him. Once again Tibor drew the bridge, drew crosses on the supports and once again mimed an explosion.

The officer's eyes narrowed. He turned and snapped commands to the soldiers. Six rushed forward immediately. One threw his arm around Milos's neck and pointed a pistol at his head. The officer pushed Tibor towards the remaining five men. Tibor understood immediately. Milos was ransom to his honesty. To show the point was not lost on him, he turned to the officer and saluted. He glanced reassuringly towards Milos and found his brother staring at him in stark terror.

Tibor led the Russians back down the road but before they reached the bridge he turned off the road on the high side. The Germans had an uninterrupted view of the low side so they could see exactly when to detonate their explosives. But Tibor felt they could sneak up over the ridge and sweep around beneath the bridge on the high side and, once there, let the Russians do whatever they had to do to neutralise the explosives. The Russians followed him, not trusting him, just obeying orders.

Once beneath the bridge Tibor pointed to where he'd observed the Germans setting explosives. Four men detached themselves to deal with them, clambering over the bridge supports as if they'd done it a thousand times before. The fifth cocked his weapon and rested the muzzle against Tibor's head. Despite being half-naked and exposed to the bitter wind channelling through the gully, Tibor began sweating. Things were now way beyond his control. If the Germans spotted the Russians and detonated the bridge, he would be shot, assuming he survived the explosion. He just hoped the Germans were watching the road and not the bridge. Otherwise ... Tibor closed his eyes, knowing he'd done his best to carry out his father's wishes.

He heard voices and when he opened his eyes he saw the four soldiers had climbed back off the bridge supports. They were grinning from ear to ear. They set off back around the rocks to start the climb that would take them back to the road. But Tibor's legs were turning to jelly. The exertions, hunger, cold and fear had sapped the last of his strength. He stumbled. Russian arms hooked under his and half-dragged, half-carried him. When they reached the tank Tibor was dimly aware of the Russian officer smiling. Smiling! The officer shouted something to him and it was all Tibor could do to wave back. He wanted to sleep for a year.

'You never told me about the explosives.' Milos was blue from the cold and shivering violently. His arms were wrapped around his chest for warmth. 'Are you okay?'

Tibor nodded and embraced him.

Two soldiers stayed with the exhausted boys while the column of tanks moved forward, the four of them perched on a rock in the weak sun as though exempted from the war. Tibor tried to imagine the faces of the German soldiers when the bridge failed to detonate. He glanced at the Russian alongside him. The soldier might have been sharing the same thoughts because his face broke into a broad grin.

'Boom!' said the soldier. And again. 'Boom!'

The four of them began laughing, two boys and their Russian liberators. The boys laughed with the release that came with the knowledge that they'd survived. Survived the Germans, the Arrow Cross, angry farmers, the deserters and, finally, their new friends, these strange Asian-looking Russians. They'd survived when it had seemed like the whole world was conspiring to kill them. Tibor gratefully accepted the bundle of clothing one of the Russians handed him and tossed a shirt and coat to Milos. He couldn't help noticing Milos's chest and checked his own. The Stars of David were now just a dirty black smudge of oil.

* * *

'Stop now,' said Lucio.

'Yes,' said Ramon. 'It is six o'clock. You've already run an hour over.'

'No,' said Milos. 'I'm not yet finished. I can't stop now. It'll change the structure.'

But Milos's skin had become grey with the effort of telling his story and reviving memories he'd worked hard to suppress. In truth, he lacked the strength to insist.

'You've given us enough to think about,' said Neil. 'More would be overkill.'

'Overkill?' said Milos. 'Overkill?'

Ramon and Lucio winced.

'Whatever,' said Neil affably. 'I need a slash and some more coffee. Anyone else need to point Percy?'

'I'll come with you,' said Lucio. 'Milos, promise me you will have a coffee before you drive home. Perhaps also a cognac,' he added solicitously.

Milos nodded. He waited until Neil and Lucio had left before turning to Ramon.

'Twice today you have forced me to change my structure. It's not right.'

'I apologise,' said Ramon gently. 'My friend, I don't like to see you like this. Perhaps you should have chosen another story.'

'No,' said Milos. 'I told you at the beginning, no? I have no choice. You had no right to stop me here. The story has to move on and you have put me behind schedule.'

'Then spread your story over an extra week. None of us will object.'

'You don't understand, Ramon. You're not listening to me. I told you before. Time is running out. There is no extra week.'

THIRD
THURSDAY

CHAPTER FIFTEEN

'Maybe it's just a war story,' said Neil. 'You guys try to read too much into the telling.'

'No, there's more to it than that,' said Ramon firmly. 'Milos's stories always have more layers than a Danish pastry. The key, I believe, is in the urgency. Why did Milos choose this story? Why does he have to tell it now?'

'That's just bullshit,' said Neil. 'Contrived so he could tell his story ahead of mine. Christ Almighty, my story needed telling too. Dwell on them too long and they lose their spark.'

'No, he has a reason,' said Ramon. 'I'm certain of it. Last week he was upset because I interrupted his story for coffee. He was genuinely upset when he ran out of time and couldn't finish the day's episode. Why the hurry, why the schedule? What are your thoughts?'

'You know my thoughts,' said Neil. 'It's his story, one he's probably never told anyone before and it's affecting him. He's reliving memories and it's taking longer than he thought. Basically he just wants the story over and done with and for us to know what an amazing bloke he was as a kid. He did okay but, for mine, it's Tibor who deserves the credit.'

'Such understanding and compassion,' said Lucio. 'Ever thought of becoming a priest?' He glared at Neil. 'Besides, I think maybe we are all overlooking the main issue.'

'Which is?' said Ramon.

'His use of the third person. The way he refers to himself as Milos. Two weeks ago you claimed that was the key, one of the foundation stones of his story. Maybe we should consider his motives.'

'I'm not so certain any more. The nature of the story, the obvious distress in telling it, maybe Milos was right. Maybe the use of the third person does contribute to his objectivity, but it is also helpful in distancing himself from his memories,' said Ramon.

'The great man admits he was wrong,' said Neil. 'Never thought I'd live to see the day.'

'Perhaps it's neither of these things,' said Lucio. 'Milos mentioned a debt. Remember? He got our attention the moment he mentioned we were owed a debt. What debt? By whom?'

'He discusses our stories with his wife,' said Ramon. 'He has told us that on many occasions.'

'So you think the debt is hers?' cut in Neil. 'It wasn't long ago that you accused him of using his wife's name to promote alternative even contradictory opinions to his own. We all know how much he hates to be wrong. You accused him of hedging his bets.'

'That's what he was doing,' said Ramon.

'Or was he?' said Lucio. 'Maybe he really was expressing his wife's opinion.'

'Damn me,' said Neil. 'Ramon wrong twice in the one day.'

The blind man ignored him. 'We have no evidence that Milos discusses the story with his wife, only his word. And he only mentions her at the most convenient times, convenient to him that is.'

'But if he genuinely discusses our stories with his wife, then it is reasonable to assume she'd have her own opinions,' said

Lucio. 'If that is the case, because she has never contributed a story herself, she may feel she is in our debt. It makes sense.'

'Bloody hell,' said Neil. 'I think you've hit the nail on the head.'

'What do you mean?' said Ramon sharply. He heard the sound of chairs being pushed back, of Lucio and Neil rising to their feet. 'What's happening? What's happening? For God's sake, Lucio!'

'Milos has brought his wife.'

Ramon started, genuinely surprised. Milos had brought his wife? Why? And why hadn't he seen it coming? Suddenly the debt was obvious, but how did that explain the urgency? Or Milos's use of the third person? A smile spread across the blind man's face which masked his true feelings. He pushed his chair back and rose to his feet, alert and concentrating, listening for footsteps, the sound of clothes brushing the backs of chairs, the reactions of his friends, trying to judge the moment. Yes!

'Gabriella, I presume,' said Ramon. He heard a brief, brittle laugh in response, younger-sounding than he expected, not forced but somehow warm.

'Milos told me you would guess. It is a pleasure to meet you at last, Ramon.' She took his hand and kissed him lightly on the cheek.

'The pleasure is mine,' said Ramon, but his mind was racing. What was Milos playing at? Even if his wife felt she owed them a debt, how did that justify Milos bringing her uninvited to their lunch? And why now? Ramon looked for clues but found few. It was so unlike Milos unless he had a purpose. And if he had a purpose, why hadn't he brought her along when he began the story?

The blind man seethed quietly, dimly aware of Milos introducing Gabriella to Lucio who was naturally effusive in his greeting. He sounded as though he was genuinely delighted to have her join them, privileged even, but how did he really feel about this unwarranted intrusion? There was a cosiness

245

and a completeness between the four of them, and a balance that could easily be disturbed. Gabriella's presence was an imposition.

'And you must be Neil,' he heard Gabriella say.

'Right on the money,' said Neil. 'It's an honour to meet you. We've heard so much about you!'

'Really?' said Gabriella.

Ramon's ears pricked up instantly, alert to the change in her voice and its nuances.

'Yes, really,' said Neil.

'You surprise me, Neil. Aren't you the one who advised my Milos to — what is the expression? — yes, "get a life" when you learned what his story would be? Didn't you advise him to get rid of all his baggage from Europe and the war?'

A smile began to spread slowly across the blind man's face.

'Didn't you tell him he should have left all his baggage behind so he could truly embrace this new country? Isn't that what you told him?'

'Maybe. In a roundabout way,' said Neil uncomfortably.

'No, not in a roundabout way at all.'

'No,' Neil admitted, 'maybe not in a roundabout way.'

'You told Milos that a smart man would have left all his baggage behind. Yes or no?'

'Yes,' said Neil.

'Then he would have left me,' said Gabriella softly. 'He would have left me behind. You see, Neil, I am Milos's baggage.'

The blind man fought back the ripple of delight that raced through his body. The game had moved to another level. He felt like shaking his friend's hand, congratulating him. Milos never disappointed.

'Please, please,' said Gancio. He pushed his way through to the table. 'I make another place alongside Milos, okay? Between Milos and Neil?'

'Thank you,' said Milos. He introduced Gabriella to Gancio.

'Anything you want, you just ask,' said Gancio. 'I have a special Italian lemon liqueur. Not for them, they have grappa, but special for you.'

'Thank you,' said Gabriella.

Gancio grabbed a chair from a nearby table and held it so Gabriella could sit down. The men followed.

'Before you say anything,' said Gabriella, 'let me apologise for my intrusion. Milos was against my coming but I nagged at him until he gave in. A wife is entitled to do this, no? I wanted to come so that I could thank you personally, not just for the pleasure your stories have given me. You see, stories are precious to me, their value goes far beyond mere pleasure. There have been times in my life when stories were the only thing that kept me going, the distraction that helped me cope with a life I could not face, a life I did not want to live. To you, your stories are fictions and a playground for rivalries, an enjoyable and also stimulating diversion in your busy lives. Milos says it is an opportunity to exercise your egos. But to me they are therapy. I don't just enjoy your stories, I live them. Every twist, every turn, every nuance. Tell them, Milos.'

'It's true,' said Milos. 'For all these past years, when you thought there were four of us sitting around this table, there have been five.'

'Your Thursdays are as important to me as they are to you,' said Gabriella. 'You have no idea how impatient I get waiting for Milos to come home. First we have dinner, a light meal because Gancio always makes him eat too much, then he relays your stories to me. My Milos has always been a good storyteller, even back in Tokaj Street. When he tells your stories, it's your voices I hear. I know whose story it is by the way he tells it. He doesn't have to say, "This is Ramon's story or this is Lucio's." I know whose it is. I hear your voices.'

'And do you help Milos construct his stories?' asked Ramon.

Again Ramon heard Gabriella's brittle laugh.

'When you know me better you would not dare suggest such a thing. You would not even think it! I am a listener. I am happy to listen.'

'But will you join in the telling?' asked Ramon. He knew he was pushing but wanted a sniff of a reason for her presence beyond what she was admitting to. Ramon liked to be ahead of the game. Anticipating the direction of a story was half the challenge and half the pleasure.

'No,' said Gabriella. 'Don't think I haven't discussed this with Milos. I have, but we both agree I am not yet ready. Almost ready, but not quite. I have made progress, lots of progress. Milos is very pleased with me. We no longer have locks on our doors, we no longer have bars over every window. I can hear a knock on the door and know it is a friend on the other side and not an enemy. I can get on a train now and not beg to be taken off. I can even listen to the eggs break, I can listen to the eggs.' Gabriella smiled and there was triumph in her voice that the blind man immediately picked up on. 'But, am I ready to help Milos tell this story? No, not in any way that would do justice to it. I wish this were not the case so I could repay my debt in person. After all, this is my story too. Maybe I can add detail if Milos agrees.'

'Scallops,' said Gancio, interrupting them with the first course. There were three scallops on each plate, on the shell, barely cooked and quivering. 'A drop of garlic olive oil, a drop of balsamic, lemon and a light sprinkle of Italian parsley, salt and pepper. Beautiful.'

'My goodness,' said Gabriella.

'Gancio leaves the scallops in the shell so Ramon can find them,' said Neil.

'Neil!' said Gabriella. 'You shouldn't say such things.' She reached across the table and tapped his hand in a pretend smack.

Once again Ramon's senses pricked up. He couldn't see Gabriella tap Neil's hand but he heard the smile in her voice.

'Ignore him,' said Lucio.

'You mentioned Tokaj Street,' said Ramon. 'Perhaps while we eat and before Milos resumes, you can tell us a bit more about your home and your early days. I have had photos described to me of Jews crowded into ghettos prior to the war. The photos were taken in Poland, Carpathia and Ruthenia which, of course, is not too far from where you lived. They were descriptions of abject poverty, of a deprived people crowded together and stripped of all but the very essentials. Yet you had a large house and people who helped with the housekeeping.'

'There were poor Jews in Hungary too, plenty of them,' said Gabriella. 'But we were not crowded into ghettos like the Polish Jews. I was also fortunate to live in sleepy Sarospatak. Did Milos tell you that Sarospatak means "the town on the muddy stream"? No? Yet at one time it was famous as a place of learning and known as the Athens of Hungary. It is a nice town, a pretty town. My home in Tokaj Street was the biggest in the street, one of the few that didn't share an adjoining wall with neighbours.

'I look back and to me it was Camelot. For years it was my retreat, the place I hid when my mind could not face the world. My poor Milos lived in fear that one day I would go there and not come back. Oh, I was tempted! It was so seductive, the prospect of letting go of reality and sinking into dreams. So very seductive. You see, I was happy back then. In my memory it never rained and winter was only an excuse to build big warm fires. There were no Germans, no Arrow Cross and no war. My home was filled with sunshine, laughter, music and, most of all, lovely, kind, gentle people who were my family. No one in my family ever wanted for love, support or affection.

'My father and brother spoiled Elizabeth and I. We could do no wrong. Sometimes my mother tried to be stern but she wasn't very good at it. I don't recall ever being scolded. We had golden days, days when Aunt Jutka and Aunt Klari came and boiled up the apricots and plums and made enough jam and preserves to last us a year. I can still remember the heat from their big cast-iron pots, the steam and my aunts' sweating faces. They used to sing lovely old songs and make us help take out the stones from the fruit. They let us lick the ladles.'

'Milos told us about the Sunday lunches,' prompted Ramon. 'They were obviously very special to him.'

'They were also special to us. We had people come to lunch every Sunday, sometimes very important rich people, but my sister and I most liked the Sundays when Uncle Jozsef brought the boys. I think we all preferred those Sundays. They were much more fun. I was madly in love with Tibor of course which helped. But in those days we had to be very demure and proper. Tibor was tall for his age and oh so handsome! My parents were always saying how clever he was and how astute but he was daring as well. You could not imagine anyone more sure of himself. Even my brother Balazs was impressed by his courage and his cunning. When I dreamed of getting married it was always Tibor slipping the ring on my finger.'

'What about Milos?' asked Lucio. 'Wasn't he madly in love with you as well?'

'Yes, and he showed it.' Gabriella once more treated the table to her laugh. 'I used to wish Tibor would be so obvious. Milos used to follow me around like a puppy dog. He had these big mooning eyes. My parents insisted that we didn't embarrass him. Poor Milos. His face used to turn as red as a beetroot when he was nervous or embarrassed. I always had to sit between him and Tibor and pay equal attention to both. The only times Tibor and I were alone together was when we played hide and seek and Milos was hiding. Milos thought he was so good at hiding but the truth was we didn't want to find him!'

'That's enough,' said Milos gently. 'Finish your scallops.'

'Two is plenty,' said Gabi.

Over the main course Gabriella recounted some of her memories but they were always pleasant things, childish, girly things. They were memories enriched and mellowed by time, like the polished top of an antique table. They gave no hint of the horrors waiting around the corner or the traumatic aftermath she'd hinted at. Ramon found it hard to reconcile the image of the happy, carefree, blessed and privileged child her anecdotes portrayed and the forlorn, desolate figure Milos had described stranded on the platform at Krakow.

* * *

Horror immobilises. The enormity of the catastrophe exceeded Gabriella's capability to respond. Paralysis deprived her legs of movement, her throat of voice and her eyes of tears. Only her brain functioned and it teetered on the very limit of comprehension. As the train began moving away, Gabriella grasped in full the completeness of her abandonment and could think no further. She didn't know where she was, didn't know where her mother and sister were going, didn't know how they'd ever find each other again, couldn't even imagine where to begin looking. Surrounding her was an alien, friendless world of hostile soldiers and slavering dogs, of terror and disbelief, of grit, smoke and a language she couldn't understand. There was nothing normal she could turn to, no anchor point to cling to. She was alone, abandoned, cast adrift. Beyond that, there was nothing.

Gabriella had never been alone in her life and couldn't begin to conceive of a life afterwards. Around her guards restrained other distraught young women who tried to run after the train, but Gabriella had no need for restraint. Her paralysis was total. Her horrified eyes remained fixed on a particular box car as it moved away from the platform, away from the station and was sucked into anonymous darkness.

The train disappeared, taking with it everything she had been, leaving her with just her name, memories, the clothes she stood in, her bag, and a terror which was absolute.

'*Schnell*!'

Rough hands grabbed her. Soldiers screamed incomprehensible orders and began dragging her to the centre of the platform. She went unwillingly, as though to move from the spot destroyed for ever any possibility that her mother would find her again. The soldiers interpreted her reluctance as resistance and called for dogs. The brutes leapt at her, snarling, snapping their jaws and straining their leashes in their eagerness to rip her apart. Gabriella screamed. She screamed as anyone would who'd been set upon by vicious dogs. In that instant, pure fear transcended all thought. She felt nothing but a desperate primal urge to flee. A soldier laughed as she leapt away from the dogs, kept laughing as she ran, stumbled and fell into line with a group of girls all as terrified as herself.

The soldiers marched them up stairs and along corridors. Gabriella dared to glance at her companions, looking for a familiar face, anyone who could form a connection with who she was and who she'd been. Some of the girls were older, some younger. One appeared no more than eight or nine. There were eleven girls in her group, two of whom Gabriella knew from school, and three or four more she vaguely recognised. This familiarity brought comfort. She wasn't alone, not entirely. When the soldiers marched them down stairs and onto another platform crowded with more young women and girls, the Sarospatak contingent automatically pressed in close to one another.

Many of the young women on the platform were weeping soundlessly, others had cried themselves out or given in to despair and hopelessness. Yet whether in their twenties, teenage or younger, the expressions on their faces were always the same. Fear, apprehension, devastation. It took a while for Gabriella to realise another thing they had in common. No one spoke. There were hundreds of young women sitting and lying on the platform, awaiting a fate they feared but couldn't even guess at, yet no one spoke. No one. The silence terrified Gabriella as much as the dogs had.

The women waited throughout the night while trains came and went. Some wept, others exchanged frightened whispers. Shortly after six they were once again herded into box cars, sixty to a carriage. They had a little more room but still only one bucket of water and one bucket as their lavatory. It took two days of sporadic travel, during which their train swung south-east to Prague, before turning north to their destination, Theresienstadt. They arrived beaten into submission by hunger, fear and exhaustion, accepting of whatever the Germans chose to do with them.

Gabriella had given up. She expected to be marched directly from the train to her execution. After all she'd been through, the rumoured death camps her Uncle Jozsef had told them about in the kitchen at Tokaj Street no longer seemed extreme but probable. She was prepared for death, prepared for anything except what happened.

Her first surprise was that Theresienstadt was not a camp so much as a town. The Germans had quickly realised the potential of the eighteenth-century fortress town which nestled into the conjunction of two rivers, the Elbe and the Eger. Both the natural and man-made barriers meant that large numbers of people could be interned there and guarded with minimal force. The Germans evicted the villagers and converted Theresienstadt into a ghetto. In other times and circumstances, Gabriella could imagine Theresienstadt being quite pretty. As it was, she was impressed by what she saw. The street they were marched along was spotlessly tidy and clean. Prisoners were busy painting the fronts of every building along the cobbled road from the station, and even in her weakened and dazed state Gabriella could appreciate the care they were taking. The buildings looked immaculate.

Her confusion grew as the guards marched them not to any place of execution but to showers. They were ordered to strip, given soap and also instructed to wash their hair. The water was cold, their time in the shower limited and their overseers abrupt. There was no concession to modesty. Yet the effect of the showers was transforming.

Once showered, the women and girls were given clean clothes and marched to a parade ground where they were each handed a lump of dry bread and a bowl of soup. There were pieces of potato and turnip in the soup, pieces not just scrapings, and there was a sheen on the surface which suggested that at some stage it had contained bones or meat. It didn't matter that the soup was weak and unsalted and tasted like dishwater. Gabriella attacked it voraciously, dunking her bread to soften it, saving some to wipe her bowl clean. Every crumb and every drop were treasure. The meal eased the craving in her stomach and provided much needed nourishment but, more than anything else, gave her heart. Optimism dared to creep in where previously there had been only despair. She imagined her mother and sister sitting in another camp somewhere with their own dry bread and soup.

After their meal the prisoners were processed and given back their bags, complete with their few possessions, taken to a barrack room and each assigned a narrow slatted bed. For the first time since they'd disembarked from the train there were no guards in sight and no dogs. Whispered conversations began as scared people dared to believe things were not as bad as they'd feared. Gabriella checked the beds around her but none of her acquaintances from school were nearby. A girl her own age just two beds away caught her eye and smiled tentatively. Gabriella smiled back.

Over the next few hours, Gabriella tried to come to terms with everything that had happened and her new circumstances, and began making plans that would see her reunited with her mother and sister. One day the war would end and when that happened, Gabriella decided, she'd somehow make her way home to Sarospatak. That seemed the logical thing to do. Just the thought of her home on Tokaj Street brought tears to her eyes. When she thought of the reunion that would follow she had to roll over face down on the thin mattress so that no one could see or hear her cry.

Having become accustomed to confinement in the box cars, it never occurred to Gabriella that she could leave the barrack room. She lay on her bed trying to ignore the pain from her swollen bladder, hoping that a guard would come and march them to the latrine. She jumped in fright when she felt a hand on her shoulder. It was the girl from two beds away.

'Will you come with me?' said the girl.

'Come with you?' said Gabriella. 'Where?'

'To the latrine.'

'Are we allowed?' Gabriella looked around to see if a guard had miraculously appeared. One hadn't.

'Yes, but I'm too frightened to go alone.'

Gabriella swung her legs off the bed.

'I'm desperate,' said the girl.

'So am I,' said Gabriella.

The girls slipped tentatively down the narrow aisle between the beds, gradually gaining pace as if their distended bladders could sense relief was at hand and had become impatient. For some reason, their urgent need to pee struck them as funny and, despite everything, they began to giggle. Gabriella held out her hand to the girl as they walked towards the latrines.

'I'm Gabriella.'

'Julia,' said her friend.

They turned the corner of their barrack and stopped dead in their tracks. Ahead of them in the queue for the latrines were groups of women, all of them gaunt and hollow-eyed, their expressions blank or haunted, their clothes threadbare. But if the appearance of the women stunned the two girls, the girls had a more marked effect on the women. Without exception they turned and stared as though struggling to comprehend what they saw. One of the women spoke to them in a language they didn't understand. They shook their heads. Another woman spoke in halting German.

'Where you from?'

'Debrecen in Hungary,' said Julia.

'Sarospatak,' said Gabriella.

'Ahh, Hungary,' said the woman. She turned and translated for her friends.

'Where are you from?' asked Julia.

'France, Holland, Austria — what does it matter where we are from?' The woman smiled grimly. 'We are here, that is all that matters.'

The latrines were little more than slit trenches into which prisoners occasionally tipped buckets of soil, but they were a vast improvement on the buckets in the box cars. On the way back to their barrack, the girls passed more women all with the same emaciated, haunted look.

'They must have done something wrong,' said Julia. Gabriella could see no reason to disagree.

Later that afternoon they were ordered to line up and each given another piece of bread. The girls ate it immediately, chewing patiently until it had softened up and was easy to swallow. Gabriella went to sleep that night wondering about the death camps and whether they were real or just exaggerations created by fear-filled minds. She thought back to her Uncle Jozsef telling her mother, Elizabeth and herself about the rumours, and how horrified, frightened and disbelieving they'd been. The very concept of death camps had seemed incredible in Tokaj Street and seemed even more incredible now. Well, her Uncle Jozsef had been wrong. Wrong then and wrong again when he'd forced her off the train. She recalled the fateful moment when her uncle had wrenched her free of her mother and sister and abandoned her to the Germans and their dogs.

For the first time in her life Gabriella hated someone and that person was her Uncle Jozsef. She knew then that no matter how long she lived, another day or a hundred years, she could never ever forgive him for what he had done. Bitter tears stung her eyes.

The following morning they were made to stand in rows five deep and were counted and recounted until the number of prisoners tallied with camp records. They were then informed of their duties. After roll call they would have breakfast. After breakfast they were to make up their beds and clean their barracks. Once the barracks had been checked, they were required to line up for work assignment. The job of counting and the instruction of their duties kept the young women standing through two hours of tedium.

Breakfast was a bowl of thin soup. Some of the young women, who the day before had greeted their bowl of soup and piece of bread as something akin to a miracle, now complained of the taste and questioned why they hadn't been given another piece of bread to mop it up. No one had any idea that they were receiving privileged treatment.

Reality came when the girls least expected it. They stood in their rows of five awaiting work assignment when one of the guards noticed a stain on a girl's dress. He immediately began screaming at her and dragged her out of the line to his superior who struck her hard across the face. The more the girl screamed the more the officer abused and hit her. He ordered her to remove her dress and kneel on her bare knees on the cobblestones.

Gabriella looked on in horror. The guards had not yet reached her section. She glanced down to inspect her clothes, hoping and praying that she hadn't been careless. She didn't think she had but would she have noticed if a drop of soup had dripped off the bottom of her spoon? All around her other girls were anxiously checking their clothing. The guards tied the hands and feet of the kneeling girl and left her there sobbing quietly.

Gabriella passed inspection and stepped forward when her name was called out, along with thirty other girls. They were lined up and marched away from the barracks back towards the road that led to the station. She didn't panic. All through inspection she'd noticed groups of women being marched away, presumably to their place of work. Gabriella's detail was halted outside the freshly painted buildings she'd noticed when she'd first arrived. This was how she'd thought the whole camp would be. Even now she assumed the painters would gradually work their way around town.

Some girls were handed buckets and cloths and told to clean windows. There was no water in the buckets and, even more oddly, the windows were already clean. Gabriella and Julia were given a broom each, led to a building and told to brush out the hallway and steps. The hallway was spotless and so were the steps, but the girls knew better than to argue. Back near the barracks one of their companions was still kneeling on cobblestones, a lesson to all. So Gabriella and Julia swept, as did other girls across the road and in the buildings alongside them, while others ran dry rags over clean windows.

'Smile!' ordered their guard. 'You must smile. You must be happy!'

So the girls smiled. Apart from anything else, they had good reason to. Only a day ago they had feared for their lives. Now they had clean clothes, two meals a day and work that wasn't really work. All they had to do was keep clean and obey orders. It didn't seem a lot to ask. If this was how she was destined to spend the war, Gabriella decided, she'd accept it gladly. Together with Julia she swept and reswept the hallway and steps, brushing away non-existent dirt and dust. Occasionally German officers passed by and examined them and their clothes and made sure they were smiling and happy.

Early in the afternoon Gabriella noticed four male prisoners carrying cans of paint and ladders coming down the street. They stopped outside the building where she and Julia were sweeping the steps for the thirtieth time. One pointed towards the top of the building while the others tried to see what he was pointing at.

'Speak German?' hissed one of the men.

'A little,' said Julia hesitantly.

'Where are you from?'

'Hungary.'

'When?'

'Yesterday.'

'Perfect!' said the man. He translated for his comrades while Julia translated for Gabriella.

'Why perfect?' said Gabriella. 'Ask him.'

'Look at you,' said the man. 'You are a lie. You are like these buildings.'

'What do you mean?' said Julia.

'A delegation is coming from the Red Cross. The Germans have ordered us to paint all the buildings along the designated route. We have done such a good job, the Red Cross must see through the deceit. They have only to look fifty metres either side to see how things really are. You, you are the icing on the cake!' He laughed.

'I don't understand,' said Julia.

'Look at you. You girls,' he waved his hands expansively, 'you are all so beautiful! Every one of you. All beautiful. Look!'

Julia translated for Gabriella and they saw the truth in what the man had said. They *were* all beautiful yet this commonality had not occurred to either of them.

'Look at your faces,' said the man, 'they are not prison camp faces. Your faces still have the look of the outside world, of freedom. Look at our faces, look at everyone else in this hell hole. Don't you see the difference?'

Again Julia translated and both girls nodded. They already knew that look.

'Soon the Red Cross will come, they will see how ridiculous these shining buildings are, see how ridiculous you look with your pretty faces and clean clothes, and they will see through the lie. They will insist on inspecting the real camp. Then the world will learn what the Germans have done to us.'

'Guard!' spat one of the other men.

Gabriella and Julia instantly put their heads down and continued sweeping while the men pretended to argue about some detail of their building. Eventually they moved off. Later that afternoon the girls were marched back to their barracks and each given a lump of bread and a little marmalade. Gabriella ate her ration of bread cautiously, saving some to mop up the morning soup. While they ate, she and Julia told the women around them what the painters had told them.

'We were taken from the train at Krakow because we are beautiful?' asked one of the women incredulously.

'Look around you,' said Gabriella.

'We are part of a lie?' asked another.

'Yes,' said Julia, 'that's what we were told.'

'If we are part of a lie, what then is the truth?'

'The other women are the truth,' said Gabriella. 'If you want the truth, look at their faces. Look in their eyes.'

The following morning the Red Cross arrived to inspect the camp. They travelled down the cobbled road past the clean, freshly painted buildings, saw the pretty girls sweeping steps and cleaning windows and did not deviate one metre from the designated route. Despite the efforts of the painters to paint their buildings like giant dolls' houses, the delegation never saw the real Theresienstadt. What they saw was a lie, no more real than a movie set. Gabriella was a part of that lie.

Almost the moment the Red Cross departed, Gabriella and all the women in her barrack were ordered to hand back the clothes they had been given. In return they were given the

clothing they had arrived in. Their clothes had been freshly
laundered so none of the women objected; in fact, many were
happier to have their own clothes. Later that afternoon, when
they lined up for their bread, their ration was noticeably
smaller and there was no marmalade. The soup the following
morning was thinner with precious little evidence of
vegetables in it. After inspection they were organised into
work groups and given new assignments.

Gabriella found herself in a factory, sitting at a long
crowded workbench assembling parts for weapons. Whether
they were intended for the army, navy or air force she had no
idea. The light was poor and her seat uncomfortable. The
women alongside her worked hard and mostly in silence.
Gabriella struggled to keep up.

During a break while they waited for a new stock of parts,
Gabriella turned to the woman next to her who, judging by
the dead look on her face, had been in Theresienstadt for some
time. She came from a town in Austria near the border with
Hungary and spoke some Magyarul.

'Why does everyone work so hard?' said Gabriella.

'We have quotas,' replied the woman. 'Everyone must work
hard to meet the quotas or be punished. Work slowly and the
overseers will notice. Make mistakes and they will notice.
Your name will be called out during selection and you will be
taken away.'

'Taken away where?'

The woman shrugged. 'Work slow and you will find out,'
she said. 'Work hard you may not.' She added bitterly, 'Hard
work is no guarantee.'

Things deteriorated steadily for Gabriella. Every day she
and Julia told each other that their lives could not get any
worse, but they always did. She got used to seeing bodies on
carts being wheeled away down the cobbled streets every
morning to the crematorium. Got used to the pathetic corpses
of small children, of the sick and those who'd grown too weak

261

to continue living. She got used to having her bread and soup rations reduced, to losing weight and strength and to wondering how long her downward slide could continue before she disappeared altogether. The other women in the camp no longer stared at her and she realised it was because she now looked like them, had become one of them.

At night Gabriella brought out her book and read it to Julia, translating from English into Magyarul. They studied the picture plates of Peter Pan, pirates and pixies, escaping for precious moments into the wonderful world created by J.M. Barrie and Mabel Lucie Attwell. But the escape was never more than temporary. When the lights went out fears ignited. There was the real world to contend with and the one thing that terrified her most. It paralysed her body and mind with unspeakable fear and, with every passing day, became more inevitable.

Nobody knew in advance when the selections would take place or whose name would be called out. Nobody knew for sure what happened to people who were selected, though it was generally regarded as a death sentence. Nobody knew the final destination of the trains that carried them away, although rumours of Auschwitz and its dreaded gas chambers had infiltrated the camp and were being spread in horrified whispers in barracks and latrines. The fact that the inmates of the sick houses were always included in the selections added currency to the rumours. The logic was brutally simple: the Germans were not curing the sick therefore they were disposing of them. Selection came to equal Auschwitz and Auschwitz equalled death.

Gabriella stood in line and heard the names of girls from Sarospatak called out, girls who shared her barrack and bunked down near to her, girls who worked in the same factory as her and worked hard. She stood expecting to hear her name called out too, dreading hearing her name called out and dreading hearing Julia's. Each time their names were omitted brought relief but also increased their fear. Each day their names weren't called brought them closer to the day when they would be. Gabriella now understood the underlying cause of the look on her face and on the faces of all the inmates. They were all dead people, dead people whose names had not yet been called.

One morning Gabriella, Julia and around thirty other women from their barrack heard their names called out at roll call. The paralysis that enveloped Gabriella during every selection gripped her. Julia and another girl virtually had to carry her out front to the assembly point. But instead of marching them towards the station, the guards took them in the opposite direction. Gabriella's spirits lifted but she remained cautious. They marched for almost ten minutes until, ahead of her, she could see three or four tables set up across the road. Two young women in clean blue uniforms sat at each table. Gabriella had no idea what was about to happen, only that they were not heading for the trains and therefore had not been selected.

The girls in blue were apparitions, visitors from another world entirely. Gabriella stared at them as she had been stared at when she first arrived in Theresienstadt. They still had flesh on their bones and their hair hadn't thinned or fallen out. They were beautiful, every bit as beautiful as she had once been. Gabriella closed her eyes and sniffed. Even at a distance from the tables she could smell soap. Soap!

The guards ordered the girls to form a line in front of each table, which they did. But their curiosity got the better of them and they gradually edged forward until they could see what these beautiful apparitions in blue were doing.

'They're tattooing numbers on our arms!' one girl exclaimed.

Gabriella and Julia hugged each other, tears forming in their eyes. The significance of the tattoo was not lost on them. Most of the women in the factory had numbers tattooed on their forearms. Tattoos were a sign of permanence. Tattoos meant that the Germans had a use for them, which lessened their chances of being selected.

Gabriella glanced at the guards who were showing no interest at all in the proceedings. They stood leaning against a wall, soaking up the sun. She took advantage of their lapse in discipline to examine the work of the tattooists at each of the tables. Some were sloppy and tattooed large numbers in irregular lines. But one girl seemed to have a talent for the task, or at the very least a greater sense of diligence.

'Come. This line,' said Gabriella and grabbed hold of Julia's arm. When their turn came they engaged their tattooist in conversation as best they could. Gabriella praised the girl's neatness and told her how she had chosen her to tattoo their arms because her numbers were smaller and neater. The girl appeared flattered and reacted as they had hoped by making certain she did a neat job on their arms. In the course of their conversation they discovered that the tattooists weren't German as they had thought but Jewish girls from Czechoslovakia. They were all quite fair-skinned and looked German. Gabriella guessed that was why they were privileged, well fed and well clothed.

Once all the girls had been tattooed, they were marched directly back to their work places. The morning which had begun in such fear had developed into a glorious autumn day with little breeze and a bright blue sky that reminded Gabriella of picnics.

CHAPTER SIXTEEN

For Milos liberation was a triumph but for Tibor it came as an anti-climax. He'd been too long at the edge and could not step back from it. He became restless and impatient and wanted to follow along behind the Russian advance, far more closely than was safe. He needed the thrill of living every day as though it was his last. Milos had only one aim, which was the whole purpose of his survival. This was to return to Sarospatak, but Tibor complained he couldn't see the point. He wanted to follow the Russians to Budapest and see what opportunities awaited them there.

'We have nothing in Sarospatak,' he argued, 'no home, no friends, no future. When Budapest is liberated it will be full of desperate people who will need food, clothing and coal for their fires. There will be opportunities for us to make something of ourselves.'

'What about Dad? What about Gabriella?' argued Milos stubbornly.

'One day we will discover where they died and put flowers on their graves. What more can we do?'

'You don't know they're dead,' said Milos indignantly. 'We can be home waiting for them when they return. We can make something for them to return home to.'

'Home? Forget home,' said Tibor. 'It's somebody else's home now. We're going to Budapest. Both of us. You are coming with me.'

'I'm going home,' said Milos. 'We are going home.'

The argument remained unresolved, a chasm between them that widened as the boys grew further apart. In the Carpathians to the north, the front had stalled as the Germans dynamited roads, bridges and railway lines ahead of the advance. Tibor used the fact that the Russians were making faster progress towards Budapest than they were towards Sarospatak to strengthen his argument, but Milos would not be persuaded. He believed that he had an obligation to his father in the event that Jozsef had somehow managed to survive, and he had a promise to Gabriella to keep. He would not be diverted.

Tibor grew tired of arguing and spent increasingly more time with the Russian soldiers. He tried to learn their language and they respected him for this. They failed utterly to realise his motives: that he was trying to learn how they thought, what motivated them, and how he could best use this knowledge once he got to Budapest.

Milos and Tibor also argued about the amount of time Tibor was spending with the Russians in light of their atrocities. The Hungarians had wanted the Germans out but not at the expense of allowing the Russians in. The Hungarians feared the fierce Russian soldiers far more than the Germans and they had every right to. When the liberating army passed through villages, women and children showered their tanks and trucks with flowers. The soldiers accepted the flowers and at night came back to rape the women.

'The Russians don't want much,' a woman from a liberated village complained to the boys, 'just to eat all our food, drink all our *palinka* and rape us. Mothers and daughters, the young and the old. Beyond that, they just loot everything the Germans left.'

The pattern was repeated in every village and town as the Russians advanced. The soldiers got drunk, raped the women and shot anyone who got in their way. Then they'd go back to fighting Germans and dying by the thousands. Yet Tibor saw another side to them. He admired the courage and discipline of the Mongolian and Kirgiz troops as much as his countrymen recoiled at the atrocities they committed. Tibor did not condone the conduct of the Russians but he was prepared to allow mitigating circumstances.

The Russians perished on the battlefield at a horrendous rate, often had to forage for their own food and were granted no leave. When they advanced they were shot by the Germans, and if they hesitated they were shot by their officers. They lived life closer to the edge than he did and Tibor respected them for that. When they stopped to eat they never hesitated to invite Tibor to share what little they had. When they had booze, they shared it with him until the bottle was empty. Then they went looking for women and loot.

Tibor quickly discovered the Russians' love of alcohol and their fascination with wrist watches and clocks. On the occasions when supplies caught up with the troops, Tibor moved in quickly as the negotiator, trading wrist watches for desperately needed food and winter clothing. When the Russians' vodka supplies dried up he traded wine, rough *palinka* plum brandy and *barack* for coarse bread, flour and sausage.

Not all the villagers could grasp that a cheap watch had exactly the same value as a fine Swiss timepiece and many felt cheated. Tibor grew tired of explaining that the Russians had never had watches and didn't know good from bad. A watch was a watch and had a value. A clock was bigger and had more value. Tibor understood that. He built up a network among the Russians, a network that was often suddenly depleted by a German counterattack. He returned the Russian soldiers' generosity and comradeship by bringing them bottles of *palinka* and not charging them. He won their trust by drinking with them until they fell over dead drunk. And all the while he learned.

Tibor was in his element now his old negotiating skills had been dusted off and once more called upon. He knew that by the time he reached Budapest he would be ready to make a killing. As his enthusiasm grew, so did his determination to impose his will upon Milos. But Milos rebuffed him. The dispute came to a head in early January 1945, when the Russian army paused to regroup for the final push to Budapest. Snowstorms swept across the Carpathians and deep into the plains of the Alfold. It was then that Milos learned Satoraljaujhely, Sarospatak and towns as far west as Miskolc had been liberated.

'You have no choice, little brother,' insisted Tibor angrily. 'I gave Dad my word to look after you and protect you. I do as Dad said. You do as I say.'

'I promised Gabriella,' said Milos. 'I can join you in Budapest later if neither Dad nor Gabriella come home. But I'm going home, Tibor, and you can't stop me.'

'How are you going to live?' spat Tibor contemptuously.

'You think I can't manage?' said Milos. 'You think I haven't learned these past months?'

'Not enough, little brother.'

They'd holed up in an abandoned and shelled farmhouse. Enough of the roof and walls remained to keep the wind and snow out of the main room. They huddled in front of the fireplace and a fire they'd made from splintered pieces of furniture, slats from shattered beds and sweepings from what had been a coal cellar. They added to the fire sparingly because their fuel had to last them through the night. The boys stared into the flames, both angry yet each wanting to break the impasse.

'We will go first to Budapest,' said Tibor eventually. 'Then, when the Russians have advanced far enough to liberate the camps, assuming there are any survivors left in the camps, we will return to Sarospatak.'

'I want to return now,' said Milos.

'No, you are coming with me to Budapest. Even if there are survivors in the camps they may not be liberated for months. You are no use to anyone in Sarospatak until then but you will be of use to me in Budapest.'

'You promise we will return to Sarospatak?'

'I promise. We will return to Sarospatak and if Gabi is still alive we will find her. Then we will ask her to choose between us.'

Tibor broke into the smile Milos hated. It was the smile of an adult indulging a child, a mocking smile that warned he'd once again been outmanoeuvred, that he'd lost.

'Gabi's choice might surprise you,' said Milos, his voice soft and lacking conviction.

'Then it's agreed,' said Tibor. 'We're going to Budapest.'

'Yes, it's agreed,' said Milos reluctantly.

'Excellent!' said Tibor. His smile softened and he hugged his brother. 'It's good that we stick together. Besides, you have a lot to learn when we get to Budapest.'

'Like what?'

'I have taught you how to survive under the Germans,' said Tibor. His smile vanished. 'Now I must teach you how to survive under the Russians.'

CHAPTER SEVENTEEN

Secrets are addictive and Istvan Kiraly had become an addict. The number of dossiers grew exponentially as he tracked down Sarospatak's missing Jews. Fourteen families and individuals now paid for his silence. It wasn't because their money brought his father release from his pain, put food on their table and bought the first new boots his feet had ever known that Istvan persisted with the dossiers, but because of the feeling of power he derived from knowing other people's secrets. Apart from the dossiers on the Jews and the people who sheltered them, his files now covered the businesses of the people sheltering the Jews, their business associates and the people who supplied materials to them. He felt exultant and infinitely superior to his quarries when patterns began to emerge. The patterns helped him identify the main players in the black market trade for industry supplies, fuel and food. He learned who was involved with which political groups, which public servants were corrupt and which gendarmes. He put everything he learned into his dossiers.

What amazed him most was how much information was available in public files if you knew where to look and what you were looking for. He visited the town hall so often the exasperated clerks finally gave him a desk and access to their files. In return, and to justify this privilege, he helped them with their filing and record-keeping. When any of the clerks or council officers asked what he was doing he replied that he was finding out how the town operated. He told them he wanted to be a councillor himself one day and was preparing the way. That answer seemed to satisfy his inquisitors as Istvan knew it would. It flattered them and politicians had always been susceptible to flattery.

He learned the details of people's private lives. Who was faithful, who was unfaithful and with whom. Along the way he made the staggering discovery that his little town of Sarospatak harboured homosexual men. It would be wrong to assume that Istvan had learned all the town's dark secrets. He hadn't, not by a long shot. But he prided himself on the belief that he knew more than anyone else, an astonishing amount for a peasant boy in his last year of school.

Istvan was convinced he had created the perfect cover for his secret life and that nobody, other than those from whom he extorted money, had any reason to suspect his true motives. He paid only cursory attention to the gendarme standing at the school gates one morning. He had no reason to suspect he was the reason for the gendarme's presence until the officer stepped out in front of him, blocking his way.

'Istvan Kiraly?'

'Yes,' said Istvan. He recognised the man immediately. He suspected him of taking protection money from a prominent black marketeer and had begun a file on him. He glanced around quickly to see where Sandor was. His brother had been trailing along behind but he managed to catch his eye.

'Come with me,' said the gendarme.

'Why?'

'You'll find out when you get there.'

'Where?'

'None of your business,' said the gendarme angrily. 'You can come voluntarily or under arrest.'

271

'Voluntarily,' said Istvan. He turned to Sandor. 'This gendarme wants me to accompany him. He won't say why or where we're going. Follow along behind us.'

'Who's he?' asked the gendarme. He looked the boy over. Not even the food shortages had been able to stop Sandor's shoulders and chest from expanding and filling out.

'My brother,' said Istvan.

The gendarme looked from one boy to the other in disbelief. 'Whoever he is, he's not wanted,' he said. 'He stays here.'

'My brother looks after my interests,' said Istvan amiably. 'In return I give him money. I understand it's not an uncommon arrangement these days.'

The gendarme's eyes narrowed suspiciously. Istvan met his gaze evenly, knowing exactly what thoughts were going through the officer's mind.

'Come on then,' snapped the gendarme.

It took only a few streets for Istvan to realise he was being taken directly to the headquarters of the gendarmerie. The question was why, and his inability to find a reasonable answer worried him. Headquarters was a modest two-storey building but rumour suggested there was a cellar beneath into which cells had been built. Istvan had never met anybody who'd been in the cells, or even seen them, but that was no reason to discount their existence. His trepidation mounted as he climbed the steps into the building.

The gendarme ordered Sandor to wait outside and led Istvan past the front desk where officers looked at him curiously. They climbed the stairs to the top storey and paused in the corridor before a closed door. The gendarme knocked three times and opened the door when he heard a response from inside.

'Istvan Kiraly, sir,' said the gendarme.

'Show the boy in. You wait downstairs.'

Istvan stepped warily into the office. If the voice had been intimidating, its owner was even more so. He was tall, broad-shouldered and thick in the arms and legs. He radiated power

272

and authority. His hair was brushed back but twisted and curled in a mass of steel grey coils that were seemingly immune to the attempts of any comb to establish order. He had a full moustache, steel-grey and bristly, that appeared welded to his face. He pinned Istvan with fierce eyes that were also grey. Istvan had never seen the man before.

The office was in disarray with filing cabinets pulled out from the walls as though ready to be moved. An electric heater glowed atop one cabinet, looking equally temporary. Istvan's mind raced as he tried to absorb everything at once but his senses were rapidly being overcome by an accelerating sense of fear. The grey eyes studied him with disconcerting intensity. Istvan felt they were stripping away his entire being layer by layer and there was absolutely nothing he could do about it.

'Come here, boy,' said the officer.

Istvan was powerless to resist. The officer leaned back on the desk which Istvan suddenly realised was also prepared for removal. There was nothing on it, no pens, no pads, nothing but a single pile of folders which, as Istvan approached, became sickeningly familiar. He stopped dead in his tracks, his short thin body dwarfed by the officer's bulk, very much the boy in the presence of the man.

'One of the clerks in the town hall works for me,' said the officer without preamble. 'Two months ago you were provided with a desk on my instruction. We collected your files after you left for school.'

Istvan felt the blood drain from his face. Amidst the fear was a sense of shame, even disgust, that he could have been under surveillance and not known it. Not for a day or two either, but for two months!

The officer placed his hand deliberately atop the stack of dossiers. 'Why?'

'It began with the Jews, sir,' said Istvan. The eyes compelled him to tell the truth. Besides, what was the point of lying when his dossiers were on the desk? 'A way to make money.'

He told the officer how one thing had led to another and how he'd become obsessed with building his dossiers, with how random information gained substance and significance when committed to paper. Under pressure from the piercing eyes he went into far more detail than was probably necessary, but he sensed an affinity with the officer and, for reasons he couldn't explain, felt a need to please him.

'After you'd found your Jews, you continued to make new dossiers on non-Jews. For what purpose?'

The officer leaned closer to Istvan, gazed at him even more intently. But Istvan didn't waver. Instead he felt a sudden surge of excitement. The officer seemed genuinely interested in what he'd been doing. There were no accusations of him acting illegally, no threats of arrest, no censure of any kind. No sense that he'd done anything wrong. His confidence began to return and his brain reassessed his situation.

'I have no set purpose,' said Istvan. 'But information is useful to different people. Its value changes according to circumstance.'

'Go on.'

'I believe I have a talent for understanding how people think and being able to predict how they will act. I began gathering information and entering it into dossiers as a way of recording my knowledge. I have always hoped that my talent would be valuable to someone.' Istvan paused in the hope that the officer would react to his last statement and reveal something of his intentions. But the officer refused to be drawn. His eyes never left Istvan's and gave no sign of softening. 'My talent is my only avenue of escape. Otherwise all I will ever be is a peasant with dirt under my fingernails and pig shit on my boots.'

'And to whom did you intend to offer your talents? The Russians?'

Istvan looked away from the officer and scanned the filing cabinets. His eyes roamed over the walls where the cabinets had been, their locations betrayed by rectangles where paint hadn't faded. He could imagine the purpose of the office and it wasn't such a big jump to imagine himself in one similar.

'I don't know who you are, sir,' he said eventually, 'but I do know you're not from Sarospatak. I don't know your rank but I know you're senior enough not to worry about buttoning your tunic. You have all these filing cabinets and I know there is a file on me in one of them.' Istvan paused again. He looked squarely into the hard grey eyes and thought he saw the hint of a smile. 'I don't know why you are talking to me, sir, but I know I've always wanted to talk to you.'

'You will call me Major Bogati.' The officer stood and began buttoning his tunic. 'There is a car outside. The driver has been instructed to take you home. You will have five minutes to pack. I am leaving for Budapest with these cabinets and your files at eleven o'clock. If you are not back I will go without you. Now leave.'

Istvan turned immediately and headed for the door, his mind awhirl. He was leaving the farm and going to Budapest? His heart pounded in his chest as he realised his talent had been recognised and his cherished dream had come true. He'd been recruited.

'One more thing.'

Istvan froze, his hand on the door handle. He realised instantly that the officer had been playing with him, that he'd been the victim of a monstrous trick designed to ascertain whether he worked alone or had a hidden agenda. So much for his talent for understanding how people think. He cursed himself for his naivety. He'd been offered the carrot and grabbed for it without considering for a moment that it might be poisoned. His disappointment was crushing. He turned around slowly, expecting to see the officer gloating.

'Tell your brother to go back to school.'

*

Istvan was recruited into the secret police, an organisation hellbent on surviving the war, the occupying Soviet army and whichever government subsequently came into power. Secrets, their stock in trade, were their means of survival. The Russians used the secret police to root out the fascists of the Arrow Cross, to capture or terminate war profiteers and black marketeers, to spy on political parties and use their secrets as weapons to influence or discourage candidates prior to elections. The secret police appeased their masters, or at least appeared to. Their existence depended equally on their dishonesty and their honesty. They infiltrated and protected selected black market networks at the expense of their competition and shared the spoils to help fund their activities. They secretly recruited thugs from the Arrow Cross as foot soldiers in their quest to retain power and influence, and sanctioned killings and beatings. They recruited Communists and church leaders, industrialists and unionists. Their weapons were hit squads, threats, blackmail and bribery and they were very good at what they did. They were determined to emerge intact and stronger whichever way the political breezes blew.

Istvan played little part in these machinations. Instead he was thrown into a training academy where he was taught the tricks of his trade: intelligence-gathering, forensics, politics, interrogation procedures, recruitment procedures and the principles of command. Though he was regarded as something of an oddity in the academy because of his diminutive stature, his talent and intelligence quickly marked him as someone to be respected.

When the Independent Smallholders Party swept into power in November 1945, Istvan believed that Hungary was set on a course for freedom, fairness and prosperity and looked forward to his state-sponsored role as protector. His father had always looked to the Smallholders Party for salvation and liberation from the landlords who bled them dry, and Istvan had grown up believing the Party was the panacea for the country's many problems.

On graduation from the academy, Istvan was reunited with his patron, Major Bogati. Even then it was clear to Istvan that Major Bogati was no mere major, that his true rank was far more exalted, but he knew better than to ask questions. His first assignment was part of a program to destabilise and undermine the Smallholders Party for the ultimate benefit of the Communist Party and their Soviet backers. He realised it was a test and determined to pass it with flying colours. His allegiance was no longer to his country, his father or the Smallholders, but to his organisation and, above all, to his inspiration, Major Bogati.

CHAPTER EIGHTEEN

Prisoners had complained about the overcrowding in Theresienstadt when Gabriella first arrived, but once the transportations began nobody complained any more. The ranks thinned out at roll call and every week more and more beds became unoccupied. Every selection was an exercise in pure fear: Gabriella and Julia stood quaking in their shoes while the names were being called out. Sometimes it was the woman in front of them, the little girl behind or the teenager alongside. Sometimes it was people with numbers tattooed on their arms. There seemed no logic to the selection process, just a grotesque and deadly game of chance. Some were called, some weren't, and beyond that there was nothing anyone could seize upon to improve the odds of their survival.

Women stepped forward with fatalism and resignation when their names were called. Few resisted and few wasted their breath on pleas for clemency. It broke Gabriella's heart when the six, seven and eight year olds stepped forward obediently but clearly baffled why anyone would want to kill them. Many had already lost their mothers and sisters and reached for the hand of the nearest adult for comfort and reassurance. It was as if they needed to know they weren't at fault and that other adults valued them. In the end Gabriella couldn't look at them. She felt too guilty because their names had been called out not hers, and too overwhelmingly relieved that she had escaped the cull one more time.

The girls' tattoos were no guarantee of survival but they were a lifeline of sorts when there was no other, provided they kept their health and strength and worked hard. Gabriella and Julia survived selection after selection but the rapid decline in the number of prisoners foreboded the inevitable. At one stage there had been more than seven hundred women in their barrack, now there were fewer than three hundred and the odds against their selection shortened.

Gabriella's and Julia's names were called on the same morning in early November. Gabriella stepped forward as meekly as all the women before her had done. She had expected a surge of panic but there was none. Just a deadness and, to her surprise, a sense of relief that she no longer had to fear hearing her name called. Her father had once spoken of the relief some of his patients felt when he told them further intervention was pointless. Some had even drawn strength from the knowledge that the uncertainty of their future was resolved. That was the relief Gabriella felt, the relief of a patient told her condition is terminal. She clutched her bag in one hand and sought Julia's hand with the other. Together they marched all the way to the station.

It was less than two hundred miles from Theresienstadt to Auschwitz but their train took two and a half days to cover the distance. Twice a day the cattle trucks were opened for toilet stops, but principally to bury the prisoners who had died en route. There were no individual graves or markers, just a hole big enough to accommodate the bodies which were buried without ceremony. The rigours of their journey prepared Gabriella and Julia for an end which they considered inevitable.

When they finally disembarked, they noticed that some prisoners were being pulled out of the line to one side and realised to their horror that they could be separated. The thought was unbearable. They held hands as they approached the selection point, each hoping that neither would be pulled out of line.

'You and you!'

The girls were too afraid to look.

'You and you!'

The voice was angry. Without warning guards grabbed her and Julia, pulled them both from the line and made them stand with the few other prisoners who had been selected.

'What's happening?' said Gabriella to anyone who had an answer. She was relieved that Julia was still with her and they could face whatever the Germans intended to do to them together. But there was safety in numbers and what little safety she'd had was disappearing with the column of prisoners marching along the muddy road away from them.

'I think we live another day,' said a young man alongside her. 'Look at us. We're all young, all strong. There's still work in us.'

Gabriella looked around her and had to acknowledge the truth. They'd been selected but somehow deselected. She was momentarily overwhelmed with relief, but it was tempered by the sight of so many others vanishing down the road. If she was to live, what was to happen to all the prisoners in the column? The rumours she'd heard suddenly acquired substance. The full horror crashed down on her and she bit her lip so she wouldn't cry out. But nothing could stop her tears. It had occurred to her that her mother, Elizabeth and her Uncle Jozsef had also faced this final selection. Neither her mother nor her uncle were young and her sister would have been barely able to stand. Had the Germans been more lenient then and less demanding in their selection? The passing parade suggested otherwise.

Of the fifteen hundred prisoners who had begun the journey in Theresienstadt only twenty-two were selected for further work. Gabriella's tiny group was marched into camp and taken to a processing centre where their heads were shaved and their clothing taken from them. They were given striped prison clothing to wear: trousers, a shirt, jacket and cap but no underwear. They were allowed to keep their shoes. Gabriella also managed to keep her book.

After processing they were left standing on an open parade ground, exposed to a bitterly cold wind and rain squalls that gusted in across the flat and featureless landscape. They stood there freezing as hours passed, forgotten or ignored. But the position of the parade ground at the junction of rows of barracks gave the prisoners some idea of the scale of the camp. The sheer size and scale of Auschwitz horrified Gabriella. Barracks stretched away seemingly to the horizon whichever way she looked. She'd thought Theresienstadt was enormous for a prison camp yet Auschwitz dwarfed it. In the distance, in the direction the rest of her fellow travellers had gone, Gabriella could see smoking chimneys. Instinctively she knew their purpose. Alongside her she could hear soft voices murmuring and knew that the others had noticed the chimneys too. Suddenly the icy cold of the wind and rain could not begin to compare with the chill in her heart. Almost immediately she became aware of the sickly, sweet smell pervading the air. She closed her eyes and did her best not to vomit.

Gabriella and Julia had been in Auschwitz for less than a week when their names were called. They had not yet come to terms with the overcrowding — there were more than a thousand women in their barrack, jammed together in rows of three-tier bunks — or got used to starving. Before Auschwitz they had been hungry but now they learned the difference between hunger and starvation. Their rations were less than half of what they had received in Theresienstadt. And they hadn't got used to the smell, the shadow cast by the chimneys or to the desperate condition of the walking dead who populated Auschwitz.

When they heard their names called, the girls had no doubt their time had come to go into the gas. They were told they were being taken to work in a munitions factory but by then nobody believed anything they were told. They'd met fellow prisoners who told them about the showers that weren't showers and confirmed the purpose of the chimneys. Some of these prisoners had survived in Auschwitz for more than a year and somehow had learned to live on little more than a crust of bread and a few spoonfuls of thin soup a day. They'd lived through selections that had robbed them of their family and friends and heard all the lies and promises that were doled out to keep the doomed passive during the final march to their execution.

Gabriella and Julia stepped forward, as passive and obedient as robots. Mercifully, horror had numbed them and fear had lost its currency. There were no tears. They were ordered to collect their things, then, hand in hand, they joined the column of selected men and women for what they believed was their last walk. Gabriella took little notice of where they were being taken. She stared at the ground or at the back of the person in front of her. Once she looked up to the sky, hoping for a last glimpse of beauty, a reminder of the way the world had been before the madness began, and how it would be when it was all over. But the sky was as grey as potato soup. There were no trees, no birds, no sun. A cold breeze chilled her and she felt weary beyond measure. Death was but another small step.

'The station. Look! We are going to the station!'

Gabriella had no idea who had spoken, only that it was a man. But the message was unmistakeable. They were not going into the gas. They were being given another chance to live.

Fortunately for them, the Soviet advance coupled with a shortage of manpower in Germany's faltering war effort had created an urgent need for slave labour and Auschwitz was an obvious source. The cattle trucks which had taken her away from her home in Sarospatak now became Gabriella's lifeline. What were the discomfort and deprivations of the box cars compared with the prospect of the gas chambers and their evil chimneys? Gabriella felt born again when she and Julia were herded into the packed car and felt the train pull away from the station. They didn't care where they were headed as long as it was away.

They were taken back west, to a camp at Urderon near Dresden, and put to work in a former textile plant turned munitions factory. They laboured twelve hours a day and slept whenever they could to try and preserve their strength. But the thin soups they were given to sustain them gradually became more watery and some days as many as three prisoners had to share one bowl. Bread kept them alive but there was never enough. Gabriella and Julia had escaped Auschwitz but they could not escape starvation. Every day they grew progressively weaker. Every day more prisoners died.

They worked alongside local people who asked them what they'd done wrong to be treated so badly and were appalled by the answer. The locals also battled rationing and food shortages but they were not immune to the suffering of the prisoners. Occasionally and surreptitiously they shared the little food they had. Sometimes it was bread and sometimes vegetables, meagre offerings received with overwhelming gratitude. Gabriella was once slipped a generous slice of potato cake which she shared with Julia later that night. There was fat in it, salt and a hint of cheese. One in five of their fellow prisoners had died since Auschwitz, men as well as women, but they were both still alive and sharing a piece of potato cake. They ate over a blanket so they would not lose a precious crumb of their life-giving gift. Both girls wept.

Late in March, with the Russians pressing from the east and the Allies advancing through Belgium and Holland, the prisoners were told they were to be moved. A rumour immediately swept through the camp that they were to be returned to Auschwitz and that this time, in their weakened condition, there would be no second chance.

Optimism had blossomed with every Allied bomber that flew overhead and with every new tale of German defeats. The local women admitted the war was almost over and that they were praying the Americans would reach them before the Russians. Liberation had seemed a matter of mere days away. Now, with salvation knocking on the door, they were to be cheated. The spectre of Auschwitz cast a blanket of fear over the entire camp.

It was a pleasant spring day when the walking scarecrows made their way to the station and the inevitable box cars. None of the guards yelled at them for straggling, no one got beaten. When Gabriella could drag her eyes up from the ground she noticed how much older the guards had become, how nervous and apprehensive. The Germans had always been so arrogant, so unwavering in their resolve. The change was monumental. She caught the eye of one of the guards.

'Where are we being taken?' she called out.

In the weeks and months past she never would have dared address a guard. She heard a sharp intake of breath from Julia. Heads lifted, curious to hear if there would be an answer and what it might be.

'Buchenwald, I think,' said the guard hesitantly. 'Yes, Buchenwald.'

'Thank you,' said Gabriella.

A murmur swept along the line of prisoners. Buchenwald not Auschwitz! Relief was palpable. But, as Gabriella soon learned from other prisoners, Buchenwald was also a concentration camp and they had no reason to expect conditions would be any better there.

That night, while their train sat in a siding, the railway lines ahead of them were destroyed by bombing. They remained there, locked in their box cars, throughout the following day and night without food. When the train finally began moving once more it did so at a snail's pace, finally diverting south. Towards evening the train halted at a siding near a village. The prisoners were unloaded and escorted to an abandoned work camp. There was no food and the beds had been stripped of bedding.

The prisoners were starving. Many, including Julia, were too weak to rise from the beds once they'd settled on them. They lay down as though to die. Some women pleaded with the guards to let them forage in the adjacent fields to see what they could find. The guards agreed and allowed the prisoners to take turns scouring the land in small groups. All they found were turnips which were pooled and distributed. With no cooking facilities, they ate the turnips raw. The guards took the same share as the prisoners.

Sometime during the night the train pulled away empty. For two more days, the prisoners took turns foraging. Their guards demanded pots and fuel from the villagers so they could make soup with the scant pickings the prisoners managed to find. It was barely enough. On the third day, the guards informed them that they'd been ordered to march on to Theresienstadt, a journey of some thirty kilometres. For the exhausted and starved prisoners it might just as well have been three hundred. Gabriella recalled her last arrival at Theresienstadt when she'd been showered, given clean clothes to wear and two meals of bread and soup. At the time she'd thought such treatment was normal; now she appreciated what a luxury it had been. This time there would be no showers, no clean clothes, and she would be lucky if there was even a bowl of soup to share.

Some men fashioned stretchers from bed boards and frames to carry the prisoners who could no longer walk. It amazed Gabriella that, even in the midst of the nightmare, some people still had the decency and strength to think of others.

She didn't volunteer for a turn carrying a stretcher. Her diminishing reserves of strength had already been claimed by Julia who needed help even to stand and Gabriella's steadying hand to walk. Julia wasn't sick, merely exhausted and near starved to death. Her body had shrunk away to almost nothing as it metabolised the last of her muscle and flesh in its bid to keep going.

That evening they were directed by locals to another lager, an abandoned work camp just north of Theresienstadt. They no longer drew comfort from the rumble of artillery away in the east, or the flashes that lit up the night sky. There was no comfort either in the American planes that flew over by day and waggled their wings to let them know that help and rescue were on the way. There was only hunger, exhaustion and death.

Gabriella volunteered to help a group forage for food but the fields had been well picked over by the locals. The prisoners were given a thin slice of raw turnip each. Gabriella gave hers to Julia. That night she read *Peter Pan and Wendy* to her. The story was unimportant because they both knew it by heart. The book had become their talisman, the embodiment of their desperation to survive. The words and pictures were a reminder of life beyond the camps, something beautiful to cherish, something to live for. Julia smiled, but even smiling seemed to sap the little strength she had left.

When Gabriella awoke the following morning, the April sun was already up and beaming through their barred window. Women stood around in groups talking softly. She rose to visit the latrine and discovered the guards had gone in the night and left the main gate open. Even as she watched she saw some men slip out and away in their striped prison clothes. When she returned to her barrack she found her companions discussing what to do. They were split in their opinions. Most wanted to remain in the camp and conserve their energy until liberated, but a few argued that they would be better off spreading out over the countryside. Who was to say that the SS would not come back, or that they wouldn't be blown up by a retreating army unit? Who was to say they wouldn't starve to death anyway before help arrived? Gabriella returned to the doorway and watched as a steady trickle of men and women slipped out through the gate. She made up her mind.

She took Julia's hand and helped her to her feet. 'Come on,' she said. 'We're going home.'

Julia smiled and a single tear ran down her cheek. The truth was, she was in no state to go anywhere. Nevertheless, they walked out of the lager, Gabriella's arm around Julia, holding her so that she didn't fall. Stepping out into freedom seemed so easy, such an insignificant act after all they had gone through.

'We are free, Julia,' said Gabriella. 'Now you must be strong.'

Julia giggled and squeezed Gabriella's hand.

From time to time on the road they passed German farmers and villagers who could not meet their eye. At midday, Gabriella boldly walked up to the door of a farmhouse, knocked and asked the old woman who answered for food. They were given a piece of dry bread slightly bigger than their combined daily ration at the work camp and some blackcurrants that would have struggled to fill a dessertspoon twice. The old woman closed the door without a word. Gabriella half carried Julia over to a barn and sat her down on a pile of straw. The bread was dry and hard to swallow but the currants were an unexpected treasure; just the taste of them promised life, strength, health. The girls ate them one by one, using them to flavour the bread, savouring every moment. Julia could hardly stop giggling. After their precious meal she went to sleep in Gabriella's arms. Later, when Gabriella awoke, she discovered that Julia's exhausted heart had stopped beating.

* * *

'It was my birthday,' said Gabriella softly.

'I beg your pardon?' said Ramon.

'It was my birthday. April 14, 1945. It was the day I turned sixteen.'

'Dear God,' said Lucio, visibly moved. 'What did you do?'

'Later,' said Ramon. 'I can hear Gancio with our coffee.'

'No, it's okay,' said Gabriella, 'I don't mind. Milos has been doing all the talking not me.' She leaned back so Gancio could place her coffee and lemon liqueur in front of her. She waited till everyone had been served. 'You ask what I did? Can you begin to imagine how devastated I felt? Sometimes I think it was my worst moment of the whole war. I'd lost my father and I didn't know whether my mother, my brother or my sister were still alive. I'd been dragged from my home in a crowded cattle truck and left alone on the station at Krakow. I had faced selection, been selected, watched as people were marched away to the gas chambers and ovens. I'd seen the chimneys. But it all came together at that moment, my worst moment, when my sweet, brave Julia died.

'I sat there crying with her cradled in my arms until the farmer came in from the fields. He lifted me up and carried me back to the house where the old woman had given us the bread and currants. He was an old man but I was just skin and bone and misery. I weighed nothing. They gave me soup and bread and promised to help me bury Julia. And they did. That evening I watched as the farmer dug a hole and he buried her. They wrapped her in an old blanket and put a cross on her grave. Imagine that. A cross for a Jew! They asked me her name so they could write it on the cross but ... but ...' Gabriella closed her eyes and bowed her head. Her shoulders shook gently as she began to sob.

'That's enough, Gabi,' said Milos gently. 'That's enough.'

'No,' she said fiercely. She raised her head and gazed

defiantly around the table. 'It is good for me to talk. I'm sorry if I have embarrassed you but it is not easy. I couldn't remember her name, you see. I couldn't remember her family name. We had become sisters and I couldn't remember her name. I told them "Julia" and her number. That's what they painted on the cross. Julia, and the number tattooed on her arm.'

For a moment none of the friends said anything. They sipped their coffee and grappa and considered the story to date, giving Gabriella the opportunity to dab her eyes with a tissue and regain her composure.

'May I see it?' said Ramon eventually.

'See what?' asked Milos.

'The tattoo.'

'Of course,' said Gabriella. 'It is not something I am ashamed of. It is just a number, like a telephone number written in ballpoint.' She rolled up her left sleeve and extended her arm across the table. Ramon used his left hand to cradle hers while the fingers of his right hand explored the inside of her forearm. 'Just writing. Nothing to feel, no?'

'There is not one number but two,' said Ramon. 'One above the other?'

'You can feel that?' said Gabriella.

Ramon just smiled and patted her arm before letting go. In fact he could feel no tattoo and had merely speculated on there being two lines, drawing on a description given to him years earlier by another concentration camp survivor.

'Let me see,' said Lucio. 'I can't feel anything. How could he possibly know there were two lines?'

Gabriella laughed and reached for her coffee. 'He is guessing, he must be. I have lived and slept with this tattoo for over fifty years. I have run my fingers over it countless times every day. It's just like ballpoint, that's all. No one can feel ballpoint. You were just guessing, weren't you, Ramon? Admit it.'

'My dear Gabriella,' said Ramon, 'surely Milos has told you, I never admit to anything.'

'No? Then you are a lucky man, Ramon.' The last traces of a smile drained from Gabriella's face and the life went out of her voice.

'Gabi, there is no need,' said Milos.

'No need? Of course there is need! You are a lucky man, Ramon, and you may never know how lucky you are. I am not so lucky. I must admit to everything. Everything! Can you imagine that? My friend the doctor has been very patient over so many years and to him I must admit everything. He takes me through hell so that I can once again greet the sunlight. Not filtered sunlight, not reflected, but warm and golden as it was when I was a child. I did not imagine anyone could go through such pain and emerge alive. But I did. And the pain took the shadows and darkness away and I can look in the mirror and know who I am. I can listen to the eggs break. I can tell my story.'

'And will you?' said Ramon.

'No!' Milos exploded out of his chair.

'It's okay, Milos,' said Gabriella.

'He is deliberately trying to provoke you!'

'No, Milos, his question is fair. I claimed I could now tell my story and he asks if I will.'

'It's not your story,' insisted Milos. 'It is my story and mine to tell.' Milos was aware of other diners staring at him but ignored them.

'Is it such a bad thing to allow Gabriella to contribute?' said Ramon calmly. 'It is her story too and, by her own admission, she is capable of telling it.'

'For God's sake, Ramon! Why are you so insistent on interrupting my story? You call coffee breaks before I am ready. You end the day's storytelling at your convenience, not mine. You have undermined me since the very first day.'

'Milos, sit down and stop shouting.' Gabriella turned towards the kitchen and waved to get Gancio's attention. She waited until Milos had settled back in his chair. 'This is what we will do. We will have another cup of coffee while Milos collects his thoughts. Then he will complete his storytelling for the day. He has told you about his schedule, no?'

She handed her empty coffee cup to Gancio. 'What do you think, Neil?'

'What? Fine. I could certainly use another coffee.'

'You have been very quiet,' said Gabriella. 'Are you bored by our wallowing in our past? Are you weary of our baggage?'

'No, not at all.'

'No? Not bored by this public washing of our linen? If you are not bored, then describe to me how you feel. I'd like to know.'

'Describe ... ?'

'Yes,' said Gabriella. 'Excited, enthralled, moved, what? How do you feel?'

Ramon couldn't help smiling.

'Fascinated, I guess,' said Neil reluctantly. 'But in a kind of appalled way. It's hard to reconcile the fact that you are the person in Milos's story, that these things happened to you.'

'Oh, they happened.'

'I don't dispute that. If I'm quiet it's because you've given me a lot to think about. Please don't take my silence as lack of interest. Far from it.'

'Good,' said Gabriella. 'At last we have your interest.'

CHAPTER NINETEEN

Tibor was a man born for the times. All his young life had been but training for the opportunities he now faced. He thrived in the devastation and chaos of poor battered Budapest. The city had been split in two by the departing Germans who had dynamited all seven bridges over the Danube, isolating hilly residential Buda on the western bank from industrial, commercial Pest on the eastern side. Infrastructure had collapsed along with the bridges. The phone service was all but destroyed, there was no postal service and trains ran only with the Russians' permission. Nevertheless, Tibor wasted no time re-establishing his contacts in the railways which, despite the fighting and bombing, still functioned. He made the railways his priority because he understood the importance of a transport system that could move goods in volume. He knew how the railways worked, and how they could be made to work for him even with the Russians calling the shots.

The city was desperate for food. The fortunate were hungry and the less fortunate were starving. Tibor did a round of the bakeries and food-processing plants that had survived and were reasonably intact and ascertained their needs. He introduced himself as a supplier of whatever was wanted.

Though not yet eighteen, he was cocky and confident in a city populated by the defeated. He spread hope where there was only hopelessness. He promised a future at a time when few could see past the end of the day. He had friends among the Russians, friends in high places and friends in the railways. He negotiated deals and convinced people that the impossible was possible. He lied without shame but, ultimately, he delivered.

Carriages carrying relief supplies into Budapest were mysteriously detached and their contents delivered to his makeshift warehouses in Pest. In this way he secured flour, sugar and condensed milk for his bakers and food processors, coffee for the cafés that struggled to provide an oasis of civilisation amidst the ruins, lentils for the desperately hungry and, the greatest of all prizes, American cigarettes. His familiarity with the Russian troops and his increasing confidence with their language enabled him to travel to villages around Budapest. The farms that hadn't been burned or bombed out had all been plundered, first by the Germans and then by the occupying Russian forces who lived off the land. He offered to buy anything anyone was prepared to sell at a better price than they could get at market. He wanted all their chickens, eggs and vegetables, pigs if they had any and as much milk as they could provide. His contacts in the railways provided transportation. Everything came back to the railways.

Tibor's enterprises grew spectacularly but so too did his notoriety and his opposition. Every city has its criminals and standover men and Budapest was no exception. The crime bosses resented his intrusion into their territory and were jealous of his success. He was just a boy, they were men, and the boy was making the men look foolish. But if he was making a fool of them, he was also making a fool of himself.

In the full flood of his confidence and with an arrogance born of youth and inexperience, Tibor believed no deal was too big for him when the truth was plainly otherwise. He found it hard to recruit the hard men to stand guard over his warehouses and protect him from his competitors. He was simply too young, too inexperienced and too dangerous to be around. Unable to hire the men he needed, he hired those who were available to him. Inevitably they proved unequal to the task.

Unwilling to put his stolen goods entirely in the hands of the hired help, Tibor took to sleeping in his warehouses, choosing his night's shelter at random to keep his men honest and his enemies guessing. Inevitably, he was betrayed. He was awoken one night by the muzzle of a machine pistol pressed hard against his temple. Having opened his eyes he closed them again immediately, bracing himself for the explosion that would leave his brains and ambitions splattered over the bags of grain he'd been sleeping on. But even in the midst of his fear part of his brain still functioned, and it told him that if his assailants wanted him dead they wouldn't have bothered waking him up. He slowly reopened his eyes.

Somebody had turned on the main lights and he saw his two bodyguards pressed up against the wall, their faces smashed and bloody. Four men stood idly by with cocked weapons. There were blood stains on the stocks. He looked away from them and into the eyes of the man holding the gun to his head.

'Who are you?' he said.

'Someone who wants to kill you.' The assailant's eyes were hard and humourless. 'But someone wants to talk to you first. Get some clothes on.'

Tibor's hands were bound behind his back, he was blindfolded and bundled into the back seat of an old Mercedes. Throughout the ten-minute journey the only comfort he could draw on came from the fact that somebody wanted to talk to him. However much trouble he was in, at least he'd have a chance of talking his way out of it.

Tibor was aware of the car slowing then turning sharply before heavy doors banged closed behind them. Men dragged him from the car and marched him up two flights of stairs where he was pushed down onto a chair and his bindings adjusted to secure him to the backrest. One of the men wrenched the blindfold from his head.

Tibor recoiled instinctively from the blinding light that shone directly into his face. Through the glare he gradually made out the shapes of men standing in a semi-circle in front of him. One man started laughing quietly and others joined in.

'So this is the little shit who thinks he can walk into our territory and steal our business.'

Tibor turned towards the voice, still dazzled by the light.

'Did he give you any trouble?'

'My girlfriend could have brought him in.'

'Turn the lamp away. Let him see me.'

The moment the lamp was turned away, Tibor focused his attention on the floor in front of him, blinking rapidly to dull the bright spots that seemed burned into his retinas. Gradually his sight began to clear but he remained blinking and staring at the floor. No matter how dire the circumstances, Tibor understood the necessity of making strong eye contact. Only when his vision was fully restored did he look up and take stock of his tormentors. There were five of them. An older man stood in the middle and Tibor was momentarily surprised by his age. He had to be at least seventy but he was the hardest-looking seventy year old Tibor had ever seen. Age had given him a stoop but made him no less imposing. One look into his eyes and Tibor knew exactly who called the shots.

'You are a lucky boy, Tibor Heyman,' said the old man. 'My competitors want you dead for your arrogance. Perhaps they have been blinded by your lack of respect. They would be happy to piss on your corpse. But me, I see more value in keeping you alive. It was only a matter of time before one of us got to you. You should be grateful I got to you first.'

Tibor nodded slightly, not trusting himself to speak and lacking sufficient information to know what attitude to adopt. He kept silent and slowly reined in his fear.

'I am Imre Vilagosi. You have heard of me?'

The name sent a shiver down his spine. Of course he'd heard of him. Vilagosi was not the biggest but still one of Budapest's most powerful gang bosses.

'This is Pal Szarbo,' Vilagosi said glancing at the man beside him who had held the machine pistol to Tibor's head. 'He is my lieutenant, my second in command.'

Again Tibor nodded to acknowledge the introduction.

'Now, Tibor Heyman, demonstrate to all of us here that I did the right thing by keeping you alive. Tell us about the railways.'

'I have contacts,' said Tibor quietly. 'I command a loyalty once given to my father, Jozsef Heyman.'

'Jozsef Heyman is your father?'

Tibor noted the surprise and delight in Vilagosi's voice, indeed, had expected it. He moved immediately to capitalise on the moment.

'I caught your attention by stealing a carriage here and there. You think that is impressive. I think it is child's play. Give me your backing and I will steal entire trains.'

'Entire trains?'

Tibor smiled. His instincts told him the dynamics had shifted. They were intrigued. 'Grain, coal, cement, livestock. Take your pick. I have the contacts to seize trains but lack the backing and the means to warehouse and distribute. Our assets complement each other.'

'He compares himself with you?' Pal Szarbo moved quickly towards Tibor and slapped his face hard. 'You want me to teach the arrogant little shit some manners?'

'In good time,' said Vilagosi. He waved Pal Szarbo away and turned his attention back to Tibor. 'What are you proposing?'

'A partnership.' Tibor's face stung as though it had been burned but he gave no indication. Blood trickled from his nose.

'A partnership!' cut in Pal Szarbo. 'For Christ's sake! Listen to him. A minute ago we were discussing whether or not to let him live!' He thumped his fist into his hand in frustration.

'What is to stop us extracting the names of your contacts?' said Vilagosi. His voice had become colder and more sinister. 'It wouldn't be difficult. Harder men than you have been persuaded to give up their mothers.'

'What good would the names do you? You can bribe and threaten as many men as you like but that won't give you a network. A network exists because it wants to exist. It is mutual cooperation given willingly for a common cause. In this instance, loyalty to my father. Of course there are pay-offs but loyalty and trust is what binds the network. That is not something I can give to you or something you can take from me.'

Vilagosi stared at him for fully a minute as he digested what Tibor had said. 'Untie him. Let him rest now. We will discuss the terms of our partnership over breakfast.'

Tibor entered a world where loyalty and betrayal often wore the same familiar face. Informers were everywhere and no one could be trusted. Vilagosi and Pal Szarbo wasted no time in teaching their new partner the disciplines of their dangerous trade. There was always someone prepared to sell them out to their opposition, to the Russians, the gendarmes or the secret police. But for the corruptibility of the Russians and the enforcement agencies, none of the gangs would have been able to operate.

Vilagosi invested heavily in his survival by buying officials, informers and bodyguards. He was ruthless with anyone he suspected of betraying him or undermining his activities. In the chaos of occupied Budapest violence and death were commonplace. There were revenge killings as Arrow Cross assassins and thugs were tracked down and summarily dealt with. There were the excesses of the occupying army, with the

Russians looting everything they could lay their hands on and killing anyone who objected. This was the world in which Vilagosi and now Tibor went about their business. Rival gangs fought over the spoils and battled for supremacy. When he'd arrived in Budapest Tibor had set out to become a middleman, a provider of the unobtainable, not a criminal who sanctioned killings and beatings. Inevitably he became both.

As the realities of his new life became apparent to Tibor, he pushed his brother further and further away. Milos was ordered to remain in the background and had little knowledge of the violent side of Tibor's activities. Violence, according to Tibor, was entirely the province of their opposition, which was why he kept Milos on the move, never allowing him to sleep more than two or three nights in the same place. At the beginning, Milos had acted as Tibor's book-keeper, keeping tabs on acquisitions, storage and sales. He also became his paymaster, keeping records of bribes, kickbacks, protection money and wages, and converted increasingly worthless cash into gold and tradable commodities. When his brother teamed up with Vilagosi, Milos became Tibor's liability.

Vilagosi offered to provide a job for Milos in one of his legitimate enterprises, but Tibor wanted Milos's separation from the organisation to be absolute. More than that, he wanted to shield all knowledge of his brother's existence. If the opposition or the secret police wanted to get at him, all they would have to do was kidnap Milos. At the same time, Tibor wanted Milos nearby so he could keep an eye on him. But Tibor's agenda took no consideration of Milos's and in the end it was Milos who solved the impasse.

Milos could never contact Tibor directly. If he needed to talk to his brother he rang a phone number, one of the few still operating, and left a message. In the second week in May, with Germany's surrender official, Milos rang the number. The brothers met for lunch in an apartment on Ferenciek Street near the destroyed Elizabeth Bridge. The apartment had once been grand but had since been abandoned and looted. It was sparsely furnished with a table and chairs that didn't match, two armchairs and a sofa with a bullet hole through the back, and heavy drapes tacked over the windows. Milos imagined the bedrooms would look much the same. The one cheery note came from a vase filled with madonna lilies on the mantelpiece above the fireplace. Tibor arrived late with his personal bodyguards in tow, wearing a heavy coat despite the warm spring weather. The coat concealed an American airman's flak jacket.

'Some of our opposition are unhappy,' Tibor said wryly. 'One of their shipments of stolen American aid somehow went astray.' He unstrapped the flak jacket and threw it onto one of the armchairs. 'Tinned ham, powdered milk, powdered eggs, flour, condensed milk, cans of peas, beans, chocolate bars and cigarettes. People put too much faith in the railways.'

He laughed but Milos found little to laugh about. He hadn't seen his brother for over a month and in that time Tibor seemed to have aged two years. The shadows beneath his eyes also suggested that sleep had eluded him.

'I take it the goods are in a warehouse?' said Milos.

'Vilagosi's warehouse,' said Tibor guardedly.

'And what am I supposed to do now that you have new friends?' said Milos. 'Keeping tabs on stock used to be my responsibility.'

'We'll find something for you,' said Tibor. 'Ahh ... just what I need.' He leaned forward to sniff the bowl of *halaszle*, a spicy paprika fish soup, that a heavyset woman placed on the table with a basket of freshly baked bread. 'I tell you, Milos, nobody in all of Hungary will eat better than us today.'

Tibor ladled soup into Milos's bowl and then into his own. 'Smell that and think of all the months on the run. This one dish makes it all worthwhile.'

'Is the flak jacket necessary?' said Milos.

'For the moment,' said Tibor. 'Now eat.'

They ate in silence and Milos had to agree: the *halaszle* was superb and the bread soft and delicious; nobody in Hungary would eat better than them. They finished the soup and even wiped the serving bowl clean with their bread. Although they now had plenty, the boys still could not allow any food to go to waste.

'It's time to honour your promise,' said Milos.

'What promise was that?' Tibor chewed absently on a crust.

'The Germans have surrendered. All the camps have been liberated. It's time to go home. We owe it to Dad and Gabriella.'

Tibor stopped chewing and stared at his brother. 'Don't think so,' he said.

'What do you mean?'

'Little brother, what do you think is happening here? What do you think I do?'

'I know what you do.'

'Any day now the Russians are going to crack down on us. Law and order will be imposed. Some of our opposition have been reckless, some have left themselves exposed. Some will be shot, some will go to prison. We are heading into difficult times but whoever prevails will emerge stronger. Everything I have worked for comes down to this moment. If I leave Budapest now I'm finished.'

'You have a promise to keep,' said Milos doggedly. 'I have honoured my part of the deal, now you must honour yours.'

'*Palacsinta*!' said Tibor delightedly. He looked admiringly at the plate of pancakes topped with American chocolate and nuts that the woman placed on the table. There was also a little jug of cream. 'Did you meet Eva? Her husband survived the war only to be caught, tortured and finally hanged by the Arrow Cross one week before the Russians reached Budapest. Hanged right here on the Elizabeth Bridge. Before the war they ran a little restaurant in Pest.'

'I introduced myself,' said Milos.

'If I was to leave now, Eva would be thrown back onto the streets with no one to look after her. You want that?'

'But it's okay if Dad or Gabi arrives home with no one to look after them?'

Tibor put down his fork in exasperation. 'You go,' he said abruptly. 'You keep your promise. Now that I think about it, that is the best course of action. You know how to contact me if either of them return.'

'I thought you wanted to marry Gabi.'

'First she has to have survived, which I doubt. You've heard the stories.' Tibor smiled suddenly, mockingly, and stabbed at another piece of pancake. 'You go and I'll stay. If she's still alive I give you my permission and the opportunity to win her over. But know this, little brother, and never doubt it,' the smile left Tibor's face, 'if Gabi is alive she is mine. One day I will come back to claim her.'

After the farmer had buried Julia he picked Gabriella up and carried her back inside. His wife heated a tub of hot water and bathed her and made up a bed for her to sleep in. They didn't ask any questions because they already knew the answers and were shamed by them. In the morning they gave her clean clothes, which were too big but far better than her threadbare camp clothes. They also gave her a cup of coffee with milk and sugar for breakfast and a piece of heavy rye bread with a sliver of cheese. Gabriella ate the thin piece of cheese immediately but kept the bread to take back to the camp. At the door, the old lady put her arms around Gabriella, hugged her and began weeping softly. Gabriella was still in the thrall of bereavement and too much of a zombie to respond.

Gabriella walked back into the camp, lost for an alternative. Her sense of volition had died with Julia. She and Julia had lived together and survived together, shared food and supported each other. They'd faced death together, prayed for liberation together and had been as close as any two people can be, two halves of a single entity forged by trial, need and affection. Gabriella sat down on her bunk but it could as easily have been the brink of the abyss. She was aware of other prisoners looking at her, wondering, guessing. Most of the women had stayed in the barrack and there were many other Julias lying and dying on their bunks. She gave the piece of bread she'd saved to a helpless young girl on the bed next to her. It was the sort of thing she'd always done for Julia and now she did it on behalf of Julia. Though the faces around her were familiar, Gabriella had not felt so alone since she'd been abandoned on the platform at Krakow.

The next day the Russians arrived. Those who could raced out to greet them as conquering heroes, but, as heroes went, they were a sorry bunch. These were no knights in shining armour but a raggle-taggle formation of exhausted men with strange, frightening faces and an incomprehensible language. Their lack of surprise or curiosity showed that this wasn't the first labour camp they'd liberated. They gave food to the prisoners, which they could ill-afford to do, and through sign language indicated that they should remain where they were. The Russians were generous and sympathetic even though their needs were almost as great and they were worn out. Prisoners who could still walk were given a boiled potato each and a piece of flat stale bread. The bedridden were given two potatoes.

Life needs incentive to persist and Gabriella had to push herself beyond her loss to find a reason to keep going. What she did next made no sense, but staying in the lager to slowly starve to death didn't make much sense either. Gabriella desperately needed comfort of the kind which could only come from one source. With the food in the pocket of her new clothes, she set off once more to walk home. To walk seven hundred kilometres across Czechoslovakia and Hungary on one potato and a piece of flat bread.

That first day Gabriella managed to walk for two hours before her strength gave out. She stopped, rested and ate her potato. Afterwards she walked for another two hours before stopping and eating her piece of bread. She walked for one more hour before accepting she could walk no further that day. She had covered maybe ten of her seven hundred kilometres and already all her food was gone. She lay down on a bed of pink, white and red blossoms beneath some cherry trees in an orchard near a farmhouse and drifted away into weary sleep.

A gunshot awoke her. She lay trembling in the dark, too terrified to move. There were screams coming from the farmhouse and men shouting in Russian and German. A woman screamed nearby, not from the house but from the other side of the orchard. Men laughed at the poor pleading woman and Gabriella didn't need to speak Russian to realise they were drunk. For hours people ran and stumbled through the orchard in drunken bawdy pursuit but none stumbled over her. Gabriella realised the terror was over when the only sound she could hear was women sobbing.

As soon as the sun rose she ran away, too scared to go to the farmhouse to ask for food. She found three mushrooms at the base of an oak, as if placed there by Mabel Lucie Attwell. Gabriella grabbed them and washed them in a nearby stream, intending to eat one and keep the remaining two for later. She scoffed the first one, barely tasting it, but it did little to ease the craving in her belly. She ate the others and washed them down with water scooped up in her hands. It still wasn't enough and she wasted precious energy wandering around the fields looking for more. Finally she gave up looking and struck out east, bitterly regretting the bread she'd given away to the sick girl in the lager. As she walked on the cravings in her body made her regret the pieces of turnip she'd given to Julia and even the piece of potato cake she had shared with her. What had her generosity achieved? Nothing. Julia was dead and Gabriella's generosity had simply made her hungry.

Gabriella saw plenty of Russians as the day passed but, despite the incident at the farmhouse, they gave her no reason to fear them. They looked frightening and alien when they passed by in their convoys but didn't harm her. Before long she took no notice of them. They were just noise and dust, the backdrop of a war drawing to a close, and she couldn't relate these soldiers to whatever had happened at the farmhouse. She walked and rested, walked and rested, dazed and zombie-like while the war rolled on past, ignoring her. But she could not ignore her weakness or hunger. Every time she sat down to rest it was harder to get up. All she could think of were food and rest. So when she saw a small group of Russians bivouacked by the side of the road that evening, she had no hesitation in walking up to them.

'Please,' she said.

It occurred to her that she didn't know how to beg for food or how to ask for their protection and to share their fire. She just stood before them helplessly, holding her hands out, saying, 'please'. The events of the previous night should have made her fear them but she was starving and they had food. She was cold and they had a fire. She was sixteen years old but starvation and the work camps had left her with the body of an eleven year old. She was a dirty, pathetic little bag of bones in someone else's clothes that were far too big. It did not occur to her that the Russians could want anything from her. It didn't occur to her that she had anything to give. Although she didn't know a word of Russian, and Magyarul was clearly incomprehensible to them, she managed to communicate her need.

'Sit!' they said and laughed. They made room for her.

It was Gabriella's good fortune that they were just preparing to eat. The Russians had made a stew using a hare they'd shot, sausage they'd stolen, and potatoes, turnips and paprika they'd gathered along the way. They'd boiled everything together in a pot balanced on stones over their fire.

Gabriella watched disbelievingly as they shared out their dinner, putting two large spoonfuls onto every plate, taking care to make sure everybody got a fair portion of meat and vegetables. The portions were so large that Gabriella despaired of there being anything left in the pot for her, and was stunned when they handed her one of the plates. Two spoonfuls of meat with vegetables, plus a piece of dried bread to eat it with.

'Thank you,' she said, so overcome by their generosity that her voice was barely audible. She started to cry.

One of the soldiers put his arm around her and gave her a reassuring hug. He said something in Russian which made the other soldiers laugh. But Gabriella ignored them and wiped her eyes on her sleeve. There was meat on her plate when she couldn't remember the last time she'd tasted meat and the odours were irresistible. A distrust bred in the camps seized her. She scooped up the biggest piece of meat with her bread and stuffed it in her mouth, chewing furiously in case the Russians changed their minds and demanded the food back. Gabriella could not get that meal inside her fast enough. The Russians watched her eat, amused by her hunger, and gave her water to drink. They also offered her some foul-smelling spirits but Gabriella turned her head away from the fumes in disgust. They cursed when they drank the spirits but they didn't spit it out. Gabriella ignored them. She had food with meat in it, bread and water, and nothing else mattered.

Tiredness set in the instant she'd scraped her plate clean and there was nothing left, not even the smell of what had been upon it. With her belly full and in the warmth of the fire she was overwhelmed by both weariness and gratitude and sleepy in the way small children get. When a soldier put his arm around her she snuggled against him, like a daughter secure in the familiar arms of her father. If anyone had asked her at that moment how she felt, she would have replied, 'Safe. Safe and happy.' The Russians had given her a real meal with meat in it and she basked in the unfamiliar sensation of having a full belly. Now all she wanted from the soldiers was the warmth of their fire and rest. She believed she was under the protection of the liberating army and safe. She was Wendy in a land of fantasy but the fantasy existed only inside her head.

Gabriella had experienced no difficulty communicating her need, now the Russians had no difficulty communicating theirs. There were seven of them and all seven raped her, one after the other. Gabriella didn't resist. She just lay still and let them do it, trying her hardest to think of the food they had given her and how it would sustain her, and trying not to cry from the pain and her feelings of betrayal. The soldiers weren't rough and they didn't hurt her deliberately but neither could they be accused of being considerate. They just used her to fulfil their needs in what they considered fair exchange. But they did hurt her. Worse, all the pushing and jiggling made her want to throw up and that was something she fought with all her might. To give up her wonderful dinner, and to have suffered for nothing, was unthinkable.

Once they'd finished with her, Gabriella fell asleep where she lay. She slept through the night and no one so much as touched her again. When she awoke the soldiers were already packed and ready to move on. They were kindly once more and gave her coffee, more bread and a wine bottle filled with water. One kissed her on the cheek. Although she couldn't understand his language, she believed he'd wished her luck. She watched them walk away down the road before struggling to her feet. The food had given her strength but the Russians had left her sore. Anyone who caught a glimpse of her walking that day would have known immediately what had happened.

Without realising it, at some point during that day Gabriella crossed the border into Czechoslovakia. She'd learned her lesson and from then on made sure that she spent every night in a town or village. She knocked on doors until she found someone who would take her in. The Czechs and

Slovaks had fought alongside the Germans yet, for the most part, Gabriella was met with kindness and compassion. The Czechs took her in, fed her and washed her. These acts of kindness were repeated across Czechoslovakia as she made her way down towards Austria and the border with Hungary. Some of the women wept and held her and tried to make her feel human again. They were kind people, good people. Gabriella couldn't help wondering where they'd all been hiding during the war.

After five weeks on the road, Gabriella was picked up by a refugee agency and put on a train heading south-east to Brno. The train was full of haunted people just like her, all on the same desperate mission to go home and see how much of their lives remained. Nobody seemed to care about fares, or maybe the relief agencies paid them. An army of skeletons swept across the continent in every direction. Wherever deportee met deportee the litany was repeated. 'Where were you? Did you know my wife, husband, brother, sister, daughter, son?' There were too many negative answers, too many missing people, to ignore the implications. Still people asked. 'Where were you, where were you, where were you?'

Workers from the relief agencies met the refugees at every stop and provided bread and soup. There were so many hungry people that they formed into three or four queues. Standing in line on the platform at Brno, Gabriella witnessed a miracle. A man left his place in line and staggered towards the next queue. Gabriella couldn't help watching because his action was so unusual: people never left their place in line in case the food ran out. But this man did, his arms outstretched, his disbelieving eyes unnaturally wide.

'Agnes?' he said. 'Agnes?'

A woman turned at the sound of her name and the familiarity of the voice. She saw the man and nearly collapsed. People around her had to hold her up.

'Thomas?' she said. 'Thomas?'

The two wrecks teetered towards one another then fell crying into each other's arms. They collapsed to their knees between the two queues, touching, not believing their good fortune, while everyone looked on. Against all odds, a husband had found his wife and a wife had found her husband. Nobody said a word. The sobbing and endearments rose above the shuffle of feet in queues, above the scrape of plates and the huffing of the engine. Still nobody spoke. The miracle was too overwhelming. It meant there was hope for the rest of them. There was still hope.

Gabriella closed her eyes and imagined her mother and Elizabeth waiting for her on the platform at Sarospatak.

The relief agencies put her on a train to Vienna and then another to Budapest. The carriage was crowded and hot but everyone had a seat and nobody complained. All the travelling had taken its toll on Gabriella's reserves and time and time again she awoke to find herself leaning against the woman sitting next to her. Suddenly someone called out that they had crossed the border into Hungary. Gabriella had dreamed of this moment and in her imaginings it was always momentous. But the reality had a numbing effect on her and her fellow travellers. It was cause not so much for celebration as apprehension. When they got home, what would they find?

From her aisle seat Gabriella couldn't see much through the windows, but others could and cried out the names of stations as they passed by, each one a friendly reassuring sound and another step closer to home. Refugees wept to be back among their own people where their language didn't occasion scorn. Somebody started to sing the Himnusz, Hungary's doleful national anthem, and the entire carriage including Gabriella joined in. In her heart she was still Hungarian, whether her troubled country wanted her or not. They were all Hungarians, weeping now for joy at being returned to their homeland. Hungarians first, Jews and gypsies second. While everyone was singing Gabriella looked around and understood what it was they were really weeping for. They were weeping for what had been lost.

Gabriella slowly came to the realisation that when she'd left the prison camp months earlier and begun walking home, she was heading for a place that didn't exist any more, except in her memory. She'd been walking back to 1940, when she still had a father and mother, brother and sister, and a wonderful home in Tokaj Street. All about her, people were singing and weeping and asking themselves the same question: 'What do I have now?'

What do I have now? she asked herself. No father, probably no mother, maybe a sister and, by some miracle, maybe a brother. Did she have a home? If she did, there would be no warmth in it, no sunlight, no beef goulash on the stove, no sizzling pork chops, no roast chicken thighs, nothing. Unless she did still have a mother, brother or sister and one of them had miraculously beaten her home. But in her heart she knew Elizabeth had been too sick to escape the gas. She had been to Auschwitz, had seen the selections, how few were called out of line, had seen the chimneys smoking all day and all night. Why would the Germans keep alive a sick girl with diarrhoea when there were others who were healthy? She knew there was little hope for Balazs too. There had been little hope even before the Germans had come and taken her away. In the space of one song Gabriella had asked herself what she had and found the answer. Nothing. She had nothing. She'd survived for nothing. That was why she cried now, why they all cried.

When the train pulled into Budapest, Gabriella had to be carried off. The realisation that her survival had served no purpose had drained her of the last of her energy and robbed her of the will to go on. She spent two weeks in a hostel for homecoming refugees, where she was kept fed and warm and looked after by compassionate Hungarians who weren't Jews and who worked hard. They were the good Hungarians whom no one could find during the war, and there were many of them. They worked off their shame by comforting, nursing and consoling Gabriella, but nothing they did could bridge the chasm of her loss. Gabriella retreated into a shell they could not crack. But she was just one lost soul among thousands and compassion had to be shared among many. When she was strong enough they put the little zombie back on the train, this time to Sarospatak.

Sarospatak. Gabriella no longer knew why she was returning there, only that it was journey's end. Sarospatak was her finishing line, the place where her struggles would be over. It was a target, an objective. She believed that if she made it home to Sarospatak then she would have survived and therefore would be allowed to die. The train emptied the further east she travelled. By the time they reached Miskolc there were just six refugees remaining in the once crowded carriage. Six husks, drained of hope and tears. When the train finally pulled into Sarospatak station, Gabriella was reluctant to get off. From the moment she'd been taken from her home, her life had been dedicated to returning and now she had returned. There was nothing left for her, neither purpose nor incentive. She was the only person in her carriage to disembark. Those remaining went on to Satoraljaujhely.

Once again Gabriella stood alone on a railway platform, this time a stranger in her own town. She sat down on the ground, collapsed really, lacking the strength or will to take one step further. People walked around her to board the train or to reach the exit. She was the piece of dog shit on the footpath that everyone avoided. She sat there with her tattered bag, mumbling incoherently. On the handle was a label with her name and destination.

Gabriella's presence was an embarrassment and an indictment. A railwayman came and tried to lift her to her feet but she resisted and instead lay down with her head on the platform. He gave up. Gabriella closed her eyes, deciding that now would be a good time to die. She had crossed her finishing line, she had beaten Eichmann, the SS, the Arrow Cross and Auschwitz. The little Jewish bag of bones had won. She drifted off to sleep or death, not caring which.

Milos waited by the exit to the station where it was easy to scan the faces of the arrivals. He did this every day a train was due from the west. Each train brought new disappointment and with each disappointment he became more convinced that his brother was right. He was wasting his time. Every morning and afternoon he walked to the town hall to check the growing lists of those who had perished in the concentration camps. Each time he feared finding his father's or Gabriella's name written there, was relieved not to find them but dismayed to see so many others, many of them familiar. He could not shake the increasing feeling of dread that each passing day brought him closer to the moment when he would see written there the two names he didn't want to read.

Today he waited outside the station with little hope or expectation. Occasionally a Sarospatak Jew had returned but there had been so few. He was about to leave when he noticed Geza Apro coming towards him. Sometimes the stationmaster invited him in for a coffee, a treat Milos never refused.

'You might be able to help me,' said Geza. 'There's this girl off the train, a returning Jew. She's too small to be the one you're looking for. Your Gabriella would be sixteen, right?'

'Same age as me,' said Milos.

'Could you have a word with her anyway? She's lying down on the platform and refuses to move. I don't want to be unsympathetic but she can't stay there.'

'I'll speak to her.'

'Thanks. I'll put the coffee on.'

Milos went onto the platform wondering who the girl could be, whether he would know her. At first glance she appeared to be just a bundle of rags. Any faint hope that the girl might be Gabriella vanished. The figure was just too small. He walked towards her, trying to think what he could say that would make the girl want to get to her feet. And if she did, where would he take her, what would he do with her?

As he drew closer he noticed she had a bag and that a tattered book was protruding from it. The girl was turned away from him so he couldn't see her face. It occurred to him that the book must be very precious to her since she'd clung to it throughout all the appalling things that must have happened to her. Perhaps talking about the book might be a way of getting through to her.

He was ten paces away when a cold shiver ran through his body, as sudden and sharp as an electric current. He thought he recognised the book's cover, battered and worn as it was. Surely there couldn't be two of them? Surely not. Five paces closer and he was certain. He didn't have to read the title or the author's name. The important thing was that he knew whose name was inside the book and who had written the sentiments preceding it.

He knew what the bundle of rags contained. His heart began pounding. It had to be her, had to be, yet she was so tiny.

'Gabi?' he said tentatively. He placed his hand on her shoulder. 'Gabi?'

Gabriella was on the brink of unconsciousness when she heard a voice say her name. She thought it was an angel calling to her, that she'd died and the sweet voice was calling her to heaven. Suddenly she realised she recognised the voice of the angel. Her fogged mind struggled to grasp the significance. The angel called her name again, so beautiful to hear, and asked her to open her eyes. So she opened her eyes, saw her angel and heard her voice say his name.

'Milos?'

'Yes, Gabi. It's me, Milos.'

He gently stroked her forehead, almost fearful in case she shattered at his touch. Her once beautiful hair was thin and patchy, no more than two centimetres long. Her once beautiful face was grey and gaunt. Her beautiful lips were thin and without colour. She was tattered and worn like the cover of her book but there was no mistaking her. His Gabi had come home. She had survived! Every night in bed Milos had pictured their reunion as a moment of unrestrained joy and love. Not for an instant had he pictured this. He wanted to hug her but feared she might break, wanted to hold her and kiss her but feared denying her breath. He wanted to sing but it was all he could do not to cry.

'Milos, are we dead?'

'No, Gabi, we're not dead.'

'We're not dead?'

'No, Gabi.'

'Not dead. Then take me home. Please, Milos, take me home.'

* * *

'Would you like a break?' said Ramon, interrupting the silence. He couldn't see Milos staring unblinking at his coffee cup, lost in his memories, but guessed what had happened.

'Milos?' said Lucio.

'What?' Milos started as though suddenly awakened. He smiled weakly. 'Forgive me. It was so long ago. Suddenly I was recalling details I thought I'd forgotten. The sun was in my eyes so I couldn't see Gabi on the platform at first, I had to shade them with my hand. Swifts were darting above her chasing insects. There was a haze, a late-afternoon golden haze. I paid more attention to the birds than the bundle on the platform. I never thought it was her, not until I saw the book.'

'What if you hadn't been there?' said Neil. 'Would Gabi have given up and died?'

'Would I have died?' said Gabriella. 'The correct question is, would I have wanted to live?'

'But I was there,' said Milos. 'The question is academic.'

'Yes, you were there,' said Gabriella. She let go of Neil's arm, which she had been clinging to ever since the resumption of the story, and put her arms around Milos. 'After all that had happened, you were there. Nothing else mattered.'

'Nothing else mattered!' said Neil. 'What about the Russian soldiers? How can you dismiss the terrible things they did to you so easily?'

'Milos, look at his arms! Look how he is flexing his arms. Like a Rottweiler's, Milos says my grip is. Like a Rottweiler's. I am sorry, Neil. You should have said something.'

'Gabi, any time you want to hold onto my arm you go ahead,' said Neil graciously. 'There is no need to apologise. Now, what about the Russian soldiers? Can you really just dismiss what they did as though it never happened?'

'It was inconsequential, Neil. Inconsequential to them, inconsequential to me. They satisfied my appetite, I satisfied theirs. That's all there was to it. It is not as though I was the only one the Russians raped. I admit there are times when I wonder how I could have been so inconsequential, how I could have meant so little to them. I wonder how could they do such a thing to a child and be so indifferent. But mostly these days I find myself wondering how they could have got pleasure from such a scrawny bag of bones. There is the mystery. You know, when I was young I had always believed there was a God who looked after little children in distress. But he was nowhere, this God of little children. Throughout the war, he was nowhere when he was needed.'

'That's enough,' said Milos gently. 'It's time for me to continue my story. I have not quite finished for the day. We have a schedule, no?'

CHAPTER TWENTY

Milos picked up Gabriella's bag, slipped his arms beneath her and gently lifted her up. Gabi was smiling but her smile was a travesty, vague, unfocused and undirected. She weighed so little, so heartbreakingly little. As he carried her towards the exit Geza Apro intercepted him, a cup of coffee in each hand.

'She is Gabriella Horvath?'

Milos nodded, not trusting his voice.

The stationmaster's jaw dropped in astonishment. 'No! But she's so small. I'm sorry, Milos, I didn't realise. Where will you take her?'

'She has an aunt on the other side of the river.'

'Milos, you can't carry her all that way. Maybe she needs a doctor.'

'She needs love, Geza, food and a home. That's all she needs.'

Milos walked out onto the street. Passers-by avoided them, avoided even looking at them. So many Jews had been taken away yet so few had returned. Gabriella reminded them of their shame. Milos stood by the kerb, uncertain how to proceed. Gabriella was falling asleep, the dazed smile still fixed on her face as though painted there. Geza was right. The little she weighed was still too much to carry all the way to the other side of the Bodrog. Milos was considering his options when a horse-drawn cart pulled up in front of him.

'What have you there, little brother?'

Milos jumped. He stared up at the driver, recognising neither the man nor his voice.

'You forget your friends, little brother. Tibor never did.'

Milos stared at the driver as memories slowly awakened. He had seen the face only once before and then by the light of a flickering oil lamp. The man had been holding a pistol. He had sheltered Tibor and him a lifetime ago and taken half of their bacon bones as payment. The man on the cart smiled indulgently.

'Your brother is very loyal to his friends. When you see him, tell him I appreciate his business.'

'Do you still live across the river?' asked Milos.

'Just tell me where you want to go.' He jumped down from the cart and helped Milos lift Gabriella up onto the seat. 'It is your good fortune that I was passing by.'

'Wake up, Gabi, you must sit.'

'Milos?' Gabriella opened her eyes briefly. She snuggled up against him, rested her head on his shoulder and slipped back into sleep. The driver shook the reins and the horse slowly pulled the cart away from the station.

'This is very kind of you,' said Milos.

'Kind!' The driver snorted. 'Little brother, you live in a strange world. Tibor asked me to keep an eye out for you in case the girl returned. When Tibor asks me to do something for him, I don't argue.'

The old horse was slow and tired but the driver was in no hurry. They plodded along the streets, across the bridge and out into the countryside, finally turning down the cart track that led to Aunt Klari's. The late-afternoon sun had painted the underbelly of the clouds red and pink as it slid towards the horizon and a cool breeze had sprung up. Milos couldn't help thinking back to a year earlier, when Aunt Klari had escorted Tibor and him home from the church and the world had been a fearful place. He'd come so far to be back where his odyssey had begun. It felt like an ending yet he knew it could only be another beginning. But the beginning of what?

Gabriella had lost her mother but she found a substitute in Aunt Klari. She'd lost her father but found another in the taciturn Andras, Aunt Klari's husband. She'd lost her home but found somewhere almost as welcoming in the little cottage. The peasant woman wept for joy that one of her girls had come back. The vine-covered mud cottage was small and basic but it did have a second bedroom which instantly became Gabriella's. Aunt Klari bathed her, spoon-fed her chicken soup with *galuszka*, tasty little dumplings, and tucked her into bed. Milos sat with Gabriella, holding her hand until she slid gently into sleep, still smiling.

'Thank you for bringing Gabi back to me,' said Aunt Klari.

Milos had joined them at the table where there was a place set for him. Aunt Klari shared the remaining chicken soup and dumplings between him and Andras, keeping only a little for herself.

'We are all she has,' said Milos.

'Don't say that!' said Aunt Klari. 'If Gabi can come home, so can Mrs Horvath and Elizabeth.'

Milos let the silence hang before replying, 'I will keep going to the town hall and to the station. I am still waiting for my father.'

'Where are you living?' asked Aunt Klari.

'I rent a room near the station.'

'What do you do for money?'

'I brought some from Budapest.' He hunched his shoulders resignedly. 'Soon I will have to find work.'

'Ha!' Andras pushed his plate away from him. 'Everyone wants work. Easy to want. Hard to find.'

'What will you do? Will you go back to Budapest?'

Milos smiled. It had been a long time since anybody had worried about him. He liked being the object of Aunt Klari's concern. It reminded him of his Sundays at Tokaj Street with Aunt Katica fussing over him. But the mention of Budapest cast a shadow. His brother had become a stranger and Milos did not want any part of the life he'd chosen. He thought of Gabriella sleeping a few metres away and his brother's claim on her. He shuddered involuntarily. What if she still loved Tibor? Gabriella had also lost a brother and he dreaded the thought that all he might ever be to her was a substitute for Balazs. That would be more than he could bear. He became aware of Aunt Klari and Andras waiting for an answer.

'No, not Budapest. Maybe someone in the railway can help me. Maybe Geza Apro or my godparents.' Even as he uttered the words Milos realised he was clutching at straws. It wasn't just a bed for a night he wanted but something more permanent. And not just a bed but food as well, when the entire population was struggling to feed themselves.

'The boy stays here,' said Andras. 'There is a loft in the barn. With work it can be made habitable.'

'No, you've done enough for me already,' said Milos hastily. He was well aware that his dinner had been intended for Aunt Klari and that he'd virtually taken it from her mouth. Life was hard enough for them and now they had Gabriella to care for. He was reluctant to add to their burden. But the prospect of staying at the farm with Gabriella made him suddenly dizzy. It was something he'd never considered, a possibility so remote and so wonderful that the idea had not once entered his head.

'You stay,' said Andras with finality.

'What about the mare?'

'She will be glad of your company. You may not be so glad of hers.'

Milos bowed his head. 'I don't know how to thank you and I don't know how to repay your kindness. But I will. I'll think of something.'

'Your brother,' said Andras, 'be more like him.'

Over the next two weeks, Milos helped Andras refurbish the loft, replacing old and missing planks with new timber and lining the roof with straw for insulation. He took time off to check the lists of the dead at the town hall before going to the station to check the arrivals. Every day brought its mixture of good news and bad. Neither his father's name nor Katica's nor Elizabeth's appeared on the lists but neither did any of them arrive at the station.

Gabriella responded to the constant care she was given. Her breakfast of coffee, bread and jam exceeded her daily ration in the camps. Lunch was the main meal, usually a stew with pieces of pork and pork fat, but sometimes with beef. She craved the meat, devoured it first, and never objected when Milos gave her more from his own bowl. Dinner was usually lunch watered down and stretched with the addition of dumplings and vegetables. Aunt Klari also brought her milk from their one cow or an egg from their few remaining hens. Gabriella began to put on weight and get her colour back. Her hair stopped falling out and there was a peach fuzz where new hair was beginning to grow. The scarecrow was slowly coming back to life.

When she was strong enough she began to tell her story while they sat around the table in the evening. She told them about the box cars and Krakow station, Theresienstadt and the selections. She told them about Auschwitz and the terrible chimneys, the work camps and the increasing hunger and deprivation as the war ground to a halt. She told a little at a time because there was a limit to what her grim-faced audience could bear.

'Enough!' Andras would say. He was a man accustomed to hard work, hardship and disappointment, but the heart beating inside his tough shell was not impregnable. At this point he would leave the table and the cottage and disappear into the night while he digested what Gabriella had said and walked off his anger.

Gabriella told them about her journey home, about the Russians who had raped her and the kindness of the families across Czechoslovakia who had taken her in. She told her story dispassionately, without tears or bitterness, little realising that one day she would be incapable of telling it at all. The only times she became animated were when she told them about Julia, the tattoo, the potato cake, and the stew with meat in it that the Russian soldiers had shared with her.

The day after Milos moved up into the loft, Gabriella asked him take her to see Tokaj Street. Milos was reluctant to oblige because he didn't want to risk upsetting her, but she insisted.

'My mother may have come home, or Elizabeth, or even Balazs,' she said.

It didn't matter how often Milos told her he'd know if any of them had made it back, she had to see for herself. Prior to her deportation, Gabriella could cover the walk between Aunt Klari's and Tokaj Street in around forty-five minutes. It took her and Milos most of the morning, with stops to sit and rest, yet Gabriella was determined not to be denied.

When they finally reached Tokaj Street, Gabriella paused, trying to reconcile what she saw with her memories. Something had happened: the street she'd known so well had become somehow foreign. There was no hiding the shabbiness. Paint peeled from window frames. Fences were missing palings. Mismatched curtains hung at windows. The once grand houses looked tired. When she found her home she had to look to Milos for confirmation. The garden was overgrown and a window was boarded over where the glass had been broken. Vague memories stirred. She recalled the night when the window had been broken by a piece of brick thrown by Jew-baiters. That seemed a lifetime ago and yet the window still had not been repaired. She stood by Milos when he rang the bell, hoping someone from her family would open the door, but knowing that would not happen.

'What do you want?' The man who opened the door was unshaven and wore only a singlet and trousers.

'This is Gabriella Horvath. She is the daughter of the family who lived here and owned this house prior to the deportations,' said Milos.

'Listen, kid, if she's come to throw us out, she can't,' said the man belligerently.

Milos fixed him with a look Tibor would have been proud of and took a step closer. 'You are as aware of your obligations as I am.' The issue of home ownership had not been resolved, but occupiers of confiscated homes were obliged by law to provide accommodation to any owners who returned.

'There's a hall cupboard left. If she wants to sleep in it, she's welcome,' said the man reluctantly. He glared at Gabriella. 'Three families live here now. There's no room for anyone else.'

'Have any of her relatives come here?' said Milos. 'She's looking for her mother, sister and her brother.'

'No!' said the man. 'Just her. That all you want?'

'If any other member of the Horvath family returns I want you to tell the stationmaster,' said Milos.

'Sure, kid.'

'At least tell whoever it is that Gabriella has been here looking for them.'

'Gabriella. Okay. That it?'

Milos shook his head in disgust, took Gabriella's arm and turned to leave. But Gabriella didn't move.

'Which room do you sleep in?' she asked.

'Front bedroom at the top,' said the man. 'What's it to you?'

'That was my bedroom,' said Gabriella.

She allowed Milos to guide her down the steps to the street. As they walked away she made no attempt to look back. They had destroyed her home but she wouldn't let them destroy her memory of it. She wanted to preserve the Tokaj Street that existed inside her head.

Milos tried to take her back to Aunt Klari's but Gabriella insisted on going to the town hall. The lists of the dead had grown but none of the names they were looking for were on it. There was another list, one which was pathetically short and bore silent witness to the scale of the tragedy. It was the list of survivors who had returned. Gabriella added her name.

'Come on,' said Milos. 'Let's go home.'

CHAPTER TWENTY-ONE

*B*e *more like your brother.*
Andras had meant well when he'd given the advice, but it had cut Milos to the core. It left him feeling inadequate and incapable. The truth was, Tibor would know what to do. Milos had always thought Tibor was cleverer than him because he was two years older, but Tibor had always known what to do and that had nothing to do with the gap in their ages. This was the thought that occupied him most as he made his daily trips to the town hall and station.

Milos scrutinised the faces as they left the station, knowing from the very first glance that they brought only more disappointment. Once the platform had cleared he sat down on one of the station's two bench seats to take stock, to figure out how he could contribute, how he could become more like his brother.

Every day there were queues outside the town's three bakeries and he was aware that most people queued in hope rather than with any real expectation of getting bread. There was never enough bread because there was never enough flour. People queued outside butcheries hoping that somehow they'd acquired an animal to slaughter. But the Russians had left little as they'd swarmed over rural Hungary, as rapacious as a

323

plague of locusts. Cobblers waited in vain for leather. Tailors and dressmakers waited for material. The town's only chemist was reduced to herbal remedies. Milos knew the kind of goods his brother stored in his warehouse and knew what he could supply. Flour, sugar, material and pharmaceuticals were relatively easy.

He considered walking into the stores and asking people what they wanted. He could argue that he'd just come from Budapest and knew people who wanted to sell product before the Russians confiscated it; that he had contacts in Budapest and on the railways and could supply what they wanted provided they were prepared to pay. Milos ran the argument around in his head. He'd be doing the town a favour and would be able to pay for his and Gabriella's keep at Aunt Klari's. Of course he'd have to pay off people in the railways and probably even some of the local police. He'd need a warehouse and a truck.

He became so engrossed in logistics that it took him a while to fully comprehend what he was doing. The realisation hit him like a slap across the face. In copying his brother he would become him. A black marketeer, profiteer and criminal, wanted by the authorities and at war with his competitors. And he'd have competitors, Milos had no doubt about that. One of them had taken Gabriella and him on his cart to Aunt Klari's. There were sure to be others. Would the time come when, like Tibor, he'd also need a flak jacket and bodyguards? Milos didn't even want to consider the issue. That was a road he had no desire to travel.

He thought back to the shops that struggled to remain open, those that had closed and the factories that ticked along at little more than idle, constrained by lack of materials. Somewhere in all this need was the solution to his problem. Tibor could always find a solution and, if he thought like his brother, so would he. He closed his eyes and his brother's voice began harping in his ear.

Think it through, Milos. Go beyond the obvious, Milos. Look for the fundamental truths and use them.

Fundamental truths! Milos didn't know where to begin. Sarospatak was a backwater, a rural outpost, a town that didn't matter except to the people who lived there. Everyone was hungry and in need of something. There wasn't enough of anything. Not enough flour, not enough milk, not enough eggs, not enough chickens and not enough meat. Milos grimaced. Until the war, he'd been raised on meat, all Hungarians were. They ate meat every day, mainly pork, beef when they could get it, chicken, turkey and fish if they could afford it. Just thinking about it made Milos hunger for a thick slice of fried pork, for peppers and cabbage leaves stuffed with beef and rice and cooked in *rantas*, a heavy roux of pork lard and flour. He smiled grimly. Look for a fundamental truth, Tibor had said, and there was the most fundamental truth of all: Hungarians were meat eaters and there was no meat to eat. Milos snapped upright, his brain whirring. He asked Geza Apro if he could use his phone.

The following morning Milos arrived back at the station just as Geza was unlocking the ticket office. The regular service from Satoraljaujhely to the main line for connection through to Budapest was not due for more than two hours. Geza made coffee while Milos waited impatiently. He was bursting to tell somebody his idea and anxious for Aunt Klari and Andras to know that he wouldn't be dependent on them much longer. But a *fait accompli* carried considerably more weight than an idea, no matter how colourfully presented, particularly one with major hurdles to negotiate. Milos drank his coffee but discouraged Geza from engaging him in conversation. He had to plan what to say to Tibor and cover all possible arguments. He didn't doubt Tibor would ring back; his brother would recognise the station number and know when to call. When the phone finally rang Milos was so engrossed in thought it caught him by surprise. Geza answered and passed the phone over.

'Hello, little brother,' said Tibor.

Milos winced. The mocking tone was unmistakeable even over the phone. It was his brother's way of reminding him of the pecking order.

'I've got a deal for you,' said Milos.

'Not so fast,' said Tibor. 'How's my girl?'

'Six breeding sows,' said Milos.

'What?'

'And a stud boar,' Milos added. He smiled. For once he'd caught his brother off guard.

'Six sows and a boar? What do you want them for?'

'Can you do it?' Milos sensed he had the upper hand for once and revelled in it.

'Of course. It's only a matter of price.'

'How much?'

'Plenty,' said Tibor. 'How are you going to pay for them?'

'In piglets,' said Milos. For a moment he thought he'd lost connection.

'Piglets?' said Tibor eventually.

'Piglets, pork chops, trotters, bacon, ham.'

'Tell me the deal,' snapped Tibor.

'You provide the six sows and the boar. In return I send you a regular supply of porkers.'

'Keep talking.'

'For twelve months I keep a third of all pigs born to cover the cost of feed, wages and transport.'

'A quarter. I'll handle transport.'

'A third.'

'After that?'

'We split the proceeds fifty-fifty.'

'How soon can you start?'

'I'm ready now.'

'Sure, little brother. What about pens?'

'You remember Andras, Aunt Klari's husband? He's building them as we speak.'

Tibor laughed at the transparency of Milos's claim. 'And feed?'

'There's plenty of stock feed around because there's no stock. One sow will buy us all we need to get started.'

'Deal,' said Tibor. 'Now, how's Gabriella?'

'Funny you should mention her,' said Milos.

'Why's that?'

'She never mentions you.' Milos laughed and was still laughing when Tibor hung up. He thanked Geza and almost danced out of his office onto the platform just as passengers began arriving for the train to Budapest. In his haste he bumped into one of them.

'Watch where you're going!'

'I'm sorry,' said Milos hastily.

The person he'd collided with was about his own age but taller and broader. He stared at Milos contemptuously. 'I know you,' he said. 'You're the Jew kid, Tibor's brother.'

'Sandor Kiraly,' said Milos. He remembered him from school and as the recipient of boots he'd grown out of. Sandor had matured into the thug he'd always threatened to become. Milos held out his hand. Sandor stared at it momentarily before deciding to shake it.

'How are you?' asked Milos. 'How's Istvan?'

'Istvan lives in Budapest now. At a police academy. I'm going to join him in Budapest and become a gendarme.' Sandor puffed up his chest as though becoming a gendarme was the pinnacle of human achievement.

'Good luck,' said Milos. 'Oh, and give my regards and thanks to your brother. He'll know why.'

Milos left the station and promptly forgot about Sandor and Istvan Kiraly. They were distant echoes from a time long past and no longer relevant to his life. He had more important things to think about.

*

In the months that followed, Budapest's black marketeers defied the government's early attempts to establish law and order and control over food distribution. Any attempts to peg prices for basic foods were doomed to failure as Hungary's currency slid into the worst hyperinflation in history, resulting in notes worth 10,000 trillion pengo entering circulation. The government led by the Smallholders Party did its best but was forced into coalition with the Social Democrats and the Communist Party by the Soviet political officers. With the army of occupation backing them, the political officers were not to be denied. To make matters worse, the Russians' claim on war reparation gathered increasing momentum throughout 1946. The entire contents of factories were put onto trains and sent back to Russia, along with entire grain harvests and the output of mines.

Vilagosi's enterprises flourished amid all the confusion as Tibor made good on his promises. Wagons filled with grain were mysteriously uncoupled en route and their contents redirected to Vilagosi's warehouses. As winter approached, wagonloads of coal disappeared, their contents passing through Vilagosi's organisation on their way to Budapest's fireplaces and furnaces. His endeavours were made easier by the bungling of Russian bureaucrats and the inadequacies of their record-keeping. Tibor became a minor legend in Budapest's underworld for his audacity. No one was better placed to take advantage of the conditions and, gradually, through his control of the railways, other criminal organisations far larger than Vilagosi's were ultimately obliged to deal with them. But fame breeds consequences as well as rewards. Other ears took note of his activities.

When rumours about Tibor began circulating through the offices of the secret police, Istvan listened carefully and did what he always did with information. He began a dossier on Tibor Heyman, entering details that not even Major Bogati could know: Jozsef's demotion from Deputy Director of

Railways and his arrival at Sarospatak as the new stationmaster, the conversion of his two sons to Catholicism, Tibor's extracurricular activities at school and the boys' narrow escape from deportation. He also listed what he considered to be Tibor's strengths and weaknesses. He compiled the dossier in his own time, even though there was precious little of it to spare.

Istvan had become an officer of the Allamvedelmi Osztaly or AVO, the Department of State Security. The AVO was officially an organ of the fledgling coalition government but in reality was an instrument of the Soviet's political arm. The Russians had little choice but to allow the majority Smallholders Party to provide the prime minister, but insisted on Communist control of the Ministry of Interior, which in turn controlled the police and the AVO. The AVO went about its business with an eye to the future and the consolidation of its power, building a nationwide network of spies and informers. Istvan's job was to identify prospects, who were enlisted by whatever means necessary: bribes, blackmail or the threat of death or injury to family. Istvan enshrined their commitment in his dossiers. In the autumn of 1946, when he was summoned to the office of his superior, Major Bogati, he took his dossier on Tibor with him.

'Your brother,' said the major without preamble, 'he failed his exam again. Speak to him, though I don't suppose he needs qualifications for the role we have in mind for him. Your brother is who he is. At least he'll be on our side.'

'Thank you, sir.'

'I believe you have something to show me.'

Istvan handed over his dossier on Tibor. The grey eyes lit up and the major smiled, an event so rare that Istvan suspected it lacked precedent.

'So the shadow finally gains substance,' said the major. 'I was curious to know how he had gained so much influence in the railways so quickly. Loyalty to the father. I never even suspected the connection with Jozsef Heyman. More than anyone, he was responsible for the resurrection of the railways. His demotion was one of Gombolini's last acts of folly. Gombos replaced him with one of his political friends, a man who couldn't run a raffle let alone a railway. There was no need to humiliate Jozsef Heyman but the fool could not help himself. Now we bear the consequences of that stupidity.'

The major turned his attention back to the dossier and read it through to the end.

'You have done well, Officer Kiraly. You continue to surprise. He is a clever fish, your schoolfriend, very elusive but still one that is undersized. For the time being we'll leave him and his master, Vilagosi, to the police and let them run for a while. But for your friend many people in Budapest would starve. Many would go without heating.' He laughed unexpectedly. 'Tell me, Officer Kiraly, who do you think supplies our coal?'

Istvan wasn't sure whether he was supposed to laugh too. The situation had never arisen before. He kept his face straight, his feet together and his hands by the seams of his trousers. The major's smile hardened. He reached into a cabinet, rifled through it and extracted a file.

'This file is now your responsibility. Flesh it out. I will make sure all new information is passed through to you. Write me a profile. Show me how he thinks. You were trained to do this at the academy, no?'

'Sir!' said Istvan. He had no need to glance at the file; he knew exactly whose name would be written on the cover. He had been handed a prize and both of them knew it.

* * *

Milos leaned back in his chair and looked towards the kitchen. Gancio's head appeared around the doorway almost immediately. Milos smiled and gave the signal for coffee.

330

There were moments when he thought the restaurateur was telepathic.

'That's it?' asked Ramon.

'For today,' said Milos. 'I'm tired and Gabriella is tired. Besides, I kept you late last week, no?'

'But what happened to your father and Gabriella's mother and sister?' Ramon paused theatrically. 'Surely their fate belongs in today's episode.'

'I'm tired,' said Milos. 'You're quite right, but I have just decided to deal with that first thing next week.'

'What about your schedule?' said Ramon.

'I give in,' said Milos wearily. 'You are determined to interfere with the telling of my story.'

'Keep it till next week then,' said Ramon.

'No,' said Milos, 'today or next week, what does it matter? The outcome is the same.' He paused for a moment to collect his thoughts.

'Milos found out on the day the pigs arrived. It should have been an occasion for joy. The pigs promised an income and a future filled with opportunities. Andras took a lot of convincing that it had been Milos's idea and not Tibor's but, once convinced, Milos went up so high in his estimation it was embarrassing. Actually the idea was not so clever. Smallholders all over Hungary wanted breeding sows because the Russians had left so few; what their army hadn't eaten had been sent back east. Milos's only cleverness was in realising he could get hold of some and negotiating a way of paying that made the enterprise viable. It was a deal only Tibor could have agreed to and then only for his little brother. Milos bought some sweet red Tokaj wine in anticipation of a celebration and Aunt Klari made some *palacsinta* with preserved fruit.'

'*Palacsinta*?' said Ramon.

'Sweet pancakes. Sometimes I think you don't listen. This was to be the day they broke the shackles of the war and, of course, it was. But not in the way they anticipated. As a matter of course, Milos checked in at the town hall on his way to the station. As always he hoped the names would not be there. But on this day the lists had grown substantially and the names were all there, typed neatly in alphabetical order. He found his father's first, then Aunt Katica's and Elizabeth's.

'No one could fault the Germans' record-keeping. The date of their deaths was also recorded. They all died on the same day, the day they arrived at Auschwitz. Their suffering was brief although their deaths must have been horrendous. They went straight into the gas.

'The war ended for Milos and Gabriella the day the pigs arrived. The living had separated from the dead. There was no more doubt, no more wondering, no more hoping against hope. The grieving could begin, so that one day it could end.'

'We found out about Balazs much later,' said Gabriella bitterly. 'It was no surprise to learn that he had died, only the manner.'

'Are you going to tell us what happened?'

'Yes, Ramon, since you have insisted upon knowing. For once, German efficiency failed. My poor brother never made it to the Russian front. None of that contingent from Sarospatak and Satoraljaujhely did. Their carriages were detached and left in a siding near Lvov. They were to be coupled to another train heading through to the front. That night a fierce snow storm broke and German communications failed. Messages were lost or instructions changed; either way the carriages were overlooked. By the time the Germans realised their error, everyone inside had frozen to death. We understand that a bulldozer gouged a hole in the frozen soil and Balazs and the rest of the contingent were buried there. Nobody in Sarospatak heard about it because none of the conscripts had lived to tell the tale. The truth only emerged after the war in a search through German records. What a waste!'

'I'm sorry,' said Ramon.

'You're sorry?' said Gabriella. 'Sorry doesn't even come close! When did you become so facile, Ramon? Have you swapped roles with Neil? He was wonderful, my brother, wise, warm and wonderful. He wanted to be a lawyer so that he could become a politician and the kind of leader Hungary has always lacked. Balasz would have been a great leader. A great leader and a compassionate one. But he died for no purpose and his talent with him. Nobody prospered by his death, but Hungary became a poorer place. The world became a poorer place for all the wonderful people who died. But I survived. Me, who had nothing to give the world but a pretty face. I survived because the Germans needed pretty faces to fool the Red Cross and my Uncle Jozsef had the wit and courage to see the glimmer of a lifeline amid all the darkness and horror. Can you imagine how that makes me feel?'

'Gabi, that's enough. That's enough now. Here is Gancio with our coffee. Drink now. Yes?' Milos put his arm around her protectively. 'Are you satisfied now, Ramon?'

'Yes,' said the blind man. 'And I apologise.'

'Like it,' said Neil in the silence that followed. The others turned towards him, puzzled by the non sequitur. 'Nice to see Ramon copping the shit for a change.'

FOURTH THURSDAY

CHAPTER TWENTY-TWO

'You must hate the Germans,' said Neil.

Gabriella smiled and shook her head. 'No,' she said, 'I don't hate the Germans. Every country has its bad people and its good people. All the Nazis did was create a situation where the scum rose to the top instead of the cream.'

'Oh come on,' said Neil. 'If they'd treated me the way they treated you I'd never forgive them.'

'My friend the doctor asked if I hated the Germans and I told him no. I told him I didn't hate the Russians either.' Gabriella rubbed her hand across her eyes then took a tiny sip from her glass of wine. '"Then who do you hate?" he asked.'

'And?' said Neil.

'Myself. I told him I hated myself.'

'What? Why? That's ridiculous.'

'Neil, you have so much to learn. All these years you have turned deaf ears to the suffering of others. If you'd listened you would understand.'

'I think I understand,' said Lucio.

'Ramon, what about you? Do you understand?'

'Of course. You made that clear last week. You hate yourself for surviving while others who you consider more deserving did not. This guilt is common. It was common in Argentina after the reign of the Generals.'

'Thank you, Ramon. You see where your intolerance has left you, Neil? Ignorant and insensitive. Yes, I hated myself for surviving, but that is only half the reason. I hated myself for not doing more with my life, for not making good use of my survival. I told you, Neil, on that first day that I am Milos's baggage. I was baggage when I arrived in this beautiful country, unable to build a future because I was incapable of dealing with my past.'

'That's ridiculous,' said Neil once more. 'You survived because a proportion of Jews survived and you happened to be among them. You have told us about the lack of system in the selections, the random elements in determining who lived and who died. It was all a matter of luck. You were lucky. There's no reason to feel guilty for being lucky, any more than there is a reason to feel guilty for being unlucky.'

'I think my friend the doctor would enjoy talking to you, Neil. I think he would find your point of view refreshing.'

'You keep mentioning your friend the doctor,' said Ramon. 'Are you going to tell us about this part of your life?'

'Yes, it is part of our story,' said Gabriella. 'It is out of sequence if I tell you this part now, but if Milos has no objection, and if it doesn't interfere with the story he has planned for today, I can perhaps tell you a little.'

'Well, Milos?' asked Ramon.

'Why not?' said Milos resignedly. 'For reasons I cannot even begin to guess at, you have again decided to usurp the telling of my story. Every day you interfere, no? Well, let's get your interference over and done with now.' He glared at the blind man and anger crept into his voice. 'Tell your story, Gabi. Leave me to figure out how to tie the ragged ends together!'

'I will only tell so much,' said Gabriella placatingly. 'I won't tell them anything that interferes with your storytelling, I promise.' She kissed Milos lightly on his cheek. 'But I am here, Milos. You brought me here and I like to contribute.'

'Milos, forgive us, but Gabriella is helping your story,' said Lucio. 'She adds colour and a relevance and because of her intimate involvement she also adds tension. It is wonderful, incredible, to look at Gabriella and know she is the Gabi in your story. It gives it another, entirely unexpected dimension.'

'Lucio's right. You tell a good story, Milos, but Gabriella makes it real. She's sure brought it home to me,' said Neil.

'Thank you, Lucio,' said Gabriella. 'And you, Neil, as always you exaggerate.'

'Your friend the doctor,' reminded Ramon. He was anxious to progress the story but realised he would have to be patient. Gancio was approaching with their entrée.

'Scampi,' said Gancio. 'From West Australia. Split down the middle and lightly grilled with a little butter, garlic and herbs. Beautiful.'

It was another five minutes before Gabriella took up her story.

'It happened the first time on the ship to Australia. My first panic attack. Of all the places it should happen. We were aboard the *Arawa*, a boat that had once carried frozen meat and now carried reconstituted human beings. My mind was in turmoil, my whole life was in turmoil, but I felt safe aboard that ship. I was leaving Europe and escaping to the new world. We had travel documents supplied by refugee organisations and these papers meant everything to me. They said who we were: Gabriella and Milos Heyman, man and wife. And they said where we were going: Sydney, Australia. There was no arguing with our documents. Amid the tumult of my mind, these were reality, the things I clung to. Our identity. Our destination. The documents were our life and our future.

'The *Arawa* also carried paying migrants as well as refugees. Some were getting off in Cape Town, some in Perth, some Melbourne, and the remainder were going on to New

Zealand. There was a lot of sadness on the ship, for what people were leaving behind, and apprehension about the future. None of us had any concept of Australia, none of us knew what it would be like, but there was also a lot of hope aboard that ship.

'I was not the only one struggling to shake off the past and embrace the future. My new life was not yet mine. I, Gabriella Heyman of Sarospatak, Hungary, was on a ship and on my way to becoming an Australian. The documents said so, and said my husband, Milos Heyman, was travelling with me. I was between two lives: one I was fleeing and another which was unknown. I was displaced, disoriented and distressed. Can you understand my dependence on my documents? My world had disintegrated. I was reduced to pieces of paper that told me who I was, who I was with and where I was going.

'For days I stayed in my cabin, which I shared with three other women.'

'But you were married,' cut in Neil. 'Why didn't you have your own cabin?'

'You think this was a cruise ship? It was a refugee ship, Neil, a migrant ship. We were fortunate to get any bed on board. Twin cabins were never an option. Now, may I continue?'

'I'm sorry.'

'Two of the women in my cabin were English and they were very kind. Mostly my new husband brought food to me from the dining room but sometimes it was these women. They talked to me about England. Lying on my bed listening to them reminded me of Tokaj Street and our English governess reading to me. One day I awoke feeling strong enough to get up and go to the dining room for breakfast. My old friend hunger had returned and I needed to eat. It's a funny thing, but I also wanted to be part of the ship's routine. Ironically, it was my time in Theresienstadt and the other camps that instilled in me a need for routine. There was familiarity in it and a sense of place. Even lying on my bunk I was aware of the routine. The set times to eat. Breakfast, lunch, dinner, entertainment and lights out in the cabins at ten-thirty. When we walked into the dining room Milos raced over and took my hand.

'"Gabi!" said the other half of my identity. "So good to see you up at last."

'"Hello Milos," said my English friends.

'Milos and Gabriella, that's who we were. Milos kissed my cheek and the cheeks of the English girls. They were very taken with him. We sat together at a table and waiters brought us bowls of porridge with cream and sugar. My friends ignored theirs but I cleaned my bowl and so did Milos. We were not accustomed to leaving food, even food so strange. My friends were entertaining themselves by trying to teach Milos English words. Milos made them laugh with the way he pronounced things so he started teaching them Hungarian words. Even I had to smile at their attempts. Magyarul is not easy. We were all like children, laughing and playing this childish game, when the people at the table behind me started breaking eggs. They'd begun breakfast before us, you see, and the waiters had brought them toast and boiled eggs to follow the porridge. I had no warning and even if I had, what would it have meant? I had no idea that listening to the eggs break would trigger a collapse.

'I screamed and covered my ears but it was too late. The nightmares had returned and with such force that every closed door in my fragile mind burst open. Nightmares, horrors and fears uncountable spilled forth. Everything I had suppressed for the sake of survival and sanity. How fast does a mind work? Let me tell you, faster than you can ever imagine. My mind embraced eight years of horrors in less than the blink of an eye. I ran from that dining room blinded by tears, thinking I was running away from my nightmares. But of course that was impossible.' Gabriella paused, staring unblinking at the plate in front of her, seeing but not seeing the two scampi shells and the bed of rocket.

'You mentioned listening to the eggs breaking before,' said Ramon gently. 'Can you explain?'

Gabriella looked up at Ramon. He couldn't see the shine in her eyes or the redness but the others could and were embarrassed.

'Explain? Yes, I can explain! But not now. It took ten years of skill and patience for my friend the doctor to get me to tell him about the eggs. Now you want me to explain after what — a few minutes? No, Ramon, you will wait. You will all wait. You will not get the explanation so easily.'

Gancio brought the main course, veal al limone with asparagus and baby new potatoes, boiled and served with a herb butter. Gabriella kept speaking as she picked at her food.

'Everyone was understanding and sympathetic although nobody really understood what was happening. Fortunately for me, but unfortunately for others, I was not the only one traumatised in this way. Everyone put it down to the war, to internment, and expected us sufferers to get over it once we reached Australia. Post-traumatic stress disorder had not been named or even identified at that time. It took the Vietnam War and thousands of grossly disturbed boys for anyone to put a label to my illness. Even if the sickness had been known, I don't think the doctor on board the *Arawa* would have treated me any differently. He gave me sedatives and put me to sleep.

'This was to become the standard form of treatment. When I couldn't face life, doctors put me to sleep. When I was asleep, I didn't have to deal with my problems and neither did they. They must have thought it was a good solution all round. But for my friend the doctor, I'd still be asleep today.

'My attacks eased as the voyage went on. We were five weeks at sea in our lovely white cocoon. There was comfort in our isolated world, in our insular little community and in the ship's routine. Every face was familiar and every minute accounted for. There were no surprises and no doubts. The ship was not just our home but our entire world and just small enough for my troubled mind to cope with.

'Who knows why phobias develop? All through the war and its aftermath I'd kept my terrors locked away in a watertight compartment. Only when I was asleep and off guard did that watertight compartment leak and I'd be engulfed by nightmares. But somewhere along the way, probably that morning on the *Arawa* when I heard the eggs break, a crack had developed and the compartment in my brain was no longer watertight.

'We arrived in Sydney and found a city that was grey and depressing with a population suspicious of foreigners. We had felt an affinity with the cities we'd passed through in Europe, but this city which was to be our home was totally alien. It frightened me. I begged Milos to take me back on board our ship. I wanted to sail for ever in my little white cocoon and never again set foot on land. Australia was our promised land but instead all I felt was terror. My mind flashed back and connected with another time and place: Krakow station when I had been left all alone in a strange country filled with strangers. Everything and everyone scared me. My watertight compartment burst open. Of course I broke down.'

Gabriella turned her attention to her lunch. She sliced off another tiny piece of veal but it had grown cold. 'Post-traumatic stress disorder. It is good that my illness has a name but the name doesn't tell you much. It is like being in a car with two steering wheels and another driver besides myself. Sometimes I steer but the other driver can override me at any time and take me to places I don't want to go. It is malicious and erratic, this other driver, and for much of my life since escaping Hungary it has been in control.'

'That will do,' said Milos gently. 'You have told enough without telling too much. Now, eat a little more and I will begin today's episode.'

He cast a quick glance at the blind man. 'With Ramon's permission, of course.'

* * *

Time heals and sleep abets, but sleep is the most contrary of allies. By June 1947, Gabriella had gained in strength and come to terms with the fact that she was the sole survivor of her family. Her hair grew back, thick and full, her body took on a shape more befitting her age. Her hips and breasts swelled but her waist stubbornly and spectacularly refused to follow suit. The thin sticks which were her arms filled out. Her spaghetti legs grew long, elegant and shapely, worthy of the fine American silk stockings Tibor had traded in Budapest. Colour returned to her face and a sparkle to her eyes. Slowly Gabriella regained her beauty. But time cannot heal what cannot be changed and the sun cannot shed light where it cannot reach. Sleep helped restore Gabriella to health and then it turned on her.

Gabriella began to fear the dark and the nightmares that reared up unbidden. Sometimes she would go weeks without one and then suffer for nights in a row. It wasn't just their frequency that was a problem but their intensity. Aunt Klari and Uncle Andras took turns to comfort the terrified girl but the sleepless nights gradually took a toll on them. When Milos volunteered to sleep on the floor by Gabriella's bed, his offer was gratefully accepted.

Andras took Milos aside and warned him to keep his trousers on, but it was a caution made purely for the sake of form and light-heartedly. Milos's conduct was above reproach and his integrity as apparent as his love for Gabriella. He hadn't pressed his claim on Gabriella nor sought any commitment from her, but allowed matters to follow a course that seemed both natural and inevitable. Aunt Klari and Andras expected him to marry Gabriella, and with good reason as daily the two seventeen year olds grew closer. And as long as Tibor remained in Budapest, there was no rival for her affections. Milos's early fears that he would become no more than a brother to her now seemed groundless and unworthy.

Milos did not move into Gabriella's room on a permanent basis but slept in the loft above the stable until her nightmares returned. Aunt Klari comforted the girl the first night and Milos thereafter until the attacks ceased. While the two had become inseparable, nothing drew them closer together than the nightmares. In the moments of Gabriella's deepest terror, when nightmare and reality fused, Milos was there. Holding her. Kissing her. Comforting her. Calming her. Telling her how much he loved her. Wiping away her tears and distracting her so that the nightmares withdrew. Some nights he read to her in his halting English from the book he'd given her so many years before, showing her the colour plates of pixies and pirates even though every centimetre was already indelibly etched on her memory. At these times, Gabriella became a child again, often speaking to him as though he was her English nanny of so long ago. Clearly her mind was seeking sanctuary in cherished memories, finding places to hide from the horrors of the camps, so Milos did nothing to discourage her. These temporary escapes brought her both comfort and relief.

Night after night Milos nursed Gabriella, stroking her forehead and hair, soothing her, talking and reading to her long after she had re-entered the realm of sleep, believing that his words could influence her dreams and keep the nightmares at bay. He stayed with her until she awoke, no matter how late, believing it was important for her to know that he was there by her side if the nightmares returned. The comfort she drew from his presence was evident in the smile she gave him when she finally awoke and found him lying by her bed, often still holding her hand. That early morning, dreamy, goofy, sleepy smile was everything his eyes wanted to see and everything his heart wanted to know. That smile told him she loved him.

Apart from looking after Gabriella, Milos had little to do. He'd taken Tibor's advice and suggested to Andras that the pigs be distributed among other farmers he could trust. Andras had seen the wisdom of it. With hungry Russian soldiers still on the prowl they couldn't risk keeping all their pigs in one place.

Milos had sold one sow to raise capital to buy feed and to pay Aunt Jutka and her husband to raise two sows and a neighbour to rear another. Andras had kept the boar and the remaining two sows, holding them in pens within the barn by day and allowing them only an hour or two of foraging by night. When order was gradually established and the occupying forces no longer had to live off the land, Andras built up the number of breeding pigs into a flourishing concern.

Milos assumed responsibility for despatching the pigs owed to Tibor and selling the remainder that weren't needed for stock building or for their own table. With everything of value being transported east, sending pigs west to Budapest was inviting attention and confiscation. Typically, Tibor had anticipated the problem and sent Milos papers which purported that the pigs were on consignment to the Communist-controlled Ministry of the Interior. The Hungarian population claimed that the Russian soldiers would steal from anyone and even steal the last breath from the dying, but they were wrong. Nobody, not even the Russians, stole from the Ministry of the Interior. As the consignment approached Budapest, the papers were exchanged and the pigs quietly removed to a safe place.

Selling pigs in Sarospatak was no more difficult, provided Milos concealed his trade from the Russian soldiers and gendarmes. Andras converted a wheelbarrow into a cart just big enough to carry a pig carcass beneath a covering of coal or potatoes. Milos could push it or position himself between the shafts and drag it along behind him. There was nothing unusual about this; with petrol scarce and so many horses slaughtered, most people transported goods in this manner.

There were few butchers in Sarospatak but all were desperate for Milos's pigs. He shopped around to see who would offer him the highest price or best deal. It was a tactic that paid an unexpected dividend. People who had lost the little they'd managed to save when the pengo crashed still distrusted the new forint, even though it had achieved an unexpected stability. Milos sold for a combination of cash, bartered goods and gold. One day he was offered in trade a piece of gold which he instantly seized upon.

'Where did you get this?' he asked.

The butcher smiled and shrugged his shoulders.

'Who knows? There is a gold watch that belonged to the tailor which I have bought and sold three times. It keeps excellent time. I once exchanged nine metres of dress material for just one kilo of pork. It was a mistake. I told my wife about the material and she claimed it.'

'What else have you got?' asked Milos.

He completed the sale by adding cash, sugar, salt, coffee and flour to the deal, items the butcher had earlier taken in trade for his meat, bacon, sausages and lard. Milos drove a hard bargain to conceal his intention and, for the first time, he pocketed part of the proceeds. He felt guilty because Aunt Klari and Andras trusted him to share the profits equally, just as they shared everything else. Andras never questioned him, simply accepted Milos's word on the deals he did. But the circumstances were exceptional and the opportunity undeniable. Milos consoled himself with the belief that once they understood his motive, they would sympathise and forgive.

Yet Milos still had little to do. Sometimes he felt inadequate as a provider, and not enough like his brother. When he voiced his concerns, neither Aunt Klari nor Andras would hear a word of it. The pigs had turned their lives around and that was something for lasting gratitude. But for Milos it was not enough. One night, while he lay in bed in the loft above the mare and the pig pen, he had another idea. It was so simple and so obvious he was stunned and angry that he hadn't thought of it before. He rose and walked out into the night, pausing briefly to listen for any sound from the cottage that would indicate that Gabriella's nightmares had returned. Hearing nothing but the deep and regular snoring of Andras, a sound as familiar to him as the squealing of piglets fighting over a teat, he walked quietly around the corner of the stable and stood among Aunt Klari's apricot trees which were heavy with ripening fruit. He picked an apricot and sniffed it. The evening was warm with little breeze and the fruit gave off a sweet and heady perfume that reminded him of his time on the run, when for almost a month apricots, plums, apples and pears had been breakfast, lunch and dinner. He let the night air wash over him, clearing the fog from his mind and sharpening the edges of his idea.

People in Budapest were still suffering from food shortages and many still subsisted on a diet comprised chiefly of lentils. Milos had realised there was a market for jams and preserves. Behind the cottage there was a vegetable garden, the care of which Gabriella had taken upon herself, and, among the vegetables, a spreading patch of gherkin cucumbers. Milos smiled involuntarily. North of Satoraljaujhely, in a shallow cave, were the jars of pickled gherkins he and Tibor had buried in preparation for their flight. They'd never gone back for them, or for the clothes they'd hidden. Milos hoped some Jews had found them, the thought of someone desperate happening serendipitously across the little hoard brought a ripple of satisfaction. But if the pickles had been treasure to fleeing Jews then, they'd be treasure to the starving people of Budapest now. He added pickles to his list of products.

Milos picked his way between the fruit trees and climbed the lower branches of an apple tree to sit and think through the logistics. He was well aware that solutions that seemed so simple by night were often buried by the complexities of reality come daylight. By shifting position he made himself uncomfortable so that he wouldn't become drowsy and be lulled into accepting false answers. He examined the issues one by one, but the dangers seemed few and easily avoidable. Why hadn't he thought of the idea sooner? When had his brain dulled? He swung his legs off the branch he was lying on and dropped to the ground.

Sleep beckoned but on the way back he paused to look up at a sky filled with stars. It was all so familiar and unchanged. The North Star hung like a beacon, just as it had when he was on the run. Milos couldn't imagine a time when he wouldn't be able to look up into a clear night sky and see the North Star looking back at him. Before slipping into the barn he again stopped and listened to make sure Gabriella's sleep was untroubled. He realised then that his brain hadn't dulled but had been distracted, and for that he had not the slightest regret.

The following morning, when the four of them sat down to a breakfast of coffee and bread with jam, Milos decided to reveal his plans.

'I have an idea for another enterprise,' he said, 'one that will draw on the special talents of Aunt Klari and her capable assistant, Gabi. Done properly, it will also involve Aunt Jutka and several of our neighbours. At least, the ones we can trust.'

Andras stopped chewing and looked at him thoughtfully. Aunt Klari put down her coffee. Gabriella began smiling even though she had yet to hear the details. None of that mattered to her; just the notion of a new idea excited her, the prospect of an initiative that would give her more reason to be proud of him. In that instant Milos realised this was one of the reasons she'd been attracted to Tibor. He took his rapt audience through his plan step by step, with Aunt Klari and Andras nodding their approval. He tried to split his attention equally between the three of them but found it hard to drag his eyes away from Gabriella's. They glowed.

'I will take our goods to Budapest myself,' said Milos. 'I'll speak to my contacts in the railways.'

'Speak to your brother,' said Andras. 'He knows Budapest.'

Milos had always intended to contact Tibor but did his best to avoid mention of his name, especially in front of Gabriella. He barely acknowledged Andras's advice. Nevertheless, straight after breakfast he set out for the station and the one phone that could get him through to Budapest. He carried with him a kilo of pork as a gift for Geza Apro.

He waited fruitlessly all afternoon for a return call from Tibor. The following morning he again fronted up at the station and, after a wait of some hours, his patience was rewarded. He told his brother how he planned to generate enough volume to make the enterprise worthwhile.

'I will have at least five kitchens working and possibly double that,' he said. 'Think back to the amount of jam and preserves we watched Aunt Klari and Jutka make back in Tokaj Street. You know how much they can produce in one day. Think how much they can produce in two or three weeks and multiply by the number of kitchens.'

'What about fruit?'

'All around us people have more fruit than they need. You know what it's like, the trees all ripen at once. These people don't need fruit; they need cash to buy meat and clothes. Even a little cash will buy a lot.'

'Sugar?'

'What I can't get here I'll get from Satoraljaujhely.'

'Jars?'

'The same.'

'Forget jam. People want substance. Send me preserves and pickles. Dried vegetables too.'

'Send you?'

'How else do you propose getting rid of them?'

'I thought I'd bring them into Budapest myself. Sell to the shops and maximise the return. Like I'm doing here.'

Tibor laughed but there was no humour in it.

'So you're just going to hop on a train? Don't you think your baggage will arouse suspicions?'

'I plan more than one trip,' said Milos hotly. 'People are leaving the country every day to find work in the cities. I'd be just another peasant.'

'That might work once,' said Tibor, 'maybe twice. The police are cracking down on the black market. Marko Street prison is full of people who had the same idea as you. Budapest is no place for amateurs.'

Milos smarted under the insult but bowed to the inevitable.

'I know how busy you are. I didn't want to trouble you over such a small matter,' he said.

'Getting you out of prison would be no small matter. The volume is barely sufficient but I can live with that. Send me everything you make in one consignment. Give me the date and I'll arrange the details.'

'How will you pay me?' said Milos.

'Take the value of the sale in pigs. Deal?'

'Deal,' said Milos.

'Take care, little brother,' said Tibor. 'And give my love to Gabi.'

That night over their evening meal, Milos explained the arrangement with Tibor. He put the best spin on the deal he could, claiming that the one shipment would reduce the risk and justified the lower price they would now receive. He said the one shipment and method of payment was his idea, but even Gabriella could see Tibor's hand in the transaction.

'Did he mention me?' she asked.

Milos was unable to lie. 'Yes. He sends you his love.'

'That's nice,' said Gabriella. 'I hope you sent him mine.'

Milos felt an arrow pierce his heart but it wasn't one fired by Cupid. This one had a sting to it: not of jealousy but fear. The fear that one day Tibor would return.

Aunt Klari contacted Aunt Jutka and together they spoke to trusted friends until they had ten kitchens lined up to make preserves. Each was told how many jars they were expected to produce. Milos undertook to provide jars and lids but each woman was required to arrange her own supply of fruit. The women seized the opportunity to become involved. Fruit was plentiful and their hands largely idle. For them it was money for jam at a time when money-making options were few.

Finding sufficient jars and lids proved more difficult. Milos wanted new jars but in Sarospatak there were few jars to be had at all. He grabbed what was available and caught the train to Satoraljaujhely. Even then he had to be cautious: anyone walking around from shop to shop buying up preserving jars would quickly be identified as a black marketeer and he couldn't afford the risk. It didn't take him long to realise that stocks of jars in the bigger town were little better than they'd been in Sarospatak. Milos could hardly believe that his scheme could falter for want of something once so commonplace, yet the evidence was compelling.

'Didn't there used to be a glass factory somewhere near here?' said Milos. He was in a small store on the way back to the railway station. The owner was an old man with failing eyesight and crippled by arthritis. The shelves of his store were hardly better off: most were empty and those that weren't carried mostly secondhand goods. There were around a dozen preserving jars on the shelves, not enough to satisfy a normal family let alone Milos's requirements.

'Levy Glass,' said the old man. 'The Jew that ran it made art glass. And it wasn't a factory, it was a studio. Fancy stuff, they made. Expensive.'

'Where was it?' asked Milos casually.

'Go back to Rakocsi Street, take the first left across the Ronyva and keep walking. Take the last street right before Czechoslovakia.' The old man grinned. Hungary's eastern boundary had shifted so many times in the past hundred years it had become something of a joke. 'My mother lives not far across the border,' he said, 'in Ujlac. She was born in the Ukraine, went to school in Hungary, got married in Czechoslovakia. Now she's living in Russia. You know what? She has lived in the same house, in the same shit hole village, all her life.'

Milos laughed politely. His father had told him a similar story when they'd first arrived in Sarospatak and he'd heard variations on it ever since. He thanked the shopkeeper and set off for the old glass studio, but held out little hope. His path took him past the Jewish cemetery which was already overgrown and in a state of disrepair. Who was left to tend it? He walked on, remembering everything that Tibor had told him about the deportations and trying to put it out of his mind. But the cemetery and the Jewish names on the doors of closed shops and businesses were a constant reminder.

By the time he'd crossed the river he was regretting the fact that he hadn't brought a drink with him. When he left Sarospatak he'd thought finding jars would be easy; it had never crossed his mind that he'd spend the day fruitlessly pounding pavements. As he drew closer to the border with Czechoslovakia his hopes diminished. There was evidence everywhere of the fierce fire fight that had taken place when the Germans tried to repel the advancing Russians. Craters in the roadway had been filled in but nobody had done much to repair the bombed-out buildings. What chance did a glass studio have amid so much destruction?

Milos made the right turn and began walking down a street where few buildings had been spared. The old shopkeeper hadn't given him a street number, so he searched for the name. Milos checked each doorway, constantly criss-crossing the road. Finally he found 'Levy Glass' written on a faded sign but the discovery brought only despair. The front of the building was little more than a doorway, a shell of what had once been showrooms and offices. Milos pushed forlornly at the door; to his surprise, it yielded. He looked around for somewhere shady to sit and catch his breath before the long walk back to the station, somewhere that hadn't been charred. The first thing that struck him was that the ruins were unlike many of the others: they'd been cleared of debris and made tidy. There was nowhere to sit.

Frustrated, Milos advanced into the wrecked building and was rewarded by the sight of broad stone steps leading up to a double door. The top three or four steps were in shade and, as far as Milos could tell, clean, as though someone had swept them. But who? And why? Milos slumped down on the top step and leaned against the door. His eyes were heavy and he was looking forward to a rest before trudging back to the station. Unexpectedly, the door gave under his weight. The hinges creaked loudly.

'Hello?'

Milos jumped to his feet. 'Hello?' he called back, peering through the doorway.

It took a moment for his eyes to adjust to the darkness within and another few moments to appreciate the reason for the gloom. Miraculously, the roof over the rear of the building was still intact. In front of him was a pile of boxes and crates, some on their side so Milos could see they were empty.

'Hello?' he called again.

'Come in,' said the voice. 'But whatever you want, we are closed.'

'Mr Levy?' said Milos.

'Yes, I am Levy.'

Milos heard the dull ring of tools being placed down on metal and the sound of footsteps on the bare timber floor. The gaunt frame of a man appeared from behind the stack of boxes.

'I am Levy,' he repeated, 'Benjamin Levy. Who are you?'

'Milos Heyman from Sarospatak.'

'Milos Heyman from Sarospatak,' the man repeated. He walked right up to Milos, adjusted his glasses and peered intently into his face. 'Tell me, Milos Heyman from Sarospatak, where were you?'

'Where was I?'

'Auschwitz, Buchenwald, Dachau, Theresienstadt, Mauthausen, Belsen?'

'None. I fled.'

'You fled?'

'My brother and I. Behind the back of God until we met up with the Russian army.'

'I should have fled. I should have fled with my family.'

'Yes, you should have. Where were you, Mr Levy?'

'Auschwitz. I lived.'

Milos nodded. There was nothing to add.

'Now, what are you doing here, Milos Heyman from Sarospatak?'

'I need glass preserving jars. One thousand, maybe fifteen hundred.'

'And you come to me?'

'There is no one else.'

'Why me? You have heard that Levy makes preserving jars?'

'No, art glass.'

'And do you know what art glass is?'

'No, not really.'

'Not really. So. My studio was famous throughout Europe, first for my art nouveau glass then for my art deco glass. I was very famous for my art deco. I was never famous for jars.'

'I'm sorry,' said Milos.

'Don't be. The world needs jars now, not art. Come.'

Benjamin Levy led Milos around the stack of empty boxes and crates, past a line of machines which were little more than large masses in the gloom, to a tiny room where the curtains were drawn back from the window and sunlight flooded in. A narrow bench and cupboards covered the far end and a table with six chairs crowded what space remained.

'Coffee, yes?'

'Yes,' said Milos.

'Jars?' said Benjamin Levy.

'Yes.'

'You saw the machines?'

'Yes.'

'They were to be our future, our leap into multiple production. Limited editions. The market for originals was becoming too exclusive, too expensive. We thought we could also do limited runs of good, simple designs and sell them in Britain and America.'

'What happened?'

'The war is what happened. When the machines arrived we had no room so we put them in storage. Nobody knew about them when they seized my business. These machines are all I have now. They are all I came home to. No wife, no family, just machines.'

'Do they work, these machines?'

'Almost. I have sugar. You want sugar?'

'One.'

'Before Auschwitz I took one spoonful of sugar. After Auschwitz I take two. It is fair, no?'

Milos smiled.

'There. Drink your coffee and we will discuss jars.'

'Can you make them?'

'I have glass in the Louvre. I have glass in museums in America. You ask can I make jars?'

'Can you make them by July?'

'Yes, Milos Heyman from Sarospatak, I can make by July.'

'Lids?'

'I have a friend makes lids.'

Milos sat and drank his coffee and told Benjamin Levy of his plans. He told him about Tibor and their contacts in the railway. They discussed cost and deadlines and how things were before Eichmann came. Finally, Benjamin Levy walked Milos to the door.

'Thank you, Mr Levy,' said Milos and shook his new friend's hand.

'Thank you, Milos Heyman from Sarospatak. Thank you for thinking of me.' The man's eyes sparkled. 'Levy is back in business.'

From mid-July and into the first week of August, Milos's ten kitchens sweltered under the heat of summer and stoves running hot. Aunts Klari and Jutka each produced two hundred and fifty jars of preserves, with the balance of one thousand spread among the remaining kitchens. Gabriella worked her heart out, relishing the smells and the industry which reminded her of happier times. For the entire duration of the bottling her nightmares stayed away.

Milos supervised the crating and paid off eight of the kitchens with cash from his pig sales. Only the aunts remained to be paid and Milos had invited them to share in the proceeds. Then, with Tibor's usual forged documentation, he despatched the entire consignment to Budapest. On his way home, he bought a bottle of Tokaj wine to celebrate. Later, when Gabi asked Aunt Klari and Andras to raise their glasses in his honour, he genuinely believed he was a hero in her eyes.

CHAPTER TWENTY-THREE

Tibor was a criminal but to some he was also a patriot. When the liberating Russian army first drove into Hungary the soldiers raped the women. Later they raped the country. *Zabra* was the word they used, which Hungarians quickly translated as 'give'. The Russians would point to a watch on someone's arm and say *'zabra'*. Maybe *zabra* was a Russian word for spoils of war, but the result was the same: whatever was *zabra* they took. They took bread from the arms of mothers who had queued for hours if not days. They took everything the Germans left behind. Watches, clocks, radios, gramophones, reading glasses, vases, kettles, household tools and anything else they fancied. They took wheat from the fields, coal from the mines and robbed the country of its industrial heart.

The Russians stole mercilessly from the Hungarian people. Tibor stole from the Russians and, in partnership with Vilagosi, sold his booty back to the people. Of course he was motivated by profit. But to a population stripped of everything but pride, his exploits also made him a patriot.

When the Russians appropriated all the leather from the tanneries that had managed to reopen, Tibor stole back enough to keep at least some shoemakers in business. When the Russians appropriated all the output from the textile mills, Tibor stole back enough to keep some clothing factories operating. Jobs, businesses and the fabric of commerce were sustained by the activities of Tibor, Vilagosi and their rivals, but it was Tibor who caught people's imagination because of his youth and his daring.

When the Russians decided to seize the stockpile of high-grade black coal from the mines of Komlo, they made a point of weighing each load and double-checking the number of coal wagons in each train. Tibor's solution was simple: he arranged for an extra train to pull up for loading. The Russians dutifully weighed the load and counted the wagons. But while the other trains headed east, Tibor's turned westward. By the time the Russians figured out that they'd loaded an extra train it was too late. Stealing trains became Tibor's trademark.

Vilagosi's empire expanded but he was wise enough to cut his opposition in on the deals. In truth he had little choice. Entire trainloads of coal or grain were too much for any one organisation to handle. He kept forty per cent of every load and sold the remaining sixty per cent in equal quantities to the four opposition gangs, leaving them free to price and distribute in their own territories.

The trade was so lucrative that the opposition went along with the deal and, for a while at least, Tibor's successes on the railways caused a fragile détente between the rival gangs. But as Vilagosi's organisation grew more powerful, jealousy and old enmities began to surface. It was clear to everyone that control of the railways could ultimately lead to control of crime in Budapest and, from there, all of Hungary.

Tibor was planning the hijack of a train loaded with brown coal when a panicked Pal Szarbo burst into his Ferenciek Street apartment.

'They got Imre!'

'Who?'

'I don't know. He was machine-gunned getting out of his car outside Gundel's restaurant.'

At that instant Tibor realised he was the heir to Vilagosi's organisation, not Pal Szarbo. Vilagosi's lieutenant should have taken charge, should be telling him what to do, not asking. Tibor seized the initiative. Pal Szarbo was used to taking orders. Tibor decided to give them.

'Was it police or opposition?'

'Opposition.'

'Then we must strike back immediately if our organisation is to survive. I want hand grenades thrown into the homes of all our competitors. If we don't know their homes, bomb their warehouses or offices. Bomb their bars, bomb their cars. Make certain every one of our opposition gets hit. Do it now and keep it up for two days. Keep our men active and constantly on the move. Deprive them of any opportunity to make private arrangements with anyone else. I'll set up a command centre in the bakery in Kobanya. Do it!'

Tibor sent messages to all the apartments he maintained telling his housekeepers to disappear for a week. In all the turmoil he had to expect that some of his organisation's foot soldiers would be turned and persuaded to reveal his hideouts. He summoned his driver and set out immediately for Kobanya. His mind raced as he tried to guess which of the opposition bosses was behind the assassination and what other moves he had planned. He expected raids on his warehouses but not all the warehouses were known. The organisation's cell structure made certain that nobody other than trusted leaders knew the whereabouts of more than half of their warehouses at any time. The organisation would survive provided its foot soldiers survived. Provided they took the initiative. Provided he survived.

For two days, during which he barely slept, Tibor orchestrated the gang warfare which exploded onto the streets of Budapest. His men hit hard and often. On the third day, when he felt he'd convinced his rivals that his organisation was nobody's easy pickings, he sent emissaries to each of the gang leaders informing them that the Vilagosi organisation was under his control. His offer of a truce, sweetened by a proposal to increase their share of the coal and grain to twenty per cent, was readily accepted.

His sources confirmed that the gang leader Mihaly Pfiel was behind the hit on Imre Vilagosi but Tibor was quick to suppress any suggestions of retaliation. A strike on Pfiel would only re-ignite the gang war. Besides, Pfiel had only done what the other gang leaders had been contemplating. His mistake had been in thinking the strength and resilience of the organisation resided exclusively in Vilagosi. Pfiel's assessment of Pal Szarbo had been correct in that the second-in-command hadn't been ready to assume command; he had, however, failed to take Tibor into his calculations. For that, the other bosses held him responsible for the warfare that had erupted.

Tibor's main problem centred on Pal Szarbo. Once order was restored, Vilagosi's former lieutenant began pressing his claim for leadership, or at least a greater say in how the organisation was run.

'You had your chance and you failed to take it,' said Tibor bluntly. 'However, that is not to say all your options are exhausted.'

The two men sat at the table in the Ferenciek Street apartment, eating a meal of pork fried by Tibor's housekeeper, Eva, but provided by Milos. Pal Szarbo was a problem Tibor had thought about endlessly from the moment the truce had been accepted. Conventional wisdom required him to get rid of Pal Szarbo before Pal Szarbo got rid of him. There was no room for rivalry at the head of any organisation. Tibor could not function if every day also brought the probability of a coup. He needed a lieutenant he could trust completely and a man who believed he'd been deprived of his right to assume control was hardly the ideal candidate.

Yet they needed each other. Tibor was still too young to command unquestioning loyalty and obedience from the hard men who were his section leaders and the men beneath them. Once his men started drifting away to other organisations he was finished. Pal Szarbo had the men's respect yet he lacked the ability to take ultimate command or to plan and develop their operations.

'What do you propose?' asked Pal Szarbo.

'We each have our strengths,' said Tibor. 'Imre Vilagosi was sharp enough to see that mine is in planning. Yours, on the other hand, is in commanding the men.'

'I won't be your lieutenant,' said Pal Szarbo contemptuously.

'But will you be my partner?'

Pal Szarbo's eyes narrowed.

'Fifty-fifty,' said Tibor. 'Joint leaders.'

'How will that work?' Pal Szarbo's eyes were filled with suspicion, but the prospect of being joint leader had clearly struck a chord.

'We each work to our strengths. Imre was responsible for planning; I will take over his role. While you are in every respect equal leader, you will continue to function as the second-in-command. That is your strength.'

'If I am second-in-command it means you are first-in-command,' snapped Pal Szarbo.

'Not at all,' said Tibor. 'We are joint commanders with the proviso that you are also acting second-in-command. We have no choice. That is the command structure that works. I can't do your job and you can't do mine. You demonstrated that when you came to me when Imre was hit.'

'I was caught off guard. I wasn't thinking clearly.'

'That is a luxury a leader cannot afford.'

Pal Szarbo seethed quietly.

'We make it clear that we are joint leaders?'

'As clear as you like.'

'And we split the proceeds down the middle?'

'Fifty-fifty.'

'I'll give it a go.'

'No,' said Tibor, 'you give it your all. You commit yourself one hundred per cent and you commit yourself now! This has to be what you want, the best solution. There can be no regrets later or resentments. I will give you total loyalty and support and I insist on nothing less in exchange.'

'Or?'

'You won't leave this table alive.'

Tibor's driver appeared in the doorway with a pistol tucked under his belt.

'You grow more like Vilagosi by the minute,' said Pal Szarbo dryly. He offered Tibor his hand.

Through the rest of 1946 and the best part of 1947, Tibor effectively ran what had been Vilagosi's organisation. He was careful to keep in the background in deference to Pal Szarbo, but nobody was in any doubt as to who was in command and who was lieutenant. The organisation prospered and Tibor began to amass wealth he'd never imagined possible. But he was a realist and understood that he only got away with doing what he did because of the post-war turmoil. The Russians' primary interest was in gaining political control of Hungary, from which everything else would flow. Centralised food production and distribution and state control of factories and banks was only a matter of time. He could see the heavy hand of the Soviets robbing the country blind, turning Hungary into a workshop for Russia and the population into little more than slaves. There would still be a place for him and his kind in the new order, but it would be a very dangerous place. Every day the AVO's network of spies and informers spread further and penetrated deeper.

Originally, his ambition had been to extract himself from day to day management by delegating more responsibility to Pal Szarbo. While his partner's courage was beyond question, there were still doubts about his ability to plan and recognise opportunities. Basically, Pal Szarbo lacked the necessary cunning and insight. All the while, alliances and allegiances were being put under increasing pressure from offers of cash to threats of blackmail. Nobody could be trusted.

Tibor quietly set about copying the tactics of the secret police and established a network of informers within his own organisation. He set his spies to catch their spies, and more spies to watch his spies. One by one he weeded out the suspect and disloyal from his organisation but could never be sure he'd got every one. The bottom line remained the same. He could trust nobody and he couldn't delegate control.

Back in Sarospatak, Tibor had always had a safe haven from his activities. He could always go home to their little cottage after his nocturnal forays. But in Budapest there was no such cottage and nowhere Tibor could call safe for more than a day or two. Gradually he'd established a more enduring coexistence with his more powerful opposition by taking care not to intrude into their activities. Now it was the AVO setting traps for him, and it was only his network of informers and his survival instincts that kept him safe.

Tibor often thought about Sarospatak and Gabriella and wished he could visit. But the inescapable fact was, the instant he stepped out of Budapest he lost the protection of his network. Once his absence was noted, his opposition would move quickly against Pal Szarbo. Once he'd decided to run, he knew he would have to take everything with him. There'd be no coming back.

As Christmas 1947 approached, Tibor made the biggest and most far-reaching decision of his life up to that moment: he decided it was time to leave Hungary. The Russians had gained control of the government and the crackdown on crime had begun. With his high profile, he realised his would be one of the first organisations targeted. He was not just a criminal but a trophy to be held up and made an example of. It would only be a matter of time before he was betrayed and caught. He'd managed to convert some of the new forints into Western currency and secreted it in a bank account in Switzerland, but nowhere near enough to justify the risks he'd taken over the previous years, or to give him the head start he needed in a new life. Yet he also realised there was a limit to the amount of assets he could convert without attracting attention. If his rivals even got a sniff of his intentions he would become a target. There was only one way out, but it was a way fraught with risk. Tibor set up the meeting that would either help him escape Budapest and Hungary or get him killed.

The man Tibor approached was the only competitor he would consider dealing with. His name was Endre Benke and his organisation was more than twice the size of Tibor's. In the limited dealings Tibor had had with his rivals, Benke was the only one he trusted to honour an agreement. As a sign of good faith, Tibor allowed his rival to nominate a meeting place. For security, they followed the convention of exchanging their trusted deputies as hostages to fair play.

They met early one morning in a private bath house in Gellert Hill near the western bank of the Danube. It was a legacy of Turkish occupation and was fed by thermal spring waters. It was one of many bath houses in the area but few were as ornate. The pool was circular and ringed by elegant stone archways which supported the high domed ceiling. The walkway around the pool was also circular, like a dimly-lit saucer around a cup. The effect was to focus attention onto the pool, which was illuminated by lights set into the domed ceiling that caused the water to glow an almost iridescent green.

When Tibor arrived, Endre Benke was already in the bath, floating on his back with his eyes closed. Tibor smiled as he eased himself into the soothing warm water. The meeting place was perfect. There were no windows and only one way in or out, a narrow stone corridor with a single solid timber door.

Behind the door, at the furthest end of the corridor, his bodyguard would now be sharing American cigarettes with Benke's bodyguard. They could not be overheard or surprised. Tibor lifted his feet from the bottom of the pool and lay with his head resting on the stone edge of the bath. Both men were clad only in their swimming costumes so there was no possibility of concealed weapons. Tibor relaxed but didn't close his eyes. Instead he seized the rare opportunity to look at his rival at close quarters.

Benke was at least twice his age, stocky and heavily muscled. Old scars criss-crossed his stomach, chest and shoulder, white ridges and lines amid a profusion of black hairs. At some stage Benke had taken a bullet through his shoulder and at another time suffered a jagged wound diagonally across his lower chest and abdomen. The wound had been stitched up by someone who had clearly never held a needle before in his life. It suddenly occurred to Tibor that Benke had probably done the stitching himself. The thought sent a shiver down his spine.

'I would come here every morning,' said Benke, finally breaking the silence. He still floated on his back, eyes closed. 'If only people like us were allowed the luxury of routine.'

'I would join you,' said Tibor. 'If only people like us were allowed the luxury of trust.'

A slight smile played across Benke's face.

'You don't trust me?'

'No. But I trust you more than most.'

Benke's smile grew.

'Then we have common ground,' he said. He opened his eyes, rolled onto his stomach and swam leisurely over to Tibor. The two men shook hands.

'Is it done?' said Benke.

Tibor nodded.

'Then why this meeting? Our arrangements are in place.'

'New arrangements,' said Tibor.

Tibor and his rivals all dealt in food and most commodities, although each had an area in which they were stronger than the others. For some it was pharmaceuticals, others cigarettes and whisky, nylon stockings and clothing or weapons. Tibor's strong point was coal.

'What new arrangements?'

'The Soviets have stockpiled more black coal for shipment back to Russia. Fuel for heating is already at a premium in Budapest, Debrecen, Pecs, you name it.'

'So?'

'Think what you got last winter for every bucket of coal you sold and double it.'

'Get to the point.'

Tibor sighed, as though unwilling to be rushed.

'It is possible to steal one of the trains. I want you to buy it, every wagonload, every single lump of coal.'

'Why would I do that?'

'Along with the train comes something much more valuable. My contacts in the railway.'

Benke pushed himself away from the wall and once again floated on his back. The man gave the impression of being totally relaxed and untroubled but Tibor could imagine the thoughts taking shape inside his head. The only question was, would Benke exploit his weakness or allow him to go graciously and with a fair portion of his wealth? Benke's eyes were closed but that was an indulgence beyond Tibor. Even relaxed, the older man was intimidating. He was a criminal and a killer by choice, not necessity. Tibor couldn't take his eyes off him.

'You defied my predictions,' said Benke eventually. He rolled over and stood staring hard at Tibor. 'I didn't think you'd last twelve months. I knew you didn't have the stomach for this work. You're nothing! Just an arrogant upstart, a piece of crap best flushed down the sewer. Did you really think that you, a boy, could walk into town and steal our business? I have children older than you. Do you have any idea how insulting it is to have you call meetings? To have you, a worthless piece of dog shit, deal us into your little schemes? You have no respect! I would have killed you if Vilagosi hadn't intervened.'

Tibor said nothing, just met Benke's eyes. Earlier he'd drawn comfort from the fact that neither of them carried a concealed weapon, but now he realised Benke didn't need one. The choice of location suddenly seemed deliberate and chilling. Benke could drown him without raising a sweat. It took all of his willpower to meet Benke's eyes and not react.

'Three things saved you,' snarled the older man. 'First, Vilagosi and, second, the fact that you were largely irrelevant. They were busy times and threw up more opportunities than we could handle. Three, you had coal. We should have killed you but what does it matter? I knew you wouldn't last.' His lip curled contemptuously.

'Lasting was never my intention.'

'Nor option.'

'The opportunity was there so I took it. But Hungary is not the only country which offers opportunity. There is all of Western Europe and America.'

'You come to Budapest, steal from me, shoot my men and now you ask me to finance your exit?'

'I never stole from you and I never shot at your men, except when Vilagosi was killed. My understanding is that neither were wounded fatally. And, yes, the deal is good so I'm asking you to finance my exit.'

'What's to stop me killing you now and taking over your operations?'

'You want the railways.'

Benke swam back towards Tibor, who braced himself for some kind of assault. He only hoped it wouldn't be fatal. Instead Benke folded his massive arms and rested them on the edge of the bath. He ignored Tibor and stared at the closed doorway.

'Tell me the deal.'

'Between twenty-four and twenty-eight wagons of black coal delivered to an abandoned railway warehouse on the outskirts of Budapest. From that point on you own the coal. You pay me for twelve wagons in hard currency at the same rate I normally charge.'

Tibor paused to let the first part of the deal sink in. He waited for a nod from Benke to continue before realising that there wouldn't be one.

'I need new identity papers. And help to cross the border into Austria. Once I reach the West I will contact Pal Szarbo with instructions to locate a package and deliver it to you. Inside the package you will find a complete breakdown of my railway network and letters of introduction.'

'What if you don't reach the West?'

'It's your job to make sure I do.'

'Supposing you make it to the West, what guarantees do I have that you will contact Szarbo? Or that he will send me the package?'

'Once I leave Hungary I leave for good. I have no need for the contacts. However ...' Tibor paused to make sure Benke understood what he had to say next. They were considerations which would never enter Benke's ruthless head. 'However, my contacts have need of me or at least a successor. My contacts in the railway are the only people in the world who trust me completely. They trust me with their lives. In return, I trust them completely and look after them. Life is not easy under this regime and barely sustainable on their pay. They need things to continue the way they are. I undertake to look after them as a debt of honour.'

'Touching.'

'Pal Szarbo was once a railwayman. I trust him not to betray me to the AVO or anyone else but I don't trust him not to make mistakes. He is very ambitious but, alas, not yet ready. If I just leave, he will try to take over and get himself

369

killed. However, he is known to my contacts in the railway. Take him into your organisation. Look after him, supervise him, make his cooperation worthwhile, and he will be an excellent go-between with the railwaymen.'

'Again, touching.'

'My men are loyal because they are paid to be loyal and my spies make sure they are loyal. If I abandon them it will only be a matter of time before they are sold out to the AVO or shot as you and your competitors fight over the spoils. Look after Pal Szarbo, reassure my men, and there will be no vacuum, just a straightforward takeover.'

'I envy you your simple view of life.'

'What's complicated? You get a trainload of coal for less than half price. You get my railway network. You get my number two and you get my organisation. There will be issues, but none you haven't faced before and overcome.'

'How do I know the AVO haven't penetrated your organisation? How do I know I won't be infecting my own?'

'I'm here, aren't I?' said Tibor. He smiled inwardly. Benke was in the bag. He was discussing the detail. He couldn't resist the deal.

'What if I refuse?'

'I'll offer the deal to someone else.'

'Who?'

'Someone else I can't trust.'

Benke smiled despite himself and slowly dragged his eyes away from the closed door. He used the wall to push off into the centre of the bath.

'Hard currency.'

'Or in combination with gold. In small ingots, not jewellery.'

'When?'

'At the warehouse. Once you've counted the wagons and verified the contents.'

'Now we negotiate.'

'The deal is already weighted in your favour. My risk is unchanged but my return is halved.'

'You came to me, boy. I didn't come to you. You are in no position to make demands.' Benke's eyes narrowed, the pupils as cold and hard as the coal they were discussing. 'Eight wagons. I will pay for eight wagons.'

'Ten,' said Tribor. 'I can't take less. There are too many palms to grease.'

'Eight,' said Benke. 'That is my final offer.'

'Ten,' said Tribor. 'And I'll throw in the pigs.'

'Pigs?' Benke's head rose sharply.

'A legitimate business,' said Tibor. 'I have been bringing sows into Budapest. They are distributed among peasants in nearby villages. I have more than two hundred and enough boars to make sure they are always breeding.'

'Go on.'

'I have no need to tell you how valuable they are. They fetch astonishing prices at the market.'

'You sell at the market?'

'Yes.'

'But why?'

'The bidding is fierce but I always win.'

Benke stopped floating and stood in the centre of the bath. Tibor could see that he was intrigued.

'You buy your own pigs?'

'Of course. What does it matter how much I pay? I get my money back, less a small percentage to the peasants, and I'm free to on-sell to butchers. Like I said, it is a legitimate business. Profitable, legal, safe.'

Benke nodded and for once his poker face betrayed him. He was impressed. More than that, he was weighing up possibilities.

'Deal,' he said. 'Ten wagons.'

'Deal,' said Tibor. This time he swam over to Benke and shook hands.

'I underestimated you, boy. I should have had you killed years ago,' said Benke matter-of-factly.

'Aren't you glad you didn't,' said Tibor.

'Comrade Kiraly?'

Istvan looked up from the pile of dossiers on his desk. He was so deep in concentration that it took a moment for his focus to adjust and his mind to re-engage the present. He was aware of other officers looking up from their desks, clearly curious.

'Yes?' said Istvan. An officer roughly the same age and rank as him stood respectfully in the doorway.

'Major Bogati sends his compliments and requires your attendance. He asks that you bring your dossier on Tibor Heyman.'

Istvan shuffled through his files until he found Tibor's. He flicked the file open and checked to see that it was both intact and up to date. He worked on it daily, either adding to it or simply digesting the information it contained. There was no reason to suspect that the dossier would be other than the way he had left it, but Istvan was nothing if not thorough, and thoroughness demanded certainty. He rose, aware that the looks on his fellow officers' faces had changed from curiosity to envy, and accompanied the young officer down the stairs and out onto the street. There was a car parked there, a black AVO Poboda. The young officer held the rear door open for Istvan.

Istvan suppressed a smile and climbed into the car. He hoped at least one of his fellow officers was observing from the window. None of them liked him and he was aware that behind his back they ridiculed him both for his size and his obsession with his dossiers. It didn't matter. It was enough for Istvan to know that they envied him, and one day soon he would be promoted far beyond their wildest ambitions. The young officer, who Istvan now realised was one of Major Bogati's drivers, started the car and pulled away from the kerb. Istvan had ridden in a car only three times. The first time in the Russian Zis which had taken him from Major Bogati's office in Sarospatak to his home so he could pack his bags. The second ride had taken him to the station with Major Bogati and the third, also in a Zis, had taken him from the station in Budapest to the police academy. The Poboda was nowhere near as imposing as the Zis but nevertheless Istvan settled back into the leather seat and did his best to make out that riding in the back of automobiles was a common occurrence.

'Where are you taking me?' he asked.

'Sixty Andrassy Street,' replied the driver.

Istvan tried to contain his excitement. He'd never been to the AVO headquarters before and envied those who had. The major had his main office at Sixty Andrassy Street and Istvan hoped that one day he would be invited to join him there. Istvan opened Tibor's dossier and began speculating on the reason for the summons. What did the major want? What did he need to know? Istvan was certain a desk in Andrassy Street depended upon his answers.

When the car pulled up in front of the AVO headquarters, Istvan waited for the driver to open his door for him, as he'd seen Major Bogati do. He realised the guards would be observing him and wanted to create a first impression that commanded respect. He strode from the car without casting so much as a glance at the sombre façade, as though it was as familiar to him as his own home.

'Officer Kiraly for Major Bogati. The major is expecting me.' Istvan presented his identity card. He was led up two flights of stairs before being shown into the ante room of the major's office. A middle-aged, grey-suited woman sat behind a drab green desk typing noisily. She looked up briefly to give Istvan a thin smile and pointed to a solitary wooden chair. Istvan sat and waited, continuing to review everything he knew about Tibor Heyman.

Twenty minutes later the door to the adjoining office burst open and Major Bogati swept through.

'Come,' he commanded.

Istvan rose from the seat as though a powerful spring had been released. He followed the major back out into the corridor and down a different stairwell to the one he'd ascended. These stairs were bare concrete and caged in by bars which reached up to the underneath of the stairs above. Istvan counted the flights as they descended and took note when they passed ground level. The change in the atmosphere the lower they went was immediately noticeable: the temperature plummeted and the air became both rank and damp. He shivered as his body adjusted to the chill. But there was something else which caused the small hairs on the back of his neck to stand on end. This was a place to be feared and the sense of fear was so powerful Istvan could taste it. At the bottom level they entered a long corridor with what appeared to be cell doors at regular intervals. As the major led him along the corridor he motioned to a couple of guards to join them.

'Open!' he commanded.

The guards unlocked one of the doors. The room was little more than one and half metres wide; half a metre of the floor space was taken up by what looked like a sunken stone bath with a heavy concrete slab lid chained against the wall. Istvan could imagine prisoners being stripped and forced to lie in the bath. He could imagine their terror as the concrete lid was lowered over them, leaving them to freeze slowly to death in tomb-like darkness and silence.

'These two valves,' said Major Bogati. He pointed to two turncocks on the wall. 'This one releases steam under pressure from the boiler next door through these outlets here at the foot of the bath. I'm told that the pain of steam on a frozen body has to be experienced to be believed. This turncock releases cold water. It is not uncommon for the water to turn to ice. Come.'

Major Bogati led Istvan to another room which contained two baths similar to the previous one but without concrete lids. Each had a single tap.

'This bath is fed from the boiler. The water is boiling. This one is fed from an underground tank and is rarely more than a degree or two above freezing. First the hot bath, then the cold, repeated at the whim of the interrogator. I find a single dip in each is usually effective. More than that can have the effect of scrambling the mind and rendering the exercise useless. Come.'

Istvan dutifully followed the major further down the corridor. The guards opened another cell. Its height and length could not have exceeded one and a half metres and its width was certainly less than a metre. His father's pig pens were bigger. There was a bunk bed barely wider than a human being, so close to the ceiling that a prisoner lying on it would not be able to sit up, and so short that no adult — not even Istvan — could stretch out upon it. No one could stand in the cell without stooping over. There was no lighting.

'Punishment cell,' said the major. 'There are several. The others are occupied. Come.'

He led Istvan back the way they'd come and into a narrow room where a row of chairs were arranged before a long thin window. Behind the chairs was a hot water radiator. A doorway next to the window led into another room furnished with a single metal bed which was fastened to the bare concrete floor in the middle of the room. The bed had strategically positioned leather straps to hold down arms and legs. A tall double-doored metal locker and a metal cabinet on castors were the only other items of furniture. The four walls were bare and featureless but for the window and doorway.

'There is a portable electricity generator in the cabinet. The locker contains the tools of the interrogator's trade. Thumbscrews, bonecrushers, that sort of thing. Comrade Vladimir Farkhas is our most skilled exponent but he has many willing disciples. Come.'

The major led Istvan back to the stairway and up two flights of stairs to another room. There was a wooden table in the middle of the room with two wooden chairs on one side and one on the other. Unlike the cells on the lower floor, the room was brightly lit by overhead lights and there was a radiator against the wall.

'Take a seat,' said the major.

Istvan moved towards the single chair on the opposite side of the table.

'Not there, comrade. That side is for prisoners. This side is for interrogators.'

Istvan sat but the major did not sit next to him. Instead he paced back and forth across the room behind Istvan.

'A good interrogator should never need to go to the bottom level. The art of interrogation is to know the answer to every question you ask. A good interrogator does not seek answers but confirmation. Understand?'

'Yes, sir.'

'The punishment cells represent a failure on the part of the interrogator, a deficiency in technique. Understand?'

'Yes, sir.'

'When you ask a question the answer of which you are not one hundred per cent sure, you reveal your lack of knowledge to the prisoner. This gives him strength and the will to resist. At that point you lose the battle and downstairs offers the only solution. Yes, you will get your answers then, but the methods are unsatisfactory.'

'Sir!'

'On the other hand, convince the prisoner that you already know everything and he will open up like a hungry little bird waiting to be fed. He will see no disloyalty in telling you what he believes you already know.'

'Sir!'

'We have brought in a man with an interesting story. He accepts our money and claims to be loyal. I believe he has told us all he knows. He was given the same tour I gave you. He sat in that chair and this is the story he told.'

Major Bogati walked around the table and sat in the prisoner's chair opposite Istvan.

'This man is a foot soldier for Mihaly Pfiel. He is a thief, a hired gun, but not, I think, a very good one and probably a liar. But we pay him for rumours and unguarded comments; for all his faults this man has good ears. He takes our money because otherwise we would send him to Gyustofoghas gaol. He is not brave. He shat himself when he was brought into this building. They had to clean him up a second time after taking him downstairs. Then I interrogated him.

'He said Mihaly Pfiel was furious because he had been offered coal by his rival, Endre Benke. He said Benke will soon take delivery of an entire trainload of coal.'

Istvan sucked in his breath.

'Yes. You see the connection? Our man also believes at least one other gang leader, Grosz, has also been offered coal by Benke.'

'He would need the railways, comrade Major.'

'Exactly. How would Benke get the railways?'

Istvan closed his eyes. There were two obvious options: Tibor Heyman and Benke had joined forces, or Benke had captured Tibor and forced him to give up his contacts. But if either event had occurred, they would have heard. Istvan would not be sitting in AVO headquarters answering these questions.

'He's getting out,' said Istvan. 'It fits.'

'Why?'

'In August he was buying hard currency and gold. Not huge amounts but enough to be noticed. Enough to finance a major crime, but none occurred that we are aware of. The suspicion is that he somehow took the money out of the country. That would be consistent. He once bragged to me how he always took out insurance. He is patient, Tibor Heyman. He thinks

377

long-term and protects himself against every eventuality. But he is also quick to react when he sees something he cannot protect himself against.'

'Such as?'

'Collectivisation. On its own, collectivisation only encourages a black market. But when it is enforced by a network of informers, a network that burrows deeper and reaches further each day, the life of a black marketeer becomes extremely difficult. One day we will successfully infiltrate his organisation and he knows that. He is not big enough to have a trusted chain of command like Benke or Pfiel so he is more vulnerable.'

'Couldn't he be dead?'

'Then where are the rest of the dead? The takeover would not be clean and there are always old scores to be settled. We would know if he was dead, or if he'd joined forces with Benke, willingly or unwillingly.'

'So how does Benke fit in?'

'Greed. If the amount of cash Tibor Heyman sent out of Hungary is insufficient for his needs, he'll want one more pay day. A big pay day.'

'So he sold the train to Benke?'

'And his contacts in the railways. Cash on delivery. Hard currency.'

'Well done, comrade Kiraly, you have given me confirmation. Now we must find out when and how.'

The major snapped to his feet. 'Come.'

Istvan followed the major back out into the corridor and up four levels, three above ground level and one above the major's office. Once more Istvan found himself in a windowless office but this one had a radiator, a large desk and filing cabinets. Two phones sat on the desk.

'My driver will take you back to gather your files. You will report here for work tomorrow morning at eight.' Major Bogati allowed a slight smile. 'I will find someone to escort you from the building.'

Istvan followed the major from the office, stunned by the speed of change. But an even greater surprise awaited him. His mentor handed him over to a guard.

'Tomorrow you will need upgraded papers. My driver has them. Earn them, because many opposed my decision on the basis of your youth. Goodbye, Lieutenant.' Major Bogati turned abruptly and strode away to his office, leaving Istvan speechless.

The driver saluted as he held open the back door of the Poboda. 'Your papers are on the seat, sir.'

Sir. Lieutenant. Istvan sat and picked up the file and opened it. The papers confirmed his promotion. He closed his eyes. He was just twenty years old and already a lieutenant. Moreover, he'd been appointed to Major Bogati's staff. His prospects were dazzling. With luck and a little information, he would be instrumental in the capture of Endre Benke and his old schoolmate, the arrogant Jew Tibor Heyman. Life did not get any sweeter.

CHAPTER TWENTY-FOUR

Railway stations are among the coldest places on earth. The engine driver and fireman waited patiently while their papers were inspected for the third time, stamping their feet and waving their arms around to keep warm. Early December snow lay in patches on the ground and turned the mounds of coal into miniature versions of alpine snow caps. The locomotive crew had no concerns other than to keep their circulation flowing. Their papers were official and in order, their train accounted for and the number of carriages verified. Still the Russians were cautious and had intensified security around the loading dock. The train eventually departed one hour late, which for a railway system that rarely ran on time, especially in winter, was as good as anyone could hope for. Tibor was on hand to observe the passage of the train through Budapest, to count the number of wagons and observe whether it was attracting abnormal interest. There were twenty-six coal wagons and a guard van at the rear which his informants said carried six heavily armed Russian soldiers. His contacts observed the train every second of its brief stay in Budapest and its transfer from the southern to the eastern network. If the police were watching the train, his informants failed to detect them.

In the early hours of the morning, the train began the second leg of its journey to Russia, swinging south-east towards Debrecen then north-east to the border at Zahony. Only the engine would reach the border. Just outside Szolnok, a small town halfway between Budapest and Debrecen, the coal train was pulled into a siding to allow other trains to pass. A train carrying low grade brown coal from the northern hills to Budapest, forced to detour by unscheduled track repair, was also diverted onto a siding. Sometime during the night the locomotives were switched. Vodka handed to the guards as a gesture of solidarity from their socialist comrades enabled the guard wagons to be switched without disturbing the guards' sleep. With perfectly valid papers, both locomotives continued on to their respective destinations, the difference being that the black coal went west while the brown coal went east.

Tibor had chosen Szolnok to effect the switch because the town sat on the intersection of two main lines, one entering Budapest through the south station, the other through the eastern. In the unlikely event that the eastbound train was stopped at the border and somebody who knew the difference between brown and black coal spotted the switch, the police would first have to figure out how and where it had occurred and then guess which route the black coal had been taken. By then the coal would have been hidden away in locations throughout Budapest.

'The train has cleared Zahony, comrade Kiraly. Twenty-six wagons of coal as per the manifest. The papers were in order. What do you say to that?' Major Bogati's steely eyes bored into Istvan.

'My information is good, comrade Major,' said Istvan.

'The coal is now in Russia,' snapped the major.

'We only believe the coal is in Russia, comrade Major,' said Istvan.

'Explain!'

'Did you see the coal? Did I?'

'I gave instructions for the covers to be pulled back. The wagons were inspected. They were carrying coal.'

'I don't dispute that they were carrying coal, comrade Major, they just weren't carrying our coal. Our coal is on the way to Budapest.'

'You seem very sure of yourself, comrade Lieutenant.'

'Tibor Heyman is very resourceful, comrade Major,' said Istvan, 'we know that. And the railways are his playground. We also have confirmation from your man in Mihaly Pfiel's organisation and further confirmation last night from one of Grosz's men.'

'Last night?'

'He was arrested for fighting and taken to a police station in Lipotvaros. He was brought here secretly for questioning. He confirmed that Grosz is standing by for his share of the delivery tonight. Yesterday afternoon he helped load a truck with sacks to bag the coal.'

The major turned away in thought. If Grosz was preparing for a delivery that night then clearly the train's load had been switched and switched a long time before the train reached Zahony.

'Rocks. Wagons filled with rocks with coal sprinkled on top.'

'Most probably, comrade Major.'

'Did Grosz's man say when or where?'

'This man is a nobody, comrade Major. He would not be told until the last moment and maybe not even then.'

'Where is he?'

'Downstairs, comrade Major.'

'His absence may arouse suspicion.'

'He was arrested for starting a fight. There were witnesses. Our man who provoked the fight was also arrested. No one would suspect our involvement. No one can make a connection between his arrest and the coal.'

'So we have no confirmation of the location or the time?'

Istvan shrugged. 'The railways are the railways, comrade Major. The coal will arrive when it arrives. But it will be at night and probably tonight. I believe that at this moment only Tibor Heyman knows exactly where the coal is and where it will be unloaded. He will use a new depot and tell nobody until he absolutely has to. Can we rely on your original informant to pass on the location to us?'

'He has 100,000 forints of ours and we have his son. He is reliable. Provided he is told in time. Provided he has access to a phone. Provided the phone works. For your sake, comrade Lieutenant, you had better pray the phone rings.'

Many people argue that Budapest *is* Hungary and the provinces merely the backyard that provides it with food. All main roads and train lines radiate from Budapest like the spokes of a wheel. Everything comes into Budapest, whether or not it is destined to remain there; Budapest imports from one province and exports to another. The rail lines in and out are fringed by the necessities of this trade: warehouses, granaries, quarries, timberyards and animal pens, many with rail spurs so that goods can be shunted directly to where they are needed or stored. Heavy industry and manufacturers also cluster around the railways.

During the Soviet siege of Budapest, many railside buildings were destroyed, either wholly or partially, and abandoned. As a result Tibor did not lack for places to offload his coal. He knew that if the police were on the lookout for his train they would expect it to approach from the east on the line to Keleti Station. For that reason, he decided to approach from the south and use an abandoned warehouse which prior to the war had been used for storing and rewinding textiles.

Tibor had been holding back from using the warehouse until a suitable occasion arose. It had the benefits of being fully enclosed with its own railway line running through the heart of it. It was also isolated on three sides which made it easy to secure. The fourth side was protected by a stone wall with steel railings on top which fronted onto a road running parallel to the Danube. A double-steel railing gate secured the only entrance and it was protected by a guard house which, before the war, had checked trucks in and out. The warehouse also had the advantage of being close to the industrial centre of Csepel Island, where trucks loaded with bags of coal would not attract attention.

The only negative was that the warehouse could handle only twelve wagons at once, which meant fourteen wagons would have to be stored in the open while the first twelve were unloaded. In mitigation, the unloading would be quick with the first wagons unloaded to one side of the tracks and the second twelve unloaded to the other. The remaining two wagons could be unloaded directly onto trucks.

The location was good, the switch of trains had gone off without a hitch and the coal was due into the warehouse yards on time. It never ceased to amaze Tibor how efficient the railways could be when there was money at stake. Nevertheless he was unusually anxious. Not because of flaws in his planning or in the execution but because of the need to share information with Benke's men. He'd arranged for Benke to have his men on standby halfway between the eastern and southern stations and had promised to reveal the location to his deputy thirty minutes before the train's arrival. Benke appreciated the security and had approved the arrangements and Tibor had no reason to distrust him. But the deputy also had people to inform and Tibor had no reason to trust them.

There was another complication. In the past Tibor had always overseen the unloading but made sure he was kilometres away before informing the other organisations of the location of the coal so they could collect what was due to them. So far there had been no breaches of security, but Tibor had always made supervising the disposal of the coal Pal

Szarbo's responsibility, just as the other bosses always delegated the responsibility of collecting their share of the coal to their deputies. The fact that the location had to be revealed before he put in his appearance was cause for concern.

Tibor sat in the unlit offices of a leather goods factory which would have gone broke if he hadn't been able to provide the owner with hides. The owner asked no questions and simply provided the keys when Tibor made his request. The office had an uninterrupted view over the old textile warehouse, the rail spur and the road approaches. Downstairs in the garage, Pal Szarbo and three henchmen armed with German machine pistols sat in a Zim awaiting instructions. Tibor's driver waited in a second Zim.

Tibor stared out into the night, mentally reviewing arrangements. If everything went according to plan, Benke's men would have him in Austria by the following morning, with a new identity and enough cash to start a new life. Milos and Gabriella also featured in his scheme: he planned to arrange their escape and transportation to whichever country took him in, once he'd set himself up in business. But even Tibor was reluctant to look that far ahead. There were too many hurdles to jump first, too many things to go wrong, and too many people knowing too many details.

Movement on the distant rail line caught his attention. He raised his German Zeiss military binoculars and counted the wagons as they passed beneath the lights at a road crossing. The train wasn't his. Within the next ten minutes he expected to see his wagons pass by, pushed from behind by a shunting locomotive onto the rail spur and into the warehouse. He turned his attention to the front of the warehouse, checking the road for any signs of movement. Betrayal now could only mean that somebody in the railways had talked. He waited and watched, oblivious to the seeping cold in the unheated office.

He watched the roadway for eight minutes before alternating his attention between the road and the railway.

Another five minutes passed with no movement in either place. He kept up his vigil as the minutes continued to tick past. His train was ten minutes late but that was no cause for alarm. The delay could be explained a dozen different ways. What was gratifying was the lack of activity on the road. The longer he watched the more certain he was that none of the railwaymen had been pressured by the AVO to betray him.

Twenty minutes after the scheduled arrival time, Tibor saw his wagons pass under the lights at the level crossing. They moved slowly, the underpowered shunting locomotive straining under the load. Right there was the reason for the delay. Tibor swung the focus of his binoculars back to the front of the building. Nothing moved. He rose, flicked on his torch and descended two flights of stairs to the garage. Because it had no windows, Tibor had allowed his men to keep the garage light on. Some were dozing and all were clearly bored. That would change.

'All clear.' He handed Pal Szarbo the address of the textile warehouse and two keys. 'This key opens the gate. This opens the warehouse. Get there as quickly as you can and park the car inside. The railwaymen have instructions to uncouple twelve wagons and shunt them into the warehouse. The time this takes will allow Benke's men to arrive. Don't unload until they have counted and inspected the wagons. I'll keep watch. If I turn the light on in the office upstairs, get away as fast as you can. Understand?'

Pal Szarbo extended his hand from the car window and gripped Tibor's. 'You should not go alone. Understand? My wife agrees.'

Tibor stared hard at his deputy before nodding. So Pal had also decided to cross the border. Tibor found it hard to argue with his decision.

'Where?'

'The hills.'

Tibor nodded. 'The hills' referred to a safe house in Pest where Tibor could contact him and let him know where they could meet once he'd reached Austria. He gave his deputy's hand a final squeeze, binding the agreement. 'I'll turn the lights out and open the door. Go quickly my friend.'

The garage plunged instantly into darkness. Tibor used his torch to find the door and open it. The driver had the good sense not to use his headlights until the car was well away from the building. Tibor closed the door and switched the light back on. He turned to his driver.

'A little patience.'

The man nodded.

Tibor raced back upstairs and again scanned the road in front of the warehouse. Nothing had changed. He swung around to check the progress of the train and was relieved to see its red rear light disappearing up the spur. As he watched the rear light blinked out. Someone was thinking. Tibor directed the binoculars back to the front of the factory and watched as Pal Szarbo's car turned in through the metal gates. It stopped and one of the men opened the door to the warehouse. When the lights disappeared inside, Tibor swung the binoculars back to the road. There was no movement. Nothing. He picked up the office phone and dialled. Nyers, Benke's deputy, answered immediately. Without identifying himself, Tibor passed on the address, listened while it was repeated back to him and hung up. He took his Luger out of his coat pocket, made sure it was loaded and put it down on the desk alongside his torch. He still had a long wait and it would be a lot more comfortable without the weight of the pistol in his pocket.

Tibor once again picked up the binoculars, not expecting to see anything until Benke's men arrived. They would be directed straight into the warehouse and the doors closed behind them. Again, there was nothing to cause alarm. He put down the glasses and rubbed his eyes. After months of careful planning everything was falling into place. His pockets were filled with the hard currency he'd been cautiously buying as he liquidated his assets. The coal was ready to be unloaded and Benke's men were standing by with payment, new papers and an escort across the border. For the first time in his life, Tibor was putting his fate in the hands of others. In that instant he understood why he'd never done it before and never would again. He smiled grimly. Surviving in Hungary had been difficult, but leaving was far and away the most dangerous thing he'd ever attempted.

Benke's deputy wrote the address on a piece of paper and called his three squad leaders over. Each had ten men under his command. They'd all holed up to wait in a bar that Benke owned midway between the eastern and southern stations. It had seemed the ideal location to prepare the men for the operation: they could enjoy a glass or two of beer or plum brandy in warmth while they smoked their cigarettes and steeled their nerves. Each of the squad leaders read the address silently, forbidden to read it aloud. Even so, Nyers had thought hard about revealing the address at all, preferring just to tell his squad leaders to follow behind his car in their trucks. But even at the dead of night with few vehicles on the road, there was no guarantee that one of the trucks wouldn't stall and become separated. There was a lot of coal to unload and Nyers wanted it done quickly. He didn't want to take the risk of losing a squad of men before the operation began.

'Everyone out now,' he ordered.

'A quick piss,' said Gyorgy, one of the squad leaders.

Everyone laughed. Gyorgy's weak bladder was the source of endless jokes.

Tibor watched the convoy of trucks arrive and held his breath as they passed through into the warehouse. The back of the trucks were filled with either Benke's men or gendarmes and only time would tell. He was too far away to hear gunfire but his man on the gate had flares and instructions to ignite them at the first sign of trouble. He waited another half an hour until he spotted a brief spill of light at the rear of the warehouse and movement on the rail line. The first twelve wagons had been unloaded and taken to a siding. Tibor picked up his torch and his binoculars and slid his Luger pistol back into his coat pocket. It was business as usual, even though there was nothing usual about this last transaction.

He directed his driver away from the road that led to the warehouse entrance and towards the rail line instead. Just before the level crossing he instructed him to turn onto a disused service road that ran parallel to the tracks and to switch off his lights. A wire fence and gate enclosed the road. Tibor told his driver to stop while he unlocked the gate. The night was colder than he expected and the wind had died away. The city would awake to frozen puddles and heavy frost. In the stillness he could hear the sounds he'd lived with all his childhood: wagons coupling and uncoupling and locomotives huffing and wheezing under load. Tibor opened the gate and allowed the car to pass through before pushing it closed. He bound the chain around the gate and gatepost but closed the padlock around a single link, giving the impression that the gate was locked. The Zim was more economical than powerful but would have no trouble pushing through the gate in an emergency.

'Drive slowly, lights off. Turn left along the side of the rail spur.'

For once Tibor sat in the front passenger seat. The overcast had begun to break up but the moon was long gone. He thought his driver might need an extra pair of eyes to find the service road by the spur and he also wanted to check for anomalies. They found the spur road and turned. Sparks flashed in the darkness ahead of them as steel wheels scraped on damaged track. Seventy metres from the rail entrance to the warehouse Tibor ordered his driver to turn off towards a straggly, stunted stand of privet.

'Turn the car around in case we need to leave in a hurry. Park among the privet. Use the machine pistol only as a last resort and make sure it isn't me you point it at.'

The driver grunted as though insulted. He had been one of Tibor's first hirings and his courage and loyalty had been tested many times. Tibor slipped away and stole into the warehouse under the cover of the arriving train. He climbed a ladder into what had been a signal box when train arrivals and departures were a regular event. The box gave him an uninterrupted view over both sides of the train and warehouse. His first glance was reassuring. Benke's men were well drilled and working hard at bagging coal. Pal Szarbo was supervising the unloading. Not satisfied with appearances, Tibor quartered the building and diligently checked distance, middleground and foreground for evidence of a trap. He spotted Benke's deputy, Nyers, at the far end of the warehouse urging his men on. Tibor noted that he was carrying a small sub-machine gun. Business as usual.

Above the rail line was a gantry once used to support the crane that lifted the heavy rolls of fabric off the wagons. The crane had been dismantled and shipped to Russia but the walkway alongside the gantry remained. Instead of descending from the signal box, Tibor climbed on up to the walkway. He couldn't help grinning ruefully as he strode above the hardworking men bagging coal, none of whom had any inkling of his presence. The sound of his footsteps was lost amid the clang of their shovels and the hiss from the steam engine.

'You know, you could hide an entire company of AVO men up here and no one would be any wiser.'

Nyers spun around to see where the voice had come from. Only belatedly did he think to look up. He wasn't amused.

'I was expecting you half an hour ago. I was beginning to think you'd double-crossed us.'

'My Luger against your sub-machine gun? I don't think so.' Tibor climbed to one of the gantry's supports and slipped quickly down the ladder onto the warehouse floor.

'Nobody's unloading the remaining two wagons,' he said.

'I'm going to bring them in and unload them in here,' said Nyers. 'What kept you?'

'A man can't be too careful. Now, you've counted the wagons, you've seen the coal. Payment and papers.'

'You know where to rendezvous?'

'Yes. Payment and papers.'

The front doors had just opened to allow a loaded truck to leave when the warehouse filled with bright white light. Tibor grabbed Nyers by the front of his coat.

'Why?' he demanded fiercely.

'Damn you! Who did you tell?' Nyers grabbed Tibor's hand and jerked it away from his throat.

'Pal Szarbo. He came straight here. I watched him.'

'No one else?'

'No.'

Nyers' eyes narrowed and scanned the men racing onto the trucks.

'Gyorgy! Here! Everybody else onto the trucks. Now!'

One of Nyers' squad leaders came running up towards them. 'Boss?'

'You just took your last piss,' said Nyers. He raised his gun and fired a short burst which cut the squad leader in half.

Nyers turned to Tibor. 'The AVO must have got to him. He was the only one I let out of my sight. The deal is off. No payment, no papers. Go! We'll keep the AVO occupied. I owe you that much.'

'Tell Benke I'll give him the railways anyway.'

Any further exchange was made impossible by a burst of gunfire from the guards posted outside. Hard-revving trucks added to the commotion. Tibor scaled the ladder back up to the gantry. When he reached the walkway he ran and didn't look back. Had the AVO covered both entrances? Had they had the time? They were the only questions that mattered. In the few minutes it took to reach the end of the walkway, Benke's men had fled the warehouse but he could hear the sounds of battle raging out front in the street. Had his luck held this one last time? He dropped as much as climbed down the ladder to the signal box, descended another few steps and jumped the rest. He ran towards the last wagon, dropped down, rolled and slipped under it.

The locomotive was still puffing but he assumed the driver and fireman had run off at the first gunshot. He scanned the darkness left and right but saw no movement and no lights except for a glow from the firebox in the locomotive's cabin. That was wrong. Why had the fireman left the firebox door open so the heat could escape? Tibor's heart was pounding so hard the sound of it seemed to resonate inside his head. He tried to calm down so he could think clearly. Maybe the fireman had been topping up the firebox when the AVO arrived. Maybe he'd just dropped his shovel and run. He pulled his Luger out of his coat pocket and eased himself out from under the wagon and began to angle away. The moment he glanced at the locomotive cabin he realised his mistake. The floor and steps of the cabin were splattered with blood. If the firebox door had been closed he never would have noticed.

'Halt! Throw down your weapon and raise your hands!'

A torch split the darkness, searching for him. Tibor needed a miracle; almost immediately he received one. The AVO hadn't had time to search the surroundings properly. They'd missed his car! He heard the engine of the Zim burst into life. Tibor didn't hesitate. He dug in his toes and sprinted. The darkness ahead of him erupted as his driver provided him with covering fire. He heard a scream above the gunfire and the torch went out. He zig-zagged while bullets ricocheted off the ground around him and hummed past his ears. When he'd shown his driver where to park, seventy metres had seemed uncomfortably close to the warehouse but now it was a gulf, so much further than the bridge over the Bodrog or the mined bridge in the Carpathians.

When his driver stopped firing Tibor assumed the man was simply obeying instructions not to shoot him by mistake. The engine of the Zim revved furiously, impatiently. Tibor charged into the privets, elated that he'd actually made it, and reached for the door. Instead he slammed up against the side of the car as though kicked there by a horse. He couldn't work out where the bullet had hit him, only that it had and that he had marginal control over his left arm and shoulder. He opened the door with his right hand and slumped into the passenger seat.

'Drive!' he yelled. But his driver was beyond hearing. The entire back of his head was missing and Tibor realised he was sitting in what remained of the poor man's brains. He reached across, opened the driver's door, put both feet against the man's body and pushed. As the driver flopped out onto the ground, the engine note died down. The driver's foot had been jammed on the accelerator. Tibor had only had two driving lessons in his life and on both occasions they'd been in fields when he'd gone to check on his sows. He stabbed his foot onto the clutch, slammed the gear shift into first and floored the accelerator. Keeping his numb left arm on the wheel, he released the handbrake and began to ease his foot off the clutch. The windscreen shattered. Tibor ducked reflexively and as he did his foot slid off the clutch and the motor stalled. Desperately he depressed the clutch and pushed the starter button, the ignition barely audible above the bullets clanging against the car's body. It was a sound he'd heard before, following behind the Russian tanks.

He released the clutch and the Zim lurched forward. He slammed the car into second gear. The doors swung violently either side of him but he ignored them. The cold night air made his eyes water and he couldn't pick out the service road. With little choice he turned on the headlights, glanced in the mirror and saw two other sets of headlights light up and begin moving. The numbness in his left arm and shoulder gave way to the most searing and intense pain he'd ever experienced. It hurt just to hold the wheel while he used his right hand to crash the gear lever through the gates into third. In the nick of time he saw the road branch right to run parallel with the main train line, cried out in pain as he hauled down on the steering wheel with his left arm. Immediately he was confronted by a single bright light ahead. His luck had finally deserted him: the AVO were behind and ahead of him. But when he looked again, he noticed something familiar about the light, something which at any other time would have registered immediately. It was a train light. Yes! There was a train on the rail line heading towards him. He pinned the accelerator to the floor with every ounce of strength, willing the straining engine to crank up a few more revolutions. The railways had always been a friend to him. Now, at this most desperate moment of his life, they offered hope of escape.

Tibor ignored his pain and stared as hard as he could into the night, trying to remember the exact distance between the gate and the road, the road and the level crossing. He checked the mirror. The AVO were closing on him, their cars more powerful and their drivers infinitely more competent. He checked the train light. Was it too close? Or too distant? How could he tell? He searched the road ahead for the gate, hoping with all his might that the AVO had left it open so he wouldn't have to crash through it. He saw it suddenly, pushed to the side, but his relief was only temporary. Flame spat at him from both sides of the road. The AVO had posted men at the gate.

Tibor ducked down as low as he could and still see the road. He was stunned when one of the AVO officers stepped out into the middle of the road and calmly and deliberately began firing at him. The Zim's left headlight shattered. A bullet passed over his head and thudded into the roof. Another smashed through the top rim of the steering wheel and deflected out through the rear window. Tibor wrenched down on the wheel and aimed the car at the officer. In the split second he lined him up, Tibor saw a face he'd all but forgotten, pinned in the light of the one remaining headlamp. The officer jumped back out of the way. The Zim missed him by mere centimetres. The man might have thought he was safe but the flailing passenger door caught him, smashed him hard against the gate post, hooked up his coat and began dragging him along the ground.

Tibor heard the man's scream but almost immediately it was drowned by the shriek of the locomotive whistle. The engine driver was warning of his approach. Tibor eased off the accelerator momentarily to line up the corner and turned hard left towards the level crossing. The Zim skidded, lost speed and power. The motor groaned and spluttered. Tibor needed to change down a gear but wasn't sure how. He simply pointed the bunny-hopping Zim across the tracks and hoped for the best. All too slowly the car picked up speed.

'Come on! Come on!' he screamed.

Behind him the AVO cars were less than fifty metres away. To his right the train was bearing down, whistle shrieking, with no chance at all of slowing.

'Come on! Come on!'

The Zim bounced onto the railway lines, the interior lighting up in the full glare of the train's headlight. Suddenly the light was above him and Tibor realised he had only seconds to live. Or escape. He closed his eyes.

The train missed the car. It whistled by, centimetres from the back bumper, buffeting the Zim with shockwaves of air. Tibor was dimly aware of the body of the AVO officer disentangling from the passenger door. He held on as the Zim finally reached a speed appropriate to third gear. Behind him, the AVO cursed and waved their fists at the seemingly endless line of wagons passing in front of them.

*

Milos felt faintly ridiculous but the goose didn't seem to mind. It followed behind him as faithfully as a dog on a lead, but Milos knew its only interest was the little inducements he handed out every few hundred metres. Every so often it banged its bill against his leg to remind him. He stopped again, reached into his pocket and brought out another palmful of grain, angling his hand so that the goose could get to it more easily. Christmas was just two weeks away and he was determined to make sure it was one he and Gabriella would always remember. The goose was destined to become part of those memories.

With Gabriella back to full strength, the time was fast approaching when he would ask her to take to the road again, this time on a journey away from Sarospatak. There was nothing left for them in Hungary and no reason to remain, other than the fact that the AVO seemed determined nobody should leave. Milos planned to marry Gabriella after her nineteenth birthday and cross the border some time in the month that followed.

They had at last become lovers, an event as inevitable as the seasons. Gabriella had simply faked a nightmare and Milos had come to her rescue as he always did. Their deception had fooled no one. Aunt Klari had simply waited a decent interval before politely enquiring when the wedding would be.

'Spring,' Gabriella had replied.

'Then tell Milos to stay in the house at night. Winter will be hard. Tell him to stay and keep you warm.'

The snow had an icy crust, making it treacherous to walk on, but it was nothing Milos hadn't experienced before. The pathway was familiar and he knew exactly where the ditches and potholes were. Nevertheless he kept his eyes on the path immediately ahead, which was why he failed to see the gendarme waiting where the pathway intersected with the cart track leading to Aunt Klari's.

'Milos Heyman,' said the gendarme.

Milos stopped dead in his tracks and looked up. He recognised the gendarme immediately. They'd been classmates.

'Matyas! What brings you and your bicycle out here?'

'Orders, Milos. I've been ordered to question you and search the house you're living in.'

'Why?'

'I'm looking for your brother.'

'Tibor! I haven't seen him for more than two years. He lives in Budapest.'

'I know.' The gendarme looked unhappily down the track to Aunt Klari's, not thrilled at the prospect of having to navigate it with his bicycle. 'Are you sure he hasn't come back?'

'Of course I'm sure! If he'd come back he would have come straight to me. What makes you think he's come back to Sarospatak?'

'Apparently the AVO set a trap for him but he got away.'

'The AVO are always setting traps for him and he always gets away. But he never comes back here. You know Tibor, he's not stupid.'

'You'd tell me if he did?'

'No.' Milos started laughing and the young gendarme joined in. 'Tell me, Matyas, why did you join the gendarmes?'

'No choice. It was gendarmes or nothing. I was tired of nothing.'

'All of Hungary is tired of nothing. Listen, do you want to come down for a coffee? You look like you need warming up.'

'Are you serious?'

'Of course. If you want, you can search the house at the same time.'

'I don't think I'll bother. My sergeant knew Tibor wouldn't be here. He was just following orders. That's why he sent me and my bicycle.'

The two men set off for Aunt Klari's, one pushing a bicycle, the other towing a goose. The coffee turned into lunch when

Aunt Klari insisted the young gendarme join them for chicken paprika. Matyas ate ravenously and gratefully, amusing them with stories about the dreariness and pettiness of his duties.

'You know the difference between a gendarme and an ordinary citizen?' he said. 'I can put my hands in my pockets without being ordered to empty them.'

Milos laughed.

'No, I'm serious. I can stand around doing nothing and not be questioned. I think this is what freedom is: being able to stand around doing nothing with your hands in your pockets.'

Andras grunted approvingly and a wry smile spread across his weathered face.

Milos offered to walk back into town with his friend, claiming he had business to attend to. Once they'd parted company, he headed straight for the station and Geza Apro's telephone. He dialled Tibor's number and waited impatiently while the operator seemed to take an inordinate amount of time to make the connection.

'Who is this?' said a voice.

Milos slammed the phone down. If Tibor had changed the person who always answered the phone, he wouldn't have changed the codes. And even if he had, the person wouldn't begin by asking who was calling. Only one organisation would do that. Milos had always suspected that one day Tibor's world would crack apart but it came as a shock to have his fears confirmed. So Tibor was on the run and his organisation had been penetrated. Where would Tibor go? Milos knew how his brother's mind worked: he'd have emergency plans and an escape route. He also realised there was nothing he could do to help him. When he was somewhere safe, probably in Austria, Tibor would contact him through Geza. Until then he would just have to wait. But of one thing he was certain: Tibor would not risk coming back to Sarospatak.

Milos put Tibor out of his mind by keeping himself busy. They slaughtered a pig, kept what they needed and turned the rest into sausages to give away to the needy. For many people in Sarospatak the end of the war had not brought an end to their suffering. Whatever else they managed to put on their plates on Christmas Day, the sausages would be the highlight.

That night, over dinner, Gabriella again asked Milos what he wanted for a Christmas present, even though he knew she'd been plotting his gift with Aunt Klari for more than a month.

'I'd like a wedding ring,' he replied. 'I can't wait until spring.'

Gabriella smiled coyly. 'You'll just have to. I decided when I was a little girl that I'd have a spring wedding. Now, I'll ask you for the last time, what are you getting me?'

'Nothing you haven't seen before.'

This answer always annoyed Gabriella but not unpleasantly. She knew it was a clue but it frustrated her that it was so enigmatic.

'Listen!' said Andras suddenly.

The banter stopped instantly. Milos strained his ears to hear any sound that wasn't everyday background noise to life at Aunt Klari's. He ignored the crackling of the fire, the moaning of the wind and the privets scraping against the windows. There was something else but he couldn't quite identify it.

'A horse,' said Andras. 'And a cart. Someone is coming.'

Milos listened and suddenly he heard what Andras had picked up. Yes, there was a horse approaching. He could hear the slow muffled slap of hooves on packed snow. And wheels. They made a hissing, crunching sound as they broke through the ice crust.

'Maybe they will just drive on past,' said Aunt Klari.

'Even if they don't, there's no cause for alarm,' said Milos. 'I'll go see.'

'No! Stay.' On the way to the door Andras reached under his bed and dragged out his rifle and a round tin. He took a single bullet from the tin, pulled back the bolt on the rifle and slipped the bullet into the breech.

'Let's talk first,' said Milos quickly. 'I'll see who it is.' He pushed his chair back and dashed to the door before Andras could object.

Milos grabbed the lantern off the wall, his mind racing. Whoever was coming down the cart track was coming to see them, of that he had little doubt. The track beyond had not been used for weeks and past Aunt Klari's the snow was both deep and heavy. He doubted the gendarmes would come in a horse and cart, but who else had any reason to come at all? The wind was bitterly cold and more snow threatened. What was so important that it couldn't wait until morning and daylight? He pushed open the door and stepped outside. The cold hit him like a slap in the face. He recognised the horse and cart immediately.

'You! What do you want?' he snapped.

'Home, bed and a hot meal. And an amenable woman. But like I told you once before, little brother, when Tibor asks you to do something, you don't argue.'

'Tibor? You've heard from Tibor?'

'You could say that.'

The black marketeer who had helped Milos bring Gabriella to Aunt Klari's glanced back at the small stack of hay on the tray behind him. Milos held the lantern up so he could look into the cart but saw nothing of interest.

'Pull back the corner of the blanket. Under the hay.'

Milos did as instructed, perplexed and unprepared for a shock.

'Oh my God!' His lantern flickered and its light was weak, but there was no denying what was in front of him.

'Hello, Milos.'

His brother, his face gaunt and grey as winter, stared weakly up at him.

* * *

400

'Well done,' said Ramon. 'A perfect time to break for coffee. Your story gains pace.'

'About bloody time,' said Neil.

'So you think the story of our friends here is dull?' said Lucio. 'You think their lives are not worth recounting?'

'I didn't say that,' said Neil defensively. 'It was always engrossing but now it's exciting. It was a victim story and now it's a crime story. I prefer crime stories.'

'I think Tibor turning up like that, half dead, was the turning point of our lives,' said Gabriella. She let go of Neil's arm.

'Why's that?' said Neil.

'Aha,' cut in Milos, 'suddenly this refugee's story is not so boring, no? Now Neil is like a child with a bedtime story, wanting to know the ending before it is ready to be told. Gabriella, tell him nothing. No, tell him to be a good boy and wait like everybody else.'

'Very funny, Milos. But I don't see how Tibor's sudden arrival was a turning point. Gabriella still married you. You'd planned to marry and escape to the West. She came to Australia with you, so I can't see what difference his turning up made. Everything turned out the way you planned.'

'The way we planned?'

'Yes, Milos, and I don't think I've missed anything. Isn't this Gabriella sitting here alongside me? Wasn't it Gabriella holding on to my arm? Like a Rottweiler, you said, and, mate, you're not wrong. In truth, the only thing that has eluded me is why Gabi married you and not your brother. I mean, Tibor was everything you weren't. He was sharp, courageous, resourceful, a real character. Gabi had many of the same qualities.'

'She still has them, Neil,' said Milos quietly.

'All the more reason why she should have given you the flick and taken off with your brother.'

'That's enough, you two. Here comes Gancio with our coffee.' Gabriella leaned towards Neil so that Gancio could serve her.

'Do you still wish Milos had told another story?' asked Ramon.

'No. I still wish I'd been allowed to tell my story. This hasn't exactly been a bundle of laughs.'

'Our lives haven't exactly been a bundle of laughs,' said Gabriella. 'But, Neil, are you better off for having heard our story, for having sat through the sifting of our baggage? Have you learned anything?'

'Learned anything?'

'Yes.' Gabriella put her hand over his. 'We have opened our hearts. We have admitted you into our past. A past we've kept locked away for more than fifty years. Does it mean anything to you?'

'I'm sorry I ever used the word "baggage". I'm sorry Milos chose to tell this story. I've seen the effect it has had on you and on Milos. But it has also had an effect on me and I admit it. I'm accustomed to going home after our Thursday lunches buoyed up and stimulated. Some of the women I've lived with have even been jealous of the lunches — I come home so high and happy. But this story, your story, it's something else. Particularly with you sitting here. I know Milos also did it tough, but you went through the camps and the selections. You survived Auschwitz. My current live-in isn't jealous of these lunches; she pities me. She sees them as an ordeal and wonders why I put myself through them.'

'Explain,' said Ramon.

'I take the story home with me, I can't get it out of my head.' Neil made the admission sound like a shameful confession. 'The things that happened to Gabi ... I don't know. My girlfriend accuses me of not listening to her, of ignoring her. Sometimes after our lunches we go out to a movie but I can't even remember what we saw; I drift off. All I see is Gabi abandoned on the station at Krakow, or hearing her name called out in Theresienstadt. I see her walking home across Europe, starving and alone, trying to survive the

Russians. I guess I kind of always knew this sort of stuff went on but having Gabi sitting here beside me really brought it home. You ask have I learned anything? Yes. I have.'

'What?' asked Gabriella softly. She took Neil's hand in hers. 'What exactly have you learned?'

'I've learned not to come here when Milos is telling a story.'

CHAPTER TWENTY-FIVE

Milos was not just relegated to second fiddle, he was knocked completely off the podium. When he insisted it was too dangerous for Tibor to sleep in the house, Gabriella overruled him and gave up her bed. Once more Milos found himself sharing the barn with the pigs and the mare. If Gabriella's life had lacked purpose since her return, she found it in nursing Tibor. She threw herself into the task with the same enthusiasm she'd shown when they'd made the preserves, but this time her dedication was overlapped with genuine concern and affection. She slept on the floor alongside his bed, exactly as Milos had done for her. When Tibor's fever raged, she was there to soothe his brow with damp cloths. When he was beset by bouts of shivering, she used her body to give him warmth. She spoon-fed him, read to him and changed the dressing on his wounds. Tibor became the focus of her every waking moment. The only thing she didn't do was bathe him because Aunt Klari ruled that inappropriate for an unmarried woman and washed him herself.

Christmas approached but Milos no longer viewed it as a Christmas to remember, rather, one to regret. The spring wedding no longer seemed inevitable. When he joined Gabriella and Tibor in the tiny bedroom he felt he was intruding and was assailed by the same feelings of inadequacy and not belonging he'd experienced as a child. He felt excluded from their orbit.

Apart from a little seepage from the exit wound where the bullet had passed through his shoulder, Tibor's main problems were a bad cold, residual infection and exhaustion. After five days, although too weak to get out of bed, he was able to sit propped up by pillows and tell parts of his story.

'I was stitched up by a vet who was the son of a stationmaster. He claimed he'd treated wounded soldiers during the war and that bullet holes held no mystery for him. He cut me open so he could stitch me up inside then sewed me back together. Afterwards he gave me a bag of oats and told me not to roll in the sandpit for a week.'

'What about anaesthetic?' asked Milos.

'Ah. If I'd known I was going to get shot I'd have taken some with me. And some American antibiotics.' Tibor closed his eyes and put his head back. '*Szilvapalinka*. Plum brandy. That was my anaesthetic.' He opened his eyes and smiled wanly. 'Milos, let me tell you something. It doesn't work.'

'You poor thing,' said Gabriella in horror.

'But you have American antibiotics,' said Milos. He picked up the bottle of pills next to the bed and tried to read the label.

'I arranged a pick-up at Nyugati Station before he operated. You won't believe how much they cost.'

'Couldn't you also have arranged to pick up some anaesthetic?'

'The vet said the operation couldn't wait, I'd lost too much blood. Maybe it wouldn't have been so bad if my nurse had been with me. Then I would have let them operate on both shoulders.'

He smiled at Gabriella and squeezed her hand. She kissed him on his forehead. Milos could take no more and left to help Andras.

Over the following days Milos kept to himself. As much as he hated leaving Gabriella with Tibor, he couldn't bear the humiliation of being in their company. He felt neglected and, worse, irrelevant. When Andras suggested he use a break in the weather to deliver the last of their Christmas orders, he didn't hesitate to drag out the cart and do his rounds of the butchers. Under normal circumstances this was a time-consuming process because he had to go from butcher to butcher to extract the best deal. But they barely had enough pigs to satisfy demand and all the negotiations had been done in advance. Milos had played the salesman, now it was time to play delivery boy.

He returned tired and cold in the mid-afternoon, as the brief grey day was giving way to night. He went straight into the barn to scrub out the cart so that it would be clean for the next delivery. His customers were quick to notice any unpleasant odours and he didn't want to give them any opportunity to demand a reduction in price. The mare was missing and its absence puzzled him until he remembered that Andras had planned to take Aunt Klari over to see Aunt Jutka before more snow fell. He scrubbed out the cart and lined it with clean straw. Before leaving the barn he put feed in the trough for the mare and lit a lantern, hanging it over the entrance for Andras.

He kicked off his boots at the back door to the cottage and entered. The fire cast a dull glow but apart from that there was no other light, no lanterns lit. Milos frowned, puzzled. He shook the snow off his coat and hung it up. His first thought was that Tibor must be feeling stronger and so Gabriella had accompanied Aunt Klari and Andras to Aunt Jutka's. There seemed no other explanation. He decided to check on Tibor before putting the kettle over the fire for coffee. He lit a lantern and stepped straight into the bedroom.

Gabriella's head shot up from the pillow. Her face was flushed and shiny as she turned towards him. The bed covers fell from her shoulder and Milos could see enough to realise she'd removed her outer clothes and was wearing only her underwear.

'Hello, little brother,' said Tibor. His face had the condescending smile Milos had grown up loathing and in his voice there was the familiar note of triumph.

'Gabi?' said Milos. He stared at her, stunned with disbelief, seeking a simple, innocent explanation. But the shame and guilt on her face belied his hopes. It tore his heart apart. In days gone by he would have run from the bedroom, fled from the scene of yet another humiliating defeat. He lowered the lantern and averted his eyes. 'Get dressed,' he said. He left them and retreated hurt and bewildered to his loft in the barn.

Milos slumped down on the end of his bed with his head in his hands. The shock had passed and now the full import of what had happened hit home. The thing he'd most dreaded had occurred. His dream was over. Crushed. Gone. He'd lost Gabriella and the realisation was devastating. Tibor had returned and made good his threat. He tried to replay the scene in his head, desperate to find the simple explanation that meant his plans, his future, his life, were still intact. But his mind was too numb to obey. He was dimly aware of the cottage's back door slamming shut and the barn door opening.

'Nothing happened!'

Her voice was shrill, desperate.

'Nothing happened! I just got into his bed to keep warm!'

Milos closed his eyes and lay back, pulling his pillow over his head.

'Nothing happened! I fell asleep, that's all!' She stood on the barn floor calling up to him. Milos waited for her to climb the ladder so she could sit beside him and he could look into her eyes for the truth. But she denied him the opportunity. There was no scrape of feet on the rungs, no sense of her voice coming closer.

'Milos, I know you're up there. Nothing happened! I just fell asleep. Say something!'

But for the life of him Milos couldn't think of a single thing to say. Gabriella left the barn crying.

'That's what happened,' said Istvan. 'That's how the Jew killed Sandor. He intended to drag his body in front of the train and drop it there but he misjudged things.'

Istvan's father stared into his glass of *barack*. He lifted his head and slowly focused on Istvan. His lips curled into a snarl.

'The Jew killed Sandor and for that you must kill him. But it was your fault that Sandor was there in the first place. Your fault that your brother was killed, you understand? You, with all your big ideas, it was your fault! Five years, you said, then Sandor will come home. I should never have listened to you. Who will look after the farm now when I can no longer work? You tell me, who?'

Istvan ignored the outburst. He'd been expecting it ever since Major Bogati had granted him leave to go home for Christmas. If Sandor hadn't been killed he would have happily stayed in Budapest. But his parents deserved to be told the circumstances of his brother's death and they also deserved what little comfort he could offer.

'Soon running the farm will not be your problem. All the farms around here are being collectivised. This farm will become part of a bigger farm. Everyone will share equally in the proceeds.'

'Huh!' said his father. 'First I lose my son and now you tell me I will lose my farm! How will we buy food?'

Istvan sighed. Gyorgy hadn't done a day's work for months and there was little likelihood of him doing any in the future. His father complained ceaselessly about his back, but the truth was, ever since Istvan had begun extorting money from the Jews, he'd made life too easy for him. His father had become an alcoholic. Whether the farm was collectivised or not, the family would still depend on the money Istvan sent home from Budapest. Only his mother and sister were upset by Sandor's death. His grandparents seemed oblivious to everything and were simply waiting to die themselves.

His mother was stoic and accustomed to life disappointing. Doubtless she grieved but her grief was swallowed up by her weariness, to be hauled out and suffered only when time and her demanding husband permitted. His sister fared little better. She was weepy and also worn out and clearly wary of their father. Istvan could easily imagine the despair and drudgery of her life. It offered little hope or prospect of betterment. She was a dull child and at best could be described as plain. One day she would exchange her tyrannical father for a tyrannical husband and her life would continue unchanged. He hoped that, even for a brief time, her husband would love her and make a fuss of her so she could feel what it was like to be worth something. Everybody deserved that at least once in their life.

It seemed to Istvan that only he truly grieved for Sandor. He'd been more of a father to him than a brother. He'd made sure Sandor always had enough to eat, clothes to wear, boots, and had looked out for him at school. Yes, he'd got him into the AVO and given him a chance at life, at living. He'd got him away from the farm and his father. And yes, in the end his good intentions had got Sandor killed. He could recall every moment of when Major Bogati had broken the news to him, still felt the bitterness and anger and hatred for Tibor Heyman.

'When we catch him, we will give him to you,' Major Bogati had promised. But they hadn't caught him and Istvan hadn't exacted his revenge.

'The Jew's brother, he's still here,' said his father, interrupting his thoughts.

'I know,' said Istvan. 'I intend to question him.'

'He's living with one of the doctor's daughters. You remember Dr Horvath? He treated my back once when it was really bad. He was the only one who did it any good. Sometimes I think we killed too many Jews. We should have been more selective. They make good doctors.' Gyorgy took another sip of his fiery medicine. 'Do you think the Jew might be hiding with his brother?'

'Anything is possible but I don't think so. We know he intended to flee to the West. We recovered the false identity papers he intended to use but we were unable to discover who was taking him over the border or where. The Greens, the AVO border guards, went on alert but Tibor either slipped through the net or he's still here. We think he slipped through the net.'

'So why go see his brother?'

'Just in case he didn't.'

Istvan was tempted to visit Milos on Christmas Day. He reasoned that since both brothers had converted to Christianity, if there was one day they would all try to be together, that would be it. But was Tibor enough of a Christian? He doubted it. Tibor wasn't the kind to put his faith in anyone or anything other than himself. Nevertheless, Milos would not be expecting a visit from the AVO on Christmas Day, even one in an unofficial capacity. Milos would have his guard down and perhaps even be a little drunk. It was a combination that appealed to Istvan. But the uncertain weather and the depth and wetness of the snow discouraged him. The chances of discovering anything worthwhile were remote and not worth the discomfort. He considered the merits of waiting a few days until the weather cleared.

By the time Christmas Eve arrived, Tibor had become accustomed to holding court. It was as though he was impervious to the tensions that had everyone else on edge. Milos ignored him while Gabriella defiantly tended to his needs, hung on his every word and laughed too loudly at his jokes. Tibor stayed in bed while the tree was decorated and the Christmas feast was prepared, then persuaded Milos and Andras to carry him to the table where he managed to sit, propped up by cushions.

'I only turned Catholic so I could have Christmas dinner,' he said.

'Rubbish,' said Milos curtly. 'Dad always insisted on celebrating Christmas.'

Gabriella chose a chair beside Tibor so she could cut up his pieces of roast pork and goose. Milos didn't object. He and Gabriella had hardly exchanged a word in the two days since he'd found her in bed with Tibor. But for his brother, there was every possibility that the meal would have passed in silence.

'The stupidity of the Russians has to be seen to be believed,' said Tibor. 'You know how Russian soldiers love watches. Well, they love clocks more. They're bigger, you see. I heard this story in Budapest — a true story — about a Russian soldier who walked into a watchmaker's with his arms full of watches. He threw them all down on the counter. "Make clock!" he said.'

Milos did his best to join in the laughter, if only for the sake of Aunt Klari and Andras, but saw through the humour to his brother's serious intent. He'd competed against his brother all his life and Tibor's motives were as plain to him as his own. Tibor hadn't come home to take Gabriella from him but because he was badly wounded and needed a place to rest. But once home, he'd seized the opportunity to press his claim on her. Being caught in bed with Gabriella had been a setback, that was all. The campaign continued. Of that Milos had no doubt. The jokes and stories were all part of a process designed to enchant her and enhance his prospects.

Tibor enthralled them with his tales of daring, about how he had hijacked trains and stolen entire shipments of coal and wheat. He told them about his meetings with the crime bosses, how dismissive they were of him because of his age, but how

411

they queued up for his coal. He told them about his one last job and his betrayal by one of Benke's men.

'But for him I would now be in the West somewhere. Maybe America. Once I'd got myself established I was going to send for you and Milos. I had the money and contacts to ensure a safe passage over the border. Then I intended to give you something, Gabi. A little present. A present to mark the beginning of a new life for you.'

'What?' asked Gabriella, clearly intrigued.

'See for yourself. I have decided to make it your Christmas present instead. I think it is a perfect and appropriate gift. I sincerely hope you will agree.' He reached into his pocket and held a closed fist in front of Gabriella. 'Hold your hands out and I will drop my present into them.'

'What is it?' Gabriella began to giggle.

Aunt Klari and Andras craned forward in anticipation, perched on the edge of their seats. Milos's heart sank. Tibor made the gesture seem spontaneous but Milos could see how he'd carefully led up to the moment. Gabriella thought it was another of Tibor's jokes, but Milos knew better. His worst fears were realised when Tibor opened his fist. A diamond dropped into Gabriella's hands.

'Oh!' said Gabriella. She stared at the diamond in disbelief. It was nearly the size of a pea and cut and polished so that it sparkled from every angle. Milos's heart almost stopped beating. He was accustomed to Tibor's surprises but not even he had anticipated this. It was a diamond for an engagement ring, the kind of gift a man gives to a woman he intends to marry. He wondered how long it would take Gabriella to realise its significance. And, more importantly, how she would respond. He avoided looking at Aunt Klari. She had recovered quickly and was glancing uneasily at him. She too had no doubt what Tibor's gift was intended to convey. Andras simply looked away, either tactfully or from embarrassment.

Only Milos had any inkling of the truth. He realised that Tibor was once again demonstrating his genius for opportunism. The diamond had not been intended for Gabriella at all but to finance his future in the West. But how could Milos convey this to Gabriella?

'I can't accept this,' said Gabriella, but she couldn't drag her eyes away. The diamond was simply too beautiful, too radiant and too special.

'Of course you can,' said Tibor easily. 'It's for all the gifts I didn't give you. While you were in the camps. While I was in Budapest. It's for every birthday I missed. For every Christmas. For our everlasting love.'

Gabriella rose and embraced Tibor, her eyes moist.

'Thank you, Tibor,' she said. 'It is the most beautiful and precious gift, but I really can't accept it. You have always given me the most wonderful presents. I still remember the record you gave me on my twelfth birthday — "Sophisticated Lady", Duke Ellington.'

Yes, thought Milos, but it was my gift you clung to when the Germans took you away. He cast his mind back to Gabriella's birthday, a lifetime ago, when he'd presented Gabriella with *Peter Pan and Wendy* and been thoroughly upstaged. Recalling that moment suddenly opened Milos's eyes to the opportunity he'd been given. Amazingly, his brother had blundered. For the first time in as long as Milos could remember, Tibor had made a tactical error. He reached into his pocket and withdrew a small package.

'Keep it for now,' Milos heard Tibor say. 'We can discuss it later.' Gabriella's fist closed around the diamond.

'Gabi?'

Gabriella turned and looked at Milos suspiciously.

'I too have a present for you, Gabi. Do you think you could accept it?'

'Of course!' said Gabriella. She gave Milos a tentative smile. 'What is it?'

'It's not a diamond, Gabi, but I think in its own way it is more precious.'

Gabriella smiled encouragingly.

Milos was aware of Tibor watching him closely. For once his brother didn't look so insufferably sure of himself.

'It's not a diamond,' Milos repeated, 'but it's given twice over with more love than you can ever imagine.'

Gabriella blushed.

'In truth, it is not just a gift from me but from Aunt Klari, Andras and someone else very special to you.'

'From us too?' Aunt Klari's face creased into a delighted smile.

'Yes, from you too. You see, Aunt Klari, I used the proceeds from the sale of one of our pigs to buy Gabi's Christmas present. It happened some months ago. This gift is equally from you and Andras. I hope you approve.'

'We already do, whatever it is,' said Aunt Klari. 'Of course we approve.'

'More precious than a diamond?' said Andras. 'I want to see this.'

'Merry Christmas, Gabi.' Milos handed Gabriella the parcel. It was wrapped in red paper and tied with a silver ribbon. He kissed her on both cheeks.

'Thank you, Milos. I really can't imagine what it might be.' She turned and kissed both Aunt Klari and Andras. 'Something I have seen before?'

'Yes.'

'And who is the someone else very special to me?'

'You'll know.'

Gabriella unwrapped the paper and held the small flat box in her hand. She hesitated, her face shining like it had years earlier when he had handed her the book.

'Go on,' said Milos, 'open it.'

'More precious than a diamond? What could it be? Look! My hands are shaking.'

414

'Open it.'

Gabriella gently prised open the lid.

'Oh my God! I don't believe it! I don't believe it!' Tears flooded her eyes and ran uncontrollably down her cheeks.

'What is it? What is it?' begged Aunt Klari.

'Oh, Milos, thank you! Thank you! How did you find it? How can I ever thank you enough?' Gabriella gave up trying to stifle her sobs and threw her arms around him, clinging to him more tightly than she had even during her worst nightmare. She cried unashamedly.

'What is it?' asked Aunt Klari again, her voice shrill.

'A gold bracelet,' Milos said matter-of-factly. 'The one her father gave her on her twelfth birthday.'

Aunt Klari's hands rose to her mouth in amazement and delight. Tears welled in her eyes and her chest swelled with pride to have been part of the giving of such a precious gift. 'Her bracelet? You found her bracelet?'

'Where?' asked Andras.

Like Aunt Klari, he was beaming from ear to ear. Tibor had bid a diamond, laid it on the table and been trumped. Andras was as proud of Milos as any father could be of a favourite son. Milos just shrugged. What did it matter where he had found it? The fact was, he'd found it. How would knowing it came from a butcher's shop enhance the moment?

'Well done, little brother.' Tibor gave Milos a wry smile and a nod that spoke volumes. It was a salute, an acknowledgement, an acceptance of defeat. 'Perhaps you should have the diamond set in a ring to celebrate your betrothal.'

'Perhaps,' said Milos graciously. Over my dead body, he thought.

That night Gabriella joined Milos in the barn. If Tibor had needed any further proof of where Gabriella's true affections lay, her decision to spend the night with Milos provided it. When they returned to the house the next morning, they found Tibor dressed and lying on his bed.

'It's time for me to move out,' he said.

'What do you mean?' said Gabriella, alarmed.

'It's not safe for me to remain here. And not safe for you either.'

'But you're not strong enough,' she protested.

'What's this?' Aunt Klari squeezed into the tiny room.

'This is not a safe place for me to hide,' said Tibor.

'He's right,' said Milos. 'I have been saying this all along. The gendarmes have already come here looking for him. They may well come again. Besides, we're not the only people who know Tibor is hiding here.'

'Don't worry about my friend,' said Tibor. 'Even if the AVO torture him he will never tell. You see, he has many secrets, dark secrets, and I know them all. If he betrays me he knows I will get my revenge. The AVO have many unpleasant ways of killing and he would certainly experience one of them.'

'Then why move?' asked Gabriella.

'Like Milos says, the gendarmes or AVO will be back. They won't give up looking for me. When they've looked everywhere else they'll come back.'

'Why, what have you done?'

'Sit down, Gabriella. There are things I haven't told you.'

Gabriella sat on the edge of his bed.

'When the AVO raided the warehouse where we were unloading the coal, a lot of people got killed. My deputy, Pal Szarbo, was killed. So were some of Benke's men. Some AVO officers were also killed and for that they hold me responsible.'

'Did you kill anyone yourself?' asked Milos.

'That's the thing,' said Tibor. 'That's why I can't stay here.' He looked directly at Milos. 'I killed Sandor Kiraly.'

'You what?' said Milos.

'I killed Sandor Kiraly,' said Tibor evenly.

'Sandor!' Gabriella stared at him in horror. 'How? Why? What was he doing there?'

'I saw him at the station when he left for Budapest,' said Milos. 'He told me he was joining the gendarmes.'

'He joined the AVO.'

'But why kill him?' said Gabriella.

'I had no choice. Sandor was never very bright but he was a tough kid and as brave as they come. I was trying to escape. My driver was dead and the AVO were chasing me in their cars. I guess they put Sandor on the gate to keep him out of harm's way while he was gaining experience. I wasn't supposed to get that far; they should have killed me as I left the warehouse. God knows, they tried hard enough. Sandor stepped out into the middle of the road and, as calm as you like, started taking shots at me with his rifle. I had no choice but to aim the car at him.'

'You ran him over?'

'No, Milos. He jumped out of the way but my car doors were open and swinging uncontrollably. One of them hit him. End of story.'

'So it was self-defence?' said Gabriella.

'I doubt the AVO see it that way. Besides, it gets more complicated.'

'How?' asked Milos sharply.

'There was a photograph in the newspaper of two AVO officers inspecting the scene; one was a senior officer called Major Bogati. His reputation is fearsome. He calls himself Major but he is far more senior than that. He gets about in a Zis and only very senior officers enjoy that privilege. Alongside him was a man described as the case officer. A lieutenant. I recognised his rat face immediately.'

'Istvan!' said Milos. The name came out more as a hiss than a word.

'We should have killed him, Milos, when we had the chance. That little prick has the ear of Major Bogati. He's not going to rest until he has me slow-roasting on a spit.'

'Why in God's name didn't you tell us this sooner?' snapped Milos. 'You've endangered us all.'

'What could I have done?'

'You could have told us so we could have hidden you somewhere else. Aunt Jutka's, for example. She's perfectly capable of looking after you. You put us all in danger.'

'Will she take me?'

'Of course she will take you,' said Aunt Klari.

'Then take me there now,' said Tibor.

'I'll help Andras get the sleigh ready,' said Milos. He left in disgust.

'So this is where you sleep?'

'It is comfortable,' said Milos.

'It reminds me of where I slept before I went to Budapest. The difference is, I had to live with cows farting. You have to live with pigs and a mare.'

'I am used to it.'

'Really?' Istvan smiled thinly. 'Then who sleeps on the floor alongside the bed in the small bedroom?'

'Gabi has nightmares. About the camps.'

'When did you learn your brother was in trouble?'

'My brother has been in trouble for years.'

'When did you learn he was on the run?'

'Matyas told me. You remember Matyas from school? He's a gendarme now. He came looking for Tibor.'

'What did he tell you?'

'Not much. Only that the AVO had tried to trap him and that he'd managed to escape. That's why he came to look under our beds.'

'What else did he tell you?'

'You mean there's more?'

'Yes, there's more.'

Istvan turned so that his eyes looked directly into Milos's. He looked for indications of nervousness, prior knowledge, curiosity, anything that would give him a hint how Milos was thinking. There was a time when Milos had been transparent

418

but that time was long gone. The trembling boy in the oversized railwayman's uniform and the young man now fielding his questions could be two entirely different people. Milos met his gaze and revealed nothing.

'Tibor killed my brother.'

'Tibor what?'

'Killed Sandor.' His eyes bored into Milos's. 'Don't pretend you didn't know.'

'Tibor killed Sandor? How? When? Matyas said nothing.'

'You link the two events — the AVO trap and Sandor's death. Why?'

Milos hesitated fractionally. Istvan sensed the indecision.

'You said there was more. I assumed one followed the other.'

Istvan stared into Milos's eyes unblinking.

'You are quite correct. I did say there was more and the two events are connected.'

'I thought so because Sandor had joined the gendarmes. Like Matyas.'

'Who told you Sandor had joined the gendarmes?'

'Sandor.'

'When?'

'I saw him at the station. When he was leaving for Budapest.'

'He joined the AVO. He was taking part in the operation. Your brother drove his car at him, knocked him down and dragged him along the road and across a railway line. When Sandor broke free of the car your brother stopped and drove back over him. Back and forth until he'd killed him.'

'That's a lie! Tibor can't drive.'

'Can't drive? How do you know if you haven't seen him for two years?'

'He had a driver. He boasted about it. He had no need to drive.'

'When did you last try to contact him?'

419

'After I saw Matyas. The same day.'

'How?'

'I rang from the station. I ring a number, leave a message and Tibor calls back.'

'Did you leave a message?'

'No. The person who answered the phone gave the wrong signal.'

'And you haven't heard from Tibor since?'

'No.'

'I have information that he came home for Christmas.'

Milos laughed. 'Tibor was never a Jew and only nominally a Catholic.'

'He came here because he was wounded and needed help.'

'Tibor was wounded?'

'Yes. Judging by the amount of blood in the car, I'd say quite badly.'

'How badly, for God's sake?'

'Badly, but not badly enough.'

'Then he'd go to a doctor. If he was wounded this is the last place he'd come.'

'Why?'

'He wouldn't do anything that would put us in danger.'

'Us?'

'Me and Gabi.'

'You and Gabi. It was always Tibor and Gabi. Could he have come back for the girl? The two of them were like that.' Istvan crossed two fingers and held them up to Milos's face, taunting him.

'Now Gabi and I are like that.'

'Really? I made a mistake, Milos Heyman.' Istvan stared at Milos thoughtfully. 'I should have interviewed the girl. I still might. Not in this cosy little barn you no longer sleep in but at AVO headquarters. If anyone has anything to say they are usually more than eager to tell us there.'

'Leave her alone. She's suffered enough.'

'Perhaps she has. But you, Milos Heyman, you haven't.'

Istvan turned and dropped expertly down the ladder to the floor of the barn, leaving Milos gasping for air like a stranded carp. Milos slumped down on the bed, heart pounding. It had never occurred to him that the AVO might use Gabriella to get to him. Just the thought of Gabriella in Istvan's hands terrified him to the point of paralysis. He knew the threat had not been made idly; Gabriella was his weakness and Istvan had recognised it instantly. Somehow he had to get Gabriella beyond his reach and soon.

Andras glanced anxiously at the sky but it told him nothing he didn't already know. High thin clouds put a yellow cast through the pale blue and the sun shone weakly from the south-east, powerless to prevent the temperature plummeting. Andras hoped anyone watching would regard his mission as prudent, but doubted it. The first big storm of winter was imminent. He knew, his mare hauling the bags of pig feed on the sleigh knew, and so did every living animal between them and Siberia. But he'd been left little choice. He shook his head. Once Milos had calmed down and thought things over, his logic had been unarguable. Tibor had to know and Andras was the only one in a position to tell him.

The mare spotted the farmhouse ahead and quickened her pace. The sooner she did her job, the sooner she'd be back in the warmth and safety of the barn. The prospect of lightening her load was all the encouragement she needed. Her breath steamed from her nostrils in twin jets.

Aunt Jutka's husband, Ferenc, emerged from the cottage to help carry the pig feed into the barn. He shot one quizzical look at Andras and wisely decided not to pursue his curiosity.

'How are you, my friend?' he said instead.

'Cold. How's the boy?' asked Andras.

Ferenc's wry grin was all the answer Andras needed. He could imagine Tibor entertaining them with his stories. Winter was a time for sitting around indoors and repairing things. A good storyteller could fill the hours and make winter pass more quickly, particularly if the stories were new and exciting.

'Take two bags,' said Andras. 'I need to talk to him.'

Ferenc nodded.

Andras took off his boots and entered the cottage. He left his coat on because he didn't intend staying any longer than it took to impart his message. The warmth inside made his face sting. He pulled a chair over to Tibor who was sitting in front of the fire reading.

'Do you know why engine drivers and firemen don't freeze?' said Tibor. 'They have a firebox to keep them warm. All you have is the wrong end of a horse.'

Andras pulled off his gloves and held his hands out towards the fire. Aunt Jutka brought him some fiery plum brandy which he downed in one swallow. He paused a moment to allow its warmth to infuse his body.

'I have a message for you from Milos.' Andras told Tibor about Istvan's visit. 'Milos believes the threat to Gabriella was an attempt to scare him into doing something rash.'

'Like contacting me.'

'Exactly. He said we had to assume he was being watched.'

'Why didn't he also assume you were being watched?'

'He did. He made me wait two days and deliver pig feed to three farms before coming here.'

Tibor smiled. 'My little brother is learning. Tell him to stay calm. I'll think of a way to draw attention off him. Tell him I think his assessment is right: Istvan was just fishing. Nevertheless, for the time being you should continue to assume someone's keeping an eye on you.'

Ferenc came in and poured Andras another plum brandy.

'If you are staying I'll put the mare in the barn. If not you'd better go. The wind is beginning to pick up.'

'I'll go.' Andras stood and shook hands with Tibor. 'Milos wants to leave Hungary as soon as possible.'

422

'So do I,' said Tibor. 'First we have to wait for spring. Then we have to mislead the AVO. We will leave together.'

Andras turned and walked to the door. Tibor called after him.

'Thanks for coming, Uncle. Could you stop off at one more farm before you go home?'

'That was always my intention.' As Andras pulled on his boots he could hear the mare stamping and snorting impatiently. Charcoal clouds green-hued with snow gathered in the east.

CHAPTER TWENTY-SIX

Tibor waited until April before putting his plan into action. His old friend with the horse and cart smuggled him into Sarospatak under the cover of night. The following morning he walked to the station wearing the cap and uniform of a railway guard. He made one phone call using Geza Apro's phone, then boarded the train for Budapest.

Now that preparation for their escape was under way, Tibor hoped his brother would calm down. All through winter Milos had been impatient, fearing a knock on the door. Only the storms had brought respite, causing every living soul to take shelter, and not even the AVO had dared venture out. Milos had wanted to make their bid for freedom in winter, arguing that the AVO would not be expecting them to try then. Tibor had countered that neither could they expect to survive if a storm blew up. Andras had backed Tibor and Milos had given in.

Whenever the weather cleared, Milos had kept himself busy selling pigs, taking gold in preference to cash so he'd have something to trade once they crossed the border. With Tibor no longer his major customer, Milos had to travel to the markets at Satoraljaujhely and Miskolc to sell his pigs. From Tibor's point of view, it was exactly the diversion his younger brother needed.

Tibor travelled towards Budapest well aware that he could no longer use any of his safe houses or hideaways. Pal Szarbo had been killed but some of his men had been captured. He had to assume the AVO had extracted every piece of information they could from them, and that every part of his previous enterprise had been compromised. He also had to assume that men he had trusted had been turned by the AVO and released to act as informants in the event that he returned. Indeed, he was counting on the fact.

As the train approached the outskirts of Budapest, it slowed deliberately to allow Tibor to jump off. All the stations were seeded with informers and AVO officers trained to look for people considered to be enemies of the state. Even in the guard's uniform, Tibor could not be certain that he wouldn't be identified. He ran from the train straight into a stand of trees. He'd chosen the spot for its isolation, but still he paused to see if there was anyone about who might have noticed him. Despite the risks he faced, he couldn't help smiling. His senses were reawakening to the thrill of danger. For the first time in months he felt alive. He was back where he belonged, tap-dancing on the edge.

Satisfied that he'd slipped off the train undetected, he changed into street clothes, put on a heavy overcoat and hat, and made his way west towards a line of poplars that marked the course of a stream. Although the water level was high the stream had carved a deep enough vee through the flat farmland to provide cover. Tibor made straight for the road half a kilometre ahead. It led to a small village which was unremarkable in every respect except that it had a tractor repair shop. All going well, the shop was Tibor's rendezvous. Despite the anonymity of the hat and coat, he felt uncomfortably out of place. His clothes were appropriate for the streets of Budapest but not suited to a quiet back road leading into an insignificant village.

Tibor had only four hundred metres to cover between the stream and the village and he walked them as quickly as he could. He knew from previous experience that no gendarmes were posted in the village and it was rarely visited by them. It simply wasn't worth their attention. Nevertheless, any exposure brought risk and he had no reason to believe that the village didn't have its share of informers. Once the fields gave way to houses, Tibor slowed his pace. The village was built around two main streets which bisected each other. He had to turn right at the intersection and walk eighty metres to the tractor repair shop. He forced himself to relax, turned the corner and immediately wished he'd been more circumspect. There was a car parked outside the tractor shop, a black Poboda, the kind provided to mid-ranking officers of the AVO. However, Pobodas weren't used by the AVO exclusively and the car could just as easily belong to the owner of the repair shop or one of his customers. Tibor proceeded cautiously, scanning both sides of the street, doorways and gardens for anyone who looked out of place. All he saw were two old women carrying shopping, their faces grim within heavy scarves. They ignored him. He kept walking, senses on high alert.

'Tibor Heyman?'

Tibor froze. Despite everything, they'd managed to catch him unawares. He'd been focusing on the car, trying to determine if there was a driver sitting at the wheel, when the two men had slipped out of hiding and come up behind him. Each took an arm and marched him to the Poboda. Yes, there was a driver. That should have warned him. The two men pushed him into the rear and sat either side of him. Their coats and hats were typically AVO.

'Drive!' ordered one of the men.

Neither had drawn a weapon on him and Tibor admired their restraint. Killers of AVO officers were not usually accorded such civility.

'Where are you taking me? Andrassy Street?'

Neither man replied, although one allowed a grim smile. When they drove into Pest one of them pulled Tibor's hat down hard over his head and forced him down in the seat. He could no longer see where they were going and wondered why they hadn't simply blindfolded him. What didn't they want him to see? Maybe they were taking him to a secret place for interrogating prisoners who weren't expected to live much longer. But that was true of Andrassy Street, of all the gaols. He heard a mournful wail which he recognised instantly as belonging to the tug boats which propelled barges along the Danube. Why were they taking him across the river into Buda? Almost immediately the car began to slow. It turned sharply and pulled to a stop.

'Get out!' ordered one of the men.

Tibor did as instructed and stopped dead in his tracks when he realised where he was.

'You bastards,' he hissed.

'Benke told us to make it look authentic. Nobody looks when the AVO make an arrest. It's the perfect cover, no?' Both men had smirks on their faces.

Tibor was told to undress and given a towel and a costume. He found Benke where he expected him to be, floating on his back in the middle of the pool. Tibor eased himself into the warm water and closed his eyes. It was a pleasure he'd not expected. The knot in his stomach slowly unwound and his muscles relaxed. More than anything he felt relief and gratitude.

'So you survived,' said Benke.

Tibor saw no need to respond.

'I notice you have acquired a few scars of the profession.'

Again Tibor did not speak.

'We bear the blame for what happened. That is why I agreed to this meeting.'

'They make it difficult,' said Tibor.

'Even so,' said Benke, 'we were aware of the rules.'

'I have come to give you the railways.'

'Why?'

'The railways need you now that I am no longer in the game. And I need papers for three people and an escort over the border.'

'Three people.'

'My brother and his girl.'

'For that you give me the railways?'

'Not quite,' said Tibor. He laid his head back against the side of the pool and stretched out. 'First we have to take another trainload of coal.'

Tibor's methods were different and the outcome successful. He acted as Benke's deputy so that nobody other than himself and the engine driver knew where the coal would be unloaded. The coal was then trucked to different sites in both Buda and Pest. After Benke had taken all the coal he could handle, Tibor put the second part of his plan into motion. He knew the AVO would suspect him of organising the train's hijack but he wanted them to be sure. Tibor contacted the other two crime bosses and told them where to collect their coal and that he wanted fifty per cent of the payment in gold or hard currency. He arranged for Benke's men to collect the payment.

Then, despite the fact that he already had false identity papers, he began negotiating new papers and a safe passage across the border with two separate groups of people smugglers. They knew his reputation and the risks involved in dealing with somebody the AVO were actively searching for and doubled their asking price. Tibor agreed on the spot and paid half up front.

He waited a week for the new papers to be prepared and then arranged the drop-offs. It was never his intention to attend either rendezvous; instead he placed Benke's men in strategic positions at each location to see if he had been betrayed to the AVO. The first drop-off was clean. Benke's men waited twenty-four hours before making the pick-up and were not intercepted. They were, however, highly suspicious of the second drop-off.

Tibor's new papers were left for collection at a ticket office in Nyugati Station, along with three tickets to Sopron on the border with Austria. All Tibor had to do was ask for tickets for Mr Esterhazy and they would be given to him. Benke's men noted the man nearby who was taking for ever to read the newspaper and the couple taking an inordinate amount of time to read the train schedules. When they finally moved on they were replaced by another couple who had similar difficulties with the schedule. Benke's men gave a schoolboy twenty forints to collect the papers for them, then watched as five would-be travellers, including the couple studying the schedules, followed the boy out of the station. Their mission accomplished, Benke's men left immediately to report back to Tibor.

The trap at Nyugati Station was all the confirmation Tibor needed that the AVO had fallen for his diversion. He collected his share of the proceeds from the sale of the coal from Benke and began his cautious return.

In three days' time Milos and Gabriella were scheduled to catch the train to Satoraljaujhely wearing hiking clothes and rucksacks on their backs. Milos's love of hiking the foothills around Mount Nagy-Milic had been established long before the German occupation. To any observers they would just be two more hikers using their Sunday to get rid of the winter cobwebs. Tibor had arranged to meet them at the Levy glass factory in Satoraljaujhely after he'd organised their escape.

'You credit Tibor Heyman with too much intelligence.'

'Yes, comrade Major.' Istvan Kiraly stood at attention staring fixedly at the major's desk.

'Things are often no more complicated than they appear. Four months ago Tibor Heyman joined up with Benke for one last pay day. We know this. We spoiled his pay day. He intended to escape across the border to Austria but we seized his papers. We shot him. He was wounded so badly he has taken months to recover. Then what does he do? He tries again. Another pay day and this time he succeeds. More papers but we intervene again. What does that tell me? Tibor Heyman now has the money he needs and, papers or not, he is going to cross the border into Austria. Agreed?'

'With respect, comrade Major —'

'So you don't agree. I should kick you out of my office. Do you know why I don't?' Major Bogati waited for a reply even though the question was rhetorical. 'I'll tell you. Because of all the officers under my command, you alone have the courage to stand there and tell me I'm wrong. Is it courage, Lieutenant Kiraly, or pig-headedness?'

'Why didn't he get new identity papers through Benke? If he had, we'd be none the wiser.'

'Trust. He doesn't trust Benke after last time. Yes, he needed Benke's help to take the coal train, but he chose not to involve Benke any more than he had to. I doubt he even told Benke about his plans to escape.'

'Why three tickets? Where did he go to recover?' said Istvan.

'You frightened his brother; you threatened his girlfriend. You had them watched for four weeks and got no response.'

'He was there,' said Istvan. 'I had no evidence, just a gut feeling. The brothers were always close. Tibor always looked after Milos when he was in trouble. When the situation was reversed it was only natural that Tibor would turn to Milos for help.'

'But you searched the house.'

'He wasn't in his brother's house but my instinct tells me he was in one somewhere nearby. I should have questioned the girl first.'

'Why are you so sure?'

'Three tickets. That was his mistake. Four months ago he was leaving by himself; now he is taking his brother and the girl. Why? Because they asked him to. When? While he was recuperating. But the tickets are also designed to mislead us. I took the liberty of contacting the gendarmerie in Sarospatak. Both Milos and the girl are still there. Why aren't they here in Budapest?'

'Tibor planned to leave without his brother and the girl four months ago and he plans to do the same again. Maybe the extra two tickets are not intended for them. Maybe Tibor was sheltered by friends in the railways and this is his way of repaying them. I hear what you are saying, Lieutenant, but the answer is not as complicated as you make out. On two occasions Tibor planned a final pay day. On two occasions he planned to escape to Austria. Those are the facts. There is the pattern of behaviour.'

'Yes, comrade Major,' Istvan said, but he was asking himself why two unknown railway people would need false papers.

'I have had extra men sent to the border. All trains, buses, trucks and cars will be stopped and searched. We will catch him this time and you will have the privilege of taking him downstairs. Now are we agreed?'

'Czechoslovakia.'

'Why?' sighed Major Bogati.

'Because people smugglers also operate in Czechoslovakia but the AVO does not. Our colleagues in Czechoslovakia will be as helpful as they need be, but they have other priorities. They have their own Tibor Heymans to contend with. They lack our imperative. I say Czechoslovakia because Tibor Heyman wants us to think he intends to cross the border into Austria. Everything he has done since he returned to Budapest has been too obvious. Benke could have hijacked the train but Tibor made sure we knew it was him. He could have hidden behind Benke and his organisation but instead chose to front

431

the operation. Even the way he tried to buy papers was too obvious. He could have used Benke but he wanted us to know what he was up to. I know Tibor Heyman. He is trying to mislead us. This is how the man operates.'

Major Bogati stroked his moustache thoughtfully.

'You are wrong, Lieutenant. But if I ignore your advice then it is an admission that I have been wrong about you. Am I wrong about you, Lieutenant Kiraly?'

'No, comrade Major.'

'How many men?'

'Five,' said Istvan.

'You have seven days to make an arrest. If you need more men, get them from the local gendarmerie. Remember this, Lieutenant Kiraly: mistakes go on your record as well as successes.'

'I should escape with you,' said Benjamin Levy, 'but look at me — I am too old and too scared.'

'You're not too old, Mr Levy,' said Gabriella.

'Ah, but I am too scared. I will not see the inside of another prison. I will not go hungry again. Ever. You see? I cannot take the risk.'

'What will happen to you?' asked Milos.

'All industry is being nationalised. They are putting me and my machines on a train and taking us to a bigger factory in Miskolc. At least my machines are not being sent to Russia, that is something. The factory is a joint venture between Hungary and Russia: Hungary bears the costs and Russia takes the profits. But I will make glass and have two sugars in my coffee. There are many dead who would gladly change places.'

'Good luck, Mr Levy,' said Tibor. 'I wish we'd met earlier. We could have done business.'

'We did business, Tibor Heyman. Through your brother we did business. Now go. It will be dark soon.' Benjamin Levy shook hands with Tibor and Milos and kissed Gabriella. 'First you ran away and now you escape. If only your head was on my shoulders. Make a good life.'

Czechoslovakia was just a few hundred metres east but Tibor turned away from it towards Rakocsi Street and the bridge over the Ronyva River. They had people to meet who would take them to Czechoslovakia via the back door. Where there were no AVO border guards.

'What have they done?'

As soon as the husband asked the question, Istvan felt the onset of panic. It implied total ignorance of Milos and the girl's intention to flee. He did a quick search of the house and barn and found clothes, good clothes, belonging to Milos and Gabriella. They were the sort of clothes anyone leaving the country would want to take with them. Mistakes go on your record as well as successes, Major Bogati had warned. Suddenly his mission to Sarospatak was looking like a serious mistake.

He left the old woman shaking in the doorway of the cottage with her husband comforting her and headed straight for the station. Five men! Five men he'd brought with him all for nothing! Istvan went straight to Geza Apro.

'Milos Heyman and Gabriella Horvath. Have you seen them?'

Geza pretended to think for a while before responding.

'They caught the eight a.m. train to Satoraljaujhely. They had rucksacks. They were going hiking.'

Istvan checked his watch. It was already approaching noon. Milos had four hours' start.

'When is the next train?'

'This evening. Five-thirty.'

Istvan turned to his men. 'Come. We'll go by car.'

Istvan kept up a brave face as he headed off to the gendarmerie. He needed two cars and he knew the captain of the gendarmes would be reluctant to give them one. But what had he to lose? If Milos and Gabriella had really just gone hiking, he'd know soon enough. If they were trying to escape, and if Tibor was with them, he'd be a hero. But it was a long shot. He realised that in his determination to catch Tibor he had been both impetuous and foolish. Maybe he had overestimated Tibor Heyman. Maybe at that very moment Tibor was sitting in Vienna, sipping a coffee and laughing at them. Maybe the Greens were already holding him for questioning. Istvan cursed silently. A wiser man would have supported Major Bogati.

He had plenty of time to cool down and think while sitting in the back seat of the Zim as they drove to Satoraljaujhely. During his school days he'd heard the brothers discussing the trails around Mount Nagy-Milic with other boys. He'd also heard plenty of tales of hikers getting lost in cloud and rain and accidentally crossing the border into Czechoslovakia. He knew the foothills were the domain of hunters who made a living out of shooting wild pigs, deer and hares and selling them. The hunters tended to be cunning rather than smart and kept to themselves. He couldn't imagine any of them turning down an offer to make good money on the side. Realising the opportunity to cut his losses was long gone, he began to formulate a plan. He needed to alert the border patrol and enlist the help of the local gendarmes, the border patrol, a hunter they could put pressure on and hunting dogs. Istvan gritted his teeth. Promotion or demotion was mere hours away.

＊　＊　＊

'I have finished for today,' said Milos.

'Bullshit!' said Neil. 'You're not going to leave us up in the air until next week.'

'It is already five o'clock.'

434

'So? The other day you talked until six,' cut in Lucio. 'If you can keep us late one day you can keep us late another. What about your schedule?'

'I have finished for today but the storytelling hasn't.'

'Explain,' said Ramon. 'No, let me guess. You want Gabriella to take over. Right?'

'No!' said Gabriella.

'Yes,' said Milos. 'You asked Gabi about the cracking of the eggs. This part leads to the cracking of the eggs. I think Gabi should tell it.'

'No, Milos, don't do this,' said Gabriella, clearly apprehensive.

'Tell the story or disappoint your friends,' said Milos. 'It's your choice.'

'No, Milos,' she pleaded.

'Then stop when you reach the border, okay? You can do that, no?'

'I suppose so,' said Gabriella reluctantly.

CHAPTER TWENTY-SEVEN

Our winter of fear had been replaced by a spring filled with hope. When we left Benjamin Levy's glass factory we were excited and optimistic. I knew I had a hard night ahead of me but I had no reason to expect any danger. By morning we would be in the relative safety of Czechoslovakia and four days later, according to Tibor, we would be in the West. He made it sound like a walk in the woods. Once we were free I was to have my spring wedding. It took the gift of my father's bracelet to make me realise how much I loved Milos and to overcome my foolishness. How lucky was I that he loved me? The Tibor I had dreamed about as a young girl had been lost in the war. The man who had emerged had fooled me for a while, but in truth he was a stranger. Hard, cold and more than a little frightening. I could never have married him. Nevertheless, I was glad he had organised our escape and was with us. This was the sort of thing Tibor was good at.

We headed north along the banks of the Ronyva before cutting north-west into the foothills. At one point I stopped and looked back. Tibor and Milos also stopped. The setting sun had dropped below the clouds and run a golden brush across the landscape. I thought to myself, if this is to be my last memory of Hungary it is a glorious lie, but a lie nonetheless. What I saw was the Hungary of my childhood. The golden landscape gave no hint of the poverty, hunger, despair and distrust. Yet that was how I wanted to remember the country of my birth, painted gold and peaceful by the sun. That was how I thought I would remember it.

'Enough,' said Tibor. 'We have places to go, people to meet.'

The people were two hunters. One was our age and the other ten years older. They were cousins. The older one was a giant of a man called Janos and the younger, thin and wiry, was Laszlo. We met them in a tiny one-room shack with wooden walls and a wood-tiled roof. We had seen similar on our walks before the Germans came and thought they were picturesque. There was nothing picturesque about living in them. The walls and earthen floor were covered by the skins of animals they'd killed. They had a table and two homemade chairs for their comfort, and two coffin-like beds stuffed with skins. I hoped we'd have the opportunity to rest but the hunters were keen to get going.

Tibor told us to take our overcoats and gloves out of our rucksacks and put them on. I remember Milos handing me his identity papers to carry, some cold pork chops and boiled potatoes. I also carried some clean clothes and shoes and a little bag with my gold bracelet and the diamond. It wasn't much to build a new life on but it was all I could carry. Milos carried the heavy things, along with his clothes: a canvas sheet, in case we were caught in a storm or had to camp out, a camping cooker that used methylated spirits, torches, knives and forks and bottles of water.

It was pitch dark when the two hunters led the way up the hill; to this day I have no idea how they could see where they were going. We could just make out their shapes in front of us showing us the way, but even so we struggled to keep up. The trails were unlike any I'd hiked before. They were narrow and covered over by bushes and low branches so we had to stoop.

It is hard to hike uphill stooped over with a pack on your back and it wasn't long before my legs were aching and my lungs burning. Tree roots crossed the path, all gnarled and twisted, so we also had to lift our feet high to avoid tripping. Sometimes not even that worked and I had to cling on to Milos to stop myself falling. I don't know how long we hiked like that, I lost all track of time.

I remember thinking this must end soon, that we couldn't have much further to go, when I heard the hunters whispering to each other, urgently, argumentatively. They stopped suddenly and Milos collided into them. The big man, Janos, grabbed him and held his hand over Milos's mouth so he couldn't cry out. I knew then that something was wrong.

I felt Tibor push past us and heard him talk softly to the hunters. I was too tired to listen and clung to Milos, my head on his shoulder, my eyes closed. For the first time I became aware of how bitterly cold it was. The cold air stung my face and burned when I sucked it down into my lungs. Milos held me tightly in his arms, sharing his warmth. He kept telling me to be strong and to be brave but his soft words were like a lullaby.

'We have to leave the trail.'

I wanted to cry out and object but Tibor, as usual, left no room for dissent. How could we leave the trail? I couldn't imagine anything more difficult than the trail we were on. We walked on for a bit and then cut hard left uphill. The hunters seemed to be following some kind of path but as far as I could see there was no trail. Branches whipped off Milos and slashed me across the face and body. My coat protected my body but nothing protected my face. I tried to fend the branches off with my hands but how can you fend off something you can't see? I pulled my hat as far down as I could and buried my head deep into the collar of my coat. I gave up trying to fend off branches and clung to the back of Milos's coat. He towed me up the hill, kept my aching, weary legs moving. I kept telling myself that Mount Nagy-Milic was only nine hundred metres high. How many metres could there possibly be left to climb?

An hour passed but the detour brought the hunters no comfort. I could hear them muttering and arguing again. But at least the going had become easier as the hornbeam and larches gave way to ash. The hunters stopped once more and just ahead of them I could see the outline of a ridge. We'd made it! We'd reached the top. I collapsed to the ground and slipped my pack off. Milos lay down beside me, the two of us gasping for air. I could hear Tibor arguing once more with the hunters. I heard Janos say how they'd followed pig trails but had found no sign of pigs. Why had there been no startled pigs or deer crashing away from them through the forest? Where were the animals? Laszlo crept up to the edge of the ridge and lay peering into the dark on the other side.

'Drink.' It was Tibor. He knelt over me with a bottle. 'Have some *barack*. It'll help fight off the cold.'

I took a sip of the fiery liquid and another. I could feel a glow all the way down to my belly. It also seemed to clear my head. I passed the bottle to Milos who gave me a bottle of water in exchange. The water was freezing. I don't think I could have drunk it if it wasn't for the *barack*.

'Is there a problem?' I asked.

'There shouldn't be,' said Tibor.

'But is there?'

'I don't know. We have a steep descent before we rejoin the trails. That is the source of the dispute. Our friends do not believe the trails are safe. They are convinced there are border patrols and that the border patrols have scared off the animals. I believe that is unlikely. However, we have no choice. The trails bisect our path; at the very least we must cross them. But we'll reach our boat a lot sooner if we use them. So that is what we will do.'

Tibor rose and rejoined the hunters, placating them with his *barack*.

I tried to listen in but the *barack* and my weariness got the better of me. The next thing I knew Milos was shaking me.

'Gabi! Wake up! Wake up!'

Unbelievably I'd fallen asleep, for how long I don't know. Everyone was waiting for me. Just as I got to my feet I heard the sound I feared most in the world. Not even the entire bottle of *barack* could have prepared me for it.

'Dogs!' Tibor spat out the word and charged towards the two hunters. 'Scum! Who did you tell?'

'No one! We told no one!' Janos was quick with the denial.

'I should shoot you and leave you here!'

Tibor was carrying a gun? Something in the hardness of his voice convinced me, and doubtless the hunters too, that he was prepared to use it. Milos let go of my arm and confronted his brother.

'Tibor, we have no time for this.'

Tibor ignored Milos. 'How much did the AVO pay you?'

Janos spat in disgust. Laszlo took a frightened step backwards.

'Who are you? Why do the AVO want you?' Laszlo turned on his cousin. 'Janos, who are these people?'

To my relief Tibor started laughing and put his gun away.

'I believe you,' he said. 'Now get us to the boat. Try to run away and I will shoot you. Understand? Now let's go. Milos, hold on to Gabi. Don't let her fall. If she falls we all die.'

The hunters leapt over the ridge with Tibor hard on their heels. Milos grabbed me and we followed. I had never been so terrified in my life, not even in the camps. I could see nothing and the hillside was so steep I kept stumbling. We slid as much as ran. How Milos held me up I don't know. I thought we were making good progress, despite everything, but the voices ahead of us were getting fainter all the time. I could hear Tibor yelling at the hunters to slow down.

'Come on, Gabi, come on!' Milos was yelling at me but I was going as fast as I could. My legs were like rubber, I had

440

no control over them. They let go when I needed them to be firm.

'Stop!'

Janos and Laszlo were standing in our way.

'Give me the girl,' said Janos. He ripped my rucksack off and threw it to Laszlo. He picked me up as though I weighed nothing and slung me over his shoulders, the way I suppose he carried the deer he'd shot. 'Try to keep up,' he said to Milos and started to run.

We plunged down the mountainside so quickly I was sure he'd trip and we'd both be killed. Again branches whipped across my face and I was powerless to prevent them. Behind us I could hear the chilling baying of the dogs. Suddenly I was praying that Janos would run faster. I was less scared of falling than of the dogs. But his breath was coming hard. He stumbled, cursed and lurched to his right. I could feel his body twist, to protect me, I suppose, but he was only partially successful. His shoulder slammed into a tree and so did my face. My mouth filled with blood but I felt more numbness than pain. Someone fell behind us and called out. It had to have been Milos but I didn't respond, couldn't respond.

'Keep going, keep going.'

I recognised Tibor's voice. He was also behind us. I assumed he was helping Milos back to his feet. I found my voice and called out, 'Milos!'

His name came out all thick and fuzzy but he heard me. 'I'm okay!' he yelled back. 'Keep going!'

Janos carried me until we reached a trail. He was a big strong man but the effort of running with me over his shoulders had exhausted him. He put me down.

'You must run now,' he said.

'I want to go back for Milos.'

'No!' said Janos sharply. 'You must run! Run with me. Your friends are coming. Listen!'

Sure enough I could hear twigs breaking and leaves scrunching underfoot. Two people were cursing. Two! That was good enough for me. I turned and ran, Janos holding my arm, pulling, dragging me. Blood blocked my nose and filled my mouth. I spat like a man just so I could breathe. Suddenly there was a burst of gunfire and I couldn't help crying out.

'Keep running!' said Janos. 'For God's sake keep running!'

But Milos was behind me. They were shooting at him. No matter what happened I wanted to be with him. If he got shot then I wanted to be shot with him. I couldn't imagine life without him. But all the time Janos had hold of my arm. Dragging me, pulling me, making me run. The track steepened without warning. I nearly fell.

'We've made it, we've made it!' said Janos.

We were running into a clearing and I thought it must be Czechoslovakia. But suddenly I found myself knee deep in water and the dark shape ahead of me was our boat. Laszlo was holding on to it, as though preventing the boatman from rowing away into the darkness. Janos lifted me up and threw me into the boat. The impact knocked out what little air was left in my lungs. I lay there, hurting, gasping for air and weeping, when another burst of gunfire split the night. I saw the flashes and heard the sharp agonised cry.

'One of your friends has been shot!'

'No!' I tried to get up but Janos held me down. I lifted my head as high as I could so I could see over the side of the boat. Someone had been shot. Milos or Tibor? Someone was coming. Milos or Tibor? I heard the splash as running legs hit the water. Heard the shouts of the pursuers, so close now. Heard more gunfire. I could make out the shape of someone just metres away. Milos or Tibor? I couldn't tell. But I wanted with all my heart for it to be Milos. Dear God, let it be Milos! Please let it be Milos! I don't know if I spoke my plea out loud or just prayed to a sympathetic God. Any God!

Whoever it was, Janos grabbed him and hauled him into the boat. I heard a thump as he landed in the bottom, heard the rasp of his breath. The oars bit into the water and the boatman pulled us out towards the centre of the river. Soldiers were shouting at us and firing their weapons.

'Milos? Milos?' I was shouting. I had to know.

I heard a groan and immediately wanted to die.

'They shot Milos,' said Tibor. 'The bastards! They killed him.'

* * *

'You're Tibor?' Neil turned the question into an accusation.

'I have suspected this,' said Ramon. 'That is why you chose to use the third person.'

'You are Tibor?' asked Lucio. He also was clearly shaken.

'Does it make any difference?' Milos pushed back his chair. 'I am Milos to you.' He put his arms around Gabriella, who had buried her face in her hands, and gently lifted her to her feet. 'Come along, Gabi. We are both tired. Besides, our friends have a lot to discuss.'

'Is this the end of the story?' asked Ramon.

'No. The story ends next week.'

The three friends sat silently, each with his own thoughts, while Milos led Gabriella from the restaurant.

'Milos is Tibor?' said Neil. 'Bastard!'

FIFTH THURSDAY

CHAPTER TWENTY-EIGHT

'Who will be telling the story today?' asked Ramon. 'You or Gabi?'

'Gabi will begin. She has yet to tell you about the eggs. I will take over to finish the story.'

'What do we call you?' said Neil. 'Milos or Tibor?'

'You call me what you have always called me,' said Milos. 'Milos is the name on my passport. It is the name on my driver's licence, my credit cards and my Medicare card. I am Milos. If you want proof I will show you.'

'Yes, but you know, and now we know, that you're really Tibor.'

'I am who my papers say I am,' said Milos. 'No purpose is served by calling me by any other name.'

'Will Gabi continue her story while we have our lunch?' asked Ramon.

'No,' said Milos. 'We will eat our lunch and then Gabi will begin. The day will be hard enough for her as it is.'

They ate in brooding silence. It was hard to come to terms with Milos's switch of identity. His friends felt betrayed.

* * *

The Hernad River is fed by melting snow from the Carpathian Mountains. In spring it is in full flood and the current flows swiftly. That is what saved us. It swept us away into the night. Away from the dogs and the soldiers. Away from Hungary. Away from my poor Milos. Janos had to sit on me so I couldn't jump overboard and try to swim back to the shore. I wanted to hold my Milos one more time, kiss him one more time, look into his beautiful face. But no one listened to me. No one took any notice. Milos was dead, we were alive. Staying alive was all that mattered.

Janos sat on me until we reached the opposite shore in Czechoslovakia. He lifted me up then and held me tightly against his chest. I don't know how long he held me but I cried until I thought my heart would burst. It could not have been long. I was just a girl, a weak link in a dangerous game. Time was precious and they had none to waste on my tears.

Janos, Laszlo and the boatman pulled the boat up onto the river bank and hid it among bushes. The boatman wanted to stay with his boat but Janos insisted he came with us until we found our Czechoslovakian contacts. He and Laszlo had to get back across the river and they didn't want the boatman losing his nerve and going without them. Tibor was worried that the contacts had heard the gunfire and decided not to wait around. Czechoslovakia also had border guards and there was no reason to expect they'd be any friendlier. We had to tread carefully but we made noise blundering through the Czech forest; at least, I did. Every step took me away from Milos and I resisted. I think they were all losing patience with me when our contacts found us.

'What happened?' they asked the boatman.

'Border patrol,' he replied. 'One man was killed.'

One man was killed. That was all my Milos meant to them.

'Tell them they still pay for three.'

The boatman turned to Tibor who quickly agreed. He must have been still in shock over Milos's death because what he did

448

next was both ill-considered and dangerous. He reached into his pocket and pulled out a wad of notes. He gave some money to Janos.

'My friend, I apologise that I doubted you. It is more than we agreed. But for you, we would all be dead.'

Janos pulled Tibor close as though to embrace him but instead whispered urgently in his ear. 'Go carefully,' he said. 'These men are Slavs. They are not to be trusted. Look after the girl.' He turned to me and took my hands in his. 'I'm sorry,' he said. Then he, Laszlo and the boatman disappeared back into the forest, back to Hungary.

'Pay now,' said one of the Slavs. He couldn't have seen much in the dark but he'd seen enough. 'Pay double. Shooting.'

Tibor peeled off a few notes. 'You get that now. More later.'

'No!' said the Slav. 'Now! Pay double!'

Tibor slammed his fist into the man's jaw. The Slav didn't see the punch coming and was totally unprepared. He hit the ground hard as he fell. Tibor grabbed the other Slav by the throat.

'Pick him up,' he snarled.

As soon as Tibor let go the Slav picked up his fallen comrade.

'Let's go,' said Tibor. 'No more trouble.' He thumped his fist into the palm of his other hand to make his point.

The Slavs led off with Tibor following close behind and me hanging on to his coat for dear life. The darkness was near absolute and tears filled my eyes but Tibor was close enough for me to notice what was missing. At some point he'd got rid of his rucksack, probably so he could run faster. My rucksack weighed heavily on my back but my heart was heavier. We were climbing again but on reasonably wide trails. Czechoslovakia seemed no different to the Hungary we had just left. Why would anyone shoot my Milos just for wanting to cross a river?

I knew we were heading for Kosice and I also knew how far away that city was. It seemed an impossible distance. The loss of Milos, the exertion and the cold had all taken a toll on me. Tibor took my rucksack and threw it over his shoulder. That helped but not enough. Every step was an effort and every one felt like my last. I don't know how my legs kept supporting me, how they knew what to do. I didn't want to go to Kosice. I didn't want to go anywhere. I wanted to be with my Milos. I wanted to die.

I don't know how long we walked but eventually the Slavs led us to an abandoned stable with only half a roof. The stable had fared better than the house, which had been reduced to rubble, but not much better. Still, it provided shelter from the wind and the chance to lie down and rest. I dropped down onto a pile of straw the moment I was inside, wanting to curl up and give my frozen body a chance to thaw out. I wanted to be left alone to weep, to weep until I fell asleep. But Tibor kicked my leg. Suddenly any thoughts of sleep vanished. His warning was unmistakeable.

One of the Slavs found and lit an oil lamp. The chimney was full of dust and cobwebs but the lamp threw enough light for me to see that the other was holding a solid length of timber like a club. The man with the lamp hung it on a hook dangling from a beam above his head. He pulled out a knife. They didn't say anything. They had no need to. Their intentions were plain: they'd brought us here to kill us. Now that I could see the men they terrified me. Their skin was dark and weathered, their hair and beards as black as the night. Their black eyes showed no compassion.

I dived behind Tibor for protection. As I landed my knee cracked painfully on a broken cart handle buried in the straw. Maybe it was a plough handle, I don't know. But it hurt and I cried out. One of the Slavs laughed. Tibor raised his hands chest high, placatingly.

'This isn't necessary,' he said. 'You want money, I give you money. See? See, I give you money?' He reached into the inside pocket of his coat. I expected him to pull out a wad of money but instead he pulled out a gun. Tibor carried a gun! He pointed it at the man with the club.

The Slav holding the knife leapt at Tibor, slashing with his knife. He was so quick, this man, so fast. Tibor parried with his left arm just as the knife flashed towards his throat. There was a deafening explosion and the man reeled backwards. Tibor turned towards the man with the club but he was too slow. The club smashed into his shoulder and Tibor fell. I heard the gun fall from his hand. The Slav was shouting at Tibor and swinging his club. Tibor kept rolling and the blows thudded into his body and arms. But the beating he was taking was fearful. He tried to roll away but his body jammed up against some collapsed timbers. I could see he was trapped. The Slav grinned and raised his club, lining up Tibor's head for the final fatal blow.

I grabbed the plough handle and leapt to my feet. I was behind them so the Slav couldn't see what was happening. I swung that plough handle with all my strength and smashed it against the man's head. He fell to his knees, dazed but by no means beaten. He turned to look at me, his face a mixture of pain and fury. I hit him again and he fell to the ground. I couldn't help myself. I stood over him and smashed the handle into his head over and over again. Over and over and over. Each blow made the same sickening sound. Like the cracking of eggs.

* * *

'My God,' said Neil. 'You killed him?'

'Yes,' said Gabriella, 'I killed him. It was terrible. More terrible than you can ever imagine. I have lived with the knowledge that I killed a man ever since. I have lived with that sickening sound.'

'My God.' Neil leaned across the table and put his arm around Gabriella, trying to comfort her.

'It was self-defence,' said Lucio. 'He would have killed you. You and Tibor. You can't blame yourself.'

'Can I get you some coffee?' asked Ramon.

'No, not yet,' said Gabriella, 'it is not yet time for coffee. I have not finished. See, I can talk about it now and my friend the doctor says it is good for me to talk about it. Milos made me have a boiled egg for breakfast this morning. Made me crack it open myself. I can do this now. Ask me and I will tell you that I am no longer afraid. Ten years it took my friend the doctor, but now I can listen to the eggs break. I can listen to the eggs.'

'Ten years,' said Ramon sympathetically.

'I didn't want to tell him. I didn't want him to open the door to that part of my mind where I kept all the things I didn't want to remember. But he found the key and I can tell my story. I can go on with the rest of my story.'

'Are you sure?' asked Neil.

'Yes, Neil. Thank you for your concern. I can go on.' She took hold of his arm.

CHAPTER TWENTY-NINE

My last day in Hungary turned out not to be my last. Without contacts and without help we could not make our way through Czechoslovakia and across the border. Tibor was badly bruised and his ribs were splintered. I couldn't stop crying. I cried for Milos and I cried for myself. I could not get Milos out of my mind, or the terrible sound of that man's skull cracking. There was blood and I suppose brain matter but I couldn't see it. It was so dark beyond the pool of light from the lamp. I could not see what I had done. I only heard it and the sound wouldn't leave me.

Once he'd recovered enough, Tibor forced me to leave that abandoned stable and once again we were on the move. He screamed at me and cursed me, kept me moving and kept me alive when all I wanted to do was die and forget the horror of what I'd done. Snow had begun falling and the wind had picked up. We stumbled on through the rest of the night, Tibor leading by instinct with no North Star to guide him and no moon to show the way. Just before dawn, he spotted a light in the distance and we headed towards it. The light came from a small farmhouse. Tibor banged on the door until a man opened it. He took one look at us and stood aside to let us in. Surely there were no more pitiable people than us in all of Czechoslovakia.

The farmer was a Slav but his wife was a Magyar, a Hungarian. They took us in. Tibor explained that we were trying to escape to the West and how our guides had tried to kill us. They bathed, fed and comforted us. We lived with them for ten days. Tibor offered to pay for their kindness but they refused. They finally agreed to accept half. After ten days, Tibor had recovered enough to move on but I was still a mess. My nights were filled with nightmares, the worst I'd ever experienced, and my days were filled with tears. I didn't want to leave the farmer and his wife but we could not stay. I had no choice.

We headed west towards the caves at Aggtelek where Uncle Jozsef had brought me one time with the boys. Tibor had gone there often enough to know the countryside well and also make contacts in the railways. Of course, that meant we had to cross back into Hungary. But Tibor argued that the AVO would no longer be looking for us; they knew we'd escaped to Czechoslovakia. His plan was to use his contacts in the railways to get to the border with Austria and then find someone to take us across.

That is what we did. We hid in freight wagons carrying crates of cherries. We hid beneath bags of grain. We hid in the guard vans of trains carrying lime for cement. We even hid in the guard van of a train carrying coal. We made it to Koszeg on the border with Austria. Two days later, with the help of smugglers, we crossed the border into Austria. We were free. I had never felt less free, even in the camps in Germany.

I soon discovered what the loss of Tibor's rucksack really meant. It had contained all the money and gold he'd accumulated to begin a new life in another country. It had also contained his papers. So Tibor seized the papers I carried.

'I am Milos now,' he said.

'No!' I protested hysterically but he wouldn't listen. It was so disrespectful to Milos and cruel to me. 'My Milos was a gentle man,' I protested, 'he was not like you. He was kind and loving. He wouldn't hurt anyone, not even his enemy. He would never carry a gun.'

'You don't understand,' said Tibor. 'Milos is dead but so is the Tibor who came back to you from Budapest. I had no choice how I lived my life. The rules were not my rules but I had to live by them or perish. But, you see, now I'm free. I don't have to live like that any more. I am no longer a criminal. I no longer have to act like a criminal. I am free. Free to be gentle and kind. Free to be loving. Free to be Milos.'

The whole idea of Tibor becoming Milos was abhorrent to me, but Tibor had made up his mind and nothing I said could change it. Everything was happening too fast. I hadn't come to terms with the loss of Milos and now Tibor wanted to steal his identity, his life and his place in my heart. I fought but I was fighting the inevitable. Tibor needed new papers and a new identity.

'Think of all the times I've helped Milos,' Tibor said. 'Milos would not hesitate to help me. He would want me to do this.'

Maybe I should have fought harder but, in my weakened state, how could I? When we reached Germany, Tibor converted my diamond into cash. He had money in bank accounts in Switzerland but said we'd need that once we'd settled somewhere. He used the money from the diamond to buy a wedding dress for me. I had my spring wedding. I cried all through the service. I should have been marrying Milos. Tibor kept reminding me that I was. He also reminded me that he was all I had and that we had no choice but to stick together. So I married a Milos and a Milos married me. This Milos told me I would learn to love him again, like I had as a child.

We did not consummate our marriage then but sometime later after we had reached Australia. Tibor was right. I did grow to love him, or at least become utterly dependent on him. In my condition the two were the same. My nightmares continued to plague me and I was always grateful that Tibor

455

was there to wake and comfort me just as my Milos had done. The nightmares were ferocious. Night after night I was burned alive in the ovens of Auschwitz. Night after night Milos was shot dead and ripped apart by dogs. Night after night I crushed that man's skull. I came to fear night and sleep, and in my fear I refused to sleep until exhaustion overcame me. And then they were there, waiting to ambush me. My nightmares.

By the time we reached England for our passage to Australia, the combination of everything I'd been through, my nightmares and sleep deprivation, had left me irrational. I probably had a nervous breakdown of some description, but such things were easily dismissed then. The doctor said all I needed was sleep and rest. Sleep, for God's sake! I clung to my identity papers like I'd clung to my book in the camps. My papers were my life raft in a very confused sea. They told me who I was, who I'd married, where I was going. I was Gabriella Heyman. I was married to Milos Heyman. I was going to Australia. When nothing else made sense, there were my papers. They were stamped and official. Unarguable. Absolute. They told me who I was.

Sometimes people make the mistake of believing their own publicity, and I think Tibor made this mistake. He avoided contact with the Hungarian community in Sydney, fearing that somebody would recognise him or somehow connect him with the notorious gangster from Budapest. But who would recognise him? Who would know his face? Some might recognise the name Tibor Heyman, but Tibor wasn't Tibor any more. He was Milos. Perhaps if I'd had contact with my own kind I could have begun the process of recovery sooner. But Tibor forbade it.

Instead we rented a house in Paddington, one in a row of terrace houses. I made Tibor put bars on the windows and new locks on the doors. I became a prisoner in my own home, as much a prisoner as I'd been in the camps. But that was where I felt secure, that was where I felt safe. I panicked whenever anyone came to the door. I'd hear them knocking and think they'd come to take me away, just as the gendarmes had come a lifetime earlier to take away my father and my brother. Just as the gendarmes came to take away me, my mother and Elizabeth. No good ever came from a knock on the door. My mind straddled two time frames and I was never really certain which one I was in.

Sometimes I would go out, but only with Tibor. The girl who had walked home to Sarospatak from Germany was now too scared to go to the shop for a loaf of bread on her own. I didn't understand what had happened to me, only that it had. Tibor indulged me. He didn't make me face up to what was happening. Sometimes he would coax me into trying something more adventurous than walking in the park or walking through the city at weekends when it was deserted. Sometimes we sat in cafés but they weren't like the cafés in Hungary and the coffee was terrible. Once he tried to take me to a movie but I couldn't bear to sit in the dark surrounded by so many people. I ran from the cinema: another mad woman from Europe. Perhaps if we'd mixed with other Hungarians I might have made friends. The friends might have helped me find my way back into life. But there were no friends. Tibor was my only friend and my only contact with life.

Tibor started a small company cleaning windows of office blocks. Most offices then had caretakers or janitors and keeping the windows clean was their responsibility. Tibor introduced them to the idea of contract-cleaning windows and later contract-cleaning of offices. But companies were slow to see the benefits and utilise his services. For many the idea was too radical or they couldn't see the value. However, enough people gave it a try and Tibor's business started to grow. But once the business became successful, Tibor grew bored with it. He sold the cleaning businesses and we bought a house in Rose Bay with the proceeds. The first thing we did was put bars on the windows and locks on the door. Our neighbours couldn't understand us at all. They couldn't understand why anybody would turn their home into a fortress.

Tibor started many more businesses. A painting business, a company that imported tiles, and he even opened a café that sold real coffee and continental cakes. The cakes were made by immigrants like us who yearned for the sort of things we were brought up with. Australians ate biscuits and meat pies, sausage rolls and fish and chips, things which to us tasted disgusting. But as each business became successful, Tibor sold it. We made money every time but neither the money nor the businesses made Tibor happy. One day he bought a Jaguar sports car and learned to drive. Every weekend after that we would go for a drive. I felt safe in the car because we were in our own little world. I don't know if Tibor was a good driver but he was certainly a fast driver. They were some of the few times he was genuinely happy. He loved the Jaguar and he loved driving fast. He loved the risk.

Tibor wanted children but I could not bear to bring a child into a world where there was so much pain. The years passed but for me nothing much changed. The pain remained. Although the nightmares eased I still couldn't bear to hear eggs break. If we needed eggs, Tibor had to break them open for me while I covered my head with pillows. My way of life became a habit and, in becoming a habit, shut off all the roads to recovery. I no longer cared why I was the way I was. I no longer cared that my life was almost non-existent. I spent my days locked in my home with only compound analgesics for company. At first I took just one or two a day. They helped me cope. When I didn't take them I missed them so I took them more often. I became hooked on the combination of aspirin, phenacitin and codeine. APCs. I spent my days in twilight, not thinking and not feeling, unable to tell one day from another. Only the weekends and the car trips brought any relief. But I always took my Vincents powders with me.

We'd lived in Australia for eight years when suddenly everything changed. There was no warning. We awoke one day to hear the news on the radio and to read it in the newspapers. It was October 23, 1956. The Hungarian people had risen up against the Russians. The Hungarian revolution had begun.

For eight years we had tried to forget Hungary and now Hungary filled every news broadcast and the front page of every newspaper. Tibor stayed home with his ear glued to the radio. When he couldn't get enough information locally he tuned into the BBC World Service on the short-wave. But our little radio wasn't powerful. Tibor wanted a short-wave radio like the ones radio hams used. He offered somebody a ridiculous amount of money to install one for us. The man came, set it up and put a huge aerial mast on our roof. Our neighbours were convinced we were crazy but we didn't care. One night, as Tibor slowly manipulated the dial, we heard a voice broadcasting in our own language. Somehow we'd found Radio Budapest and the station had been taken over by freedom fighters.

From that moment the radio was never turned off. We cheered when we heard about Russian tanks being destroyed and AVO officers being hung in the streets. But the broadcasts were intermittent and often meaningless to us. Ordinary people used the station to send messages or make appeals to the West. Sometimes, mostly during the day, all we could hear was a wall of static, but we were too frightened to turn the radio off in case we missed something, and too scared to play with the tuning in case we lost Radio Budapest altogether. On the morning of November 1, we heard on our little kitchen radio that the Russian army was returning to Hungary. Thousands of tanks and thousands of troops were crossing the border to crush the revolution. We even heard Satoraljaujhely mentioned. Tanks were rolling back through the border town.

We ran to our short-wave radio but all we heard was static. Tibor was beside himself with anger and impatience. I knew he wanted to be there, fighting the Soviets. But we were so far away and, besides, Tibor could never leave me.

Later that night we picked up Radio Budapest again. The student revolutionaries were begging the West for assistance, pleading for NATO and America to come to their rescue. It was so hard to listen and not be able to help. For me the broadcasts were torment because they awakened so many terrible memories, but I couldn't turn away. I sat listening while tears streamed down my face. Once again my poor country was being destroyed. We sat there into the early hours of the morning, hanging on every word, living every moment.

On the night of November 4, we heard gunfire and explosions in the background and the announcer's fear as he relayed the news that tanks and artillery had opened fire on Budapest. People interrupted his broadcast to send desperate messages to relatives in America and Canada. Sometimes the announcer excused himself because he had to run to a window to help defend the building. It was shortly after four in the morning, when the announcer had just run to pick up his rifle, when we heard another voice come on air, another poor, defiant soul sending a message. We stopped breathing, Tibor and I, and stared dumbstruck at each other. My heart did a somersault and ended up in my throat, beating so hard I was sure it would burst. There was no mistaking the voice, even over the thousands of kilometres, even with the ebb and flow of static.

'H-hello,' it said, 'is anyone listening? This is Milos Heyman. Milos Heyman from Sarospatak. Gabi, Tibor … if you are listening, I am alive. I am alive.'

* * *

'I knew it!' said Lucio delightedly. 'I could not see how the Milos we know could be the Tibor you described. I said so last week after you left.'

'Lucio's heart always rules his head,' said Ramon. 'But for once it seems he was right and I am happy to have been wrong.'

'And you, Neil?' asked Gabriella.

'I think you've cut off the circulation in my arm.'

'Oh! I'm sorry.' She released her grip.

Neil turned towards the kitchen to catch Gancio's eye but once again the restaurateur had anticipated their wishes.

'I think we should toast the resurrection of Milos with our grappas,' said Lucio. 'And, I suspect, the resurrection of this beautiful lady.'

'Indeed,' said Ramon. 'I must confess that I too prefer the company of Milos to the company of Tibor. But I'm curious. How exactly did this resurrection of Milos come about? It doesn't ring true. You were shot dead. Tibor saw you. He'd seen enough dead people to know who was dead and who was merely wounded.'

'Don't be ridiculous,' said Milos dismissively. 'Do you think he had time to see if I was breathing? Do you think he waited, with bullets flying around his head, just so he could check my pulse? The bullet that hit me struck my collarbone right beside my spine and exited just below my throat. There was enough blood to convince anyone I was dead. Besides, the impact hammered me to the ground. I hit my head and compounded my injuries by knocking myself unconscious. Tibor would have tried to help me up, seen the blood around my throat and perhaps even noticed that my eyes had rolled back. But I doubt it. I doubt he saw much at all. It was too dark and he could only have had time for the most fleeting examination. The blood and my limp body would have made him assume the worst. Bear in mind that he was panicked, exhausted and riddled with guilt. It was his fault that I'd been shot. The AVO were after him, not me. In his guilt and the panic of flight, he assumed I was dead.'

'I have no trouble with that,' said Lucio.

'So who is going to tell us what happened? You or Gabi?'

'Patience, Ramon,' said Milos. 'Here comes Gancio. First you may toast my resurrection and, yes, Gabi's also. After we have drunk our coffee I will tell you how I survived.'

'Will you persist with the third person?' asked Ramon.

'No. That device is no longer necessary.'

CHAPTER THIRTY

Under any other circumstances, I would have been finished off by the border guards and my body dumped into the Hernad River. But, in an ironic twist, the guards mistook me for Tibor. Istvan had made it clear to them that he wanted Tibor alive if at all possible. The guards carried me on a makeshift stretcher made from saplings and the waterproof canvas in my rucksack.

Istvan's disappointment that the guards had captured me and not Tibor was tempered by the fact that he now had evidence to offer Major Bogati which justified his actions. He ordered the guards to take me to the hospital in Satoraljaujhely. A dead Milos was no use to anyone. A live Milos would save his career. Two weeks later, with my shoulder strapped and the fragments of bone and bullet removed, I was taken under guard to Budapest. My old schoolfriend Istvan gave me the tour of the torture chambers downstairs at Andrassy Street but it really wasn't necessary; I'd already decided to cooperate. I told Major Bogati everything I knew, lying only to protect Aunt Klari and Andras. When the major asked me where Tibor had gone to recover after being shot I denied all knowledge and emphatically denied sheltering him. I told them Tibor had only approached me in early spring with an offer to help us escape to the West.

Whether they believed me or not was academic. They weren't interested so much in where he'd been but where he was going. I told them Tibor wanted to go to America, which was what I believed. They charged me with helping a known criminal to leave the country illegally, with attempting to leave the country illegally, with subversion, black-marketeering, disseminating anti-Soviet propaganda and as many other charges as Istvan could think up. I readily admitted guilt, knowing they'd extract confessions one way or another anyway. I expected them to shoot me or gas me so what did it matter what I confessed to? But again I underestimated my old schoolfriend. Istvan Kiraly had other plans. He wasn't interested in me but in revenge.

One day when I was taken from my cell to be interrogated I found myself alone with him.

'Major Bogati has no further use for you,' said Istvan. 'He suggests I take you downstairs. In two days you will confess to raping your own mother.'

'I confess now. What's the point?'

'What is the point?' Istvan never raised his voice. He didn't need to. The hatred I saw in his eyes turned my legs to jelly. 'You ask what is the point? Your brother murdered my brother. That is the point! Do you think I care what you confess to? One hour downstairs and you will be begging for death. After two days you will crave it. But your death will not come quickly, Milos Heyman, and your pleas will fall on deaf ears. If our interrogators are skilful and patient, you could last four days. What do you say to that?'

I couldn't respond. I was speechless with fear. I had seen what they could do to me down there and it took all my strength not to empty my bowels. Istvan just watched me, enjoying every moment.

'Do you love your brother?' he asked suddenly.

I stared back at him blankly. My mind couldn't adjust to this shift in his questioning.

'Well?'

'Y-yes. Of course I love him.'

'Good,' said Istvan. 'So you should. You would have been picked clean by worms years ago but for your brother. He looked after you like I looked after Sandor. I protected Sandor like Tibor protects you. He must love you a lot, your brother.'

'I believe he does.'

'He would risk his life for you?'

'I believe so.'

'Good. Do you know anything about India, Milos Heyman?'

'India? No.'

'They have tigers in India and sometimes these tigers steal into villages and kill people.'

He looked at me for a reaction but I couldn't follow his thoughts. Mine were still locked on the basement below.

'Do you know how they catch these tigers, Milos?'

'No.' And I didn't care.

'They take a live goat into the field and tether it to a stake. They use the tethered goat as bait to lure the tiger into their trap.'

I still didn't see what the tigers had to do with me.

'It is a primitive tactic but effective,' said Istvan. His eyes glinted cruelly. 'Major Bogati has no further use for you, but I have. You will be my goat, Milos Heyman. You will lure your brother into my trap.'

The iron fist around my stomach tightened its grip.

'You are worthless, Milos, worthless to everyone in the world except to your brother and me. You will bring him to me. I don't care how long it takes. Patience and persistence are the stock in trade of all good investigators. You will bring Tibor to me and then I will take him downstairs. And you, Milos Heyman, you will watch what I do to him.'

*

I was sent to the prison at Vac on the eastern bank of the Danube, about thirty kilometres due north of Budapest. Before Tibor could rescue me he had to know where I was. Istvan made sure my sentence was published in every one of the city's newspapers. From then on, my gaolers sent reports every month back to Istvan. There were informers everywhere within the prison, desperate to provide any information that might lead to a reduction of their sentence, more food or better accommodation. They kept a record of who I spoke to and who so much as uttered a word in my general direction. Those prisoners were tortured to see if there was any link back to Tibor. Word quickly spread throughout the prison that I was to be avoided at all costs. Years passed but no information was forthcoming. Yet a report was prepared for Istvan every month without fail, and every month they interrogated me as a matter of course. Istvan had patience and persistence in abundance.

I was kept in that prison for eight years, the first four of them without seeing daylight. Vac was the most notorious prison in all of Hungary. If there is a greater hell on earth I cannot imagine it. It was built alongside the Danube and water seeped into the cells on the lowest levels. I spent three months lying on a bed in a cell in pitch darkness where to stand meant standing in thirty centimetres of icy water. In winter the water froze. Many prisoners did not survive in those cells. Men froze to death in there, went mad or died from pneumonia. I knew men who rejoiced when they were taken upstairs to the interrogation cells to be tortured. The interrogation cells were heated. Never in my life could I have imagined that people could be so cold, so obsessed with the need for warmth, that they would welcome torture just to feel a little heat on their bodies. But they did. It was my good fortune that I didn't have to spend winter in that cell because I could not have survived it.

Torture and beatings were routine. The political prisoners fared worst; I probably owe my life to the fact that they chose to regard me as a common criminal. Most of the political prisoners had done nothing wrong. They were victims of a system whereby informers had to identify enemies of the state or be accused of being an enemy of the state themselves. Innocent people were sent to Vac, tortured and driven mad there. When I close my eyes at night I can still hear the screams of the tormented begging for mercy. Sometimes it is my voice I hear, my screams. They tortured me regularly every month as part of my interrogation to see if Tibor had made any attempt to contact me. They also tortured me on the rare occasion when anybody spoke to me in case they had given a message. Tibor never did try to contact me but Istvan Kiraly needed to be sure. Patience and persistence, Istvan had said, patience and persistence. How I cursed his persistence.

Food became an obsession. In the mornings we were given a mug of coffee and a pound of stale bread. Twice a week, around eleven-thirty, we were given soup with meat and vegetables. There was never much meat but it was the first thing we looked for. Grown men cried if their spoon came up empty or they were given less than their fair share. I've said before that Hungarians are a race of meat eaters; that we believe the consumption of meat is essential for strength. Hungarians also eat a lot of fat in the belief that it insulates the body against the cold. It was fat the prisoners in the lower levels looked for. In the afternoons we were given a meal of vegetables. The portions were always small. We probably ate better than the Jews in Auschwitz, and better than Gabi did in Theresienstadt, but it was still far from enough. The beatings became more painful the thinner we got.

There were no friends in gaol. There were too many informers to trust anyone. Besides, there was always the risk of speaking to the wrong person and being accused of being an accomplice. But we learned in the midst of that horror who

467

could be relied on when we were sick or needed help. One man sought me out and managed to talk to me without appearing to. He said his name was Nyers and that he knew Tibor. I thought he was an informer and ignored him for fear of the beatings it could bring. Yet this man Nyers fed me my meals when I was too sick or weak to feed myself. When I was fevered he gave me his blanket and one time he lay with his arms around me all night to share his warmth. Such humanity and generosity was rare. But for him I believe I would have died that night. Still I ignored him but now as much for his sake as mine.

One way or another, I lived with death, torture and the numbing, grave-like cold for eight years. Eight years without hope or reason to hope. In our hermetic world we heard nothing of the outside. There were no newspapers or radios. Then one day a group of prisoners in the cells alongside the river heard someone shouting to them. It was October 17, 1956, and somebody had taken the enormous risk of rowing a boat beneath a prison window.

'Political prisoners!' called the rower. 'Do not despair. All will be free within two weeks!'

Can you imagine the effect this had on us? Fevered speculation raced around the prison, reaching into even the most remote and terrible underground cells. Suddenly there was hope where there had been none. Suddenly there was the prospect of a future beyond those walls. Every day we waited for something to happen. Nothing did but our sense of expectation did not diminish. Then, on October 24, machine-gun nests appeared on the prison roof and we were all confined to our cells. Something was happening but we couldn't imagine what. Someone said that there was a war and the Americans were coming. We did our best to believe the rumour; it justified the machine guns. But why hadn't we heard shooting? We all knew what war sounded like.

Our guards became increasingly nervous and we began to notice changes. Within a couple of days of the machine guns appearing, the red stars vanished from the front of the AVO officers' caps. Such a small thing but it signified so much. Then the guards exchanged their green uniforms for police uniforms. A prisoner who had the privilege of a cell with a window overlooking the street saw a man standing on the opposite side of the road calling to the prisoners and waving the Hungarian flag. The hammer and wheat sheaf emblem had been cut out of the middle. This was news almost beyond comprehension. The prisoner told those in the cells on either side of him what he'd seen and they passed the word on till every prisoner had heard the unbelievable news. Someone started singing the Himnusz and soon every prisoner joined in. Even more unbelievably, our singing struck terror into the heart of the guards. They dragged prisoners from their cells and beat them in the corridors to silence them, but the prisoners kept singing even as the boots thudded into their faces and bodies. The guards gave up on the beatings and ran.

The guards ran from us! If we needed proof that something momentous was taking place, that provided it. As dawn broke, the thousand prisoners in Vac began their own uprising. We broke up the furniture in our cells and used it to force open the doors. The freed liberated others. We brushed aside the terrified guards and dashed in a wild screaming mob for the street. Not all of us made it. There was a doctor in Vac, a Doctor Adam, who was a cruel and merciless AVO officer. As we dashed for the gates he began machine-gunning us. Prisoners who had spent years in Vac and were on the very threshold of freedom went down in that withering hail of bullets. Other prisoners, defying death themselves, climbed the walls to his position and killed him with an iron bar. The bastard kept firing up to the instant his brains splattered onto the concrete.

Suddenly the gates were open. I confess, I stepped over the fallen bodies of my fellow prisoners as I seized this chance for freedom. Nothing could stop me, but I wasn't alone. It was a stampede. I had no objective in mind other than to put myself on the other side of the prison walls. As we ran away down the streets of Vac, people applauded and cheered us. At that moment the world was utterly incomprehensible. Ordinary citizens were applauding gaol-breakers? I saw a woman standing in the doorway of a shop weeping with joy.

'What is happening?' I asked her. 'Why am I free?'

That was the first I heard about the uprising. I was standing there, slack-jawed in amazement, when Nyers grabbed hold of my arm. I'd last seen him scaling the wall to get to Doctor Adam. He might even have been one of those who killed him.

'Come on!' he said. 'We have to get to Budapest.'

Budapest. It's a strange thing. As soon as he mentioned a destination I knew where I wanted to go: back to Sarospatak. But no sooner had the idea entered my head than I realised that was the very last place I could go. That was where Istvan would look for me. So I went with Nyers to Budapest.

Nyers was very resourceful, much like Tibor. All of my life I had been accustomed to following close behind and not asking too many questions and that is what I did again. Nyers talked our way onto a coal barge which was carrying vegetables and fruit to feed the revolutionaries in Budapest. For the first time in eight years my world was defined not by walls but by sky. A cool breeze brought fresh air to my lungs and it tasted unbelievably sweet. So this is what freedom tastes like, I thought. Why had I never tasted it before? I sat down on the deck and leaned against the wheelhouse. Nyers sat beside me. I spoke my first words to this man who had saved my life. 'Thank you,' I said.

He shrugged dismissively.

'Why did you take so many risks to help me?'

'I owed your brother.'

Tears ran down my cheeks but I also started laughing so hard I nearly choked. Tibor was still looking after me, it didn't matter that his help came indirectly. Despite the torture and the monthly reports, we'd beaten Istvan Kiraly.

The captain and his two men celebrated our freedom with us. They gave us most of their lunch — thick beef stew and stuffed peppers cooked in pork fat. We weren't cold any more but we couldn't help ourselves. Meat was strength, fat was warmth. We gorged ourselves. The crew also had more *barack* than was good for them and we drank until we were drunk. Drunk on freedom, drunk on warmth and drunk on *barack*.

We were welcomed like heroes into Budapest because we came with food. The crew wanted no payment; the fruit and vegetables had been given to them by peasants in the north to feed the freedom fighters. Everybody wanted to help the revolution. Nobody wanted payment. Students took the food away to hospitals and barracks and food distribution points. Nyers and I wanted to help with the unloading but we were too weak. When the students heard we were political prisoners freed from Vac they refused to let us work and lifted us high on their shoulders. At first light that day we had been prisoners; now, at dusk, we were heroes. This world we had come back to was very strange. That night, after we'd said our goodbyes and given our thanks to the crew of the barge, we discovered just how strange.

There were open boxes on the pavements outside buildings to collect money to fund the revolution. They were unguarded. Even while we were watching, people emptied their pockets but nobody stole a single coin. Shopfronts were shattered but there was no looting. Buildings had been reduced to rubble but nobody was picking through the remains. We passed places where food was being given away. All people had to do was queue up and they were fed. People took the minimum they needed, aware that there were many others who were hungry and that the available food was limited. We saw children, boys and girls between twelve and fifteen, running around with rifles and siphoning petrol out of cars into bottles. Neither of us realised it at the time, but we were looking at the frontline troops of our revolution. The Russians had insisted that Hungarian schoolchildren be taught the art of guerrilla warfare in the event of a NATO invasion. Ironically, what they'd succeeded in doing was teaching the young people of Hungary how to overthrow them when the time came. It was these young children who destroyed and disabled tanks. It was their broken little bodies that lay in the streets and in the shallow graves in the parks.

Nyers couldn't find a phone that worked so we trudged from place to place looking for a bar that was open and a face he knew and could trust. Occasionally we saw dead AVO officers hanging from lampposts and from trees. Many had notes worth hundreds of forints pinned to their uniforms. Blood money. Budapest was a very strange place. Eventually Nyers found somebody who knew how to contact Benke. Next thing we knew we were in a Mercedes racing through Pest. From time to time we were stopped at roadblocks manned by armed students, police and sometimes even Hungarian soldiers. But on this night two escaped 'political' prisoners in a car owned by a notorious criminal were not arrested but applauded. We didn't realise that Benke and his cohorts were fighting alongside the revolutionaries.

Benke greeted his ex-deputy with genuine affection. Apparently Nyers had been given a script to follow in the event that he was captured by the AVO, referring to properties that could be sacrificed to give the illusion of cooperation, and had stuck to the script despite the best endeavours of his torturers. Benke took us to a house in the hills of Buda and put us in the hands of an elderly couple who were instructed to give us anything we wanted. We were told to rest, eat and put some meat on our bones. Under normal circumstances those arrangements would have been fine. But we were in the middle of a revolution, what was almost certainly the most momentous event in the history of our sad, suffering country. Nyers and I were agreed on what we would do. Yes, we would rest and eat and get strong. We gave ourselves two days to build up some reserves. Then we wanted to fight. I also wanted to find Istvan Kiraly and wring his scrawny neck. In the meantime we listened to Radio Free Budapest.

It was October 27 when we escaped from gaol and November 2 before we made our way back into the heart of Budapest to fight the Russians. Despite our bravado we were still weak. It had taken eight years to turn me into a living skeleton; this could not be fixed in a few days. We heard that Andrassy Street had been raided and that all the AVO officers who had not escaped had been killed. The Party Headquarters in Republic Square had also been raided. The prisoners in the cellars had been released and the AVO officers upstairs hanged. Nobody could give me any information on the whereabouts of Major Istvan Kiraly or Major Bogati. What I did learn was that the freedom fighters had discovered that many high-ranking AVO officers had secret escape passages in their homes and offices. Imagine that. In their hearts they knew there would come a day of reckoning yet they still didn't change their ways. They built escape tunnels instead.

We thought the fighting was over and that, against all odds, the uprising had succeeded. We thought we were too late to take up arms and contribute. Like most people, we gathered around radios to hear Radio Free Budapest. It broadcast the demands and conditions for a free Hungary. Acceptance of the conditions was a prerequisite for a truce with the Soviets. The radio station kept people informed of the political manoeuvrings and directed armed volunteers to trouble spots. It told people where food was being distributed. It served so many purposes in a city where communications had been devastated. But Radio Free Budapest also relayed rumours.

Some of the speculation was wild. One minute the Americans were coming to save us, another it was NATO. But only one rumour carried any conviction and it was the one we least wanted to believe. Despite all their assurances that they were leaving peacefully, the Soviets had begun massing tanks and troops on the eastern, northern and southern borders. It was

473

apparent that Hungary's glorious days of freedom were drawing to a close. We knew the Americans weren't coming to save us and we knew the Russians would not tolerate such a rent in the iron curtain. We knew Budapest and Hungary were doomed.

For years Nyers and I had been kept in isolation and denied all contact with the world. For us, Radio Free Budapest symbolised everything we were fighting for. It didn't take a genius to realise the station would be one of the first targets the Russians would attack. We decided there and then to help fight for its survival.

The Russians opened fire on Budapest at four in the morning on November 4. In 1945 I had witnessed the ferocity of the battle between the Germans and the Russians over the occupation of Budapest. This time the fire was all one-sided. The Russians had artillery and tanks. We had small boys and girls with bottles filled with petrol. We also had a population armed with rifles and a few machine guns, but rifles and machine guns could not stop tanks. From the windows of Radio Free Budapest we saw boys run out from buildings to drop Molotov cocktails down the turrets of tanks and directly into their petrol tanks. We saw tanks destroyed along with their crews, but we also saw young boys blown up with the targets they'd attacked, immolated by their own bottles of petrol or gunned down by supporting tanks. The courage and sacrifice of those children will live in Hungarian history for ever, but not all the children in Budapest could stop the Russian tanks.

Shells exploded in the radio building but I remained at my post, firing non-stop while a girl of about twelve reloaded rifles for me. But our efforts were more symbolic than effective. Nyers called to me and pointed out a group of four tanks which had halted in a nearby square. The barrels of their guns were swivelling directly towards our position.

'Run!' he said. 'Run and don't stop until you reach Austria.'

I didn't need telling twice. There was no way I was ever going back to prison. I preferred death to prison but I didn't want to die either. I dropped my rifle and ran. Others did the same. It was then that I noticed the unattended microphone in the studio. I didn't know if it was switched on or not but I had seen others send messages and wanted to send one myself. I wanted to tell the world that I was alive and trying to escape to Austria, in the hope that somehow Gabi or Tibor would hear of it. I grabbed hold of the microphone and started speaking. But how could I say I was heading for Austria? I had to assume the remaining AVO would be monitoring every word spoken on Radio Free Budapest. Istvan Kiraly would learn of my intentions. I decided to mislead him. When I gave my name I said Milos Heyman from Sarospatak, in the hope that he'd conclude I was heading back there. It never occurred to me that in trying to mislead Istvan I was making a catastrophic mistake.

The building was falling down around me as I ran. I never saw Nyers again or the twelve-year-old girl who'd reloaded my rifles. I hope they had the good sense to run too. A piece of shrapnel clipped the back of my head but I hardly felt it. All I knew was that my hair was sticky with blood. When I reached the street it was filled with rubble from collapsed and burning buildings. The smoke and noise was terrifying, but I knew where I was and knew I was heading west. As I left the city centre I heard a car coming up behind me, weaving around the rubble, tooting its horn. I thought it was the AVO after me. In all the chaos of Budapest I thought the AVO had heard my broadcast and sent a car after me! I turned around to see if I could outrun it or try to escape by running through a damaged building. The car was a Mercedes and there was a French flag flying from one of the side windows. The car was full of reporters, French, German and English. They tried to drive around me but I blocked their way.

'Take me,' I begged them. 'Take me out of Budapest!'

The reporters argued heatedly. The driver apologised and said it was too risky for them. So I stood in front of their car and refused to move. The reporters became more agitated. The English reporter offered to give up his seat for me.

'Okay,' they said, 'lie down in the footwell of the rear seat.'

They put their coats and equipment on top of me and told me that Budapest was ringed by tanks and the Russians were stopping anyone from entering or leaving. They said they were going to try to pass me off as another reporter and to keep my mouth shut and pretend to be unconscious. By this stage the back of my head was covered in blood. At least their ruse would have some substance.

We drove straight through the Russian lines without being stopped. I think the Russians were happy not to have foreign reporters witness the fall of Budapest. But we knew there'd be more Russians ahead and more roadblocks. It was only a matter of time before we'd be stopped and, in all likelihood, my flimsy disguise would be revealed for what it was. I asked the reporters to stop on a quiet piece of road where there were trees for cover and let me out. That started another argument, with the English reporter insisting that they should take me all the way and smuggle me across the border. Even I knew that would only get us all arrested. They dropped me off just east of Gyor and gave me some bread and cheese which was the last of their food. After watching them drive away I circled wide around Gyor and headed for the border south of Sopron.

The countryside was swarming with people trying to escape. I met up with a family of five, a husband and wife and three small children. She was carrying one child on her back while her husband was struggling with the remaining two. They were exhausted and on the verge of giving up. Weak as I was, I took one of the children and some of their bags. Unwittingly, I also took over command. I became their Tibor. I realised that we needed rest and food more than anything and marched up to the door of a farmhouse. I asked the farmer if we could hide in his barn until it was dark.

'Hide,' he said. 'Don't ask. I never saw you.'

He asked me about the revolution and I told him it was over. He closed his eyes momentarily and nodded. It was easy to imagine this scene being played out all over the countryside. Once again Hungary would be forced to do penance, but most Hungarians believed their country's penance was disproportionate to its sins. The farmer gave me some bread and some stew for the children.

That kindness was repeated all the way to the border. For one brief moment the flag of freedom had flown over Hungary and the peasants were determined to help those who had put it there. Young men volunteered to guide us through the lines where they knew the patrols were least frequent. It snowed the night we crossed over into Austria. Border patrols had been stepped up but the storm limited their activities. I crossed into Austria on my hands and knees with a little boy stuffed down the front of my jacket to keep him warm. He slept right through the night. We made it, and for that I had to thank my months on the run with Tibor.

Even on that terrible night, in the snow and cold, ordinary Austrian citizens were patrolling their side of the border looking for people like us so they could help us. They gave us blankets and hot coffee and took us to the Red Cross. We were too cold and exhausted to feel any elation over our newfound freedom. The family I had helped were sent to a refugee hostel. I was sent to hospital with pneumonia.

I had dreamed of freedom. Freedom had always been more than just an ideal but something tangible, something I would feel with my heart and every fibre of my body. In my dreams it had always been something uplifting and triumphant. And, in my dreams, Gabi had always been by my side. But Gabi was not by my side and neither was Tibor. I had no idea where in the world they were or how I could ever begin to look for them. I felt as if I had escaped into a vacuum. I had lost my home, my country and the flesh off my body. I was a homeless, stateless skeleton with pneumonia in a hospital where I knew nobody and, apart from the occasional interpreter, nobody even spoke my language.

Milos slumped back into his chair. He took a sip of his coffee but it had long grown cold.

'You know, Neil,' he said, 'on the first day of my story, during our first break for coffee, I said how much I envied you. How I envied the fact that you will never know fear as I have, never suffer my deprivations, never be in a situation where life and death stand as equals and not care which of them the next day brings. When I said that, I was thinking of Vac.'

Neil nodded, unsure how to respond.

'I envy the fact that you, in this lucky country, never had to go through what I went through.'

'But you escaped and made your way to Austria. You survived. All credit to you.'

'Yes, I survived. But what you call baggage and I call my past does not acknowledge borders. I'd escaped from Hungary, but not from the horrors, not from consequences and not from obligations.'

'What did you do?' asked Neil.

'I did nothing.'

'Nothing?'

'That's right, Neil. I did nothing. For two weeks I did nothing. Then they told me I had a visitor. In the space of minutes I went from boundless joy to despair. It was then that I learned the tragic consequences of my mistake.'

'I'll get Gancio to bring you another coffee,' said Lucio.

'Let's all have another,' said Ramon. 'Gabriella, I take it you are going to continue the story? You are going to tell us about this mistake?'

'Yes, Ramon. Milos has convinced me to share the telling. And coffee is a good idea.'

CHAPTER THIRTY-ONE

Milos's desperate message on Radio Free Budapest affected Tibor and I differently. Of course we were both stunned at first but, once we'd got over the shock of hearing Milos's voice and discovering that he was still alive, we were overjoyed. But we were also frightened out of our wits. We could hear the battle raging, hear the explosion of shells and the last desperate pleas for the West to intervene. We looked at each other in horror. I could not imagine how anyone could survive such a bombardment. At the very moment we learned my Milos was still alive it seemed we were about to lose him again. It was so unfair. Suddenly, Radio Free Budapest ceased transmitting. Both Tibor and I knew what that meant but Tibor refused to believe it also meant the end of Milos.

'I taught him how to survive,' he said fiercely. 'He is alive, I know he is. He has survived the Russians before. He can survive them again.'

I knew Tibor was voicing hope more than conviction, but that is what I also wanted to believe and believe with all my heart. I hoped desperately that Tibor was right, that my Milos was still alive. Can a few words revive a love, bring it back stronger and deeper after so many years? Of course they can! Those few words took me back to Aunt Klari's, to the nights when Milos slept by my bed and his love was all that stood between me and insanity. They took me back to my last Christmas in Hungary, when Milos gave me my father's bracelet and I realised how much I loved him. People say love conquers all. Maybe it does. All I know is, hearing his voice snapped me out of the stupor I'd descended into. Suddenly there was something in my life more important than me. Suddenly I had something to live for.

But I was alone in my euphoria. Tibor became increasingly agitated. During all the years we'd lived in Australia we had believed Milos was dead and had made no attempt to find or help him. The news that Milos was still alive delighted Tibor but also devastated him. He believed he'd failed his brother and the duty of care his father had entrusted to him. He turned on himself for not having made sure Milos was dead, for not having made enquiries, for not having helped Milos when it was obvious he'd needed help. He paced around the house and refused to settle. He ignored the coffees I made for him. Later that morning he dashed out of the house without saying where he was going. He returned that evening with two air tickets to London.

'We have to find him,' he said. 'After all this time, we have to find him! We must do this even if we do nothing else with our lives.'

At that stage we were cashed up. Tibor had sold all his businesses except his Jaguar dealership and he instructed his solicitor to sell that in our absence in case we needed more money. Five days later we took off for England on a Qantas flying boat. There I was, too scared to leave my house, sitting on an aeroplane. The flight to London was prohibitively expensive but even so we were lucky to get two seats. People had cancelled, fearing that Europe was once more on the brink of a war. From England we flew to Austria. Tibor was determined that no expense would be spared in our quest to bring Milos back.

The problem was, while we'd heard from Milos we'd heard too little. Tibor read more into Milos's words than were ever intended. Milos had mentioned Sarospatak and Tibor convinced himself it was Milos's way of telling us where to find him. If he'd stopped to think, he would have realised that Milos would never risk going back to Sarospatak, but he didn't stop and he wouldn't listen. He was determined to make up for everything that had happened to Milos from the time he'd persuaded Milos and me to escape from Hungary with him. Only a truly heroic act could compensate for the years in which Milos had been abandoned. Tibor planned to cross back into Hungary and make his way to Sarospatak and was deaf to any argument.

I didn't argue too hard, I must confess. I wanted my Milos back, whatever it took. I would have agreed to anything, no matter how dangerous or foolhardy. There was no stopping Tibor anyway, his mind was made up. It had taken almost a week to get to England and another two days to get a flight to Vienna. We were told that the telephone system in Budapest had been destroyed, but Budapest isn't the whole of Hungary. Tibor kept ringing around until he found a line that was working and somebody he knew answered it. That person got a message to Endre Benke.

Benke managed to call us back at our hotel. He was adamant that Tibor should not return to Hungary. He offered to send people to Sarospatak on our behalf to find Milos if he was there. But Tibor wouldn't listen. Benke told him to try all the refugee hostels first, but again Tibor wouldn't listen. He felt he'd lost too much time flying over. He was worried that Milos would think we hadn't heard his message. He feared that Milos would despair of ever being rescued. But in hindsight, we know the real reason Tibor insisted on going back. It was the risk. The thrill of the danger. That was what had been missing from his life in Australia. That was why he hadn't settled. Tibor needed to stand on the edge and look over one last time.

Benke arranged for Tibor to meet with contacts who could smuggle him back into Hungary. He left that night with his pockets stuffed full of English pounds and American dollars. I kissed him goodbye and begged him to take care but I don't think he even heard me. He'd reverted to the Tibor who had come back to us from Budapest. Only his mission to rescue Milos mattered. Nothing else. Not even me.

He left me in Vienna by myself. A woman who for eight years had been too scared to venture outside to the corner shop. He left me alone to cope in that strange city and, to my utter surprise, that is what I did. Perhaps the sound of all the German-speaking voices awakened something in me and I drew upon the survival instincts I'd developed in the camps. Benke had told Tibor to try the refugee camps and that was what I decided to do.

There was no way I could find my way across town to the relief agencies alone, nor hope to communicate successfully once I'd got there. So I did what Tibor should have done the instant we arrived in Vienna: I made my problem the hotel manager's problem. He was most sympathetic and placed a young woman who spoke English at my disposal. I sat with her all morning while she phoned around the hostels and aid agencies. The Austrians, like the Germans, are good record-keepers but even their resources had been stretched by the sheer numbers of Hungarians who had used the uprising as an opportunity to escape. But my young woman was polite and thorough. By lunch time we knew Milos was not registered at any of the refugee hostels. 'Have you tried the Red Cross?' one man asked. My helper suggested we ring the Red Cross after lunch.

She was calm, my young woman, calm, patient and thorough and I thought I should try to be like her. I wasn't anxious or desperate. I expected my search for Milos to take days, if not weeks, and even then I did not feel confident of success. Tibor's obsession with going to Sarospatak had almost convinced me that he would find Milos there. Tibor was my strength and Tibor was not often wrong.

The young woman and I ate open sandwiches and salad and drank a glass of wine each. I talked about Sydney and our beautiful harbour. I told her about kangaroos and koalas, cockatoos and lorikeets. The young woman was fascinated. After lunch we went straight back to her office and she dialled the Red Cross.

'Yes,' they said, 'we know the whereabouts of Milos Heyman.'

They told us which hospital he was in, which ward and the visiting hours. In just one morning I'd found my Milos! I could not move from my chair. I'd found my Milos. Just like that! Tears flowed down my cheeks. I couldn't stop crying and I couldn't stop smiling. Crying and smiling, that was all this foolish woman could do.

The young woman took me back to my room so I could wash, change and make myself presentable. Now I was excited. Now I was impatient. My hand shook so much my new friend had to apply my lipstick for me. She came with me in a taxi to the hospital, walked with me to the ward and tactfully waited outside the door. I tiptoed inside. My Milos, my beautiful Milos, was asleep on the bed in front of me. After eight years my Milos had come back to life. My heart went out to him when I saw how pale he was and how thin. I was too scared to touch him, too frightened to wake him. I started crying again and, as I stood there my Milos opened his eyes.

However long you know Milos, you will never see the smile that I saw that afternoon in Vienna. It was brighter than all the suns in the universe. No matter how long you live, you will never find two human beings more glad to see each other. I ran into his arms and we embraced each other, held each other and cried like babies. Ask me the happiest moment in my life and I will tell you: it was sitting on that hospital bed in Vienna. Not even the tragedy that followed can diminish it.

Milos slowly released me so he could look again at my face and into my eyes. 'Where's Tibor?' he asked.

Of course Milos was distraught when he heard. He wanted to go back into Hungary to find Tibor and warn him. He shook uncontrollably at the thought of what Istvan Kiraly would do to Tibor if he captured him. Fortunately, Milos was still too weak to go anywhere and there was no way I would have let him go anyway. With the help of the Red Cross, we managed to put a call through to the station at Sarospatak to ask Geza Apro to find Tibor and tell him that Milos was already safe in Vienna. But Geza Apro was no longer stationmaster and Milos's godfather, Mr Zelk, had retired. We asked if somebody could take a message to Aunt Klari but the answer was no. Nobody wanted to help us.

Milos asked for and got the number of the AVO office in Sarospatak. His hands shook as he dialled, gave a false name and asked to speak to Major Kiraly. He was told Major Kiraly was out of the office on AVO business and to leave his number. Milos hung up and held his head in both hands. Istvan Kiraly had survived the revolution and returned to Sarospatak. We both knew what had taken him there: Milos's broadcast. The goat had managed to slip its tether but had foolishly left a scent behind. That scent had lured Tibor into a trap.

Milos and I should have been rejoicing at our reunion but instead all we could think of was Tibor and the terrible fate in store for him. A cloud settled over us as dark as any I have known. For five days I divided my time between Milos's bedside and the telephone in my hotel room, willing it to ring. And then, on the night of the fifth day, when hope had all but faded, the telephone rang. It was Tibor. First Milos had come back from the dead, now Tibor.

'Tibor!' I screamed. 'Where are you? Don't go back to Sarospatak! Can you hear me? Milos is here! I have found him!'

'You have found Milos?'

The phone line crackled and Tibor's voice was faint but even so I heard it rise with disbelief and delight. I told him how I had found Milos in the hospital, how he was recovering from pneumonia.

'You found Milos. You found him.' He kept repeating these words over and over as though savouring them, but there was also wonder in his voice that someone as useless as me had accomplished this miracle. I told him about ringing the AVO office in Sarospatak and discovering that Istvan Kiraly had set a trap for him.

Tibor laughed. 'When I arrived in Budapest I rang my friend in Sarospatak. You remember my friend? He has exchanged his horse and cart for a truck, a Skoda. He told me Istvan was back in Sarospatak and that plain clothes AVO were watching the trains. We both realised why.'

'Where are you now?' I asked.

'Not over the phone, Gabi. I am safe, trust me. I will give you a number for Milos to ring.' Tibor slowly recited the number while I jotted it down. 'Tell Milos to ring me at ten tomorrow morning. That's all for now.'

'Don't hang up!'

'I have to go, Gabi. And Gabi ...' There was a long pause which should have told me something. 'Take good care of my brother. Promise?'

'Of course!' But the phone had already begun buzzing as I made my promise. Tibor had hung up.

My mind was awhirl with questions. What did Tibor mean when he told me to take care of Milos? Where was he? When was he coming back? And what would happen then? It was too late to rush to the hospital and tell Milos the news that Tibor was still alive. That, like my questions, had to wait until morning.

I think it was learning that Tibor was still alive that finally drove the pneumonia from Milos's body. It was the best medicine he

485

could have had. He could not stop hugging me while we waited for the operators in Vienna to make the connection with the number Tibor had given me. Milos had so much to say, but when Tibor's voice came on the crackling line it was Milos who did most of the listening. Sometimes it is possible to know what people are talking about just by listening to one person's responses, but, with so little to go on, I learned nothing. At first there was joy and tears as they exchanged their first words for eight years, but then Milos's face grew serious and he hardly uttered a word. The call ended before Milos was ready, exactly as it had done with me the night before. Milos stood stunned. I had to take the phone from him and replace it on its cradle.

'He's not coming back,' said Milos, his voice barely a whisper.

'What?' Tibor not coming back? It didn't make sense.

'He's decided to stay on with Benke and steal more trains.'

My jaw dropped in disbelief.

'He made me promise to look after you. "Look after your wife," he said.'

Look after your wife. My eyes filled with tears as I realised what Tibor had done. He'd given me back to Milos. He'd accepted responsibility for our separation and was now making amends in the only way possible. When had he made his decision? It had to have been while he was talking to me on the phone; once he'd learned Milos was safe and outside Hungary. The significance of his silence and the promise I'd made to him the night before suddenly became obvious. Tibor had realised that if he came back he would be an obstacle between Milos and me, an impediment to us taking up the life we'd been denied. But what a sacrifice! He'd cut himself off from the two people he loved most in the world and who loved him in return. And what would be the price of his magnanimity? I shuddered involuntarily. Tibor had been my husband, my friend and the mainstay of my life. I had to face the reality that I would never see him again.

Milos took me in his arms. Undoubtedly, similar thoughts were going through his mind. Weeping, I consoled myself by remembering how anxious Tibor had been to return to Hungary and how, for all the freedom Australia had offered, he'd been unsettled there. Tibor was a man for a time and a place and, in truth, his place was not Sydney but Budapest.

Tibor made no further attempt to contact us. That silence spoke volumes. I took the initiative and decided we should return immediately to Australia. Eight years ago Tibor had stolen Milos's identity and now Milos took it back. He pretended to be Tibor pretending to be him. It made everything so simple. He applied for a new Australian passport on the basis that he'd lost his. Milos looked enough like his brother to pass himself off as a sick Tibor, and I had copies of Tibor's 'Milos' signature for Milos to practise. The consulate did not hesitate to provide us with travel documents that would get us into Australia. After all, as far as they were concerned, Milos was an Australian citizen, had a house in Rose Bay and an Australian wife. Our papers said so and papers were unarguable. That was the part Milos liked best: he had an Australian wife and the wife was me.

Tibor set us free to live our lives together. He never wrote to us but he did keep in touch with Aunt Klari from time to time. Through Aunt Klari we learned that he'd returned to his old ways and was up to his old tricks. Sadly, and perhaps inevitably, it was also through Aunt Klari that four years on we learned of his death. Somebody had talked, or was blackmailed by the AVO into providing information. Tibor was ambushed unloading a train and, when the hopelessness of the situation became apparent, turned his own gun on himself. Aunt Klari and Andras read about it in their local newspaper. Andras claimed Tibor's body and buried it at the back of the farmhouse. We drew comfort from the fact that Tibor never saw the inside of Andrassy Street or any prison. We drew comfort in knowing that he was never tortured and that, with his last act, he had denied Istvan Kiraly the revenge he craved.

* * *

'I have known people like Tibor,' said Ramon quietly. 'People who must risk everything just to feel alive. Inevitably the time comes when they risk too much.'

'Some of the partisans were like that,' said Lucio. 'They looked forward to skirmishes with German soldiers. My Aunt Colombina used to say they laughed in the face of danger. When the war ended they had nothing. Many of them turned to drink. Thank you both for your story. Thank you for sharing it with us and for letting us into your lives so intimately, especially since the telling was often so distressing. I feel privileged.'

'My sentiments exactly,' said Ramon.

'We haven't finished,' said Milos.

'There is more?'

'Yes, Ramon, there is more. I told you at the very beginning of my story that I had no jurisdiction over subject matter. I told you there was the matter of a debt to repay.'

'Ahh, the debt.'

'Gabriella insisted.'

'And it is her debt?'

'Yes, Ramon, it is Gabi's debt and hers to repay. Perhaps we should let her get on with it, no?'

CHAPTER THIRTY-TWO

Happy-ever-after endings are not confined to fiction, but in life they are sometimes a long time coming. When Milos and I returned to Sydney I tried my best to be the wife he had always imagined I'd be. We made a new start so that Milos could have his own life and not simply inherit Tibor's. We sold the house at Rose Bay and all the furniture and moved to Bellevue Hill. I did my best to shed some of my baggage. I didn't object when Milos refused to put bars on the windows or double locks on the doors. In those first few months, with Milos beside me, I was strong. His love made me strong. Of course he wondered why I ran and hid whenever we needed eggs broken. He laughed about it and asked why. But I couldn't tell him. I couldn't tell anyone about the eggs. Maybe if I had, things might have turned out differently. My inability to face up to my torments was a warning that I refused to acknowledge. I thought time would heal but it only brought periods of remission.

Milos's presence gave me strength but it was ridiculous to expect that he would be present every minute of every day thereafter. Nobody in this world is entitled to a free ride, no matter how deserving they may think they are. Milos, like Tibor, was amazed by the opportunities he saw. Coming from a land of deprivation to a land of plenty, he was astonished by the waste all around him. People abandoned cars which in Hungary would still have years left in them. They threw away tyres that still had tread. People threw away washing machines and sewing machines because they were considered too old or not worth repairing. They did the same with bicycles and prams. Milos was fascinated by this waste.

'If people think it is rubbish,' I told him, 'then it is rubbish. Rubbish is rubbish.'

'Rich people's rubbish,' he said. 'Poor people's treasure.'

Milos started a business buying up old cars. He repaired those that could be repaired and uncovered a ready market for good cheap cars. The cars he couldn't fix he stripped for parts and uncovered a ready market for cheap parts.

'Even in a land of plenty there are poor,' Milos said. He catered to the poor.

After the car yards came bicycle repair shops and appliance repair shops. There was nothing he could not squeeze more life out of: washing machines, vacuum cleaners, heaters, you name it. Milos didn't do the repairs himself. He lacked the knowledge and the skills. He gave the work to people who were desperate for it, almost always immigrants who had the skills but nothing else, often not even a good grasp of English. Milos made sure he covered his costs and made a small profit. He made lots of small profits and they all added up.

But these were not businesses which ran at arm's length. Most people worked a forty-hour week but Milos ridiculed the idea. 'Only in a rich country,' he said incredulously. He worked ten-hour days and a half-day on Saturdays. You can admire his determination and his work ethic, but it had the effect of leaving me where I least wanted to be. Alone.

Milos was the pillar I clung to, but my pillar left me for ten hours a day and half a day on Saturdays. I tried to keep myself busy but there were too many empty hours and too many opportunities for memories to resurface. Once again I found refuge in my Vincents powders. The nightmares returned, more vivid than ever, as though invigorated by their time away. Once again I stood out in the cold in my prisoner's striped uniform and heard my name called out. Once again I was burned alive in the ovens of Auschwitz. Once again Milos was shot and his body ripped apart by dogs. And through it all, through this nightmare, came the sound I dreaded most: the cracking of eggs. Where could I find consolation and relief but in my powders? I began to withdraw and for a while Milos, my precious guardian angel, was too busy to notice.

Once Milos realised what was happening to me, he started spending more time at home. He learned to use his time more wisely and to conduct his business by telephone. We worked together to overcome my demons. Every morning when the sun beat down on the front of our house, he made me open the door and leave it open for one hour. The idea terrified me but, with Milos by my side, I could do it. If there was a problem at one of his yards and he had to go, I kept the door open and counted the minutes until the hour was up. Gradually we extended the hour to an hour and a half, then two hours. Sometimes I even managed to forget the door was open. We went out for walks every day. Milos insisted on it, whether it was sunny or raining. Once again Milos put himself between me and my fears.

We made progress. We had good weeks, good months and, on balance, even good years. In a moment of inspiration, Milos got me two Hungarian housemaids. They came twice a week, down from the Blue Mountains by train. Such a long way to travel but they didn't seem to mind. Their names were Martha and Maria but to me they were my Australian Aunt Klari and Aunt Jutka, and like my aunts they were as round as Russian dolls. They had come from a village near Apafa, almost due south of Sarospatak and near the border with Romania, but their lives had not been dissimilar to Aunt Klari's. They worked hard and every summer we made preserves and jams from plums, apricots and peaches. Preserves and jams were cheap in the shops but we made them for the sheer pleasure of doing it. For days at a time, our home in Bellevue Hill became the Tokaj Street of my childhood. They helped me and Milos helped me. But all they were doing in reality was sustaining remission when what I needed was a cure.

For almost thirty years we lived the myth that I was getting better. We were happy. But the truth was, I was dependent upon Milos, my two Ems — Martha and Maria — and my powders. I had survived Eichmann and escaped Soviet Hungary. I had come to a new country which took freedom for granted, but I was still not free. I was not free of my fears. One day Milos told me he was taking me to see a doctor. It was a new doctor, not our regular doctor, and for a long time I didn't understand why Milos took me to see him. I went twice a week, every Monday and Wednesday morning for one hour. At first the hours were very pleasant. The doctor became my friend. He asked me about Hungary and I told him about my family and Tokaj Street. All we did was chat for an hour and then Milos took me home. This went on for months.

'Why do I have to go there?' I asked Milos. 'Why do you take me there?'

'Don't you like going?' he replied.

'Yes,' I said. 'What is not to like? My friend the doctor is a nice man. We chat. I do most of the talking and he does most of the listening.'

'Do you trust him?'

'Of course,' I replied. 'What's not to trust?'

'Good,' said Milos. 'One day your friend the doctor is going to set you free.'

I believed Milos but I couldn't see how my friend the doctor was ever going to set me free. All we did was talk about our Sunday lunches at Tokaj Street and the crush I had on Tibor. I talked about Aunt Klari and Aunt Jutka and how we made wonderful preserves. My friend the doctor always listened attentively and smiled and laughed. I looked forward to seeing him for my two hours a week. Then one day he asked me about the day they took my father away and the sun disappeared behind a cloud. It wasn't long before the cloud darkened my sky and the storm burst. My happy hours with my friend the doctor became hours of pure hell.

I would do anything rather than go to see the doctor. But Milos made me. Every Monday and Wednesday he dragged me kicking and screaming to the taxi and held me tight all the way there while I shook and cried. My friend the doctor asked me about the train that took me away, about Krakow station, about the camps and the selections. He asked me about Auschwitz and he asked me about Julia. Julia, for heaven's sake! My friend from Theresienstadt. I had tried not to think about her for years. He prised open all the doors in my mind and dragged out the pain. But even then there were things I could not tell him, things I was not able to face. I told him about the Russians who raped me, and how I had learned that I was the only member of my family to survive. I told him about my guilt for surviving when there were others so much more worthy. I told him so many things, but I could not tell him everything, and I certainly could not tell him about the cracking of the eggs. One day, about four years ago, he gave me a boiled egg and a spoon.

'Crack it open,' he said. 'Crack open the egg.'

I screamed and cried and fought and I would not do it. I would not break open the egg. When Milos brought me home I lay down on the sofa and curled up into a ball. I stayed like that for hours while my mind sought a safe haven. It took me back to Tokaj Street, it was so sweet there and pleasant. So safe. There were times when my mind retreated so deeply Milos could not awake me and he feared he'd lost me. For six months, my friend the doctor gave me an egg and a spoon each time I went to see him. It was torment, but slowly it occurred to me that each time the torment was a little less than before. One day I summoned all my courage and broke open the egg. That sound! That sickening, wet sound! The egg opened and so did the floodgates. I cried and screamed and remembered every detail. I relived every second of that terrible night. My hour became two, became three. I told him about the eggs and about everything else I had hidden from him. The doors burst open and everything came tumbling out. My friend the doctor took me in his arms and told me I was the bravest woman he had ever met.

He was wrong, of course. My friend the doctor had set me free like he had promised to do, but by then I had acquired more chains. All those years of taking compound analgesics had finally exacted their toll. My kidneys failed, destroyed by the powders and tablets which had helped me cope. Three times a week I needed to be connected up to an artificial kidney, a dialysis machine, to have my blood taken out and washed. It is a humiliating, drawn-out and often painful process. I could not bear to do this in hospital so Milos learned how to operate the machine.

Home dialysis was better but not good. I hated that machine. It took out my blood, washed it and gave it back to me, but each time my blood lost a little of its vitality. It kept me alive, that machine, but alive is not the same as living. My skin turned sallow and yellow. I endured the most terrible cramps as the machine stripped water out of my body. Afterwards my skin itched so badly Milos had to rub me until I fell asleep. It governed our lives, this infernal machine. Milos used to joke about it. 'Time to have your oil changed,' he'd say.

To keep my spirits up he told me stories. He used to tell me stories to take my mind off my visits to my friend the doctor, and now he told me stories to distract me while my blood channelled through the machine. Milos has always told wonderful stories, even when he was a child visiting us at Tokaj Street, but four years ago his stories got better, more varied and more stimulating. That was when he met you and you began your Thursday lunches. I cannot begin to tell you how much I looked forward to Thursday afternoons when Milos brought your stories home to me. They were the most precious of gifts. I learned how each of you speak by listening to the way Milos retold your stories. I learned the way you think through the way you constructed your stories. We would argue, Milos and I, always trying to guess the ending or uncover hidden agendas. Your stories helped me forget the pain of having my memories raked over. Your stories helped me forget that I was dependent on a machine. They gave us moral dilemmas and made us look deep inside ourselves to find the truth. They helped me forget that I was growing weaker and that soon I would die.

For five years my life depended on that machine while I waited and hoped for a transplant. Salvation came two years ago, tragically, on the back of a motorbike. We had all but given up hope when a young man riding home from work in the rain skidded and crashed. His head hit a lamppost, causing massive brain damage. The doctors kept him alive on life-support machines while they sought permission from his grieving family to remove his organs for transplant. What a gift! What kindness from strangers! My heart went out to that young man's family. A young girl in Melbourne received one of his kidneys, I received the other.

Milos told me your stories as I lay in hospital while my new kidney made up its mind whether it would work for me or not. Sometimes the level of toxins in my blood was so high they'd think about putting me back on dialysis. The threat was always enough to get my kidney working again. I refused to go back on that machine. After six weeks I was well enough to come home.

The last two years have been the best of my adult life. After all these years I am free. Free of the machine and free of my fears. Imagine that. After so many years! Of course I still have nightmares occasionally but I can deal with them now. They are almost like old friends and I would miss them if they went away. I take every opportunity to demonstrate my freedom. I leave both front and back doors open all day in our house in Bellevue Hill and the sunlight streams in. I leave the windows open. I go shopping by myself. I ride with Milos on the train to the city. I speak to strangers. For the last two years I have been living my life to the full. I sit in theatres and cinemas. I can walk in crowds. But for all the new things that I do, Thursday evenings are still the most precious. When Milos tells me the next instalment of your stories.

* * *

'That is very flattering,' said Ramon.

'Flattering? Why would I flatter you? I know your stories are just a pleasant interlude in your busy weeks, but for me they are much more. They were diversions when I most needed diverting. They were the crutch that supported me through my troubles. They made me use my brain when it wanted to shut down and retreat. They gave me reason to live. How could I possibly allow myself to die in the middle of one of your stories? How could I, before I knew how it ended? No, I didn't come here to flatter you, Ramon, I came here to thank you. To thank you all and repay my debt to you in the only way that is appropriate — by telling you my story.'

'Gratifying. Perhaps that is the word I should have chosen,' said Ramon. 'It is always gratifying to learn that we have helped someone whether or not that help was intended. It was never our intention to put you in our debt, but you have repaid us many times over. For us, telling our stories requires only skill. Telling your story required courage.'

'Great courage,' said Lucio. 'Whatever debt existed has been repaid with interest.'

'You are both very kind,' said Gabriella.

'Perhaps,' said Ramon, 'but there are a few points I don't understand.'

'Such as?' said Milos quickly.

'Why the urgency?' said Ramon. 'Why did you have to tell this story ahead of Neil's?'

'Yes, Milos, why the hurry?' cut in Neil. 'You did the full drama queen number and I for one would like an explanation.'

'Drama queen number?' said Gabriella. 'You are saying my Milos is a drama queen?'

'Damn right! You should have heard him. He went off like a cheap alarm clock. And what about your precious schedule, Milos? Why did the story have to be finished today?'

'I told you, I had no choice over the subject matter and no choice over the timing of the story,' said Milos.

'Time is running out, that's what you said,' prompted Neil. 'You used that as an excuse to jump the queue. And you ordered a cognac before your meal. Pure theatrics. Bloody hell, if I'd known where you were going to take us, I'd have ordered one too.'

'I thought you appreciated our story,' said Gabriella.

'Ignore him,' said Lucio. 'He enjoys being insensitive.'

'There is a deadline,' said Milos doggedly. 'And time is running out.'

'Explain,' said Ramon.

Milos slumped back in his chair and ran his hand through his hair.

'Tomorrow Gabi and I fly back to Hungary. To Sarospatak, to be exact.'

If Milos had announced they were going to the moon he could not have silenced his friends more effectively.

'Visiting, or something more permanent?' asked Ramon tentatively.

'Both,' said Milos. 'I am going back for a visit. Gabi … Gabi is going home to die.'

'What?' said Neil. The colour drained from his face. Gabriella still had hold of his right arm and he covered her hands with his.

'Yes,' said Gabriella.

'But you're cured!' protested Neil. 'You've got your new kidney and you've got your head back together.'

'Now do you understand, Neil?' said Milos bitterly.

'Understand?'

'Why I had to tell this story and why I had to tell it now?'

'Of course, but —'

'Do you still think it was a wallow? Another boring serve of European tragedy?'

'Of course not!' He turned to Gabriella. 'Gabi, I'm so sorry. But what happened? What's wrong with you?'

'My kidney is failing, Neil, and I will not go back on the machine. My story was my gift to you. My farewell gift.'

'Jesus Christ,' said Neil.

'Why are you so upset? Five weeks ago I was just a bagful of bad memories best left behind in Europe.'

'I never said that.'

'Oh, but you did.'

'I never meant it.'

'Oh, come on!' An edge crept into Gabriella's voice. 'You accused Milos of feeling superior because he had suffered and you had not. You accused him of being proud of his suffering, of wearing it like a badge. Get over it, you said. Have a bit of counselling, a few sessions with a shrink, and get over it. That's what you said, wasn't it?' Gabriella let go of Neil's arm and put her hands on her lap, distancing herself. 'That was the total extent of your sympathy.'

'She's right,' said Ramon. 'That is what you said.'

'I was just winding Milos up,' said Neil. 'I didn't mean it.'

'You meant it,' said Milos.

'I agree,' said Ramon. 'You were openly hostile to the idea of Milos telling his story. Scornful, even. Time heals, you said, where there is a will to heal. By implication you accused Milos of self-indulgence, of not having the will to heal. By implication you accused Gabriella as well.'

'That was not my intention,' said Neil.

'Then what was your intention?' pressed Milos.

'I was just speaking generally. The comment wasn't directed at you specifically.'

'Rubbish. You had no compassion, Neil,' said Gabriella. 'That is what hurt us. You had not heard our story and didn't even want to hear it. You made no effort to understand us or the events that have shaped us. You were dismissive of them as if they had no relevance. You were dismissive of us. You had no compassion for Milos, for me, or anyone else driven to this wonderful country by suffering. You hadn't heard our story and you didn't care. You hurt us, Neil, you really hurt us.'

Neil recoiled as though stung. But Gabriella wasn't finished with him.

'Five weeks ago my life meant nothing to you. Now you claim you are upset because I am dying. What am I supposed to believe?' Her hands renewed their grip on Neil's arm and, by doing so, begged a response.

'We're waiting,' said Milos.

'Believe both,' said Neil eventually. 'What you say is true. Lucio says I am insensitive and I suppose I am. Five weeks ago I didn't care, but your story's made me care. And care deeply. Whatever you think of me, I'm not made of stone.'

'None of us are,' said Gabriella.

'You think I wasn't moved by your story? Christ Almighty, your story would bring a tear to a bookmaker's eye. It sure stuffed up my Thursday nights. You know it did. I said so earlier during one of our breaks.'

'Yes, he did,' said Ramon.

'I'm sorry, Gabi, if I hurt you. And I'm sorry if I hurt you too, Milos. It was unintentional. I accept my comments were born of ignorance.'

'We know. That much has always been obvious. You have always worn your ignorance like a badge, a source of pride,' said Milos, his irony deliberate. 'But where do you go from here, Neil? We aren't the only people who've suffered. We aren't the only people who've come to this country weighed down with baggage.'

'Where do I go?'

'For God's sake, do I have to spell it out for you?'

'I don't know what you're getting at.'

'Have I been wasting my breath these past five weeks? Has Gabi? I'm sorry, but I thought we'd manage to topple your edifice of ignorance. Or at least open up cracks in it.'

Neil hung his head. 'What do you want me to say?'

'I don't *want* you to say anything,' said Milos angrily. 'But let me ask you this. When I return from Hungary, what will Gabi's legacy be? Will I find a new tolerant, compassionate Neil? Or does your newfound compassion extend only to us?'

'Milos is asking if you will try to be more understanding,' said Gabriella. 'Will you? For me?'

Neil nodded but wouldn't look at her.

'More tolerant and compassionate?'

Neil closed his eyes and appeared to struggle for control.

'Yes, I'll try.'

'Try? Is that all?'

'No,' said Neil heavily. 'I will be more tolerant and compassionate.'

'That would be wonderful.' Gabriella pulled Neil towards her and kissed him on the cheek. 'I'd like to believe that, Neil, I really would! What a wonderful legacy that would be.'

'I wish Milos had brought you to our lunches sooner,' said Neil, trying to deflect attention. 'We meet you then lose you. It's just not fair.'

'Unfair, perhaps,' said Gabriella, 'but I am not afraid of dying. I have won, you see? Despite everything that has happened to me, I will go to my grave a free woman. That is my victory. It is cause for celebration, not tears.'

'Then we should celebrate,' said Lucio. 'Open a bottle of champagne and drink to your story, your life and your victory.'

Gabriella shook her head. 'That is a lovely thought, Lucio, but I am tired. Telling my story has been a bigger effort than any of you could possibly realise. I need Milos to take me home.'

She rose wearily to her feet. The four men stood immediately.

'Goodbye, Neil,' said Gabriella. She embraced Neil and kissed both his cheeks. 'Remember my legacy. Keep your promise.'

'Goodbye, Gabi,' said Neil. There was a tremor in his voice and a redness to his eyes. Except for the blind man, his friends looked away in embarrassment. This was a Neil they'd never seen before.

Gabriella let go of Neil, turned and embraced Ramon.

'Goodbye, Ramon, it has been wonderful meeting you. I knew I would be impressed and I have been.'

'Now I am flattered,' said Ramon.

The blind man bided his time, waiting patiently as the remaining farewells were made, taking note of the sadness in the voices.

'So when will we see you again, Milos?' he asked.

'Six to eight weeks.'

'Not sooner?'

'No.'

'Doubtless you will visit Tibor's grave?'

'Of course. Anything else?'

'Yes. Something of little consequence. But I was wondering. I have a friend whose son was on dialysis before his kidney transplant. He had a device called a shunt implanted into his left arm to make it easier to insert the canulas. I was wondering, Gabi, just out of curiosity, which arm did they put your shunt in?'

'Does it matter?' said Gabriella warily.

'Indulge me.'

'My left arm.'

'The arm with the tattoo?'

'Yes.'

'That's odd.'

'Why?'

'Because when I asked to feel your tattoo I felt no shunt. They are quite prominent. Difficult to miss.'

'It was removed after the transplant.'

'Really? I felt no scar either. If I could feel your tattoo, surely I should feel a scar?'

Neil and Lucio turned to look at Gabriella as the implication of Ramon's words slowly dawned on them.

'There is no shunt,' said Gabriella. 'I had no kidney transplant. I am not dying.'

'What?' said Neil. 'You're not dying?'

'Why don't we all sit down,' said Milos.

'Milos has a habit of underestimating you, Ramon, and I'm afraid he has done it again. The part about the kidney transplant and my imminent death was an embellishment. I argued against it, but Milos believed it was necessary to teach Neil a lesson.'

'Teach me a lesson? Why me? What do you mean?'

'Let me guess,' said Ramon. 'Your insensitivity and lack of compassion towards refugees finally irritated Milos to the point where he decided to do something about it. Am I right?'

'As always,' said Milos.

'Milos shares our stories with Gabi and she was equally outraged. Disgusted even. She became Milos's willing accomplice. I suspected something that very first day. Milos knew how you would react to another European tragedy, as you so insensitively put it, and he knew you would press your claim to tell your story. You were set up, Neil, deservedly so.'

'Your story was for my benefit?' said Neil.

'To teach you a lesson, yes,' said Gabriella. 'To teach you tolerance.'

'What about the rest of your story? How much of that is true?'

'Do you think this tattoo on my arm is fake? Do you think I would fake a thing like that?'

'What about your escape to Czechoslovakia?'

'Milos, take off your tie. Show Neil the bullet hole.'

Milos unbuttoned his shirt and revealed an ugly but old scar at the base of his neck.

'What about Tibor?' asked Neil.

'We are leaving for Hungary tomorrow, like we said. We are going to visit his grave.'

'But were you married to him before you married Milos? Or is that another embellishment?'

'I married only once and that was to Milos. But it was Tibor who first slipped this gold band on my finger.'

'So all the rest of your story is true?'

'Neil, don't be so naive,' said Ramon. 'You know better. Milos and Gabi are storytellers. How do you know if Gabi's answers are the truth or a continuation of a fiction? You don't know. Like all good stories, significant elements are true, but it is up to each listener to gauge how much and which parts.'

A sly smile spread across Neil's face. He looked from Gabriella to Milos and back again.

'Congratulations,' he said. 'I'm flattered that you think I'm worth the effort. I suspect most of your story was true, which makes me all the more appreciative. But as far as teaching me a lesson goes, you miscalculated. You got the balance wrong.'

'Nonsense,' said Milos. 'We opened your eyes, no? Be man enough to admit it. We had you on a piece of string and forced you to confront your prejudices. Didn't we just hear you make a promise to Gabi?'

'Yes, but you weakened your lesson with your embellishment. You made me feel ashamed of my attitudes but not as ashamed as I should have been. My shame was overwhelmed by shock and sadness at the prospect of Gabi dying.'

'I heard shame,' said Lucio. 'It didn't sound overwhelmed to me.'

'And I hear a desperate man making a pathetic attempt to salvage his ego,' said Ramon.

'The point I'm trying to make is that I was more upset by the prospect of Gabi dying.'

'Does that mean you intend to go back on your promise to me?' asked Gabriella.

'Not at all. I was just saying —'

'You've said enough, Neil,' cut in Milos. 'The fact that we've made you promise to change your attitude means we didn't miscalculate.'

'He's right, Neil,' said Ramon.

'I agree,' said Lucio.

'Maybe,' Neil conceded.

He turned to Gabriella. 'The important thing is, you're not about to die.' He covered her hands with his again. 'I can't tell you how relieved I am about that.'

'Dear me,' said Gabriella. 'Milos was right. You really are a sucker for a happy ending.'

ACKNOWLEDGMENTS

Lunch with the Stationmaster is a work of fiction, though clearly it has its roots in history and in the experiences of Holocaust survivors. As Ramon remarks, every good story contains significant elements of truth and it is up to the listener/reader to determine what is fact and what is the product of imagination.

Gathering the facts would have been a lot more difficult but for the help of Alan Gold, author and Anti-Discrimination Commissioner, who cherry-picked through his library for reference books which were invaluable.

I would also like to thank those who gave up their time to tell me their personal experiences.

It would be less of a book but for the thoroughness of my editor, Nicola O'Shea, who allowed no page to pass unimproved.

Thanks also to my agent, Margaret Connolly. Every author needs someone like Margaret on their side and I pity those who haven't.